God

J.A. Marley

A Danny Felix Adventure

First published in 2018 by Bloodhound Books

www.bloodhoundbooks.com

Print ISBN :- 978-1-912604-19-7

Also By J.A. Marley

Stanstill

Praise For J.A. Marley

"This is a book that I really enjoyed, it was a very well thought out and executed plot, some great characters and twists." ***Yvonne Bastian - Me And My Books***

* * *

"Standstill really is a refreshing read, the action is jam packed, the secrets, lies and twists are deliciously exciting, the characters are spot on." ***Dash Fan Book Reviews***

* * *

"A hugely impressive debut novel from a talent to watch." ***Mark Wilson - Author***

* * *

"Standstill is well written, easy to read and fast-paced. It is a gripping story throughout which builds up into an explosive finale." ***Gemma Myers - Between The Pages Book Club***

* * *

"I can heartily recommend Standstill to existing thriller fans and those looking to discover why thrillers have so many dedicated readers." ***Susan Corcoran - Booksaremycwtches***

* * *

"I was really surprised when I realised that this was the author's debut, it reads more like a book from a well-established author with several works of this very competitive genre under their belt!" ***Donna Maguire - Donnas Book Blog***

* * *

"Standstill is a clever and gripping thriller, with an interesting cast of characters. If you like UK crime fiction then this is definitely a book to add to your list!" ***Kate Moloney - Bibliophile Book Club***

* * *

"A truly great debut novel by Marley and he shall be on my to watch list for more reads to come." ***Alexina Golding - Bookstormer***

* * *

"The standstill that is brought about is excellent and unexpected. It'll have you thinking about it for a while after you've finished the book." ***Mark Tilbury - Author***

* * *

"The story is a wonderful introduction to the London criminal underworld, through the various characters and locations mentioned throughout the book." ***Steve Robb - BookieWookie***

* * *

"Standstill is an impressive debut. There are characters that we care about, a pace that is unrelenting with a clever and twisted plot." ***Jo Worgan - Brew And Books Review***

"Since no one really knows anything about God, those who think they do are just troublemakers."

Rabia of Basra Circa 717 – 801

For HJ

1

❖ A Mini - Mart Adventure ❖

When the scruffy-looking kid pulled out the gun and pointed it at the chump on the other side of the cash register, Danny Felix thought, *Here we go.*

He felt his heart stir, his stomach muscles flex and his balls tighten.

Danny couldn't deny it. He was excited.

Here he was, in the presence of a stick-up merchant, waving a gun around like they'd seen too many cheesy Jean-Claude Van Damme movies.

"Nobody muthafuggin move!"

Wild eyes sat atop a scarf wrapped in a hoodie, Old Navy sweats pulled high to the waist. Filthy, worn-down Converse sneakers completed an overall look that screamed desperation and deprivation.

Danny could smell the funk of nerves, bravado and good old-fashioned fear emanating from the would-be thief. It was a familiar smell, one that he had, undoubtedly, emitted himself in his early career. He watched as the gun thrashed around. If he wasn't mistaken, it was a replica. It looked like a World War One vintage revolver, a Webley Mark IV.

To Danny's mind, anyone who possessed a genuine Webley wouldn't need to knock off a Tom Thumb mini-mart off Florida's Highway One.

The bandit whipped the fake gun around for added effect, to make sure anyone present would know this was the real deal. It caused Danny to flash back, a gun in his own hand, faces filled with terror, suddenly compliant. He had to drag his attention back to the here and now.

Danny was the only other customer in the shop.

The stoner kid behind the counter looked bored, resigned to having to stick around after his shift to tell cops about a robbery they would, from his bitter experience, do jack shit about.

Danny swept the store with his eyes, his head not moving, his own familiarity with such events allowing him to clock where the closed-circuit cameras were positioned. They were usually all in the same type of spots. He was certain that they had caught an image of him as he entered through the door from the side, and the one behind the stoner's head was probably making a movie star of both him and the stick-up merchant right now. But, still, Danny thought he could have a little fun.

"You're making a right fucking mess of this."

It was the smallest of movements, but Danny knew he had the thief's attention because they turned their left foot slightly towards the door.

"Shut yo face muthafugga, what kin' of turnt accent be that? I'm the bitch pointing the gun right atcha, so do as I say!"

Danny shrugged. *Bitch? So, this is a bandita rather than a bandit.* Danny adopted a look of sympathy. "I would, but I can't stand to see someone making such a pig's ear out of a blag that should be so simple."

The filthy left sneaker twitched toward the door again. The eyes above the scarf widened then hardened in almost the same instant.

"Look at this, yo' punk ass bitch. See this. I'll smoke yo' ass all over this sto."

"You're about to fail, bandita. First, you've wasted time chatting to me, enough to allow Captain America here to reach under the counter and hit his store's panic alarm. The local coppers are probably en route right now. Secondly, you haven't covered the angles behind you in the aisles since you stormed in. You don't know about the bloke who is about to crack you across the head with a baseball bat."

She flinched, glancing over her shoulder enough for Danny to make his move. He closed the distance between them in one sweep, gripping her gun hand, bending the wrist back beyond its natural angle. He pivoted his hips onto one leg, his other sweeping away her feet just above the ankles. As she dropped, the gun fell. Danny simply extended his left hand, the satisfying heft of the replica revolver meeting his palm, while his right arm locked around her head, pulling her off the floor. He tucked her head into the crook of his arm as you would a football.

"See, you didn't know if there was someone there for sure. Pig's fucking ear. "

The girl thrashed about, trying to scratch and pull at Danny's hair. He simply tightened his grip, denying her airways full capacity. Her fight soon waned.

Nearly limp, he lowered her to the floor.

"What you should have done, quick as you like, is march straight to the cashier. The gun should have been practically down his throat whilst scanning the store to make sure that there really was only the three of us in here. Then, demand the money, asking for it to be done fast and, if needs be, pull the hammer back on the revolver to show you mean proper business."

As he said it, Danny carried out the instructions.

Stoner Kid's eyes were wide with his arms in the air. He almost reached down to pop the cash register open until Danny gently shook his head at him. Bandita had pushed herself into a sitting position, her breath coming in short rasps.

Danny continued: "Except you couldn't pull the hammer back on the gun because it's a bleeding replica. And as for your accomplice? He or she is taking a month of Sundays to work out you might be in trouble. I haven't heard a squeal of tires yet, which means… three, two, one…"

On cue, the shop door flew open. Bandit number two entered like a whirlwind, with another ancient-looking handgun being waved around.

The accomplice didn't scan the scene either but came straight at Danny at speed.

Danny shifted his weight, matching the oncoming velocity of the attacker. They met halfway. Danny put all his weight into a straight-arm punch. It arrowed onto the bridge of the accomplice's nose.

The explosion of blood was like a scene from a Rocky movie. And as suddenly as it had all kicked off, it was over. Danny turned to the stoner kid behind the counter.

"That… that was fucking cool, dude." The stoner pushed his lank, greasy hair away from his eyes. "Man, this is fun and games, but I'm the asshole who's still gonna have to hang around to answer dumb cop questions. Except…"

Danny couldn't believe it as the kid slapped his own forehead. "Oh man, I forgot to push the panic button…"

Danny cocked his head. By Danny's assessment, the stoner kid probably had a brain that was ten percent water and ninety percent THC. "What's your name?"

"I'm Colt… Hi… What's yours…?"

Danny strode to the door and flipped the 'open' sign to read 'closed.' "We can play this one of two ways, Colt. You can go out back and call the Old Bill, the cops, and we can waste the rest of our evening talking to Bozo the Donut Eater, or you could go back there and erase the last hour of your CCTV and report a malfunction in the little log book you keep. You have one of those, right?"

Colt nodded slowly.

"And, in turn, I will dispose of Bonnie and Clyde here for you, in a non-lethal, community-relations kind of way, and we can all go about our lives."

"I dunno, man. I should really report this…"

Danny spread his arms wide, making a face like a cheesy De Niro in one of his later, dreadful movies.

"You won't hurt 'em, Mister…?"

"As God's my judge, kid…"

Colt's face warmed with a grin. He nodded his agreement.

"Okay, Colt. Give me your belt." Danny was already taking off his own. Colt hesitated as if to protest, but then obliged.

Danny secured the two would-be rip-off artists with the belts. Securing the late-arriving accomplice, he was surprised to discover they were both female and white, despite the attempts to sound ghetto tough. He grabbed a magic marker from a nearby shelf and pocketed it.

"When I'm gone, Colt, park their car up in one of your furthest parking bays. Make sure when you erase the CCTV that you erase all the cameras, even the one that covers the forecourt. too. "

Colt nodded again enthusiastically as they exited out into the parking lot.

Danny bundled the pair into the back cab of his pick-up truck. Colt watched, a question hovering on his lips as Danny slid behind the wheel.

"You sure you won't hurt 'em?"

"Promise."

Danny reached inside his pocket, pulling out a hundred-dollar bill. "This should cover my bottle of bourbon, the marker and the Funyuns, plus your belt, too, Colt..."

"Uh, okay... and hey, Mister... How'd you know their names were Bonnie and Clyde?"

Ten miles further north in Founders Park, a local festival was in full swing, with an old fashioned drive-in movie in progress.

Danny drove straight into the park.

He looked up at the temporary big screen, impressed by the clarity of the picture on this early spring evening. Early spring? Who was Danny kidding? This was Florida, it was about nine-thirty at night, and the temperature was a balmy seventy-eight degrees.

"Whatchu doin' to us, mofo? You some kind of rapist or sumthin?"

Bonnie and Clyde – or rather Bonnie and Bonnie – had been grizzling all the way, but only now were brave enough to go full volume.

"I'm not going to hurt you. At least not physically. But I am going to teach you a lesson."

"What the fugg?"

Danny's pick-up bounced across the field, past the mass of cars all pointed at the screen, turning directly under a giant image of a robbery in progress.

With the engine running, Danny leapt out, came around the cab and yanked open the back door. Before hauling the two useless thieves out onto the grass, he took a moment to scrawl something across each of their foreheads with the magic marker.

"You can't fuggin leave us here… What the fugg, man?"

"Next time, if you're going to rob, do a proper job. Can't have the likes of you giving good thieves a bad name."

Danny leapt back in the truck, horns beeping as the reflected light off the screen showed up the two girls trying to stand. A few stewards jogged towards them.

As he turned his pick-up to leave, Danny's headlights picked out the *banditas*, revealing their faces, complete with the word 'thief' written across their foreheads in black ink.

Danny laughed.

As he pulled away, he looked in his rear-view mirror. The Dead Presidents were on the big screen, leaping over the bank counter, telling the employees to put 'em up. Danny laughed again.

"*Point Break*. Great film. Bank robbing like it used to be… but with added sky diving." Danny felt nostalgic. But that thought was soon replaced by another. "Jesus, if this is my idea of great night out, my life really has become fucking boring…"

2

❖ Coming up for Air ❖

"Jesus Christ, I mean… Jesus H. Christ."

Vincent Cardell was not easily shocked, but the guy zip-tied to the chair was all kinds of fucked up.

Cardell's mind raced.

They had taken care to not draw any blood, but the victim was a mess. His eyes were swollen shut. Ugly raised welts showed across his naked torso where an electrical cord had been used to whip him. There were cigarette burns on his hands, chest, lips and ears. Cardell could not wrench his eyes away from the wounds. His tongue rested between his teeth, slightly protruding from his mouth.

He stepped into the small concrete room, having been careful not to let anyone see him enter. He pulled a pair of latex gloves tighter to his hands as he surveyed the claustrophobic space.

There were three other guys in the room. The biggest looked at Cardell, following up his stare with a negative shake of his head. Cardell sighed. Nothing was ever easy. He bent close to the stricken man and spoke gently.

Cardell's voice was a deep, rich, southern states drawl. He spoke with a tenderness that contradicted the situation. "Emmanuel, Manny… My Lord, why did it have to come to this? You could have made this so much easier for all of us, especially yourself."

Even with two swollen, rotting apples for eyes, tears flowed down Manny's cheeks. The sound of Vincent's hypnotic voice was enough to move him to weep.

"Uh… uh… bebeed unyu. Uh payed wiyu."

"Pardon, Manny? Was that you believed in me? Now, Manny, it was the Lord's light combined with my prayers that gave you your life back."

"Uh… ohhhhhhh… Uh lobbed yu."

"And you can love me and the Lord again, Manny. You know how He has a merciful heart, as have I. All you have to do is tell me. Tell me how long you have been talking to them and exactly what you said."

More tears. Manny was getting agitated, pulling against the zip ties biting into his wrists and ankles, but holding him firmly in place. "Uh neber tawked no one. Neber!"

Cardell looked up at the biggest of Manny's tormentors who could only shrug in reply, a look of uncertainty on his face. Turning back, Vincent laid a gentle hand on the stricken man's arm, reaching under the chair with the other.

"Okay, Manny, okay. Take it easy, I believe you, I do. I'm only sorry we had to do this. But, you know, we had to be sure. There can be no room for doubt. Our work. It's too important. I promise you. We'll make this up to you. We'll put it right."

With his eyes the way they were, Manny wouldn't have been able to see the roll of duct tape Cardell had picked up. Flicking at the end of the tape, he got his gloved index finger under the start, and with his other hand, he slowly unravelled a good length of the silver insulation material.

Taking his cue, the biggest torturer quickly swept a thick, black, plastic masonry bag over Manny's head, and before Manny's struggling could begin in earnest, Cardell wound the duct tape around the bag and his throat, sealing it to his victim's skin as surely as any weld.

Manny bucked in the chair, panicking at the sudden darkness. Terror would have been pushing his heart-rate sky high. Vincent could only imagine how, in this moment, Manny's head would suddenly fill with the lies he had been told. All of them. In one chilling, heart-breaking moment, Manny would know all his trust had been betrayed. His devotion, his recent life, all built on sand.

It took all four of them to keep Manny upright and in the chair. Cardell was entranced by the way the heavy bag pulsed flush with Manny's mouth every time he attempted to breathe.

It took less than three minutes for the convulsions to stop. The air in the tight little room was heavy with the odour of their joint efforts.

Slowly, Vincent stood upright, and stepped away from the lifeless figure in the chair. He carefully snapped off the surgical gloves.

"Am I all right?" He raised his arms out from his side, slowly turning in a circle for the others to inspect him, then he smoothed his tie and hair.

"Yes, Mr Cardell. You seem to be fine."

"Check the corridor."

"All clear, sir."

Cardell slipped out of the room, glad to be out of the fug of the small room. He walked down the long concrete corridor. Bare pipes and insulated ducting lined the low ceilings above him. He progressed through the bowels of the huge complex, turning from one corridor to another, soon starting to encounter other people. He kept his gaze straight ahead as he passed them. A few reached out to touch him lightly on the shoulder or back. The air grew fresher the further he walked.

Sounds were increasing, every step brought him closer to the noise, the excitement. His heartbeat slowed as he approached. He could feel it: 'inspiration' settling on him, calming him. He was, once again, ready to do what he was on this earth to do.

He felt invincible.

People clapped his shoulders, applauded his presence. They told him that he was great, devoted and sincere.

He arrived at a huge curtain. He accepted the microphone which was pressed into his hand by a young, eager helper.

And then, out he stepped onto a stage. He felt the rush of the balmy air of the outdoor stadium.

Bright lights filled his eyes, and a wave of adulation washed over him. The noise, the cheering, the applause, the hysteria, the energy. The sheer forceful excitement his mere presence generated in this sprawling amphitheatre seemed to jump like electricity from the crowd, straight into his body, his veins, his heart.

Raising his arms wide, looking this way, then that, every single one of the thousands of souls before him leaning forward. Each believed in that moment that he was looking at them and only them.

Finally, Vincent Cardell lifted the microphone towards his mouth. The crowd duly settled for him. Breath was exhaled and then held, waiting for the first words to come from his lips.

"My Friends. My Florida Friends. All praise to our Lord Sweet Jesus. I am here with you tonight to bear witness to his holy, healing light!"

The crowd went wild.

3

❖ Heeby Jeeby ❖

Deputy Sheriff Amparo Sosa of the Monroe County Sheriff's Department turned her attention back to the young, and she had to admit pretty dumb, store clerk who stood shuffling in his oversized jeans.

"Look, Cody, bro. I didn't mean to get you into trouble here, but what did you think would happen if that abandoned car sat there for more than a day?"

"It's Colt…" He shrugged, staring intently at his battered sneakers.

"Let's step outside, *hombre*."

He followed her out into the car park, staring dolefully as two men hooked up a battered Camry onto their tow truck.

"Go ahead. Have your cigarette, I know you are Jonesing…"

Colt instantly scrabbled for the pack of Marlboros in his pocket, lighting up and inhaling in a rush of eagerness.

"So, let's go over this again. Stick-up artist number one comes into the store waving a gun around. Super Customer, the only one in the store at this point, tells them they are messing up. Then, he disarms the stick-up artist and turns the gun on you for a second. He then predicts the arrival of stick-up artist number two, who then arrives and runs straight into customer's fist. Really, Cody? I mean, *Ese*… seriously?"

"Pretty much… unhuh… errr… it's Colt."

Deputy Sheriff Sosa started to gently chuckle, shaking her head. His eyes followed her dark ponytail, a faintly mesmerised look coming over his face.

"So then, Super Customer suggests that you erase the security camera footage and that he will clear the mess up, and you could get on with your night without having to worry about cops and questions and your boss, Mr Tomaski, calling you a dumbass. And you agreed? Dude?"

"I… I had somewhere to get to, Ms Sosa… Depu… ah…"

"Mr Tomaski might have a point here, Colty. I could be hooking you up for obstruction of a criminal investigation."

"They… they didn't take nuthin'… The big guy, he… he stopped all that. I just thought no harm, no foul… and my name…"

Sosa stared at him. He tailed off… staring back, focusing again on her hair.

"Colt, you gotta give me something more, man. Else I'm going to have to haul you back to the Sheriff's Station. It could become an even longer night, and into a few days, until I can get to the bottom of this. See the car… the car's your problem."

She pointed at the Camry being towed away from the store. "It's on my BOLO list. Know what that means?"

He shook his head, all lank hair and sullen resignation.

"Be On the Look Out for. It's been used in a couple of robberies across the bottom half of the state. That puts this automobile high up my priority list. And when you decided to listen to Super Customer… well, you just made my priority list, too, Colt. And that's not a list you really wanna be on."

"I… I done told you all I know."

"No, you told me what happened, and then, you told me Super Customer was real big, but I need more than that."

Colt's eyes were wide now. She could see she was scaring him and that was exactly what she wanted.

"If I search your car, Colt, will I find anything else that will push you further up my priority list? Maybe a little recreational plant product?"

Colt's eyes were now threatening to break free from his head. "Uh...uh, hold on, I remember... I remember."

"Remember what?"

"The dude. He was… was… big yeah, but he had a weird voice too. Even the robber bitch… I mean, the robber… she even said it was weird sounding, too."

"Really? What kind of weird?"

"No, no… he was like not from around here? Dude sounded a bit like the spy… in the movies."

"The who?"

"The double-oh one, the one who always wins and gets laid…" As he said the last bit, Colt swallowed involuntarily, his throat clicking as he did so.

"James Bond?"

Colt nodded furiously.

"He sounded British? He had a British accent?"

"Yeah… an accent… which made it even crazier."

"What? What was crazy?"

"He was a British dude… but he drove a pick-up…"

At that, the walkie-talkie on Sosa's hip squawked, a garbled but insistent voice breaking the moment. "Sosa! Sosa! Where in the name of all Christ's saints the hell are you?"

Sosa sighed out loud, embarrassed by the interruption from her dispatcher. "This is Sosa… Annie, what have I told you about…?"

"Never mind all that horseshit… they need you down at the festival drive-in. Some kind of crazy clusterfuck's happening…"

Sosa sighed again and looked at Colt. "You're going to have to give me a moment here, Colty…"

"Uh… okay… I just need to… to check on something…"

As Sosa turned to reply into her radio, Colt shot to his car like an Olympic sprinter. She presumed it was to dispose of something recreational and plant-like.

She glanced at her watch… it was still only midnight.

As he pulled onto the oyster-shell drive to his home, Danny could feel it starting. He had been thinking about his own flashback as the first bandita had waved the gun around in the store earlier. His memories had played out like one of his beloved movies. Holding the gun. People's compliance. The control he had over them. Their fear. Fear. That's what triggered him.

It was happening… again.

Set back from the main road through the narrow strip of land that made up Islamorada in the Florida Keys, it was his safe haven, a bolthole. But right at that moment, he couldn't step out of the truck.

His knuckles, wrapped so tight around the steering wheel, were glowing white in the night air. His heart hammered, his ears filled with a rush that felt like his head was about to explode, his breathing faltered. It came in sharp, jarring shudders.

Danny was having a panic attack.

What made these episodes worse was that once he was in one, he was both terrified and powerless to stop them at the same time (and they were gradually increasing in frequency).

"Come on… come fucking on… stare at something. Pick a spot and stare at it and breathe!"

His mind was suddenly full.

This was the bit he hated most. His brain became a tumult.

Images of flames reaching high into a London sky. Ear-piercing screams. People's faces melting before him. A thick acrid cloud of explosive dust seemed to be swirling around him, billowing into his eyes, up his nose, into his ears, leaving a stench of blood, burning flesh and gunpowder within the pores of his skin. Like a waking nightmare, Danny couldn't help but be overcome by his own terror.

And then, nothing.

It was as if a switch had been flicked in his head and heart simultaneously. These fits always ended as sharply as they began.

Danny howled as his lungs finally found their ability to inhale and exhale in a sledgehammer moment of normality, and as his primeval scream subsided, the tears came. They always did.

Huge, wracking sobs causing fat, hot tears to cascade down his face, and a tide of desperation to match them settled in his chest.

Danny eventually managed to open the door of the truck, almost falling out of it. Twenty minutes earlier, he had been chuckling to himself at the sight of two would-be robbers. Now, he was a quivering wreck.

He'd come to know the symptoms, able to spot the build-up of his "heebie jeebies" as he now called them, but not with enough warning to stop them coming, or even have time to seek refuge. They swept over him whenever, and wherever.

Danny slid out of the suddenly stifling air of the truck. He half crawled, half walked to the porch of his clapboard house, collapsing into a swing chair where, most nights, he loved to sit, drinking Bourbon and listening to the sounds of a Florida night.

But now, he was weeping. Feeling drained, sub-human, he realised that the images he had just conjured in his own head, along with the millions of pounds he had brought from London, were the real legacy of what had happened there. They were his heebie jeebies… and he believed he deserved everything they could throw at him.

4

❖ The Lord's Work ❖

The set was brightly lit.

A white-haired woman sat off to one side behind an old-fashioned wooden church organ. On the other side, a bank of ten volunteers were on telephones, frantically scribbling down credit card details on yellow legal pads; donations were pouring in as fast as the old organist could play *What a Friend We Have in Jesus.*

In between was a six-foot-high cross made from plastic, the facade designed to mimic stained glass. Coloured light spewed from behind its facia, reaching right down onto the floor of the set itself. Sat amidst the "holy light," three presenters were gripping red, leather-bound bibles, earnest looks on their faces.

A grey-haired man with a thickening waist, the anchor, was clutching his bible to his chest.

"There is no love, if there is no Word. There is no life, if there is no Word. There is no hope, if there is no Word. The Word is all, and without it, we are but leaves in the wind. Praise be Jeeee-sus, our Lord." He elongated the name, like it was tearing his very heart out when he spoke it aloud with his rich, Georgia accent.

Two guests, who sat next to the anchor, quietly amen-ed at this. The host stood up, his guests following suit, cameras adjusting so not a single moment was missed.

"I'd like to take this opportunity to thank this great man of God, Vincent Cardell. In joining us today, he has brought added grace to our annual Century Crusade Drive here at Shining Light. And thanks also to his beautiful wife, June."

Smoothing down his tie and puffing out his chest, Cardell responded. "Zachary, June and I both know how vital the work is that you do here. It is nothing but God's Glory in action. It's our privilege to come and bear witness with you and all the mighty pilgrims here..."

Cardell turned to the camera with the little red light on top, knowing it would reframe and zoom into his close-up. He focused his mind on the lens, putting the sparkle in his eye by shifting his feet slightly so that the key light up in the ceiling of the studio was beaming right onto him, making it hard for him to see properly. Exactly as he wanted it. He knew that now he had the 'twinkle' going full pelt.

"These pilgrims are spreading the Holy Word, breathing good back into our troubled and Satan-obsessed world. If you value lost souls, if you value Scripture, if you value your own souls, you'll pick up that phone today and you'll donate whatever you can..."

As he said this, he reached out with his arm, resting it on the attractive, brunette-haired woman next to him, pulling her into his shot, intensifying his stare a further notch.

"It's the right thing to do... it's the Lord's work."

June Cardell took her own, deep breath. "And remember, South Floridians, you'll be able to join my husband and I, and a dazzling array of young evangelical talent, at our annual Soul Reclamation Prayer Meet at the beautiful Miami Urban Convention Centre in just six short weeks. But in the meantime, please keep praying and keep helping Zachary Getz and his faithful flock reach out to those who need the Lord's touch the most."

All this was delivered in a voice that was caught somewhere in the middle of the Atlantic Ocean, the lilt of an upper-class English accent mixed in with the elongated vowels.

"Praise be and God bless you, Vincent and June. Let's finish this hour of our prayer and fund-raising drive with Martha's beautiful music..."

Zachary nodded at the white-haired woman who immediately launched into *Lord of The Dance* as though her very life depended upon it. The lights dimmed slightly, leaving the protagonists on the set silhouetted by the multi-coloured cross as they shook hands and hugged their on-air goodbyes.

Zachary whispered into Cardell's ear as he drew the man close, making sure his mouth and lips were averted from the line of the camera's sight and his mic muffled. "If you raise as much fucking money up at that convention this time as you did last year, I'll know the devil is married to a Brit..."

"The Lord's work, Zach... The Lord's work."

Then, it was June Cardell's turn, not failing to notice Zach's hand brushing her ass as he pulled her in for her hug. She benefited from the whisper treatment too.

"When you want a man with a real cock, you just come a-running, June dahlin'..."

"Now, Zach, you know I couldn't possibly handle you. From what I hear, you're circumcised, and yet, you have all these people thinking you aren't Jewish by birth."

Zach stepped back and chuckled as he appraised her. A floor technician declared that they were off-air.

House lights came on, and the set became a blur of movement as cameras were repositioned, and a lady armed with make-up fussed around Zachary Getz.

"We hope to see you in Miami, Zach. Your presence always brings in a few more souls..."

"I'll be there, Vincent. If only to see this English rose of yours..."

June sidestepped the second hug, managing to avoid another ass grab as she did.

A serious young woman in a trouser suit appeared beside them, looking at the couple over the top of her iPhone.

"I know, I know, Ms Kravitz. June and I are needed somewhere else right this second..."

"You are both due at the Everglades City Country Club in an hour, Mr Cardell. It's for the local Baptist community mission drive launch. And that's fifty minutes from here..."

"The Lord's bidding never rests... Zachary, God Bless, we'll see you in Miami..."

❖

They swept out of the industrial pre-fab unit that housed the small studio. Vincent noted the warmth of the outside air, which for this time of year, still felt unusual to him, a native of Nashville, where early Spring could still mean frost and snow.

As they walked, the atmosphere between the Cardells changed. Vincent thought the mood could match that Tennessee air he had just been recalling.

Neither he nor his wife said a word until they were both in the back of the black limo that was waiting for them.

Ms Kravitz rode up front with the driver, and, once settled in their seats, June made sure the divide between them and the others was fully closed before she spoke. "Are we any closer?"

"You know the answer to that."

"What do you suggest we do next? What are you going to do? Kill all of them? Torture them until someone owns up out of sheer agony? I can't believe where we are with this."

"We've grown faster than I envisioned. What were we supposed to do? We needed people."

"We? We? If you had listened to me, we wouldn't have that Zedillo woman asking the kinds of questions you cannot afford to answer. These people do not fuck around. Someone has talked. Someone you brought in, someone we couldn't trust."

"Stop panicking, June. It is time for calm and collected thinking. We can sort this."

"No, Vince, you sort it… and if you can't, if you don't, I will."

June sat further back in her leather seat, turning away from her husband as she did so. She thought she would need a divine miracle if she were to walk away from all of this with a life she could enjoy, on terms that she would set.

5

❖ Fisher of Men ❖

"How long yo' had this bidness?"

Simeon Duvall was staring at Danny Felix whilst peeling the label off his numbingly cold beer bottle. It was his third, and he had a very pleasant buzz going. The sunshine of the Gulf of Mexico combined with the gentle sway of the boat was helping.

"A little over a year now. It serves me very well." Danny was sitting on the gunwale of his little fishing cruiser. He had a Dr Pepper in his hand, some crushed ice flowed down the side of the plastic bottle.

"A whole damn year? I musta bin one of yo' first customers! I wouldn't put yo' down as a fisherman, Danny. You seem more of a…" Simeon circled the top of his bottle in the air as he searched for the right word. "… an urban type. Yo' look and move like you got plenty o' street smarts."

Danny chuckled. It amazed him how, no matter how long you spent not talking about yourself, people sooner or later lost their patience and started digging. "Simeon, do I look like a city wideboy? I don't even have a pair of proper shoes, mate."

At just under six feet, Simeon was all muscle. His face was round and handsome, quick to smile, even quicker to light up with laughter.

He ran his hand over his close-cropped hair and slapped his thigh. "You're a mystery. That English accent. The way yo' appeared out of nowhere. That iddy biddy advert in The Key West Citizen and the hand-painted sign on the roadside the only proof yo' exist... yo' don't even have one o' dem cell phones, brother."

"You never seen a drop-out before? Someone who didn't like being around too many people all at the same time? This is the Florida Keys..."

Simeon sat back in the pedestal chair. Danny could see he was starting to think about casting out into the blue water again, see if he could get a bite. So far, the fish had been pretty shy.

"If I were a gambling dude... which I am not, I would say yo' ex-military. Or a cop of some kind. Something that requires cojones."

Danny stared out across the sea, taking a sip of his drink, hoping nonchalance would close this avenue of conversation down.

"You look to be fit. Dropouts normally have a little beer baby goin' on. Usually a hint o' the bong water about them. Yo'? Not so much, Brother..."

Simeon's arms glistened and flexed as he swung his fishing rod high over his head, flicking it at exactly the right moment, the bait and lure arcing away from the boat, the sun glinting off the end.

Danny went on the offensive. "I'd say you know more about me than I do about you. I don't even know what you do for a living."

"Go ahead, brother. Take a swing o' the bat. What is my current occu-pa-tion?"

"Jesus... I wouldn't know where to begin, guv."

"Yo' made a damn good start... better than yo' think."

Danny cocked an eyebrow at him. "That's cryptic..."

"Yo' got my boss's name right."

Danny wasn't often surprised. "You work for Jesus? You're some kind of... pastor?"

"A priest... I'm a priest..."

Danny laughed. He might have guessed Simeon was an engineer or a lawyer. Someone with an education, a little money. But a priest? Never. "A fisher of men... a holy Joe. I could have been guessing forever. I wouldn't have had a Scooby."

"What yo' say? Scooby? You've gone all limey on my ass."

"I wouldn't have had a clue. Scooby Doo... clue. So, you say mass, give out the last rites, communion... all that stuff."

"A priest who doesn't wouldn't be much use now, would he? Yes, I do all those things. I attend to the needs of my flock. I even hear confession. How'd you like a go at that? Got a few stories to tell? A few little secrets you need ironing out, you can talk to me, and we can get God to let things slide, tidy that soul of yours up a little. What yo' say?"

Danny was standing now, hands out, pushing an imaginary wall away from his chest. "Whoa. No offense. But I've seen, heard and felt enough that was done in the name of some version of God, Gaia, Allah and whoever else to know that I don't trust any of it."

"So, I guess that makes us just fishing buddies. We go back to being mysteries to each other. Shame, shame, I was beginning to like yo'." Simeon sighed and Danny realised, for the first time, that he liked the man, and the respect was obviously mutual and growing.

"Fishing buddies works for me, mate."

Simeon's smile returned. "At the very least, that's a start and… wooooo, hold on… I gotta bite…" And suddenly, his line was taut, and the reel was racing.

Danny was happy for the distraction.

"What time you get finished up last night, sugar tits?"

Amparo let the clipboard she was holding slowly drop to her side. She had only just checked in for her shift, and already, it felt like it was going to be a long day. Starting with the usual crossing of swords with Annie the Dispatcher. She was about to lecture her, but Annie thrust a steaming cup of coffee under her nose.

Annie Drummond just didn't add up. White-haired, a grandmother, a volunteer retiree, a heart of gold, but a mouth that constantly swore like a chain gang boss.

"It was gone one a.m., Annie. And thank you, how are you doing today?"

"Oh, ya know. My bladder infection's flared up again, so I'm pissing like a racehorse, and my knees tremble, even when they're not getting any action. Growing old sucks donkey dick."

Amparo's eyes shut as soon as she heard the word "bladder." She dropped her voice. "You know, Annie... we really need to work on your language skills a little here..."

"Hey, I came down here from New Jersey for the sun, not to be polite... those girls that came in from Founders Park. Any of that make any sense in the end? It sounded like Krusty the Clown was jerking us off until we were suddenly getting twenty calls all saying the same thing. They really have shit scrawled across their foreheads?"

Amparo decided to roll with the punch in this conversation, sighing as she did so. "Yes, they had the word 'thief' written on their foreheads. They did corroborate what the mini-mart kid was saying. The *muchacho* who turned them loose that way had a weird accent. Could've been British, they said."

Annie took a long, noisy slurp of coffee, her white eyebrows arching as she did so. Amparo wasn't sure if that was the effect of the hot coffee or the fact that they had an English vigilante on the go. "Jesus wept. The number of tourists go through here from across the pond, you bet your cutie Latina ass there are about twenty thousand suspects."

Amparo's patience was beginning to drain, but she took another slow breath. "Except the stoner kid at the convenience store said the man was driving a pick-up truck. Like a real, honest to God, *Yanqui*."

"Holy shit... really? I'm only aware of one Englishman round these parts, local type deal, I mean. He runs a little fishing outfit. I only know cos my parish priest goes fishing with him now and then. He told me at the whist drive last Thursday. Says he likes him. I hope they ain't gay... I like that priest."

Annie casually upped and walked away, off to start despatching in her own inimitable manner.

Sosa's mouth hung open. She didn't know which she was more surprised by. The fact that Annie had just delivered her a slender lead, or the fact that this woman who could make a hooker blush went to church.

6

❖ Meetings of Minds ❖

Vincent Cardell watched in silence as the blue waters of Biscayne Bay sparkled in the sunlight. The limousine carrying him sped over the I-195 bridge, leaving downtown Miami behind. He was on his way to South Beach, where the beautiful people flocked to see and be seen. Not that Cardell was looking forward to his appointment there. Quite the reverse.

His head was like a washing machine. Thoughts, plans, worries and possible scenarios thrashed around his mind, colliding, torturing him at a time when he knew he would have to be as calm as the waters beneath him.

His wife's last words as he left rang out amongst the jumble in his head. "Give nothing away. Be scant on detail and turn on that wretched charm of yours… it's about all we have left…"

The limo pulled onto the smaller streets of South Beach itself. Hotels rose up high on either side. People on the streets a mixture of tourists and panhandlers all flocking to the sun-kissed strip of land. Some were there to have a day of fun, others trying to profit from the generosity the atmosphere might generate.

Cardell took in the sight of a bedraggled-looking vagrant. The man stood by the traffic light that stopped his progress. At first glance, you could have been forgiven for thinking that the homeless man was one hundred years old. His hair was wild, sand-coloured, his face was lined like asphalt cracked by a blistering sun. Looking down, Vincent noticed that instead of shoes, he wore wads of newspaper taped to his feet. Bony legs led up to a pair of filthy board shorts and a T-shirt with Mickey Mouse flipping the bird at the world on the front. Vincent suddenly felt the cold of the air-conditioning in the car. The chill made the hairs on the back of his neck and arms stand up. The homeless man couldn't see Vincent. The limo was swathed in privacy glass, yet it felt like the homeless man was staring right into his eyes, deeper, further, going right to the core of him. The traffic light changed. Vincent felt the transmission of the long car engage, and as they pulled away from the corner, the homeless man held up the piece of cardboard he had been holding down by his side. In scratchy, spidery letters, the words on it hit Vincent like a slap to the face:

"'What would Jesus do?"

Suddenly, Vincent found his moment of calm. The Good Lord had come to him in his moment of need. A sign... a reminder that Jesus shone his great light on those who believed and spread his word. No matter that he was about to meet with Ines Zedillo. Vincent knew he could deal with her now. He had been chosen. Chosen by God to lead. Chosen to do this work, to spread the Lord's word. He had the might of God's will on his side.

What would Jesus do? If he had to... why, perform a miracle, of course. When all appeared insurmountable, Jesus trusted, and God had always shown a way. And that was exactly what Vincent intended to do. That day and every day from then on. And if Ines Zedillo was to get in the way of God's plans for him? Vincent would simply kill her and any she sent after him. After all, he was God's instrument, he was on this earth to do His bidding. Nothing would stand in his or his Lord's way.

As Vincent was having his moment of revelation, June Cardell was travelling to a meeting of her own. The venue was a strange one. Since moving to America and marrying Vincent, she had grown accustomed to eating in high-end restaurants and country clubs; the kind of places that required long trousers, collar and tie on the gentlemen and elegant blouses, skirts and heels on the ladies. Porky's Bayside BBQ in Marathon Key wasn't that type of place.

June felt more than a little self-conscious as she made her way from the parking lot into the roadside eatery. Her black, flowing maxi dress and matching Prada pumps were at odds with the boards declaring specials of conch fritter and beer-butt chicken. However, the need for privacy and discretion at this stage was a price worth paying for having to set foot in a place she felt beneath her. There was no chance that a paparazzi or journalist would be staking out Porky's.

She pushed up her sunglasses into her shining brunette hair, squinting slightly against the sudden glare of the sun, Scanning the tables, she looked for the reason she was setting foot in a place that had picture menus and plastic-topped tables. She soon spotted him. At a corner table set flush against the open windows, looking directly out onto the boat dock that separated the place from the Gulf of Mexico.

With the slightest nod of his large, clean-shaven head, the man she'd come to talk to beckoned her towards him. As she sat opposite, she was able to check that her lipstick was still immaculate in the reflection of his sunglasses.

"What a delightful bistro you've picked…" She was about to say his name but stopped herself. The need for caution and secrecy prompted her to bite her tongue.

"This is one of South Florida's finer establishments, love. Don't knock it until you've tried the fried pickles… quite something." His English accent made June feel a little homesick, but she brushed the flash of that emotion away as you would shoo a fly. Home was not somewhere she ever expected to see again.

At that, a server appeared next to her. Tall, gangly and way too old to be wearing the shorts with red braces holding them up, his belly touched the edge of their table while he was still standing a foot away from it. Still, she thought, he had what Americans called a perky disposition.

"Welcome to Porky's. We hope you enjoy our relaxed island atmosphere. What can I getcha to drink…?"

"Coffee," came the reply from behind the reflective shades. June tried to not stare at the size of the waiter's stomach at eye-level beside her.

"I'd like a glass of rosé wine, please." As soon as she said it, she regretted her choice.

"Ma'am, is that the pinky-coloured one?"

"Errr..."

"She'll have iced tea." The gruff tone of the London accent was all the waiter needed to hear. He beetled off to give them the privacy they required, hollering the order across the bar as he did so.

"So, Mrs C. It's a joy to see you. It's been a while. Not since your fun 'n' games back in London. How can my special brand of talents serve you today?"

"It has been a while. From what I hear, you had more than a spot of bother in London, too. How'd you get thrown clear?"

"When you know as many people of privilege as I do, most problems can be made to disappear. Especially when you can remind those people exactly how well I know them and their... what shall I call them? Dirty little secrets?"

"Yes, but getting into the US..."

"You made it... and we both know butter wouldn't melt in your mouth now, don't we... more likely it would sizzle..."

June was about to register a little indignation but suddenly, the belly was back and drinks were being served.

"Now, how about some lunch today?"

"We need a little longer with the menus. The choice... too many good things to eat, mate."

Mr Belly got the message, once again, and off he went.

June leant forward, an intense expression on her face. "You listen to me. I was never so much as arrested, never mind charged, back in London. I have a new life here now, a fresh start and a successful one at that, and that's why I need your help. I want to preserve that life, and I'm having a little... difficulty."

Once she had said it out loud, June realised that she had been holding the weight of anxiety in her stomach for quite some time. Her companion waved a large hand gently in front of his own face.

"What now? Mr Jesus Freak not paying you enough attention… or just not paying?"

"Fuck you. If you came here just to insult me, you're wasting both our time. But I know there always has to be something in it for you. You're working an angle by meeting with me. You need something, too, or else you wouldn't have shown that wide-boned face of yours."

"Don't get your knickers in a twist, love. A wise man once said that opportunity dances with those already on the dance floor. Your cry for help is simply a chance for me to have a little dance."

"Oh God… I'd forgotten how full if it you are."

"What exactly do you want from me, Mrs Jesus Freak?"

June sat back, knowing it was now or never. She either had to trust this man or change tack and come up with another idea. Except she was the one who had reached out to him, once she'd heard the rumours that he was in America. She knew time was against her. She had no choice. "Okay. It is about my husband…"

"Over the side, is he? A little indiscretion or something that you just cannot ignore any longer?"

"If only it were that easy. I couldn't care less if he was having it away with the staff. Sadly, it's a little more complicated than that. "

"Money? Filthy lucre?"

"And where we get it from…"

"Souls living in fear of never walking through those pearly gates tend to be easily parted from their dosh."

"They are, and they do… but that is not our only income stream."

The big man sat forward in his seat, removing his sunglasses. June had to suppress a little gasp as she saw, for the first time, how his left eye was a mangled blob of white and yellow in its socket. It looked like an egg that had been broken in the pan.

"So, we are talking a little dirty money?"

"It's dirty when it gets to us. It's clean when it leaves."

"Now I know why you wanted to talk to me, Mrs C. When the money is from somewhere a touch exotic, there are always complications. Let me guess. Has your God-fearing other half been taking a little slice off the top?"

June just looked. She took a sip of the iced tea and grimaced at the foul taste. Cold tea… seriously? But then, she thought the nasty flavour somehow seemed instantly appropriate.

"And tell me, young lady, whose money is your husband taking his extra commission from?"

June took a deep breath, this was it. The ultimate moment of trust.

"So, what can I get you to eat? The Conch fritters are terrific!"

Mr Belly was back, with all the timing of a heart attack, and June's shaven-headed collaborator roared with laughter.

The Delano Hotel on Collins Avenue was one of South Beach's most chic. Vincent strode through the lobby, with its muted tones and long flowing linen drapes. The fabric billowed, caught by a breeze that flowed through the entire lobby, from its huge French windows that lead to the pool and on to the shore itself. He shared the lift with a beautiful, young woman, wearing an off-the-shoulder sundress. Her skin was the colour of warm caramel, her voice just as smooth as she wished him a great day and exited on the tenth floor. He kept going up to the top of the building, arriving at the door of the penthouse suite. Taking a moment to compose himself, he fixed on a smile and pressed the doorbell.

He was ushered in by a large Latino man wearing a suit that looked at least a size too small for his hulking frame. The interior was simply, yet stylishly, furnished. More muted colours on both the walls and the furniture served to radiate serenity. The lounge filled with light from the open doors which led to a large terrace that afforded breathtaking views of the golden strand that made South Beach such a magnet for sun seekers of all types.

Ines Zedillo stood to greet him. Before her, a table was arranged with an exquisite lunch – seafood, salads, a bottle of champagne in an ice bucket and bowls of exotic fruit.

"Señor Cardell. It's always a joy to see you."

"Señora Zedillo. The pleasure is all mine. This looks like a fine spread; the Lord certainly has provided."

"*Sí*, my friend, he does… when my guests arrive, they will be well looked after."

Cardell's face flushed at his own presumption and the knock-back that met it, but Ines went on as though she had not noticed.

"*Vamos*. Let's take in the vista. It's such a beautiful day, no?"

Ines moved towards the glass panels that framed the edge of the terrace, beckoning the preacher to follow. As he joined her, he was struck by how elegant she looked. Tall, in great shape, despite the fact that he knew she was at least sixty. Her hair had lost its original raven-black sheen, now highlighted by grey in many places. Her long face and bright eyes radiated intelligence, whilst her blood-red, manicured fingernails hinted at a ferocity to match it. The glint of the crucifix at her throat on its simple gold chain reminded him of her Catholic faith. It was a stripe of Christianity he neither trusted nor saw as anything other than a collection of smells and spells. For him, the true Christianity came from the bible and nothing else. Not from some old man in Rome.

Ines raised her face to the sun, letting the breeze shift her hair. She closed her eyes to the warmth on her skin. Cardell stood waiting to hear why she wanted to meet. As he regarded her, for a second, he imagined her naked. What would she look like if her were to draw a thin-edged blade across that long, clear-skinned face of hers? He shook the image from his thoughts when she spoke.

"Señor Cardell. How long have we had our arrangement?"

"I believe it is three years now, *señora*."

"And you have enjoyed our… support. We have taken your mission and backed your expansion. We have invested in you, making you a man of God with a significant flock, no?"

"Of course, *señora*. The resources you have brought to bear have made it easier for many to hear the Lord's word."

"And we have treated you fairly *simpatico*?"

"Yes, and we have done all we have been asked to. It is a… business arrangement as well as a spiritual one."

"And in six weeks, we will have your big *fiesta*. The time in which we can move the most significant amounts of our funds. I trust the preparations are all in place?"

"Indeed. We are expecting our largest crowds ever, and at the same time, we are, as always, ready to serve you and your colleagues with the usual financial arrangements."

"No problems? Not even a small wrinkle in your plans?"

Vincent felt his guts tighten. Whatever she knew or thought she knew, was it about to come out? That thin-edged blade appeared in his mind again, albeit briefly. He held his hands out in an assured manner. "All is fine at my end, *señora*. Have you heard otherwise?"

Ines ignored his question, producing a long, elegant cigarette and a zippo. She touched the flame to the end, letting the first smoke roil out of her fiery red lips. "You met Arturo? On the way into the suite…"

Cardell just nodded, thinking, *Who the hell is Arturo?*

"Arturo has been my guard and friend for almost… *Madre de Dios*… ten years. How time passes. But Arturo has just had some awful news. Come… see…"

Ines took Vincent by the elbow, leading him back into the suite, back to a long table that dissected the room. On it was a large envelope, nothing else.

"Arturo has a cousin, one very dear to him, his mother's sister's only child. Only children are always treasured. You feel it, no? So, when Arturo got the bad news, he had to break it to his own mother, and she now cries as if she has lost one of her own… *Mira*…"

Zedillo gestured to the envelope. It was the very last thing of this earth he wanted to touch, let alone open. But Ines's stare was enough to make him reach out. Automatically, slowly, taking the envelope in his hands, he felt the slight weight of what might be inside.

The seal had not been stuck down, so he was able to simply slide the contents out onto a table that the hotel's designer could never have imagined would see such a moment.

Photographs.

Two of them. In colour. Photos of a badly beaten, wet, naked corpse. A dead man. The first picture a full length shot, showing how chains had been wrapped around the corpse's feet, yet had obviously not been enough to stop it re-emerging. The second picture was the kicker, though. It was a close up of the face. A man's face. A man's face that had bruises and burns across it. A man's face bloated by time in the sea, but if you looked closely enough you might be able to recognise it as the face of Manny. The last time Vincent had seen that face was as he had helped to pull a black, plastic bag over it. The pictures held Vincent in their thrall for a beat too long. He realised he was staring.

"My Sweet Jesus." Cardell's response was a whisper. He knew he had to up the emotion in his own voice. "Is this… is this Emmanuel? Manny? The Manny who works for…" Cardell let his voice trail. His face was slack, and he made a point of unsteadily leaning on the arm of the sofa behind him. "I… I… what in God's name happened here? "

Zedillo was watching him very closely, trying to gauge the level of sincerity in the shock that he was exhibiting. "Your guess is as good as ours, Señor Cardell. His mama, she called Arturo to say he had not been home in days. So, we ask questions, to seek help from our contacts. And yesterday, we get this from some *hermanos* in the Miami police."

"But… but I saw him. We prayed together at the start of the last mission, the one in Coral Gables. He was the sweetest soul." And, at this point, Cardell pulled off his masterstroke. A single tear gathered in his right eye. Swelling, breaching the lower lid, it slowly traversed down his cheek.

"I'm sorry, Señora Zedillo, but this is heart-breaking news. I must pray for his passing, that the Lord may seem him safely to his eternal reward."

"Señor Cardell, I can see you are shocked, but do not worry. We will find out exactly what happened here. But you can see now, no? I need, *you* need, to be sure that there are no problems between now and your Mission next month."

"I can assure you, Señora, this is a shock and will be for all my team. We loved Manny… but surely you don't think this has anything to do with our operations?"

"I hope not. But it is better that you know and know to watch closely. What you and your team do for us, Señor Cardell, is *muy importante* to me and my associates. We will let nothing, nada, get in the way of what we have built with you… the faith we have shown in your faith… *claro*? *Claro*, Señor?"

"Crystal, Señora… quite crystal. Can we prepare a visit to the family? He was, after all, like a member of ours."

"I will leave that to you. Now thank you for your time. I will be watching… *adios*…" She blew a cloud of smoke at him, the sweet fumes causing him to blink whilst confirming his dismissal.

Once alone in the elevator, Vincent thanked Jesus. At first under his breath, but then slowly, his voice rose, until, as the doors opened on the ground floor, the people waiting to enter could hear his prayers before the metal doors opened.

Ines Zedillo returned to her spot on the terrace, her face once again taking in the warm afternoon sun. Arturo came and stood beside her, handing her a glass of water as he did so.

"Señora, forgive me, but I do not have a *primo* called Manny…"

"*Muchacho*! I know that, but I wanted to push our little preacher. I wanted to see how he would react."

"And what did you see, Señora?"

"See? *Yo no se*… I don't know… but I know that a man cannot hide behind God and his bible forever. If he is lying to us, we will know… we will know. *Entonces*… what time is the senator due? This lunch is going to waste…"

7

❖ Step in Time ❖

Danny had enjoyed his trip. Simeon had proved to be excellent company and was unlike any other priest he had met.

The day had been punctuated by laughter, easy silences, and relaxed conversations on everything from music to climate change to celibacy. They'd even chatted about what Simeon liked to call 'soccer' while Danny kept correcting him by calling it 'football.'

Back at Danny's clapboard home, they were enjoying another easy silence as they unloaded the trash, fishing gear and the solitary fish they'd managed to land.

Once they'd finished, Simeon gripped Danny's hand in a shake that was both strong and sincere.

"You're a badass mofo, Danny… That was a fine day's fishing… I only get one day off a month, but I figure I know what I'll be doing when it rolls around again."

"It'll be a pleasure to see you then, Simeon. You are, as they say where I come from, a top geezer."

Simeon's booming laugh was a great response, but what he said next took Danny by surprise. "You could always swing on by and see me at my place of work. Mass is every Sunday morning at ten or eleven-thirty. Yo' could even sit yo' ass in my confessional, like I suggested. Sometimes, it's good to get a little something off our chests… know what I'm sayin'?"

Danny considered the holy man, and his reply, before opening his mouth. "That's an interesting offer… but, really, Father, I know what I think of God, and I am sure he knows it too. We leave each other alone. It works best that way for all concerned."

"God, consciousness, the Force... I don't give two shits what people wanna call it. So long as they know it's there, Danny. And you know. Something in your life gave you a glimpse of it. You wanna take a closer look, have a proper talk about it... you'll find me over at St Justin the Martyr in Key Largo. I promise not to bite... See ya later, my man... Keep it real."

And with that, Father Simeon squeezed himself into his bedraggled Ford Taurus and drove off, leaving Danny standing there on his oyster-shell drive thinking that he might just have been given the most individual call to prayer any human had ever had.

Deputy Amparo Sosa almost missed the turning. The road sign was so small as to be self-defeating. But at the very last second, she spotted it, spraying gravel as she pulled off the highway and onto the narrow drive. Almost immediately, she had to swerve to avoid a battered Ford that was coming towards her at speed.

Another time, she would have buzzed her lights and pulled over the driver to warn him about putting the "pedal to the metal," but right now, she was too curious about meeting the mystery English guy whose little sign promised an excellent day's fishing at competitive prices.

The drive, which was flanked by Camellia bushes, soon widened to reveal a little clapboard house complete with a veranda with an old swing chair in one corner. To the left of the house was a boat dock which gave out onto one of the many channels that gave Florida Keys' residents access to the Gulf of Mexico. A modest-sized fishing boat was tied up, gently bumping against its moorings. On the right side was a battered-looking carport. A vehicle sat there with a tarpaulin covering it. It looked dusty, as though it hadn't been pulled aside in a very long time. She couldn't tell from the shape whether it was a truck or not. That was okay, she aimed to find out.

It hadn't taken long to discover where this little fishing operation worked out of. One of the fire fighters who shared the depot with the police at Founders Park had heard of the English guy and spotted the sign a little further down the road past Marathon Key.

As she stepped from her cruiser, making sure she had her rover radio clipped to her belt, a tall man came around the corner of the house from the boat side. He was hefting a dripping cool box. Amparo was instantly struck by the man's gait. He carried himself with ease, despite his height. His hair was close cropped, unlike many of the dropout fishing types who ran such businesses.

His legs were muscular and lean. As the breeze caught his T-shirt, pushing it against his frame, she noted that didn't have the little beer belly that other fishermen often had either. Too many Tecates in the sun, but not for this charter man. It then struck Amparo that she was paying maybe a little too much attention to what this guy looked like.

"Can I help you, officer?"

"That confirms it. I've found my Englishman."

"I beg your pardon?"

"I'm Deputy Sosa from the Monroe County Sheriff's office… and you are?"

Looking him directly in the eye, she reached out her hand and noted the strength of the handshake she got in return. He was less than an inch taller than her, so maintaining that eye contact was easy.

"My name's Danny… Danny Franklin. I hope this isn't an official visit, Deputy. I can't recall running a light or being at the scene of a dodgy crime recently."

"Dodgy?"

"Sorry, I mean suspicious circumstances… that sort of thing."

"I am here on business, Mr Franklin. I'm following up on an incident that was a little strange up at the Tom Thumb on Highway One… the store by mile marker seventy-nine?"

"Excuse me for saying, but one Tom Thumb kind of melds into another. They're hardly Harrods Food Hall, now, are they?'

"Harrods? I'm not sure…"

Danny held up his hands, an easy smile spreading across his face. She could see he was having a little fun here at her expense. "All right, all right. I'll stop with the British references. It'll make your life easier. Mind you, haven't you ever seen Dick Van Dyke in Mary Poppins? Step in toime?" He laced the last phrase with as much comedy cockney as he could.

Sosa felt even more confused, but she also had to suppress a little smile. "Mr Franklin, this is a serious matter I'm investigating. There was an attempted armed robbery."

"And how does this involve me, officer?"

"A member of the public stepped in. Stopped the robbery. Witnesses said he had an English accent."

"So, you're looking for this gentleman to give him a medal? With the number of visitors you get round here, that could be a long old search, don't you think?"

Sosa felt she had lost the initiative in her questioning. She didn't want to admit it to herself, but she was enjoying listening to the man speak. His accent… it was… anyway. She tried a different tack.

"Would you mind showing me what's under the tarp in your carport?"

Danny raised an eyebrow. "Are you a petrol head?"

"Sir, I would appreciate it if you would stop talking to me in riddles."

Danny laughed. "Okay, okay. I promise, but answer me this. Aren't you supposed to have some kind of a search warrant before snooping under a person's carport?"

"If you have something to hide, I can go away and get that warrant."

"And if this bloke stopped a robbery, why are you so intent on finding him? Did he rob the shop, too, after foiling the first attempt?"

"No, sir, but we have reason to believe there was an over-zealous use of force involved."

"So, this would-be, have-a-go hero punched somebody?"

"Are you going to let me see under the tarpaulin or not?"

"Okay, officer, okay. As you have asked so nicely."

The two of them walked over to the carport. Danny pushed some foliage aside to reach his corner of the tarp. "Here we go, officer. You take one corner, I'll take the other."

Sosa still couldn't tell what was under the covering, but she wasn't optimistic. It didn't look the right shape to be an honest-to-god American truck.

They peeled back the green canvas, slowly but surely revealing a battered ex-military Jeep underneath. It was a flatbed, but it wasn't anything you could mistake for a modern shit-kicker run-around.

"This what you're looking for, officer?"

Sosa felt a little crestfallen. She'd been pleased that her detective work had taken her this far, but disappointed that she had ground to a halt so soon.

"Thank you for both your time and your co-operation, Mr Franklin."

"Please, call me Danny. The pleasure has been all mine."

"Mr Franklin, if you are going to drive that jeep, can I recommend you get that taillight fixed, it looks cracked. I wouldn't want to have to write you up a ticket."

"There might be worse things…"

"I beg your pardon, sir?"

"I mean, there could be worse things I had to fix on my jeep."

"Oh, okay, well, good evening, sir, and thank you again."

As she walked back to her cruiser, Danny watched, taking in the way she moved. She was tall, just a little shorter than him. Dark hair, some of which had escaped the confines of a severe ponytail, had been moving lazily along the curve of her jaw in the breeze. Despite the bulk of her bulletproof vest and the various bits of kit that hung from her utility belt, he could tell she was fit; a runner's habit was obvious from her size and shape. And then, to top it all, her eyes. Dark, but with a light in them. Something about them had caused him to stare a little.

At the same time, Danny was feeling pleased that he had taken the precautionary measure of parking his truck in a rented garage he kept down in Key West. He knew he had to do a few other things, now that his knee-jerk reaction to boredom a few nights earlier had brought him unwanted attention, and so quickly.

Why had he enjoyed toying with her so much? Was it another case of anything to break out of his boredom?

He watched as she turned her squad car in a wide circle, driving away, him wondering if she'd taken a moment to watch him in her rear-view mirror.

"Step in toime. Look lively, step in toime," he said gently. "I don't think you're finished with me yet, Deputy Sosa… not just yet."

Colt was staring idly at the mosquitoes that were dancing around the sole spotlight that illuminated the car park in front of the Tom Thumb convenience store where he had just worked his last ever shift.

He thought his job had been secure (after everything that had happened in the attempted robbery), especially when that nice lady cop had spoken to Mr Komaski, telling him not to fire him. However, that evening, Mr Komaski had come right in and sacked Colt's ass, telling him the only reason he hadn't done it earlier was that he knew he didn't have anyone else to cover the shifts. Now, he had found some other bozo, Mr Komaski's words, not his, it was time for him to get the hell out. Motherfucker!

Colt was so intent on watching the dancing flies that he didn't notice the figure standing in the shadows just behind his old beater of a car.

"Hey, Colt…"

Colt nearly lost his guts right there and then. The voice scared the shit out of him, his nerves still jangled from all his troubles and the considerable amount of weed he had dedicated his life to for some time.

He was then doubly afraid when he recognised the voice. It was that Brit dude… the one who had just about ruined his life this week.

"Awww, no, no, no, no… not you, no way, man… noooo."

Colt was fumbling with his car keys, dropping them in his haste to get the fuck away from this guy. He'd had enough trouble to last a lifetime already. Plus, since he had told the cop about the dude, in a very rare moment of lucidity, it had occurred to him that it might have been a mistake. A bad one. And now, here the guy was. Probably ready to beat the shit out of him… or worse.

"Hey, Colt… calm the fuck down." Danny didn't move from his spot in the shadows. He had been careful not to be caught by the security cameras as he waited for the young clerk to come out.

"I didn't… I… I didn't tell nobody nothing, dude… Okay?"

"Colt… Chill. The. Fuck. Out. Okay, I know you spoke to the police. They came to see me. I'm cool with it… no problems from my end, sunshine… okay?"

"Why are you standing back there? In the dark… I mean… creepy…?"

"Listen, I need to talk to you. Just clear this all up… Take me for a drive."

"I'm not, you know… stupid. You're gonna kill me."

"Oh, Colt. For fuck's sake, mate. I'm not going to kill you. Stop being so dramatic."

"Dramatic? You just cost me my job, you… you… son of a bitch.'

Colt said the last bit in a way that made Danny think it was probably the bravest thing Colt had ever done in his life.

"That's what I want to talk to you about. Put it right. I've caused you nothing but trouble. Now, I want to make it up to you."

Colt paused, as if unsure what to do. Danny stepped up to the passenger door of Colt's car. Out of force of habit, Colt slipped the key into the old car's lock and opened it up, instantly thinking, *Why the fuck did I do that?*

Danny slid into the car. Quickly, Colt did the same.

He looked at Danny and wailed. "Mother… fucker… how did you… how did you make me…? I mean… Jesus H. Christ…"

"Colt, shut your bleeding mouth. Drive this hunk of crap out of the car park will you… please."

Once they were on the road, Danny sat at an angle, looking directly at Colt as he nervously steered the car.

"Where do you want me to go?"

"Anywhere, Colt. I only want to speak with you.'

"Are you a spy?"

The question made Danny laugh. "Jesus, Colt. How did you guess? I mean, how have you seen through my cover…?"

"I knew it!" Colt thumped his steering wheel for emphasis. "I told that nice lady cop, you reminded me of that spy dude out of the movies… who else but a freaking spy knows how to punch like you do."

"Calm down for a second and listen. I am here on official business, which is why I need to keep a low profile. Talking to police officers is not low profile. You hear me?"

'Yeah, dude… I'm sorry I had to… had to tell her something, she was gonna search my ride… That's not righteous…"

"Stop worrying about that now. Listen, they could still come back and ask you to identify me. I can't have that happen. My cover is in enough trouble already."

At that point, Danny laid an envelope on the seat between him and Colt. The flap was half open, a thick sheaf of dollar bills showing inside. "Colt, have you got family?"

"Only my maw, but she lives up north, Fort Lauderdale. I ain't seen her in an age, on account of that asshole she's living with. He's not my dad."

"So, how about this. How about you take a trip? Somewhere nice. Somewhere you've always wanted to go."

"I can't afford to go nowhere, especially as I… you know… ain't got no job no… no more."

It was at that point that Colt noticed the envelope.

"And I feel responsible for that, Colt. I truly do. So, to put it right, there's fifty thousand dollars in that envelope…"

Colt swerved the car, other drivers blaring their horns as they moved to avoid him. "Holy shit! Fifty thousand… Holy shit…"

"Colt, Colt… you're supposed be chillin'. Careful, man!"

"Oh, sorry… yeah, sorry… dude… but… come on! Fifty thousand!" Colt struck his steering wheel. He hit it twice this time to show Danny he was truly in awe.

"And all you have to do, Colt, is let me drive you home, get packed, and then, I'll drop you at the airport, and you can go wherever you want."

"I've always… always wanted to go to Colorado."

"Yeah? I hear the mountains are beautiful…"

"Screw that. They made… they legalised… marijuana…"

"Of course, they did. What a fine state." Danny was smiling. "This is going to be easier than I thought, man. You'll be happy there, and my cover will be safe. At least now I know I don't have to kill you."

Colt nearly crashed the car again.

Danny roared. "Relax! I'm fucking with you. Okay, so let me take you home. You can pack a case and I can drive you to the airport."

"Oh… oh… I ain't got no case. Don't have that many clothes so I've never needed a case. Any… anyways… I never been nowhere, so never needed no case. We can… we can go straight to the airport…"

"Straight to the airport it is, then, Colt. Straight there…" Danny celebrated his luck.

"Can I… can I ask you a question, mister?"

"As long as it's not about my mission, Colt. Go ahead, sunshine."

"Does your car have… you know, have… machine guns in the fender?"

❖

At about the same time as Danny was starting his chat with Colt, Deputy Sosa was cruising Highway One in her squad car. Another shift, another night where the most exciting thing that happened was rousting a local using the central median of the road to pass a tourist out of sheer frustration. That's if you didn't count meeting a mysterious Englishman.

She was thinking about taking her meal break when her radio chattered into life.

"Sosa? You got your sweet ass ears on?"

"Annie, this is Deputy Sosa. Go ahead."

"I'm about to go off shift, Honey. Got some Hush Puppies in the refrigerator with my name on 'em. But thought you might like to know something before I get the fuck outta here."

Sosa winced, but her curiosity demanded she follow up. "Go ahead, Annie. But the clean version, eh, *por favor*?"

"Honey, do you want to know about the fancy pants Miami lawyer who just turned up, flashing dental work that cost more than my goddamned condo?"

"Miami legal?"

"Jesus, Mary and Joseph, that's what I'm telling you, girl. Talked to the captain for about twenty minutes. He called the jail sergeant and those two girlies from the drive-in? They's in the wind, sister."

"Huh? But there's reasonable suspicion…"

"The fancy lawyer must've had some moves on him… Charges dropped… They are gone… like my water retention… did I mention getting old sucks donkey… oh, hold on… you wanted it clean."

Sosa had pulled her car to the side of the road so that she could sit and stare at her radio, not quite believing what she had just heard. Miami legal muscle? Someone had money, and influence, to burn. Or just money… lots of money…

It was late when Danny arrived back home. He had seen Colt off at the airport, waiting until he saw him hand his boarding pass to the lady at the end of the jetway to be sure he had gone to Colorado. Danny then had to stop on Highway One at the convenience store that had the one last public telephone for at least twenty miles. He rang the cell phone number, and his lawyer confirmed that he had worked his magic, and he would pick his fee up the next time he drove to the Keys for a little R and R. Which would be soon… Danny paid well and in cold hard cash.

All in all, he was pleased with how quickly, and tidily, he had managed to shut down the lady cop's line of interest. There was now nothing in South Florida to connect him to the convenience store incident, and he could go back to living that low profile again.

But something was gnawing at the edges of his instinct. Something… or someone was coming. He could feel it. His powers of intuition were always stronger than most, and even though there had been little call for them in a long while, it surprised him at how keenly he could feel an oncoming storm. And feel it, he most definitely could.

And, as if he needed it, some physical proof showed up almost immediately.

He was fantasising about a large shot of Blanton's Bourbon with a little ice as he climbed the steps of his house, fumbling with his key fob to unlock the door, when he kicked something with his foot. It made a metallic rattle as it pinged across his porch. Danny looked. In the gloom, he couldn't spot what he had connected with. When he flicked on his porch light, his breath caught in his throat. No wonder he couldn't quite see it in the dark. It was black. It was metal. It was a small toy car. A little model black London taxi, complete with yellow light on the top and an advert for the famous Hamleys toy store on the side.

Danny knew a message when he saw one. And as he picked the model car up, he noticed his hand was shaking. Then, the sweats came, and suddenly, his mind was convulsing, dread rising in his chest. A panic attack consumed him.

As he sank to his knees, he knew there was nothing he could do to stop it.

8

❖ Sins of the Flesh ❖

June had to be very careful.

But she knew exactly how far to push things. Many of her female friends back home would have been disgusted, but she thought it was terrific. After all, it meant that she had to do relatively little.

Plus, if she was really annoyed, it was a great way to purge irritations out of her system. And lately, her husband had become increasingly annoying, to the point where she had to remind herself "Be careful." She was never allowed to leave any marks.

So, as she angled the candle over her husband's prone torso, she counted out only five drips of the hot wax onto his, admittedly still slim, belly. He writhed where she had earlier secured him to their bed. She couldn't hear his protests, as he was gagged using a rubber ball they had bought online encased in one of her stockings. A blindfold and ear plugs completed his sensory deprivation.

She watched as his erect member twitched at the burn, wondering, for the umpteenth time in her marriage, how anyone could find this erotic. But Vincent surely did... and besides... it meant she didn't have to fuck him. Not that she had wanted to do that for a very long time. That didn't mean to say she didn't enjoy sex. She preferred it a little less weird and with men who were a little younger, fitter and who didn't pray to Jesus each time they orgasmed.

Vincent grunted, a feral noise that she couldn't quite understand. Was it their safe word? She couldn't be sure. As she poured more wax, this time onto his favourite bit of anatomy, the moaning and the groaning convinced her it had not been. He was almost at that point. The point. The moment when she could just leave him frustrated and on the edge for at least half an hour. She reached up and violently gripped his hair, yanking it so his head was pulled back further into the pillow. She could see a snarl form at the edges of his mouth, her stockings protruding as his teeth and tongue pushed them. With her other hand, she savoured the swish as she brought the one-dollar fly swat they'd found in a Wal-Mart in Coconut Creek down with vicious intent. The contact was firm, enough to make Vincent squirm. Mind you, it was his balls she was swatting. That had to hurt. His fists were opening and closing frantically. They always did in these moments, and, not for the first time, June wondered what he was imagining those hands doing? It never looked gentle.

She felt her mobile phone vibrate in her pocket. It gave her an idea, but then, she brushed it aside. Lately, she had been in no mood to indulge her husband any more than she had to.

No, he was cooked for the moment. She took the phone from her jeans and walked towards the door leaving him to his mixture of frustration, anticipation and difficult breathing for the next thirty minutes or so.

She wanted to read her text message. It simply said, *Call.*

June made her way to the kitchen of their cavernous house which overlooked Tampa Bay in Tierra Verde. The huge French doors opened up onto a terrace and garden that sloped down to the water side. It was a view she loved and never intended to tire of. That was why she was making the phone call as instructed.

The cell phone only needed to ring once before it was answered. And in her ear, she heard the words she was hoping for, delivered in a rough London accent:

"I've found the man I told you about. The one we can work with. You will go and see him."

Danny realised he had to start asking questions. He was in trouble, and he knew it. The attacks were getting more frequent and severe. Sooner or later, he would have to try to seek help.

If someone had found him, he needed to know who. It was time to ask around and see if any strange faces had appeared on the scene. He needed to get a fix on who liked leaving toy taxi cabs on his front step.

He had been keeping a low profile since his arrival in the Keys, but it didn't mean that he hadn't done his research. He knew where to go when you needed to talk to someone with a flexible attitude towards law and order. He had assumed that, sooner or later, he would have to plug back into that community, so, occasionally, he had let his presence be seen and known as someone also flexible when it came to matters of the illegal kind. Not too many details, but enough.

And where did you go when you wanted to get a little information from the types who liked to push the boundaries of the law? Danny knew exactly where. You went to where you could see one of the most extraordinary sights in the whole of Florida... possibly even America.

Woody's was a ramshackle strip joint right on Highway One in Islamorada. An establishment of questionable taste that proudly sold itself as the only nude and full liquor joint between south Miami and Key West. It should, Danny thought, be equally proud of the sight that was one of their dancers... the improbably monikered Slow Tina. And what was so remarkable about her? Tina was well into her seventies, hence the reason why she was called slow. She still danced nude... but at a much-reduced pace. As well as being a local legend, Danny had heard that she was a mine of information about the Keys' more dubious residents. He had made a point of befriending her.

Ducking into the neon lit interior of the bar, Danny was surprised to see how busy it was. Tina only danced the early evening shift these days. She couldn't handle the late nights anymore, and normally, her audience would be in single figures, but that day was a little different. She was in the middle of the crowd, managing to look regal and aloof despite her surroundings. Danny caught her eye.

Tina sidled up to an empty bar stool and Danny took the cue, he joined his favourite septuagenarian.

"How come it's crowded, Tina?'

She took a moment to rearrange the string bikini and sarong she was wearing, then took a sip from some hellish-looking blue drink. Danny tried to keep his eyes at shoulder level and above. Anywhere else led to madness.

"Honey chile, it's coupon day. They get everything 'too-fer' up until nine pm. You can print them right off that computer thingy they all got these days. You not got no coupons?"

"Too-fer?"

"Sure, sweetie… dontcha know… 'too-fer'? They don't do two for one in liddle ole London town, evah?"

"Oh, I get it… I'm not sure… maybe at the supermarket, Tina. But you sell a different type of service in here."

A cackle born of too many Marlboros rose from her throat at that. Her hair was almost all white and looked dry like straw. She reminded Danny of how Bette Davies looked in *Whatever Happened to Baby Jane?* all pancake make-up, vibrant lipstick and more wrinkles than an elephant's trunk.

"How's Morty doing?"

Danny knew it was always polite to ask Tina about Morty, her Chihuahua dog. She loved that animal, and you didn't dive right into asking favours with a Southern Belle. Manners were everything with Slow Tina.

"That dawg… he'll be the death of me. Keeps thinking he can hear ghosts in the middle of the night. Barking and yellering all over my bed at four in the morning. Still, he's the only one don't get scared when he sees me with no make-up on."

It was Danny's turn to laugh. He signalled the bartender, motioning for him to refill whatever it was that Tina was having.

"It's called a Blue Marlin, darlin'. They make 'em specially for liddle ole me"

Danny would never dream of tasting anything that colour.

"And a Woodford for me please, Sal…" If you can't beat them… he might as well join them.

"You're too kind, my handsome Brit. Is this a social visit, or we looking to talk a liddle turkey?"

"Oh, now, Tina, it's always a delight to come and visit you."

"You think I just floated my way up the Florida Straits in a bubble? Leave the flim flam for them college boys. They don't know no better."

She playfully slapped his shoulder as she said this. Danny noticed that she left her hand there, beginning to gently stroke him after putting him in his place.

"I declare, I remember the days when a young man like you would be taking me in those Vee I Pee rooms out back. You are a fine specimen, Danny. You make me feel all pre-menopausal, even in this humidity."

"Oh, Tina, that would have been my honour back in the day."

"Honour? Screw that, honey, it would have cost you all of five dollars for one song and a little touchy feel. Now, what do you need to know?"

"Okay. It's a long shot, but I think I may have had an unwanted visitor last night. So, I was wondering, if you had heard any rumours. Are there some new faces hanging around?"

"Nobody famous, sweetheart. You know the type I mean, tend to get their photies on the wall of the Sheriff's office…"

"The type I'm talking about, Tina, might not be so… careless…"

"Oh… a talented individual? Now we're getting a little more specific. But unfortunately for you, I've not heard anything… except… maybe…"

Danny leaned a little closer. The DJ had started to play *Cream* by Prince just as he and Tina had reached the crux of their chat. On the stage, a dancer flung herself around a pole like a woman possessed.

"Well… Fat Tony… you know Tony? Sure, you do… on the run for burning his strip mall down in Poughkeepsie. God Bless Florida's lax attitude to other's states arrest warrants. Well, now, he manages Porky's Barbecue joint down the Keys away… tasty conch fritters. Anyhoo, he and I were bitching a liddle about how the tourists don't tip so well like they used to. He said especially the Europeens, they just don't know how. So, he tells me about this couple who just came in the other day. They were both English, but arrived separately, her looking a million dollars and him all muscle and sunglasses. They didn't even leave a nickel behind. But what made Tony pause was that he could have sworn the man was law enforcement or military of some type. Something 'bout the way he carried himself. But those who carry a badge usually do the decent thing with their change."

"What did he look like, Tina? Did Tony say?"

"He didn't say too much, except he remembered he had a head that looked too big for his body. Oh, and something about a weird eye. One that wasn't all there."

Danny's mind was racing. Tina's confidantes had a knack of spotting detail and recognising a lawman or a specialist when they saw one. English? Possible cop or ex-military?

Not wanting to jump to conclusions, Danny knew he needed to find out more but was probably done for the moment with Tina.

He pressed a folded up one-hundred-dollar bill into Tina's hand as she started to gather her drink and her little stripper handbag off the bar.

"You're too kind, honey chile. Gotta pay my bills. Have to go now, you should nevah keep your public waiting too long… what should I dance to, Danny? A liddle Aretha? That one she did with your English boy? George Michael? That him?"

"That was him, and it sounds just perfect, Tina. You'll keep your ear to the ground for me, won't you?"

"I never deny a gennelman… especially when he's payin'…"

Tina gave him a lascivious wink that belied her years, and, not for the first time, Danny thought if he had met her when she was younger, it would have been a lot of fun to take her out back to that "Vee I Pee" area.

But now? He paid his bar bill and stood to leave. He didn't need to see Tina strut her stuff at three miles per hour. Danny left Woody's feeling worried. But at least he was in motion. He was on the hunt.

9

❖ Old Timey Gospel ❖

When Vincent Cardell felt troubled or off centre, he always returned to what he knew best. He made a few phone calls and soon he was on his way to a little revivalist tent that was touring around the upper half of Florida State. A preacher he knew had been taking the message of the bible to communities across northern Florida and into Georgia for the last three years. The small operation was run by family, literally pitching a tent in a local farmer's field and proselytising to whoever showed up.

It was Old Timey Gospel. The kind of blood and thunder Christianity that talked of the serpent Satan, the Book of Revelations and the second Coming. Would y'all be prepared when Jesus calls again?

The car journey up may have taken three hours, but, to Vincent, it was more than worth it. He was here to proclaim the precious word of The Lord. The service was in a marquee on the outskirts of White Springs. This tiny town lived in the shadow of Jacksonville but didn't share any of its more liberal attitudes to life.

The tent was stiflingly hot. Mosquitoes buzzed in the air. A smattering of faithful sat on plastic folding chairs waiting to be given the keys to the pearly gates, which many of them were not too far away from seeing.

As he took to the platform that was made out of hay bales and old wooden pallets, Vincent could feel his crisp white shirt sticking to his back. He surveyed the thirty or so audience and took a deep breath. There was no microphone or lectern to hide behind. He had his red leather bible and his own convictions. They were enough.

He spoke and wanted to talk about his true passion. He needed to hear it himself as well as for the glory of God. He needed to re-affirm his mission in life before his God, before these sinners… before his own soul.

"Pilgrims… Fellow Sinners… Fellow Penitents… I am truly blessed to be here tonight with you. Preacher Lucas was very kind to extend his hospitality and blessings to me tonight. I'd like to thank him for that."

A few half-hearted hallelujahs welcomed him.

"But let's talk, you and I, about being thankful. What is it we have in our lives to be thankful for every day? We have our families? We have our faith? It is the love of God, Jesus our saviour and the Holy Ghost. We have that every day, every time we take a breath…"

Vincent looked up from his red bible, feeling the attention of the congregation on him. They knew he was about to begin in earnest.

"But what have we got to be thankful for beyond that? Pilgrims, we live in a time of sinfulness that makes Sodom and Gomorrah look like a July fourth picnic. Men begat with men. Women with women. We have lawmakers, who we pay our hard-earned tax dollars for, sitting in their ivory towers, talking about bathrooms for tran-sex-u-al people. Abominations in the face of Adam, Eve and all that God created. We have television and the media pushing messages of tolerance for heathen religions and portraying sexual congress and drug taking as glamorous. Young minds are exposed to the in-ter-net. If ever the devil wanted to write his own script, he would surely do it on a laptop computer."

The smattering of hallelujahs was beginning to gather pace. Vincent felt his righteousness build in his chest.

"Satan's serpent moves amongst us, slithering amongst our schools, allowing the teaching of beliefs that question the Lord's Bible. The world is millions of years old? That's not what God wants us to know. A different message says we should stand side by side with other, supposed, holy books that deny our Christian rights, our heritage, the sacrifice of the Crucifixion, and the very fact that Jesus died on the cross for our souls! High and mighty charlatans teach of science with no role for divinity. They deny God's hand in our beautiful country, our beautiful America!"

The congregation was truly warmed up, their fervour growing to keep pace with Vincent's own.

"And they do all of this, safe in the knowledge that they believe they are right. Not God. But they don't know their Bible! They don't know God saw them coming. On ho-mo-sex-u-ality: *If a man lies with a male as with a woman, both of them have committed an abomination; they shall surely be put to death; their blood is upon them*. That's Leviticus twenty chapter twenty and verse thirteen. Abomination!

"On false idols and religions: *The sorrows of those who run after another god shall multiply; their drink offerings of blood I will not pour out or take their names on my lips*. That's Psalms sixteen four. Their sorrows multiply! On God and our beautiful America: *But ask the animals, and they will teach you, or the birds in the sky, and they will tell you; or speak to the earth, and it will teach you, or let the fish in the sea inform you. Which of all these does not know that the hand of the LORD has done this?* That is the book of Job. Chapter twelve, I do declare. The hand of The Lord! God knew… he knew where our vanity and our soullessness would lead us."

Each bible quote was greeted with shouts of "Praise be" and "Praise Jesus", Vincent building towards his final message, his eyes burning bright, sweat beading on his brow.

"Jesus himself said it, Pilgrims, he said it with his own mouth, the wisdom falling from his sacred lips, for us to hear, not to turn a deaf ear towards. He said: *and then many will fall away and betray one another and hate one another. And many false prophets will arise and lead many astray. And because lawlessness will be increased, the love of many will grow cold*. Lawlessness will be increased! We see this every day. Jihad. Suicide bombers. All trying to wipe away our Christianity. But our Divine Saviour will prevail. And we can help. It is our duty… our mission to help. We must take up the positions that will prevent lawlessness. We must put Christianity back into the hearts our leadership! Jesus commands it… he demands it!"

At that point, Vincent lowered his voice to a harsh whisper. He knew they were with him in the room. He had them.

"So, the next time you're in that voting booth, be it to elect a sheriff, a congressman, a senator or a president, take a moment. Are they Christian? Do they hold the blessed hand of Christ in theirs? Will they lead from the bible and not from the sinful, latter day Sodom our country has created? Will they put Jesus to the fore? Will they serve us as we serve our Lord? For, as it says in the second book of Peter, *The heavens and earth that now exist are stored up for fire, being kept until the day of judgment and destruction of the ungodly.*"

The room had fallen silent. Heads nodded to replace the shouts and cries of devotion.

"Elect leaders who will bring that fire. Become leaders who will bring that fire. Unleash the Fire on the scientists who tell us climate change will rob us of the land and water that God gives us. Our God would not abandon us in such a way. Bring fire upon the gays, the transsexuals, the deviants who promote sodomy and subversion of God's way. Bring fire unto the false prophets, the Jihadis, those who would deny our great saviour's light! Bring Fire! Rain fire down on them so that our America can be a beacon of Christ's way and Christ's love for us. That is our calling! Bring fire, pilgrims, fire that can cleanse and return the righteous to the very heart of our nation and our families. Rise up for Jesus… it can be our only salvation! Bring fire! Bring that holy fire!"

Vincent was shouting, his passion making his voice crack and lips spit. The congregation joined in with him, leaving their plastic seats, pleading for the destruction of fellow human beings, shouting the deadly mix of fundamentalist Christianity and patriotism into the air. Just as he wanted. Just as Vincent Cardell wanted for himself. For some day, he hoped to be the name on that ballot, the name against which these souls could put their tick. And that was why he wanted all that money. Politics, he knew, was an expensive game, one that required risk. He was prepared to take those risks, and if that meant using sleight of hand, or more, to fool the likes of Ines Zedillo and her masters, then he would take it. He would be as Christ's champion on earth. He wanted this more than anything, because he knew it was what God wanted.

The journey back to Tampa was long, Vincent felt exhausted as he always did after preaching, whether it be to thousands at one of his big rallies or a tent in the middle of nowhere to a handful of souls.

The air conditioning of the car was a welcome relief after the muggy air in the tent earlier. But despite his fatigue and need for a shower, Vincent's work for the night was not yet done. His driver steered down the I-75. The three-hour drive home would be lengthened by a detour into the city of Tampa to meet with the head of security for Vincent's operation.

Staring out of the car window, watching the night fly by, Vincent was struck by how far he had journeyed. He had never suspected that he would need a head of security. But his ferocious ambition had propelled him to places, alliances and situations he could never have foreseen. And as his attempts to realise his ambitions grew, they brought him into ever murkier waters.

They met regularly, once every two weeks, and that night was the night. He would have various updates for Vincent, but on this occasion, there would be an extra element to the usually straight forward proceedings.

They pulled into the car park at Riverfront Park. The soccer pitches and tennis courts were long empty after the evening sports fans had gone home. Vincent's limo drew level with a black four-door Mercedes, decked out in privacy glass. A driver stepped out to open the rear door. The security manager made the switch from the Merc to the limo, joining his boss for their update meeting.

"Good evening, Pastor Cardell."

Vincent regarded the tall, greying man. They had been working together for over two years, and it was only now that he truly felt he could trust him. Mind you, recent events had increased the need for trust.

"Mr Norby… good to see you. Do you have what I asked for?"

"Yes, sir, as requested."

"Good man. Shall we do the update first, before other business?"

"Yes, sir. I'm due to meet with the guys at the Miami Conference Centre this coming week to finalise plans for our upcoming mission. But everything seems to be in place. There is not much to adjust from last time."

"Excellent. Now, what about that journalist?"

"The lady in question has been told, again, that her requests for an interview will continue to be ignored. We have identified a fellow believer in the higher management of the *Miami Sun Times*. He will be apprised of the situation later this week. That should be the end of it."

"I want to know the moment that happens. We can't let a hack trying to dig up anti-Christian dialogue disrupt our work."

"Of course, sir."

"And… my wife?"

"Nothing much to report this week. With the exception of one thing. She made an un-diarised stop at a barbecue joint one lunchtime in the Keys."

"A barbecue joint? My wife?"

"We weren't there to witness it, sir. It stood out when I reviewed the log from the tracker on her car."

This piqued Vincent's curiosity. Norby did not know June that well. A barbecue joint? She was more likely to stab herself in the eye than to eat somewhere with anything less than a Michelin star on the menu.

"And nowhere unusual before or after?"

"No, sir. Straight there, straight home."

"Are we still tapping her phone?"

"Not since she lost her handset a month ago."

Vincent remembered it. The big fuss she made of having misplaced it. The handset never showing up, despite having a tracking app activated on it. It was as if the damned thing had just vanished off the face of the planet. She had acted considerably upset, lamenting the loss of her contacts and photos, telling him her last back-up had failed.

"We'll try and get back into her new phone this coming week, sir. Perhaps while you are both on an engagement or a TV appearance."

"Okay, good. Keep a close eye on that tracker… And now, more delicate business."

"I'll just get him…"

Norby exited the limo, leaving Cardell to briefly puzzle over his wife's lunch habits. Cardell had ordered the tracker for June's car as soon as Norby had started working for him. It wasn't that Vincent suspected anything, but he liked the idea of being sure. He felt that way about most people he kept close, the numbers of which could be counted on the fingers of one hand.

The door of the limo opened, and Norby ushered in a bulky man dressed casually, an uncomfortable expression on his face.

When both men were sat and settled opposite Vincent, he spoke. "Mr Ferragamo, thank you for joining us. I apologise as to the lateness of the hour, but I have been busy reconnecting a few souls with our Lord's wishes."

"I… it's perfectly fine, Pastor Cardell. It is important work."

"That it is, Mr Ferragamo… that it is. I just wanted to take this opportunity to thank you. We have recently called upon you to do some… how can I put it? Extraordinary duties? Would that be fair to say?"

"Yes, Pastor. In my old life, it was something I was well used to doin'."

"Indeed. I recall, I met you at one of my missions in Raiford, the Florida State Prison, did I not?"

"Yes, Pastor, I was finishing a ten stretch. Armed robbery…"

"And, how was it? Raiford, I mean?"

"It was okay, I suppose… I had rough moments…"

"Did you belong to… a gang? Where did you stand in the yard at exercise?'

Ferragamo was looking puzzled. The Pastor had never spoken much to him directly, never mind plucking him from his favourite bar in order to meet in the middle of the night and talk over prison yard politics. He looked down at his shoes, his reflection looking back at him in the shine. "I was affiliated to a biker gang, Scorpions…"

"Not to a… *famiglia*?"

"I have no Sicilian blood, Pastor… I was more into… well, my buddies… meth and the like. In the outside world. But now I know Jesus, Pastor. I want to reassure you of that."

Ferragamo looked as though he felt he was on some kind of back foot here, trying to say things he thought the Pastor might want to hear.

"Did the Scorpions ever make use of any of your… special talents?"

"I'm not sure I'd like to say…"

"Oh, come now, Mr Ferragamo. We are all made equal in the eyes of Jesus, and I have made use of those talents myself. Don't be coy."

"Maybe, Pastor. A lot of things went on in Raiford. Sometimes stuff had to get done… you know… to stay alive."

"I see. And what would your friends in the Scorpions have done had the task you'd been set turned out less than an unqualified success?"

Ferragamo was in full on panic mode, sweat breaking on his brow. "I've done all that was asked. I held Manny down. I helped clean up. I ditched the body myself."

What he hadn't noticed during the conversation was that Norby, sitting beside him, had donned a pair of see-through plastic gloves. Something that flashed in the internal limo's light was now in those plastic-covered hands.

Norby made a grab for Ferragamo's left wrist, exhibiting surprising levels of strength as he did so, clamping the arm under his. Gripping a wrist with one hand, with his other, Norby slotted a nasty looking pair of pruning shears around the ex-convict's pinky finger, easing pressure onto it so that the shears bit into the skin. Ferragamo knew instantly not to struggle.

"Look at me, Mr Ferragamo, not Mr Norby. It would be best for you if you pay attention to me. Right now."

Ferragamo's head swivelled like he was in a dream, in slow motion. Panic made it hard for him to shift his focus any faster.

"The body, Mr Ferragamo. It showed up. Rather too quickly, it so happens. And the wrong people found it… also rather too quickly."

"I did what I was told… I did everything… I don't know what could have happened. I put stones in the coat pockets, I lashed chains to him… I don't… I didn't…"

"When the very people I do not want finding that particular body suddenly produce photos of it, I get a touch suspicious."

"I swear to you, Pastor. On my life, on the Holy Bible… I did all I was asked. I don't even know who you were trying to stay clear from…'

"Mr Norby has already assured me of your associations, Mr Ferragamo. But, you see, we are engaged in some deeply serious work on this project. And I can't have failure. You must realise that. We can't let others in our brotherhood see that mistakes are left unpunished. We can't let complacency take root like poison ivy in our midst. So, come now. Accept what you have brought onto yourself. If it helps, we can pray together, you and I, as Mr Norby does what cannot be avoided."

Ferragamo was wild-eyed, the shears biting further into his skin. He had begun the journey to Christianity with this so-called pastor as a way of getting his jail time reduced, but slowly, he had found a certain solace and logic in his words. The charisma and the way the organisation had reached out to Ferragamo on release, when no one else would, had made for a seductive package. But now, here, in the back of this big car with his finger bleeding and the Pastor opposite him reciting the Lord's Prayer, Ferragamo looked aghast.

"You… you bastard. This ain't Christian. This ain't Jesus' way. I thought I had joined a church, but fuck you. You're nothing but another gang, one as brutal as any I ever saw in prison."

"Say 'Amen' with me, Ferragamo, at least give the Lord that much respect…"

"Wha? You motherfu—"

Cardell nodded to Norby, who squeezed with all his might.

The crack as the bone severed and the spray of blood that accompanied it caused Cardell to shift quickly in his seat. Cardell stared at the red splatter that had fallen on the seat next to him. The bright shock of it against the black leather enthralled him. Almost absentmindedly, he spoke again.

"Mr Norby will see to your wound. Goodnight, Mr Ferragamo. I trust you now know the depth to which I require my brothers to feel our mission. I wouldn't like to be in your shoes if you ever let me down again. Mind you, I doubt you will. God bless you, sir. God bless us all as we attend to his work." His face was plastered with a beaming smile as he said it.

10

❖ Hook, Line and Sinker ❖

Danny hated planking. Locking his core muscles as he lay face down on his elbows and the tips of his toes, legs rigid to support his weight. He knew it was good for him, a fiendishly effective exercise that delivered. Still, he fucking hated it. He had completed the other rounds of his morning routine. He had boxed with a bag that hung behind his carport, flung weights around to keep his arms, shoulders, back and chest taut, and finally abdominals and the dreaded plank for his core.

Any distraction from his complaining muscles was welcome. It was a chance to let his core relax, give in to gravity and let his body settle back onto his hands and knees. The crunch of a car's wheels on the oyster-shell drive heralded the arrival of a fancy-looking car pulling up to his house. He figured this was a pretty good excuse to stop planking.

The Florida sun was low in the morning sky, so it was still cool in his front yard, but the sweat was pouring from his head, his damp training vest clung to his chest as he approached the car.

The door opened, and a slender leg emerged. Danny was curious. It was a feeling which only grew as the leg was completed by a tall, brunette-haired woman. She held her head high as she walked towards him. Her chin jutted out, a little elevated to show him she was a confident woman.

"Have I caught you at an inconvenient moment, sir?"

Danny realised he must look like he'd been dragged to hell and back and mopped his forehead with the towel hanging over his shoulder. "No, not at all. Just finishing the hardest work of my day. I quite like excuses to stop trying to 'plank'."

"Oh, God. I hate those. My personal trainer is forever banging on about how good they are. Torture is what I call them."

Danny instantly caught the English accent buried beneath a burgeoning transatlantic twang. In the recent past, it might have excited an interest, but that morning, it made every alarm bell in his subconscious go off like there was an electrical fire breaking out in his brain.

"Mind you, being strong in that position can be useful in so many ways. My name is June Cardell. Are you the fishing man?" The brunette extended a hand towards him, which Danny responded to by gesturing to his sweaty demeanour.

"You might want me to wash my hands before shaking yours. And yes, I am the… fishing man."

"Nonsense. A little sweat never hurt anyone. Pleased to meet you."

She moved in close for the handshake, the smell of her perfume wafting towards him as she did so. He was struck by how long it had been since he had spent any time in the company of a woman.

An awkward pause followed as Danny collected himself. June Cardell swept a stray strand of hair back behind her ear.

'Err, so how can I help, Miss…?"

"It's Mrs… Mrs June Cardell. I was hoping to charter you for a day's fishing. It's what you do, after all…"

"Oh, right. Yeah, that's… indeed. I fish. When were you hoping to go?"

"Today would work for me. I think the weather looks perfect. I have the time, and I came looking. Your sign on the roadside seems to be all you advertise with. I tried googling you before I pulled up onto your drive."

"I run a low-key operation here, Mrs Cardell. If you don't mind me saying, you don't look dressed to go on a fishing trip."

June looked down at herself, as if taking stock of her knee length skirt and blouse ensemble. "Oh, this outfit? Don't worry I have some cut-offs, T-shirt and pumps in my car. Are you free?"

Danny didn't know what to say. He was used to tourists seeing his sign and pulling in off the road. He always had the boat ready to go for just such a scenario. Plus, he liked to go out on the Gulf of Mexico on days like this one, when the water was calm and the sun sparkled on its surface like jewels on a crown, whether he had a paying customer or not. But this woman was making him feel wary. His mind flashed back to his thoughts of an oncoming storm. Was this woman the first signs of that storm?

"I can pay. I have cash. You probably prefer cash. Who wants to pay taxes and write up receipts?"

"I…" Danny couldn't think straight; she was blindsiding him.

"Why don't you go and have a shower. I can change in the back of my car. I've got all that privacy glass, so I won't be putting on a show."

June Cardell didn't wait for his response. She turned away, making straight for her car, and Danny couldn't think of anything else to do but go and have that shower. It looked like he was going fishing, and with a paying customer.

The deputies of the Monroe County Sheriff's office worked solo in their cruisers, but there were always at least two on duty on that stretch of road at any given time. So, in a way, you did have a partner, and you came to be buddies with them, because if things got a little interesting out there, they would usually be the first on any scene to help.

Amparo Sosa felt very lucky because her shift buddy was someone she trusted and could call her friend. And there was nothing more she liked better on the job than breaking for lunch or coffee and catching up with her fellow Deputy Sheriff, Cheryl Costanza. They were at their usual lunch haunt, Lazy Days, just before Tea Table Key. Cheryl loved the coconut shrimp, but Amaparo preferred the chowder. That day, they were making each other laugh.

"I tell you, that sonofabitch, he says to me, 'Deputy, you don't have the jurisdiction to write me up.' So, I just started writing him up. 'Here, here's your moving violation… one hunnerd and sixty bucks. Thank you so very much.'"

Cheryl was giggling at her own story. "I mean, Amparo, if you could've seen this jerk's face as I handed him the ticket and reminded him I wasn't state and that he was in my territory. You know when a kid is sucking on a Twinkie and you take it away from him? He looked just like that."

Sosa joined in her laughter, easily recognising the face she was describing. How many times had a tourist made that mistake?

"It was like that time I stopped that *hombre* on over by the State Park at Indian Key…"

"Which? The gang banger?"

"No, that was outside Woody's. No, the *Touron* with the battered, white conch cruiser. I think it was a Hyundai. His girlfriend was so out of it, she didn't even know I'd pulled them over. And he goes – I ain't got nuttin' in the automobile, Sheriff… and as he says it, she comes round and asks him for the baggie!"

They were laughing harder now.

"So, I ask him to get out the car. You know, *amigo*, just do yourself a solid and step out slowly. He starts to whine, 'You ain't got no right!' All I had to do was rest my hand on my baton. He got out of the car like a jack rabbit. Anyway, I find nothing, no baggie, no blunt ends, nothing and just as I'm about to give up, his girlfriend starts saying something. He's trying to shut her up, until eventually she goes, 'The smokie didn't look in back, did she?'"

Cheryl blew Mountain Dew down her nose at this.

"So, lover boy is now cussing and swearing. I open the trunk… at least forty pounds of *mejor cocaina*… all packed up nice and pretty. It's like Captain Corey likes to say over and over… the dumber they are…"

Cheryl finished their boss's mantra for her. "The smarter we look… Amen to that, sister. Amen."

They laughed a little more, until a question passed across Cheryl's face.

"*Que, hermana*? You have a question?"

Cheryl looked at her, a little sheepish. "Did you ask Captain Corey? About the drive-in girls? It's been nagging at me since you told me. I don't figure the Captain to be a pushover..."

"Yeah, yeah, I did ask him. I don't think he was letting anything slide. When the fancy lawyer showed up, he had about eight sheaves of paper all filled with reasons why we couldn't hold or charge those girls. No DNA. An unreliable witness, who is now nowhere to be found. No video surveillance footage and the car we towed wasn't registered to them. Plus, a bunch of legal bullshit to go along with it. Captain said he was going quote the Constitution at him if he hadn't let them go."

"You ever seen the Cap look so unnerved?"

"No, *hermana*, no way. But what can we do? It's like the day I pulled that *Touron* over with the dumbass girlfriend. I just knew, when I saw their car... I knew. Something was *muy malo*..."

Cheryl looked at her friend and colleague from over the tops of her sunglasses. "Yeah, I hear ya. When something stinks, it stinks."

"And you know... Florida Keys... the sunny place, for shady people."

The two cops clinked glasses on that note, both taking comfort from their shared understanding.

"But, hey, sister, from what you told me, the Brit guy you found? He's a good-looking guy, this Brit? That's gotta be enough for you to take another look. I mean, strictly professional interest here."

They laughed again.

"What was it you said? Oh yeah... 'He had this hot voice'... who even thinks that?"

Amparo swatted at Cheryl, her friend pulling back at the last second. The blush came easily to the young deputy's cheeks. She collected herself, noting on her watch that their lunch break was almost up.

"He had more than just a hot voice, *muchacha*... I can tell you. But he did make my radar ping. I think you might be right. I might need to take a second look. C'mon. We gotta get back to pushing the green and white."

Sosa was right, their time was up. They had to return to keeping the peace.

As she climbed back into her green and white liveried police car, she started to talk to herself, aloud, gently. "*Sí, señorita*, I think we might just take another look at *El ingles*..."

It was a beautiful day. Danny's boat was drifting aimlessly, having left Florida Bay behind and entered into the deeper waters of the Gulf of Mexico. He loved it when the sea was like this. A perfect blue in the sunlight, with a surface like glass, with only the wake of his own boat disturbing the calm.

However, he was having a hard time enjoying it that day. Every time he tried to engage his customer on the subject of fishing, of even trying to fish, she seemed disinterested. Taking the time instead to stretch out those long legs of hers, now clad in cut-off denim shorts, the sea breeze pushing the hair straight back on her head. She had her sunglasses on, meaning he couldn't get a real fix on her facial expressions. Danny was having trouble reading this woman, and he didn't like it. Not one bit.

In the end, he gave up the idea of even casting a line into the sea. He cracked open one of his coolers and offered the lady a drink.

"Do you have any wine?"

Danny began to shake his head before she cut him off.

"Oh, for heaven's sake, what am I asking... a beer? I'll take a beer."

Danny passed a bottle of Coors Light to her. Ice was sliding down the glass adding its own twinkle to the afternoon. "So... Mrs Cardell... what part of England are you from?"

"I was wondering when you'd pick up on that. I'm a good old-fashioned Home Counties girl. Bucks, through and through..."

"But that accent…?"

"It only really comes out these days when I talk to the likes of you. You're a London boy… proper cockney, innit?'

Danny allowed himself a smile and nodded, pulling the tab on his can of Dr Pepper.

"Not joining me in a cold one, Mr… Franklin?"

"I like to keep my boat, and guests, intact whilst out here on the salt."

"How super responsible of you. And where exactly are we?"

Danny crossed from his perch on the side of the boat to where she was sitting, in the pivot chair that was supposed to help the fishing fan battle with whatever took a bite of their bait. Right now, June Cardell was using it to work on her already impressive tan.

Danny stood next to her and pointed. "Back that way is up into the Everglades. Unless you want to get stuck in a swamp and meet alligators, I'd steer clear of there."

He turned, using his foot to swivel her chair at the same time so that she kept pace with his pointing hand. "Go further up and you are on the way to Tampa. Go left a bit, there's Tallahassee, and if you really wanted to keep going, you can get all the way over there to New Orleans."

"New Orleans? Isn't that a den of iniquity? A place filled with hard liquor, hot jazz and loose women?"

"Forgive me for saying, Mrs Cardell, but you don't strike me as a woman who would shock so easily."

June angled herself a little further back in her seat, as if taking him in before responding. "I'm just a country girl from England. What would I know about 'juke joints' and 'flop pads'?"

Danny was surprised by her use of the "N'awlin's" slang terms. She was full of surprises.

"In all seriousness, Danny – and as I'm calling you that I hope you will start to call me June – I really don't frequent the seedier cities that North America has to offer."

"Okay… June… I think I've got that message but answer me this. Why are you here? Today? With me?"

"Simple, I have lived in Florida for at least six years now, and not once have I been out on a boat, to fish or… anything else really. That's a bit like visiting London and never setting foot in a black taxi, isn't it?"

The mention of a London taxi tweaked Danny's gut instantly.

'I suppose. But you could have gotten onto any boat. There are a lot more well-known charters than mine."

"I have a habit of doing things on the spur of the moment. Spontaneity is one of my favourite ways to behave."

"And how does… Mr Cardell, take to all this 'in-the-moment' behaviour?"

June turned to look at him, pushing forward in her seat, her bare leg touching his. "Is that what is making you seem… on edge, Danny? Are you worried what my husband might think… or do?"

Danny smiled and moved his leg away at the same time. "Listen, Mrs Cardell, I don't tend to worry about what anyone else may or may not do, or how they may react to a situation. All I care about is when someone is playing a bit of a game with me."

Danny was warming to his theme. He felt he was about to discover exactly what this English woman was doing here on his boat. Was she the one leaving toy cars on his porch?

"Are you a man of Jesus, Danny? Have you accepted him into your heart as your Lord and Saviour?"

Danny was thrown off balance by the curveball question. *Why does everyone who shows up on my boat turn out to be into God these days?* "Mrs Cardell, excuse my blunt language, but I don't fuck with Jesus, and he doesn't fuck with me."

"How very refreshing…"

At that, June Cardell hooked her leg round Danny's and pulled him towards her. At the same time, she pushed out of her seat with the other leg and met him full on. He could smell her hair, the rise of her breasts against him. Tightening her grip, she gave him a long, open-mouthed kiss, her hands running over his chest as she did so. Danny couldn't help but respond, meeting her strength, kissing her back.

When she was done, she held his arms by his sides and threw her head back, gently laughing. Danny was, in every sense of the word, gobsmacked.

"Have you never met a woman who simply takes what she wants, Danny?"

Danny looked down at her, not really knowing what to say next, so he decided to do what he wanted instead. He pulled her against him and kissed her, this time running his hand down her back to her rear, using the waist of her shorts to tighten the contact between them.

"I kiss better when I know it's coming, Mrs Cardell, and now I'm pretty sure I'm being toyed with. Who the fuck are you?"

He let her go, and she sat back down into the pivot chair, rearranging her hair as she did so.

"That was most enjoyable, Danny, but I think you should start by telling me who you are. London boy, shows up in the Keys out of nowhere? Lives in a little roadside shack, yet has enough money to buy a boat and, probably a passport and driver's licence with a different name on it…"

Danny took a long, slow swig from his Dr Pepper and regarded the woman with a cooler eye. She was asking exactly the kind of questions he had managed to avoid for almost two years. He didn't intend to start answering them now.

"Has it occurred to you that we are out on the salt, in the middle of nowhere? And you start asking me questions? Did you come here to fish, or fish around me?"

"No need to come over all London gangster on me, Danny. Cool your jets. I'm just having a little fun. Aren't you? Don't tell me that kiss wasn't fun?"

"I never mix pleasure with business."

"Well then, our association is going to be very boring. You're starting to remind me of my Jesus-freak husband. Let me tell you about him."

And she did.

❖

As Deputy Sheriff Sosa pulled off Highway One onto the oyster-shell drive that led to Danny's house, she didn't know why, but she cut the engine on her green and white, and let the car drift a few yards to a natural stop. Why had she done that? She wasn't sure, but it had felt the right thing to do. This *Ingles* wasn't official business… at least not now, but she was still intrigued. Was that professional curiosity or something else? Or worse… a bit of both? Sosa didn't want to answer her own question.

She stepped out of her car and made her way slowly up the drive. She was being careful to stay close to the Camellia bushes that bordered both sides of the drive. That way, she was shielded from view of the porch. She walked far enough to see the front of the house but still be obscured when she spotted movement ahead of her. But, to her surprise, it wasn't the man she was expecting. This was a huge man, bigger than the Danny she had met, broader, slightly taller, with a head that was wide and clean shaven. He was squatting to set something down on the stoop of the porch, and then, he was off, making his way to the side of the house that led to the boat dock.

Sosa waited until he had disappeared around the corner of the house before she moved closer. She heard the rasp of an outboard motor on a small boat, leading her to believe the tall man had departed. She jogged to that corner of the house in double quick time. As she peeked round it, she managed to see a skiff leaving the dock where it met the local channel. The man was alone.

It was only then that Sosa realised that she had her hand resting on the butt of her service pistol. She let out her breath in an audible blow. Turning, she took stock of the front yard of the modest dwelling. There was an expensive-looking Mercedes SUV out front that she hadn't seen last time she was there. She made her way back towards the steps of the porch, looking to see what it was that the tall man had been left.

She bent down, looking at the little flash of red sitting there. A model of a vehicle of some kind. Bright red, like a big coach or bus. She went to pick it up but then hesitated. On closer inspection, she realised it was a toy. She had seen one in a film once, something romantic and funny… Was it that Christmas one? *Love Actually*? She couldn't be sure.

Why would someone leave a toy bus on someone's stoop? And why had she felt tension as she had watched the man do it? She had been holding her breath, her hand still on her gun.

Everything about *El Ingles* enveloped him in further mystery as far as she was concerned. He might just be worth keeping tabs on for all sorts of reasons.

11

❖ Business or Pleasure? ❖

As soon as she began to make her play, Danny knew that June Cardell had form, a past. Still, it surprised him when she told him it all right off the bat.

Sitting at the back of the boat, she shared the story of her life in England.

"I'm a Buckinghamshire girl… little village called Seer Green. Growing up, I was bored, so it was too easy. Too easy to fall for the wrong man at the wrong time. His name was Don. It was all infatuation, lust, excitement. In a very short time, he managed to blur my boundaries and convince me that my family didn't love me. Only he could. The more they tried to intervene, the more I believed him."

Danny listened intently, now and again, little stabs of recognition punctuating her words. Hadn't he, too, been bored? He, too, had chosen a lifestyle his family felt alien.

"Soon, I was involved in his less-than-well thought-out drug distribution network. It was exciting, dangerous, and I have to admit, I liked a puff and sniff myself. But he was an amateur. Within six months, other gangs were circling us. He was so sure he could ride out anything, he could use his balls and brass neck to face anything the mean streets of Bucks could throw at him. Turns out that when others show up, the streets of Bucks aren't all that. He disappeared overnight, and I got woken by the loudest of policeman's knocks."

Her eyes had gone a little glassy, the reflection of the blue water and even bluer sky giving her a wistful look. Danny had to stop himself from chuckling. *She could win Oscars, this one.*

"I talked, gave the Old Bill the evidence they needed. All they had to do was find him. Then, one night, one of the coppers showed up at the woman's shelter they'd dumped me in. Took me to a pub, bought me some food, made me feel a little human again. Then, he offered me a different kind of deal. One that would sort out any worries I might have had if they did catch my ex. If he did his time, afterwards, would he come looking for me?"

"Let me guess. He offered you a more permanent solution, one with no comebacks?"

She nodded, not looking at Danny, staring off to the horizon. "All I had to do was ask around, do some sniffing. If I could find my ex, I was to tell the copper where other interested parties might find him before the Old Bill did. In return, I'd be given cash and a plane ticket. A chance to start over.

"It didn't take long. His mates were never really his mates, and soon, they were spilling their guts to me, telling me where he was. A week later, I landed here in America. I was staying in a boarding house in Washington. I chose there, because, for some reason, to me, New York felt too obvious a place to hide. A few weeks later, a brown envelope was delivered to me by courier. Inside, it was a single page from the *Evening Standard*. On the front was a photo of a yellow Range Rover full of bullet holes. I knew the car instantly. My ex was most definitely now ex."

"Guilty?" Danny watched her carefully. This answer would tell him more than anything about who he was dealing with.

"Not a shred." Her face changed, hardening as she said it. "He took my life and used it like toilet roll. I was his little trophy. He traded on my looks to impress his so-called mates. It was like I was a shiny sports car. Just another status symbol he felt he needed to cement his own self-worth. Yes, I was complicit, but I was too young to know any different."

"What did you do next?"

"I kept moving. I thought it best. I drifted down the East Coast, spent some time in a weird, hippy commune in North Carolina, whacked out on quality cannabis. All the clichés: nights chanting around a campfire, sleeping under starlight. It soon wore thin.

I was thinking about moving on again, when one morning, a relatively new camp member asked me if I believed in God."

"A Damascene moment…"

"You know a little bible then, Danny?"

He shrugged in reply.

"Why am I being so open with you? Is it the sultry warmth of the afternoon or the sway of the boat?" She was studying him. He could feel her eyes as they swept up and down the length of him.

"What can I say, June? I like a good story…"

"If only it were just a story, Danny."

"What answer did you give the woman? About God…"

"What God would want anything to do with me? Especially as I had blood on my hands… and not just Don's… my ex… I'm sure others died because of the smack we sold to them."

June swept a stray strand of hair behind her ear, looking a little lost in her own reverie.

"Anyway, when I quit the commune, I went south. Almost by accident I started going to church. Proper ones at first. It didn't matter whether it was Catholic or Episcopalian, I didn't care. I just liked the stillness. Then, one day, in North Florida somewhere, God knows where, I stumbled across a little revivalist tent, you know the type. All blood and thunder from the pulpit. I had realised I was running low on cash. Anxiety was creeping up on me, keeping me awake nights. I was getting desperate. So, there I was, almost broke, weighing up what few options I had when I met him."

June shifted her position, letting the sun fall flush on her face as she reminisced. "He was blood, thunder and fire all wrapped up in scripture and charisma. He was handsome and passionate. He plucked me from my seat in the fourth row. It was easy, mind you; there were only about fifteen people in the tent. He looked at me and told me I was lost. He put his hands on my head and prayed. He said that only Jesus could wash away the blood in my life. I was gobsmacked. How did he know? What could he see?"

Danny cleared his throat. She paused, looking back at him, frowning. He raised his hands. "I wasn't going to say anything. I just needed to clear my throat."

"No, you were going to say something like, 'Isn't that just a typical, Old Testament kind of thing a preacher would say?'. The answer is yes… but also no. He was looking at me… into me. He knew. Vincent Cardell knew more about me in that moment than I knew about myself."

June stood up and walked towards Danny. Her hair caught the last rays of the afternoon sun, her eyes were shining, her feline gait making Danny swallow involuntarily.

"At the end of the revival service, I waited to speak to him. He told me there and then that he could show me, through Jesus, that I could repent and be whole again, that I could admit my failings and find a path forward. Three months later, we were married in a little white church in St Augustine. Shortly after that, things got a little more… intense."

She stood directly in front of Danny, close enough to feel her breath on his face. He wanted to shift back a little, but he was already on the gunwale of the boat. The next step would be a wet one.

"As we grew to know each other, I soon realised that Vincent wasn't just driven in his faith in Jesus. He's driven in practically every facet of his life. He has… appetites. A dark side. Driven. Firstly, for scripture. I knew that. But what I didn't know was that he was also hungry to spread the word of Jesus in more ways than simply preaching. Vincent wants power. Political power. And that hunger and drive brings ruthlessness with it. Ruthlessness to fight for the one thing that kind of power feeds off in America."

Danny laughed softly. "A shit load of money. That is what it takes to acquire a position of real influence."

June nodded back. Reaching out to him, she took his hand, pulled him up off his perch on the side of the boat. She led him towards the "fighting chair" that faced out to sea at the back of the boat. It was the scene of many conquests, all of the sports fishing kind.

She sat him down in the seat and stood over him, continuing to talk. "So, we needed money. Lots. Vincent was becoming something of a star on the Evangelical circuit, pulling in bigger crowds at bigger churches. Invitations to appear on Gospel TV shows rolled in. A few at first, then more and more, until two years ago, we launched the 'Miami Mission'. Eight thousand people crammed into the 'South Beach Tabernacle'. And that was night one. We held another, six months later. Bigger venue. More nights. Twelve thousand people a night. But still, even with donations and T-shirt sales, Vincent wanted more."

"I can see where this might be heading. Did your Vincent climb into bed with someone? A little business arrangement?"

"Indeed he… we… did."

June moved closer to him. She traced the line of his beard where it swept down the side of his neck, touching the slightly frayed collar of his Lucky Brand, Johnny Cash T-shirt. "You smell delicious, a mix of the smell of sea salt and heat."

Danny swallowed.

"Being a follower of Jesus is a thriving business, Danny. Money flowed in. Lots of it. Donations, all paper ones, flooded in at our mission events. It would be an easy thing to pad those returns out with the proceeds of crime. Cash in dirty, profits out clean. Charitable disbursements to schools and hospitals and orphanages in Eastern Europe, North Africa… Central and South America. Shit, we even actually built a few of them for real. Meanwhile, our partners reclaimed their clean cash, and we kept a percentage of the action. We now had real juice."

She leant into him, sliding an arm around his neck, steadying herself so that she could use her other hand to unfasten the button on her cut-off denim shorts. Watching her shimmy out of them had Danny transfixed, especially when he realised that she wasn't wearing any underwear.

"So, tell me, June. What was the point at which you realised this was all going to go Pete Tong?" Danny put his hands on her hips, running them down over her thighs as she straddled him.

"I was always nervous about it. I mean, we were getting in to bed with serious players."

"It seems to me that getting in to bed with a player might not be all that alien to you..."

She playfully slapped his shoulder in response, then followed by lowering her full weight onto his lap. "But what really made me doubt the wisdom of all this was Vincent's impatience. He decided our cut wasn't enough. We weren't amassing the political war chest quickly enough. So, he started skimming off the top. Just a little here and there. Putting it down to bribes at first, then local expenses at the foreign ends of our ventures and finally under-reporting the churn of funds. Given that crime is mostly a cash game, he believed they'd never really know how much we were actually laundering."

"But you think they do know." He could feel her, the heat and pressure of her body on him creating exactly the kind of reaction he knew she wanted.

"Yes. They either do already, or they will soon. I think Vincent believes he has the righteousness of Jesus on his side. This, after all, is for the greater glory of his word and testament. Only through politics and leadership can you really promote a White, Christian, American agenda. And I think he's also in it for the thrill..."

She rotated her hips slowly, noticing how he flexed his thigh muscles to accommodate her weight and movement. His shoulder muscles rolled as he helped her lift her T-shirt over her head.

"And you aren't a thrill seeker, June?"

"It's one thing being a thrill seeker. It's another ripping off a Mexican drug cartel."

And there it was. The moment of truth Danny had been waiting for. The real reason why June Cardell had found her way to Danny's little house and onto his boat, ending up on his lap. She wanted him to help ease the situation with their enemies in some way.

She slid her hand up his back onto his neck, pulled him in close and kissed him fully on the lips. Danny let her and then joined in, matching the urgency of her kisses.

"I thought you just told me you didn't mix business with pleasure? You're sending me mixed messages, sir."

"You told me you were a follower of Jesus, they tend not to break the sacred institution of marriage…"

"No, I said I went to church and married a preacher. I never said I became stupid when I found the love of Jesus… Vincent may have been able to look into my soul… but it's still my soul. My experiences back home in England taught me to always be my own woman." She reached down and pulled at Danny's shorts.

"And so, you sought me out. How can I help, June Cardell? How can I help this God-Fearing yet earthy, married yet independent woman?"

June suddenly sat still, leaning back away from him. "Why that's easy. Firstly, you're going to help me rob my husband…" She kissed Danny again, adjusting her balance as he pushed back.

"And secondly…?"

"Secondly, we're going to make him think he's in on it…"

"Tricky… but go on…"

"Well… that's enough for now, except… now, now, you're going to fuck me…"

And all Danny could say gently was, "Fuck me!"

12

❖ God Loves A Sinner ❖

Once Danny had tied the boat to his dock, the twilight had well and truly gathered. Magic hour. The time of day great film directors loved to shoot in most. And Danny thought the Florida Keys did 'Magic Hour' better than any other place he had ever visited.

The sky was suffused with purple and pink. Distant thunderhead clouds giving the colours the perfect contrast, their billowy whiteness tinged with darker greys where the rains sat heavy and ready to fall. A heron, perfectly silhouetted by nature's light show, arced over his head.

Danny was struck that, in a film, this would be the beginning of a romantic interlude. The lead man would sweep the leading lady off the boat and into a kiss that would be framed by the twilight sky, both parties resplendent in their close-up moment. Except, in this instance, the leading lady had just suggested the leading man rip off her husband but only after she'd pounced on the lead like a wrestler in a championship bout. Romantic? Perhaps not.

Danny blew out his cheeks and turned to look at June. He had enjoyed the afternoon's fireworks, but somehow, they had only served to pull into sharp focus a fact that Danny had long been trying to ignore. He was lonely. And this woman was not any kind of answer to his solitude.

"That's a very serious face, Danny. Are you scheming already? Have you decided to take on my little project?"

Danny held out his hand to help her from the boat to the dock. "A bird shows up, occupies your entire day, asks you to pull a blag on her husband and then gives you a good seeing to. That'll leave most men's heads spinning."

"Such a way with words. I was led to believe you're not most men."

"And that's exactly why I have my serious face on. You were sent to look for me. You show up and lay this out, and now, I am busy trying to work out the angles. Who sent you? Why? And where is the person who picked me out for you?"

Danny motioned for June to walk with him, to escort her to her car. They made their way around the wooden deck to the front of his house, pausing at the top of the steps.

"You have a low opinion of women, Danny? Are you one of those men who think that we're all just make up and ditzy smiles?"

"No. But I'm a very specific target. Your story doesn't lead me to believe that you found me without help. Not without a very precise steer."

June was nodding, smiling. "If you want work done on your house, what do you do? You ask a friend to recommend a builder... request a few references. I did the same thing. After all, I do need someone with a very particular skill set."

June stepped closer to him, her hand snaking over his shoulder. "Danny, this could be a great adventure for us. The start of something beautiful. We could have fun, we'll enjoy the money, we'll live our lives out on the big canvas."

"Have you ever seen a film called *Double Indemnity*? A sexy Barbara Stanwyck talks Fred MacMurray into a scheme to bump her old man off for insurance money."

Confusion registered on June's face.

"You're asking me to rob your husband, but I know, next up, you'll want him dead. It doesn't end well for Barbara and Fred. Your project won't end any differently, either. I'm not the man you're looking for. You can tell whoever sent you my way that I'm not interested in anything they, you or anyone else might want to try and tempt me with. And, while you're at it, ask them to stop leaving me little gifts, too."

Danny stopped and picked up the model London bus that he'd spotted as soon as they'd come around the corner of his house. He'd half expected that something would be there, waiting.

June looked even more confused at the sight of the little red toy in his hands, but she pressed on regardless. "I'm not a woman who takes no for an answer. What I've shared with you today is an honest-to-god, once-in-a-lifetime opportunity. It would be flying in God's face to turn such a thing down. I'll let you think on it. You know I'll be back, Danny, and soon. In the meantime, pray on it...the Lord will show you the right path."

Danny laughed. Putting both hands on his head, he wondered at just how crazy this woman might be. "You ask me to rip off your husband, fuck me and don't even raise so much as an eyebrow when I mention murder, and yet, you still talk about God?"

"Yes, I do, because God made us... made us in his image, and that means all of us, every last one of us. That includes sin too, Danny. Haven't you ever heard the expression, 'God loves a sinner'? And anyway, if God didn't want us to sin, why'd he make it just so delicious to do so? See you soon, Mr Fisherman, whether you like the idea or not."

June Cardell kissed him on the cheek, then, with one hand, squeezed his ass and patted it for good measure. Danny was, for once, speechless.

As she walked away to her car, he stared at her, sashaying back to her other life, and he grew angry. He knew in that moment his quiet life in his perfect little corner of the Keys had just been turned completely upside down.

13

❖ Fight, Flight or Freeze ❖

Danny had a lot on his mind. Not only the situation developing around him, but the fact that he was performing a headstand was also a factor.

He was controlling his breathing. He tensed his core, his feet lightly braced against the clapboard wall of his house, the headstand causing the muscles in his neck to burn. Slowly, he straightened out his elbows, performing a handstand press up, keeping the push up and dip back down slow, controlled and graceful.

He could feel the blood pumping in his upper body, sweat glistening on his skin, even in the cool of the early morning. He steadied himself again and counted to three before repeating the push and dip, the ninth time he had done so that morning.

When he had to figure out a problem, he did so while occupying his body in some way. Sometimes, it was through exercise; sometimes, he practised his lock-picking skills; sometimes, it was with the aid of a long, loud conversation with himself while out alone fishing.

That day, exercise was the best option. So far, he had racked up two hundred press ups, countless squats to high kicks, and now, he was upside down, enjoying the heat of the blood accumulating in his head. His intuition had been right. His oasis of peace had been hit by a storm. He had felt it coming, but when it arrived, even he was surprised that it was in the shape of a crazy, sexy, Christian woman.

But she was just the support act. Danny needed to direct his focus. He suspected he knew who had sent June Cardell his way. And if he was right, he had to consider his options, and fast.

He pushed and dipped his body for the tenth and final time, his arms shaking as he did so, his shoulders telling him he was about done.

Once upright, he took a moment for his balance to settle and his vision to clear. Heading to the punch bag hanging in the carport, he snatched up his sparring gloves and beat out a fast one, one-two rhythm, dancing on the balls of his feet as he circled his target.

He believed there were only ever three options to be considered: flight, fight or freeze. Danny could take flight. He knew for certain that no matter how this problem would play out, his Florida days were now, surely, numbered. That didn't mean he had to run now, right away. But soon. Someone had found him.

Fight was his second option. He could flush out the source of his problem and, when the time was right, get the in first punch. This strategy was full of risk. But then, Danny was at his most comfortable when the stakes were high.

He paused his routine, took a deep breath, giving his body a few seconds to recover, before re-engaging with the bag. This time, he threw in a series of spinning high kicks followed by a volley of rapid jabs, twenty each time, trying to keep the pace and power uniform.

He wasn't one for freezing, usually, but this time, it might be best to sit still, wait it out and see what happened. During the wait, he could at least set all his ducks in a row.

Danny stopped again. His chest heaving, he sucked in lungfuls of air, registering that the temperature was starting to climb. Another fine Florida day was in progress.

Stepping out from under the car port, he squinted, taking in the deep blue sky, feeling the breeze cool upon his chest and face. Fight, flight or freeze?

Fuck it, he thought. *There's only one man who could find me, and I've fought him before and won. Where's the harm in a little rematch? Come get me, Harkness…*

❖

There weren't many things that Ines Zedillo felt squeamish about, but for some reason, eye injuries or deformities made her feel queasy. But when the man at her table took his sunglasses off to wipe his eyes, she couldn't help but look away.

She didn't like the unnatural milkiness of his eyeball. She didn't like the way it swivelled independently of its counterpart, and most of all, she didn't like to think of what ugly act had left such an unpleasant legacy. He was a big man, shaven-headed, but someone, somewhere, had bested him. The eye was a legacy of it.

When the shades were securely back in place, she felt able to continue their conversation.

"Tell me, señor..."

"Harkness..."

"Tell me, Señor Harkness. How do you know that some of our financial matters have been compromised?"

"Did you know, *señora*, that when he was secretary of the UN, Kofi Annan said that 'knowledge is power, information is liberating'? I want to liberate you from a highly inconvenient difficulty. My source is well placed in one of your expansive laundering operations. How I came to the knowledge is not important. How I can help to eliminate the problem is."

Ines took a sip of the Bloody Mary in front of her, savouring the heat of the spice and the cold of the mixture as it hit the back of her throat. She had always liked the taste, a morning drink laced with alcohol, the indulgent decadence of it appealing to her. She inspected her impeccably manicured fingernails as she gripped her glass, the light click of them against its surface somehow reassuring. She felt in control.

"Señor, you know who I work for, you know what we do. You show up here, telling me my organisation is in trouble, and you are the only man who can help me. I have always heard that the English were arrogant, and you seem to be proving it. I suppose, in solving this... issue, you propose to charge me a certain amount of money?"

"A good piece of work is worth paying for, and I prefer to be described as confident rather than arrogant. I have all the tools, the contacts and the skillset to help you. Plus, if your organisation was so powerful, how would you find yourself with this skimming problem in the first place?"

Ines laughed, amused at this gringo's *bravura*, and also his stupidity. "You have *huevos grandes*, Harkness. Talking to me as if I am small time. Your offer would only make sense, if the amount you charge me is smaller than the amount I am already losing. By your logic, that would mean I am losing a lot more than I am happy to admit."

"And my source has shown me proof that you are. And losing face is always a bitter pill, isn't it? Now, let's stop being polite and talk frankly shall we, Ines?"

She bridled at the use of her first name, her frame visibly tensing. She clicked her nails against her glass, watching him shift his weight towards her. His head looked a little too big for the rest of his body, his arms long and solid. She suddenly felt like she was in a room with a circus tiger; outwardly tame but, inwardly, still capable of sudden violence. She flashed her disdain across her face, deciding to show him she was still in control.

"That's the Ines I want to speak to, right there! Not the designer-clad, dripping in jewellery, charitable foundation Ines. I want to talk to the street-savvy drug dealer. The one who clawed her way out of Culiácan to be here and didn't give a fuck whose throats were cut along the way."

She sat silently, seething, but not letting him see the depth of her indignation. She would show him just how angry she could be when it suited her.

Harkness sat further forward, dropping the volume of his voice so that only she could hear him, not the two bodyguards who stood just off to one side.

"How do you think those animals from the Barrios are going to react when you have to tell them you've been haemorrhaging significant amounts of their cash? Your head will look very pretty, lying severed on a Miami beach. I'm here to remind the street-smart Ines what's at stake and help her to clear it up. Yes, I've done my research. I've heard the stories about where the developer cum socialite got her seed capital from. Street chatter can be fucking loud in this town. I know an awful lot about you. If nothing else, that makes me worth your fucking attention. You also might try not talking to me like I'm dog shit on your shoe."

"*Aguas*, Señor Harkness. You are in my home. I will treat you with respect, once you have earned it. Now, tell me, *cabrón*, If I do have such a huge problem, how do you propose we solve it?"

Harkness gently clapped his hands together and laughed. "*Cabrón*? Now we're talking, Ines… now we are talking! As for your little problem, I have already started work on the solution… I've found exactly the right man to sort it for us…"

"One man? He must be very special if he can solve this… puzzle all on his own."

"Oh, believe me, Ines, he has exactly the right kind of strengths. We will both enjoy watching him at work."

Harkness stood to leave.

"And what of price, Señor Harkness? You don't want to set one, *ahora*?"

Harkness kept walking.

"I think you need a little more time, señora, to realise just how valuable my friend and I might be. Maybe I need to convince you just a little more. *Hasta luego*."

14

❖ Let Us Pray ❖

From experience, June knew that timing was everything. She honestly believed that whatever happened in life, it did so at the moment it was supposed to. Her troubled romance and its violent conclusion back in Britain were a perfect example. They signalled the start of a chain of events that had brought her to a better life in the US, and they were now culminating in a chance to cement the lifestyle she had become accustomed to. A life without the need for a man hanging around telling her how she should be living.

She trusted in that timing implicitly, believing in fate. She was willing to let it play out its hand. But she also believed that when you could control the timing of something, give it a little encouragement, then that could be advantageous too. If she could pick and choose when, she spent a long time judging the best moment to commence. And this fine morning was no exception.

She knew exactly where he'd be. Knew exactly what she had to do. Knew exactly how he'd react. Despite his ruthlessness and single-minded focus on power, she knew him. She understood him. His sexual proclivities and lust for her gave her an influence and power over him that no one else held. She showered at precisely eight am and then used the body cream she knew he liked. Slipping into a long silk robe, she checked her hair in the mirror before setting off to find him.

The prayer room was on the ground floor of their split-level house, dominated by a floor-to-ceiling window overlooking the Florida Bay. Hanging in front of the window was a huge wooden cross, its surface intricately carved with quotes from the New Testament. Beneath it was a long, wooden church style kneeler, the low platform looking utilitarian, no padding or cushion to rest your knees on, just hard, bare oak. She found it mindboggling that anyone could remain kneeling there for long periods of time. The sun was streaming into the room, silhouetting Vincent Cardell as he prayed, head bowed beneath the cross.

June closed the door silently, then tiptoed over to stand behind him. She could hear him uttering his invocations under his breath, she couldn't be sure but she thought it was Psalm sixty-two, the one about "God alone is my rock and my salvation". It finished "Power and love belong to God".

Vincent had a stillness to him that she found almost unnatural. She wondered how his knees and back could take such discomfort.

She slipped out of the silk robe. Slowly, she gently raised it over his head, bringing it down over him. He gave a small flinch.

"June…"

"Shhhhh."

She leant on his shoulders, keeping him in place on his knees.

"Darling, let's pray together, shall we? Let's show our Lord how much we love each other."

She then took his hand, pulling it back towards her, placing it between her thighs, letting him feel her nakedness. His breathing quickened.

She reached around him, finding his belt and, unhooking the buckle, unbuttoned his trousers.

"Pray, darling… don't forget to pray…."

And Vincent did as he was told, his voice a little hoarse to begin with. He started to recite the Lord's Prayer just as June freed him from his boxers. She knew he'd be able to smell her body lotion as she pressed her naked form against him. She, too, joined in the prayer, moving her hand in time to the rhythm of their speech, the residue of the lotion on her hands helping her do exactly what she wanted.

She stepped around him, kneeling down, taking him in both her hands, raising her voice to match the volume of his as he started to recite "The Lord is My Shepherd". She quickened her pace, touching him in exactly the way she knew he liked, pushing him towards the inevitable conclusion, but making sure she was in control of the timing of it. Yes, she had even thought that through.

Vincent was ecstatic, his voice booming out the scripture. "I will fear no evil: For thou art with me; thy rod and thy staff they comfort me."

She whipped the silk robe off his head, grabbed the back of his head and forced his face between her breasts.

Her other hand was still busy, the prayer more muffled. Soon, she knew it was time…

"I will dwell in the house of the Lord for everrrrrrrrrrr."

His orgasm convulsed through his body. She leant back, using their weight to roll off the kneeler and onto the floor. Vincent landed on top of her, her arms round his neck, her fingers running through his hair. The great cross loomed over them. Silence settled into the room.

After a few moments, June brushed the hair away from one of his ears and whispered, "I've been thinking about our little problem, and I want you to meet someone… I think I have worked out a way to make it all go away. Will you indulge me, darling? I think I've been a rather clever girl…"

A smile broke across her face as she felt him nod an affirmative into her chest, his head still nestled there in his post-orgasmic glow.

Timing… is everything.

Danny was hanging the phone up at his usual roadside call box when the police cruiser pulled up alongside him. He was grateful that he had concluded business with his pet lawyer before the arrival of law enforcement. But when he saw who was driving the green and white cop car, he was surprised. He had felt a flutter of excitement.

Deputy Sosa ducked her head a little so that she could see Danny out of her passenger window. "I thought that was you, Mr Franklin. How we doing today?"

Danny leant on the frame of the car, savouring the chance to look at her. "It's another beautiful day in paradise, Deputy. Hope yours has been a good one so far?"

"Not long started, but I'm sure it will be the usual, either a fender bender or a tourist driving like a crazy person. I'm about to take an early break. Want to grab some coffee?"

Danny cocked an eyebrow at her. "Official business? Am I still on some kind of list?"

"Guilty conscience? Let's just say, I have a question to ask you, *amigo*. Not strictly a professional matter, I would like to satisfy my curiosity."

"Such a charming invite. Hard to turn you down. Where?"

"Midway has good coffee, mile marker eighty point five?"

"Yes, I know it. See you in ten."

Danny jumped back in his jeep, the ex-military one that was converted into a flatbed. He was pleased that he was still driving this newer vehicle and not the truck she had been looking for earlier.

He pulled into the parking lot of the coffee shop. Deputy Sosa was already waiting for him at the roadside.

The inside of the shop was a riot of pastel colours, pink, lime green, soft blue all taking the Florida chic to its logical, explosion in a paint factory, conclusion. Danny blinked a few times to adjust his eyes.

"It wouldn't be good to have a hangover in here, would it?"

Amparo laughed. "Yeah, they used every pastel coloured tin in the paint store. Coffee? Or do you drink something more exotic? Hot tea?"

"Regular coffee is fine. You lot don't know how to make tea."

They took their drinks outside. The picnic tables under the trees echoed the colour scheme from inside, but at least out there they weren't so intimidating.

"I have to admit, Deputy, you have me curious, too. If I were a cat, I'd be dead by now. Go ahead, ask your question."

"Okay, I was driving by your place on duty, making my rounds, and I was wondering why a man would be leaving a little model bus on your front stoop?"

Danny sat back, blowing gently on the liquid in his to-go cup. He paused before answering. "That question begs a few more in response, Deputy..."

"Call me Amparo. I did say this is not strictly official business..."

"Okay, Amparo. Why did you feel the need to stop at my gaff? Sorry, my home?"

"When we're on patrol, we are on patrol. We check out whatever we feel needs checking out. When I think about you, my cop's instinct kicks in, and when that happens, a good cop normally follows it. It's something I've had drilled into me since my academy days."

"Fair enough, I get it. I've tickled your... spidey sense. So, you saw the person leaving me that little present?"

"I did. He didn't see me. He came and then left by boat at your dock. There was a fancy car parked in your drive, too, a Mercedes."

"A regular 'Amparo of the Yard,' aren't we?"

Danny could see that she didn't get his British detective reference. He made a mental note to tone down his British expressions around her.

"My answer is that I am as mystified as you are. I have no idea who is doing it, but I suspect it's an old friend indulging their English sense of humour. The bus was the second one they left; I also got a London black taxi cab a while back. Could you describe my little gift fairy for me?"

"He was tall, a strong looking man. I only really saw him from behind."

"Shaven-headed?"

Amparo hesitated for a second. "*Sí*... sorry, yes. I think so."

Danny counted his blessings. This happy coincidental meeting with the deputy had just confirmed that James Harkness was attempting to slip back into his life. It was a little troubling. Much as he liked Amparo, and he was admitting to himself that he did, he hadn't yet shaken off her cop's interest in him. If that was what it really was.

"I think I know who it is. Yes, a friend of mine, playing a little prank."

"Something else, though, Mr Franklin..."

"Danny..."

She smiled, her face lighting up. "I noticed that there was no phone line going to your house. No TV service. These days... that's a little odd?"

"I'm not a redneck, if that's what you're wondering. I don't think Englishmen can be rednecks, can they? I don't have a sofa or a fridge on my front lawn, do I?"

This brought another smile from Amparo. Danny liked making this girl smile.

"But you run a business. Surely you need at least a telephone?"

"My little sign on the roadside seems to bring me enough. I have an advert in the local paper, too, from time to time, and I do all right. I make enough money. That fancy car you mentioned earlier was a customer's, actually. Maybe you should come out, fish with me sometime, see why I have such a strong customer base."

She started to shake her head.

"*Que Padre*! I'm a dry land kind of girl, like to keep my feet on solid ground. All that pitching and swell... makes me feel a little *chuke*... sick. If I'm going to have a good time, I go dancing. There's no chance of drowning on a dance floor."

Danny liked the sound of a dance.

It was time to make a move. Now he knew what was going on, he had to up his game and the schedule to go with it. He stood up.

"I am to dancing what David Duke is to race relations... but if you want to try and discover your sea legs someday... you know where to find me."

She was laughing again, watching as he fished his key ring from his pocket, feeling for the jeep key he would need in a second.

He instantly regretted the move, because he caught a flicker in her face.

"Have a great day, Mrs Amparo."

"I'll try and thank you for answering my questions… and it's Miss, by the way…"

As he climbed back into his jeep, Danny looked down at his key ring, confirming his suspicion about the flicker that had passed over Amparo's face. He still had the key to his other truck on the ring. The huge GM logo stood out proudly on the back of the plastic fob. And he was pretty sure she'd clocked it.

Danny sighed. He was still giving this delightful deputy reasons to keep sniffing. And with everything that might happen, that was a complication he didn't need.

He drove back to the call box he had visited earlier, punching in the number of his lawyer for the second time that day. He had one more job for him, a task he had hoped he wouldn't have to put in play, but with Harkness's presence all but confirmed, it had become "Hobson's choice".

As the assistant placed his call on hold, Danny said a little prayer to the patron saint of criminals that the man whose help he wanted was still around and able to come.

15

❖ Friends Reunited ❖

At night, the Florida Keys collaborate with nature to pull off one of its favourite tricks. As twilight descends, cocktails are mixed, tourists and locals like to kick back and enjoy the sunset. Moments of undeniable beauty occur. Darkness then falls with all the immediacy of someone flicking off a light switch.

And that evening was no different. No sooner had Danny settled on his porch to watch his favourite time of day play out than he found himself sitting in darkness with nothing to show for his intentions but an empty bourbon glass and the sound of a mosquito flitting around him, hunting for a fresh bloodstream to dine on.

He was contemplating a refill of the Blanton's, the Kentucky whiskey's rich, woody taste a luxury he loved to savour. He was about to go to the kitchen when a noise changed his mind. It was subtle, but he recognised it instantly. It was the gentle plop of a paddle dropping into water, guiding a skiff. It came close to the edge of his dock, followed by a gentle bump as the craft hit home.

The boatman was being careful, but listening when in near silence was something Danny cherished and excelled at, so when even the smallest sound broke through, he was alive to it.

But this was a visitor he was expecting sooner rather than later. Given the description of the man Amparo had provided, the sudden appearance of June Cardell, and even what Slow Tina had said, Danny knew who this could be.

And he was ready for him.

Danny was impressed. For a big man, Harkness moved stealthily along the dock and up onto the wooden porch. Not even so much as a creak gave him away. Danny decided to greet his guest first.

The loud click of the Desert Eagle forty-four Magnum as he cocked it was enough of a welcome.

"Danny, Danny, Danny… there's no need to be like that."

"Give me a single reason why I shouldn't put a bullet in your fucking chest right now, Harkness."

"Is that any way to treat an old friend? Did you like my little gifts? The taxi? The bus?"

"I prefer the gift I gave you in London. Do your friends often leave you with an eye that looks like a half-sucked gobstopper?"

Harkness's face was clear, lit by a crescent moon and framed by the midnight blue sky overhead.

"You know the rules, Danny. When you play rough, you have to accept that you might get hurt."

Harkness leaned back against the porch rail, no sign of any tension or fear in his voice. Danny reached high up behind his head and hit a switch. The veranda was flooded with light. The big man instinctively put his hand up before his face, shading his vision from the sudden illumination. When he finally dropped the hand, Danny felt more than satisfied with the souvenir he had left on his enemy's face.

"I take that back. It doesn't look like a gobstopper, it's more like a rotting lychee. Why, and how, are you here, you fucking cocksucker?"

"Napoleon said that 'the truest wisdom is a resolute determination.' You inspired that resolution in me, young Danny. After our… little tussle in London, I just couldn't get you out of my mind. Me being here? It's your fault."

"Oh, fuck me sideways… I forgot how much you love a speech."

Inwardly, Danny was wincing. He knew Harkness was right. Danny had read a lot about an idea called systemics. It posited that all things in life were systems. Families, friendships, companies, communities, even whole societies were all systems that grouped together to form a whole. Within those systems, certain rules could be defined and would then play out to their logical conclusion, no matter what. From his understanding of systemics, unresolved issues in our lives are like floodwater breaching the hull of a sinking ship. You plug one hole; the rising sea will simply find another one to overwhelm you. Leaving Harkness lifeless and in the hands of the boys in blue back in London was obviously not enough to stem this particular tide.

"I should have killed you when I had the chance."

"But you didn't. You see, I know you love me, really. That, plus all the coppers running about. You didn't want to look bad in front of that detective bird… What was her name?'

"Chance… Christine Chance."

"Yeah, her… If she knew I was here now, she'd just about self-combust."

"And how did you get here?"

"You should be able to guess. Having done the things I have in the name of our beloved government, over in places like the Sandpit, Northern Ireland, everywhere and anywhere, you get to call in a few favours with a few big names, know what I mean?"

"You sound like Bryant. 'If you're not cop, you're little people.'"

"What?"

"Never mind, it's from a film… *Blade Runner*."

"I like my little speeches, you still like your movies… *plus ça change*, eh?"

Danny thought he'd heard it all now, Harkness speaking French.

"… and I wasn't just Old Bill, Danny. Military ops under a black flag give you a lot more pull. Fuck, I was even able to specify which open prison they put me in."

"You did a deal? You landed Dexy with it all?"

"Ah, Dexy. Fine woman, thought she was a criminal mastermind, when in reality, she was only a club owner. You stitched her right up, Danny, not me. I didn't have to grass Dexy up, I was just… brushed under the carpet. Too many stories I could tell, too many people shitting themselves at the thought. And now, I'm here to see my favourite blagger."

Danny wanted to test something, right now, when Harkness would least expect it. Without warning, he suddenly tossed his empty bourbon glass in the Big Man's direction. Harkness caught it. Effortlessly. He snatched it from the air.

"You managed to compensate for the one eye, then?"

"'If thy right eye should cause you to stumble and sin… pluck it out.' If it's good enough for the bible…"

"Talking of which, how did you come across the bible bashers?"

"Oh, did you like June? I know her from back in Blighty. She had an ex-boyfriend… naughty boy, thought he could become a big-time drugs Charlie. She and I helped put him back in his place. What did you make of her?"

"Does she really believe all that Jesus malarkey?"

"Hard to tell, isn't it? Did you bang her?"

Danny looked away.

Harkness roared with laughter. "You did! You fucking did an' all! 'Have at it' is what I say. She's on the more mature end of the scale for my tastes but I bet she was… enthusiastic?"

Danny ignored the question. "I could smell you from a thousand miles away, Harkness. As soon as she started talking about the husband, the money, I knew you were involved."

"What can I say? Always at the centre of the storm, me. This job is sweet as a nut, Danny."

"I danced to your tune once before… I haven't forgotten how that turned out."

Danny stood, closing the space between them in an instant. He brought the big sliver handgun right up under Harkness's chin, pushing it hard into the soft flesh. Harkness, caught off guard, strained onto his tiptoes, trying to lessen the pressure Danny was exerting under his chin.

"Did you think I would let bygones be bygones? Did you think I'd forget how you wound Big Man Boom up and set him loose on London? All those deaths? All because you wanted to throw me under the fucking proverbial bus?"

Danny was squeezing the trigger. He could feel the slack go out of the mechanism, sense that he was close to the biting point of the firing pin. One more little squeeze and Harkness would be dead, his brain pan flying high into the Florida night air.

But something had begun to stir in Danny. A flutter around his heart.

"You're full of shit, Danny. You brought the ex-IRA bomb expert into play, you miserable fuck. You invited the psycho-terrorist to the table. All I did was remind him who he was. All that blood is on your hands, too. If you'd kept me in the loop, I'd have trusted you more, and maybe, all that Semtex wouldn't have been needed."

And that is when Danny felt the full force of it. Like a trapped bird at the back of his brain. His chest convulsing then constricting. A fug seemed to gather around him. His knees weakened. He closed his eyes for a second, trying to ward off the panic attack that was building.

"You played him, Harkness. You made it possible for all those people to get sideswiped. I planned to scare London; you set it alight. You… you… "

The emotional deluge was too great for Danny to hold back.

Images of burning people assailed his brain. His heart felt like a panicked rat, thrashing against his ribcage, his breathing convulsing, air refusing to enter his lungs, the furious violence of what happened in London tearing through his mind.

Harkness shifted his weight, and Danny just folded off him and onto his knees.

Harkness's face was a picture of amazement. To see the blagger in all kinds of trouble, his face drained of colour, ashen and unable to even speak was a shock. He moved towards him, about to try and help him up, but Danny was suddenly able to catch some air.

He inhaled in a howl, his faculties finding a little purchase from God knows where, the feel of the gun and the realisation of his current vulnerability bringing him back some focus. As Harkness reached for him, Danny jerked back the gun and let off a round. The noise was ear-splitting between them, the smell of gunpowder rank in the air, Danny feeling something warm and sticky on his fingers. All of this in a heartbeat. And then, he heard it.

Harkness. Screaming.

Looking up, Danny could see that his wild shot had caught the side of Harkness's head, blood was pouring down the side of his face from where the top half of his left ear should have been.

That was the moment that Danny's brain decided to shut down.

16

❖ Stoning Birds ❖

When he came to, the first thing Danny saw made him involuntarily sit up a little straighter. He then realised that as well as staring into Father Simeon's hazel-flecked eyes. He was sitting on the floor of his porch, his back propped up against the wall of the house.

"Good morning. Welcome back to the real world. How ya doin', my man?"

"Err… that would be telling. Did you say good morning?"

"People tell me all sorts of things, Brother D. Comes with the priest territory along with the funny looking collar, and yes… good morning."

Danny's memory kicked in. He must have lain there all night. He looked down at his right hand, expecting to see his gun, not surprised that it wasn't there.

"Looking for something?"

"Uh… no, I'm not."

Danny looked at Simeon. He wasn't holding the gun either, so that could only mean that as well as giving Harkness a new scar, he had a new gun, too.

"Y'all hit the sauce a little hard last night?" Simeon gestured towards the shattered remains of the Bourbon glass on the porch floor.

"Something like that. Are we fishing today, Sim?"

"Uh-uh… I just stopped by to invite you to a little happening I have this coming weekend."

Danny pushed himself up. Using the wall to steady himself, he hoped Simeon wouldn't notice that he needed the support. "A knees-up? Kind of you."

"Whatchu sayin'? Knees... wut?"

"It's London speak, for a party... a knees-up is a party..."

"You are one curious mutha..."

"Said the catholic priest. The only one I know who has a mouth like a sewer... mind you, you are the only priest I know... Come inside, I'll make you a coffee..."

"You look like you need it more than me."

As they turned to go, something caught Simeon's eye. Dark splashes on the wood just to the left of the remains of the tumbler. He stopped, crouched down, reaching out to touch the marks, trying to see how fresh they might be. His fingers came up dry, a little grit on them. Simeon straightened up, a question hovering on his lips. Danny pre-empted it.

"I see you've spotted the result of my attempts at DIY." He held up his left hand, showing a scabbed finger as proof.

"Must've been a deep cut to leave so many splashes o' red..." Simeon slowly shook his head, letting a breath out as he did so. "You should know better than to fool around with shit you have no idea about. Stick to fishing, Brother D."

Danny knew he didn't believe the explanation, but he was relieved Simeon didn't pursue it.

"Coffee. Come on in."

Danny realised the instant he walked into his living room that he was tense. For a fleeting moment, he had expected to see it trashed. That whilst he had been out cold, Harkness would have rampaged through the modest abode. But everything was as he'd left it the night before.

As he started the coffee maker, Father Simeon perched against the small kitchen table, watching Danny go about the simple chore.

"So, what's this knees-up in honour of, then, your holiness?"

The smell of brewing coffee started to fill the air. Simeon pulled out a chair.

"Our little tête-à-tête about God, the universe and everything on the boat the other day bothered me."

'I didn't mean to offend, but when it comes to religion, I'm a mind-made-up type."

"I geddit, I geddit, but I do think yo' might be missing something. I think yo' might be cutting off a whole side of yourself. It could be something beautiful, man. I know when I meet someone who has good bones. You got those type o' bones, Brother D."

"Listen, Simeon…"

"No, no, now, hear me out… let a dog bark. I know you got all sorts o' stories runnin' in yo head 'bout how religion does nuthin' but make men hate one another. But I think I can show what else it can do. Show you an iddy biddy peek of the good that can happen. People might just surprise yo' ass. So, I wanted to invite you to my little event. Show you how religion ain't made up of theology. It's made of people, and all of 'em have hearts. And you might have some fun along the way. Kill two birds, and all that jazz…"

Danny poured the coffee, enjoying the sight of the black liquid nectar swirling into the mug even if he didn't often drink it. Tea was more his thing, but he wanted a bigger caffeine hit.

"That's all very nice, Simeon, but like I said before, I've got a lot of personal data that supports my worldview… and as for having good bones? It might be time to get that radar of yours recalibrated, mate."

"Now, listen up. I ain't asking you as a priest, or a spiritual adviser. I'm inviting you as a brother, a friend. Come take a look. What's the worst that could happen?"

Simeon was staring at him. He had a sincerity on his face that almost made Danny flinch, a reaction that was alien to him.

"Okay, I don't know what I'm being invited or saying yes to… but I'll come. Bless me, Father… for I have RSVP-ed."

Simeon's face cracked into a huge smile, his big fist accepted the mug of coffee being passed to him, the other clapped Danny on the shoulder, almost knocking him off balance.

"My man! My Brother D… I swear you're just gonna love it…"

"Yeah? That might be, but you still need to get that radar checked..." *Because*, Danny thought, *my bones are riddled with our people's screams and you can't even see it.* He took a sip. The coffee tasted hot and bitter in his mouth.

Ines Zedillo had to wait until the afternoon before making the call. The time difference between Miami and the south of France was an inconvenience, but when your boss might be imprisoned and given the death penalty the minute he set foot on American soil, it was a small price to pay.

She'd sent her boss the latest briefing document a few days earlier via Fed Ex, and today, he would have the chance to discuss its contents with her. She listened to the ring tone on the satellite phone they used for such conversations. Not a hundred percent secure method of communication, but better than any mobile, landline or online connection.

Thousands of miles away, the other end of the connection chirped. She could picture Alvaro Montoya as he set aside his demitasse of coffee to answer it. Nestled in the Provence countryside, she imagined he'd be sitting at the breakfast table on the terrace of his beautiful villa. Even at this early hour on a spring morning, she knew the sun would be warming him along with his coffee.

"*Bonita... que tal?*"

"*Jefe... muy bien... y tu?*'

Despite the caution of satellite connection, they would converse without names and be circumspect with their choice of words.

"*Chica*, I received the detail. Thank you. The numbers look fabulous. As always, I'm in your debt."

"We can improve them now we have a new player on the field."

"*Sí, sí...* I think he's a striker, no? Only a goal scorer would have the ego to turn up and play uninvited."

"He thinks he is a better player than the ones we already have. As I mentioned, he wants to solve a problem he thinks we have not spotted. A tactical one, so to speak. Should we give him a chance?"

"*Chica*, you know my views on weak tactics. If they are making it easier for our opponents to score against us, then we change them… shuffle the line-up. I know this new talent is not one of 'our' players, but if he is skilful, sign him on loan, no?"

"But what if the new player is not so tactically astute?"

"Give him a trial. If he turns out to be a loser, we ditch him. *Sabe, señora*?"

Alvaro was being quite clear, despite the footballing euphemisms. She was to give Harkness the go ahead to fix her skimming problem. And if he turned out to be useless, or worse, even more trouble than the skimmer, the cartels had ways of making problems disappear. And if he solved the problem, then perhaps he might be useful, or perhaps she might let the cartel machine dispose of him too.

"The new player wants to bring his own coach with him… someone he says will be a catalyst for the team."

"*Que suerte, chica*… you always bring us luck. I'm sure you will know how to handle these players, even if results go against us. *Hasta luego, bonita*. Get me results."

The line went dead. And Ines let the phone drop to her side. She stepped out onto the patio. This one overlooked the waters of Biscayne Bay. The sun was starting to dip beyond the horizon. As with all problems, opportunities also presented themselves. She was beginning to think that with Harkness, and whoever this man he wanted with him was, she might be able to kill more than a few birds with just the one stone. And her boss, from his luxurious exile in Europe, had just given her permission to do so.

As always, problems presented her with opportunities. It was one of the factors that had made her so successful in the treacherous world in which she walked. She was able to spot where advantages could be gained, even in the face of adversity. She relished such challenges, and here was another. And, as usual, Ines liked her own odds of success.

17

❖ Scarlet Billows ❖

The band was giving it everything they'd got. The brass section was puffing with all their might, the drummer looking to thrash out the irresistible rhythm. The lead singer was wrapping his voice around the lyrics, his tune unctuous and seductive. The revellers on the dance floor were playing their part too, moving hips and feet in time, all elegant dresses and razor sharp tuxedoes.

The glamour of the Royal Ballroom in Miami added to the decadent feel. You could have been forgiven for thinking this was a party scene fresh out of the demob happy days straight after World War Two. It's lavish drapes and chandeliers were like props from a Hollywood musical. Except it was the twenty-first century and the partygoers were there to raise funds for an ultra-right-wing think tank called 'Forethought'. Political respectability needed clout. Clout cost money. Huge amounts of it. And it didn't matter if your blog movement dressed up views that had been around since the heyday of the Klan. If you paid enough for your emperor's new clothes you might end up hanging out with the emperor himself.

And in the middle of all this 'whiter than white', 'righter than right' party, Vincent Cardell was doing a passable job of a hybrid foxtrot and quickstep. June's hair was flicking round her head as he led her on a very merry dance.

The music ended with a flourish and the dancers stopped to raise their hands in the air, applauding the band, the singer, themselves. Vincent reached out and took June by the wrist. A smile beamed across his face, flush with the exertions of dance that his father would have called 'the Devil's distraction'. He pulled her close, kissed her full on the lips, not noticing the way her body tensed ever so slightly as he did so.

"So, set it up. If you think you have someone who can clear up this Zedillo mess, then I want to speak with him, June."

"When?"

"This Sunday. He can watch us preach God's true, holy word and then I can work out if he is our 'Godsend'?"

"He can be. I'll sort it…"

And this time she kissed him. Feeling him react against her hip, his mind flooded with thoughts that could distract a devil, just as the singer took to the mic, announcing the last song of the evening.

"There's only one song that can polish off a celebration like tonight, folks. Let's go all Bobby Darin, and I'll tell you about a man named… Mack the Knife!"

And the band kicked in.

Danny felt annoyed rather than surprised when he heard a car pull up onto his drive, tyres crunching on the oyster shells. He had just been trying to decide which movie he was going to watch. Was it going to be Richard Gere's breath-taking villainous turn as the ultimate corrupt cop with Andy Garcia on his tail? *Internal Affairs* was always a compelling watch. Or was he going old-fashioned yet up to date as Jeff Bridges broke out his gruff sheriff act for *Hell or High Water*, a film Danny was yet to watch but had heard great things about. Now, by the sound of it, his plans were about to be screwed.

He stood out on his porch, letting the headlights of the deep red Ford Mustang sweep over him as it pulled to a stop. Shading his eyes, Danny could see a familiar bulk and shape climb out of the car. The broad shoulders. The bullet neck and head that was close-shaved and looked that bit too big for the rest of the body. Instinctively Danny reached for the back of his jeans. He realised too late that there was no pistol there, no chance of the secure feel of cold steel to greet his hand.

Fuck. You don't need a gun to watch a movie. He grimaced.

"I can see you looking, Felix... there's no need to panic. I owe you for that half a fucking ear."

Harkness stepped into Danny's car lights. Backlit, Danny could see the ear he had mangled with his reckless shot.

"I've only just gotten used to my new look. Come with me." Harkness said it in a tone of voice that made it obvious this was not an invite. It was a command.

"And why should I do that?"

Harkness came to the foot of the steps that led down from the porch. Looking up at Danny, he showed no sign of malice or nervousness at the vulnerability the height difference left between them.

"I'll tell you why. You, my fine young thief, are experiencing panic attacks. I know one when I see it. And that is why I'm not that pissed off with you about the whole ear deal."

"It's less than a whole ear..."

"Fuck off with your smart-arse mouth. In the car. Now. We're going to cure your 'screaming ad-dabs'."

"How would you know what's best for me?"

"You're fucked in the head, Danny. You fell off the horse. Perceived wisdom tells us to get straight back on it."

"It's been eighteen months since I've had so much as an angry thought. But as soon as you show up they seem to blossom."

Harkness laughed. Looking at his feet, he stepped up onto the porch. "A little of what won't kill you can do you good."

"But you're a killer, Harkness, dark as night. A stone-cold madman who kills anyone who gets in your way."

"You're bored, Danny Felix. I can smell it on you. I can see it in your eyes. You wouldn't be melting into your own thoughts with every little stress if you weren't. You wouldn't be fucking damsels in distress when they show up on your boat. You wouldn't be even having this chat if you weren't bored out of your tiny little scheming mind. You need some juice. A little action. And I can provide..."

Harkness let it hang in the humid night air. The words, out there in the world, were taking on a life of their own, finding purchase in Danny's head like an ear worm song from a worthless pop star.

"I'm not getting involved. You can keep your little Jesus freak woman, Harkness. Keep her money, her job, and her 'Jesus is my homeboy' husband. I'm done, I'm out… I'm twice as quit today as I was when you first showed up leaving little toy cars on my porch. Go fuck yourself…"

"At the very least, Danny, look at it as a way to finish the business you started back in London. You know you have to kill me, right? This may be the only way you can find a route to that particular loot."

Harkness was laughing, clapping his hands, a sound that Danny never wanted to hear again, ever.

But the reality hit him, made him stop and pause. Harkness was speaking the truth. This had to end. And there was only ever going to be one way.

"Come on, Danny. Where is the adventurer who brought London town to its knees? Where is the blagger who brought a little style back to the art of thieving? You with your panache. Your balls and brass neck. You're an artist, Danny. Don't let that go to waste. Come with me. Have some fun and those night sweats will be a thing of the past. Get back in the game… you never know, you might get a swing of the bat at me in the process."

Danny considered the man he hated most, save his own father, standing now in front of him, trying to cajole him into another bad situation. And yet the logic stacked up. The only way to keep Harkness at arms-length was to walk beside him. See where his plans lead and then take the best opportunity to stymie them. And then, this time, take him off the board once and for all.

Danny couldn't believe he was about to say this: "Where?"

"I want us to pay a little visit to some regular heroes. Cause a little fuss, raise a little hell. Put a dent in someone's plans that might just help us a bit further down the avenue…"

"I don't kill. That's over for me. No guns, no bombs. I can work smarter than that now."

"Holy fuck… Am I asking the Dalai fucking Lama out on a job? Hold on, will these do instead?"

Harkness stepped back down to his car. Opening the boot with the key fob, he delved in and emerged with a pair of baseball bats. "They aren't lethal if you use them right… right, Danny?"

Oh fuck, here we go, was all Danny could think.

Harkness had driven north to a residential area just outside Florida City, a part of south Miami that had resisted every attempt at redevelopment. The neighbourhood was one that even Danny would think twice about entering without the protection of serious weaponry and some back up. Having glanced into the boot of Harkness's car, Danny knew, on this occasion, he had plenty of both.

The target was nondescript. A typical half-breezeblock half-clapboard bungalow that had a drive, a garage, and a porch sat above a small garden out front. The only thing that marked the house out as different was the number of floodlights that sliced open the dark of the night every time a car went past. And when the lights came on, Danny was sure he could see two little cameras above the front door.

"What is this place? A crack den? A drop? A safe house?"

Harkness shifted in the driver seat, trying to stay comfortable but keep his line of sight to the house clear. They had been sat there for at least an hour.

"It's a money drop. El Banco del Cocaina. Anytime now, scrag-end little dealers are going to start pitching up, unloading what they've made for the day. Cold, hard drug cash. There will be a steady stream of the fuckwits until about four in the morning. At which point the wanker bankers inside usually light up a bit of recreational salad, and end up off their tits. You can tell it's a drop. Have you spotted him?"

"Who? The kid on the edge of the roof? The one who's sound asleep?"

"Yep, he's their spotter. If they catch him like that, they'll kill the little wanker. He supposed to raise the alarm if the cops or another gang show up."

"And you want us to go in… right?"

"See, you might be bored, Danny boy, but you've not lost it."

"You're fucking stupid and nuts, Harkness. They'll be tooled up like no tomorrow."

"We got bullet-proof vests. You gone chicken on me, son? Besides, once the adrenalin hits, you'll have a hard-on the size of the Isle of Dogs… Admit it… you have soooo missed me."

Even in the dark of the car, Danny could feel the grin on Harkness's face.

'You want to go in there, swinging baseball bats, wearing Kevlar and not much else and expect to come out alive and with the money…"

"Yep…."

"Okay. Hopefully you'll get your face blown off in the process, save me a job while we're at it…"

Harkness chuckled and blew Danny a kiss.

'She'll be in touch again soon. You know that, right?"

"I told you, Harkness, I will not help June Cardell rob and kill her husband."

"After tonight's festivities… you will. The fun factor will grab you by the balls again… mind you, so will June. Besides, she's not asked you to kill her old man. Just rip him off. Her next step will be to introduce you to him. He'll want to run the rule over you himself, he's that type. Just don't mention my name. I'm more a background player on this one."

"If that's the case, why are we here? I thought tonight was connected?"

"Let's just say we are covering off more than one angle on this, okay?"

Danny's heart sank. It was going to be as dangerous and tricky as always with Harkness, and now, Danny was in the middle of it.

The night lengthened. They put on the Kevlar vests. They were bulky and uncomfortable, especially in the warmth of the Florida night. Danny closed his eyes now and again, power napping. Running what might be about to happen through his mind, he tried to keep the excitement down. He did a lousy job. Each time he inhaled he could feel the butterflies in his chest. The stomach knot tightening. But what was more worrying was that these symptoms didn't feel like the ones he experienced just before he had a panic attack. No, these were hunger pangs. Hunger for action. Hunger for excitement. Hunger for adrenalin.

He came out of his reverie and looked at his watch. It was three-thirty in the morning. He looked over at Harkness. He was awake and still staring at the front door, his one eye illuminated by a green glow that came from the display of the car radio. It was on but at very low volume. The tinny noise of the radio distracted Danny because he could barely hear the song playing but thought he still recognised the melody.

Harkness spoke over the tease of music. "When the next dealer turns up to dump his cash, we go in too."

At that, the spotter kid roused himself, climbed down from the roof and went inside.

"What luck… pee break."

After a few minutes, car headlights flashed as it progressed up the street. An old Pontiac Grand Am passed them, drawing to a stop in front of the drop house. Harkness glanced at Danny.

"Hammer time…"

Silently slipping out of the car, Harkness passed Danny a baseball bat, ducking back into the car to retrieve another two for himself.

"I presume you want me to go through the door first?"

"You read my mind, Harkness. This is one hundred percent your clusterfuck. Jesus Christ what am I doing here?"

"Jesus Christ? If you want his help, we could always stop and pray? Actually, you know what, I have an even better idea."

As they crossed the street towards the house, Harkness started to hum, causing Danny to quietly exhale with a shake of the head.

What happened next exceeded all the levels of craziness that Danny had experienced in his relatively young, eventful life.

The Grand Am pulled away, a dealer made his way up through the little garden towards the entrance of the unit, a weighty looking backpack slung over the shoulder of his dark hoodie. Harkness and Danny crossed the space between him and them in quiet, double quick time, managing to get within ten feet of him just as he said something into an intercom on the right frame of the door. As that door swung open, the dealer was startled by a sound and spun around. Danny was startled too. Until he realised the sound was coming from Harkness.

"*Abide with me; fast falls the eventide; The darkness deepens; Lord with me abide*" Harkness was singing. And not just singing, but singing beautifully. His voice was that of a fifties crooner, delicately enunciating the words, and at a volume that could entertain a room without a microphone. And at the end of the lyric he swung the first of his bats straight across the dealer's stomach, changing the look on his face from startled to agony. And suddenly the hymn was playing itself out in Danny's head and he was singing along and aloud too, as the pair of them conducted their own recital of mayhem. "*When other helpers fail and comforts flee, help of the helpless, O abide with me.*"

Harkness went through the door into a long straight hallway. He dealt with the guard behind it with a vicious poke of a bat, causing his nose to burst all over his face before his hand could reach the gun hanging at his side. "*Swift to its close ebbs out life's little day;*"

Immediately to his right, another figure was emerging from a doorway. His gun came up, only to be met with a swing down from Harkness's Louisville slugger, the clear crack of bones snapping in the man's hand as wood crushed flesh against the carbon stock of a mean-looking automatic rifle. At the same time, Danny was behind Harkness, kicking past him to send a coatrack falling in front of another man, thwarting his attempt to get a bead on both of them with a sawn-off shotgun which would have turned all in its range into mincemeat.

"*Earth's joys grow dim; its glories pass away;*"

Danny met the shotgun man's knees with a sweep of the bat, his scream of pain blended with Harkness who was still making like a Sunday school teacher. Claret was now smeared all over the bats both men held. Danny was amazed as he saw Harkness passing him, twirling the two sluggers over his head, like a deranged band majorette, one bat smashing a wall mirror while the other caught some good luck and the head of thug who happened to be hopping in panic from the toilet. His trousers were halfway up his legs, his other hand bringing an Uzi into play. He was out cold before he hit the ground, with a huge gash opening on the top of his head.

"Change and decay in all around I see; O thou who changest not, abide with me."

Harkness and Danny flattened themselves against either side of the next doorway, just as a hail of bullets peppered the wall and floor between them. The air filled with the sharp smell of cordite and someone yelling in Spanglish, accusing them of being 'motherfucker pendejos'.

What Harkness did next struck Danny as a move of genius. He screamed. A blood-curdling, ear-piercing shriek of prolonged pain, which brought the shooter to the doorway, in anticipation of a kill-shot. All he got for his troubles was baseball bats to the face and balls simultaneously.

From behind them, the shotgun guy Danny had dealt with decided he could take a pot-shot despite his broken kneecaps. Buckshot whizzed through the air, nicking Danny's left ear, a hot buzz of noise and pain felt as it did so. Yelping, Danny turned, instinctively launching his bat end over end at his assailant. The slugger caught him right in the throat, an ugly thump and gulp, followed by gurgling gasps as the man was left to fight for air.

Crouching, Harkness went through the last door of the bungalow unit, into a kitchen dominated by a table that was just about the right size to allow access to the cooker and cupboards. Calmly sitting behind it was a young man, hands held in the air. He had a huge joint hanging from his lips, tattoos all over his face and neck. The sweet smoke made Danny's eyes sting.

"Yo, *Ese*… take what you wan'. Eh? I got no beef wi' no DEA…"

On the table in front of him was piles and piles of cash, roughly stacked with a few Tecate beer bottles dotted amongst the money, and a nasty looking Mauser machine pistol lying on its side.

Harkness ventured into the room, twirling one of his bats in a lazy, slow arc. His eyes never left the toker as he sat, impassive. He sang again, only this time gently, turning his tune into a lullaby.

"*Hold thou thy cross before my closing eyes; Shine through the gloom and point me to the skies.*"

Danny joined him in the tight kitchen space, the aroma of marijuana cloying in his nostrils. He looked down at the guy behind the table. The dealer looked bemused by the singing. Harkness tapped the table with the end of a bloodied bat.

"Did you make the call, mate?"

He exhaled a huge cloud of smoke before nodding slowly…

"I don' they keel me right after joo, no?"

Danny could see the logic of it. Harkness stepped forward…

"*In life, in death, O Lord, abide with me*!"

And he sledgehammered the guy with his slugger. His head snapped back from the force of the blow, blood rocketing up the cupboard doors behind him.

"Danny, my boy. Open some cupboards, find me a bin bag. We need to oh-one-two-one fucking do-one out of here in the next three minutes…"

It wasn't an order or a bark. It was a gentle admission that they were on the clock.

They were back in the Ford Mustang in four minutes and roared away with a shit load of cash in a black bag before any drug dealer back up could even see their tail lights.

"I hope the good Lord heard our tuneful prayers this evening, Danny!!" laughed Harkness.

As they careered away in the car, Danny could feel the hot urgency of an erection in his trousers.

18

❖ Paradise Lost ❖

Overnight, a thunderstorm had blown through the Keys. On waking, Danny enjoyed the sound of moisture dropping off the trees and clicking onto his wooden roof, the breeze causing the droplets to descend. It made him think of the expression "pennies from heaven".

After boiling the kettle, he padded around his modest home with his tea, bare-ass naked, enjoying the cool morning air. He opened all the doors of his home to fill it with the freshness before the humidity and the heat of the day came.

It was only when he absent-mindedly scratched at his hairline, and the pain it caused, that the events of the previous night rushed back into his mind. Going into his living room, he saw the black plastic bag filled with cash sitting there, confirming his memory of blood, baseball bats and Bobby Darin.

Jesus, what a night.

He knew he had some thinking to do, lots. But he also felt strangely calm, in a way that had eluded him for some months, if he was honest. This thought did not fill him with any pride. Was he just an adrenaline junkie? Living for the psychopathic high of violence and danger? He had never considered himself to be that base… that lowest common denominator. Yet, Harkness's prediction that "mayhem maketh the man" in his case seemed to be more accurate than he would have ever thought.

But still, he knew he was in jeopardy. His life was now possibly in danger, no matter what kind of animal he might be. Harkness was nothing but trouble. June Cardell, the same. Danny suddenly felt glad that he had contacted his lawyer a few days earlier. He had put in motion a call for help whilst also laying the groundwork for an escape route. But, for the moment, he wanted to enjoy his Florida home.

Sipping at his tea, he went out onto the deck, confident that he could stand here at the back of the house without any one sliding by and discovering him naked. From here, he could enjoy the movement of the slow, green water in the canal. Leaves and sticks lazily drifted by, making patterns in the eddies of the flow as it made its way out into the Gulf of Mexico. Its shimmering waters were framed by the vegetation in front of him and a sky decorated with puffball clouds and a blue that almost hurt to look at.

Lost in his thoughts, he didn't hear the car pull onto his drive. The breeze was ruffling the bushes to mask it from him.

And because she was wearing gym gear complete with a pair of Nike running shoes, June made it all the way up onto the porch, through the open doors of his house. She stood in the kitchen doorway where it gave out onto the back porch before Danny knew anyone was there.

Startled, he turned, tensing his body, getting ready to strike out until he saw that it was her. She leaned against the doorjamb, a huge smile on her face.

"I know you were taking in the view, and now, so am I. Is this how you greet all your guests, Mr Franklin?"

At first, Danny felt vulnerable, but then, he suddenly thought… *What the fuck.* He sipped his tea and leant against the rail of his porch decking as if nothing could cause him a moment's concern. *Think of the devil and she shall appear*, Danny thought. "It's a beautiful day in the Keys. It could only be ruined by an unexpected guest. Didn't we talk about you not coming back, June?"

"Talk is cheap, love, you know that. And besides, if you had a bloody mobile phone, I could have called you."

"And if my aunt had bollocks, she'd be my uncle."

June chuckled in reply. She then stepped towards him. Standing close, she used a fingernail to trace a line from his collarbone to his abdomen, stopping before she reached where she had just been looking.

"I wanted to stop by and extend an invitation to you. Except it's not so much an invitation as one of those things the Queen used to have back home. What were they called? Oh yes, a Command Performance."

"I don't go anywhere I don't want to, June."

"Harkness said you'd be difficult." She stood on tiptoes and kissed Danny on the lips, careful not to let her body touch his. "Mmmm, Earl Grey tea this morning, very English. My husband wants to meet you. To talk business. He wants you to rob him, just like I do. Except he thinks he'll get the money back... but we can discuss all that later. You. Me. Harkness."

"Have you fucked Harkness, too, June? Or are you holding that little move back for a time in which you feel you'll really need to?"

The slap she delivered to the side of Danny's face was a good one, making his eyes water and see stars at the same time. And then, she was leaning against him, her Lycra-wrapped thigh pressed against his cock. She pulled his head down to hers, her perfume filling his senses as she whispered in his ear.

"You will find, Danny, that I am a twenty-first century woman. I make my own decisions and live how I choose. Stop being a sexist fuckwit and listen. Vincent will send a car for you tomorrow, Sunday. You will get in it. You will come and listen to him preach our Saviour's word, and you will meet with both of us after to talk... business."

"And if I don't?"

"I'll have you killed. And I don't need my husband's permission or Harkness's help to do it, either." She stepped back, looking him up and down. "And that, Danny, would be a shame, because I want to have a lot more fun with you, whilst we do the Lord's work. And, by the way, can I start calling you Danny Felix now? Not Franklin? Harkness has told me all sorts of lovely stories about you."

And with that, she walked away. Danny watched as she went back through the house to her car.

He sighed. Like all criminals, he hated loose ends, and he had a feeling he had just become one for all concerned in this plan.

Bollocks. What was that classic Milton poem called? Oh, yeah… Paradise Lost.

19

❖ Mysterious Ways ❖

On a bright and shining Saturday afternoon, there is one thing Americans really love to do.

Barbecue.

And if you are ever in any doubt, the large, hand-painted sign that was strung across the entrance to Founders Park declared that everyone was welcome to the "Annual St Thomas More Society Alzheimer's Cook Out!"

The heat of the day was being nicely tempered by a breeze which carried with it a delicious medley of smells. Hamburger, spicy chicken wings, sausages and corn on the cob all fought for sensory attention as families gathered to have fun in the name of a good cause.

In the middle of it, Father Simeon was like a cheerful MC, greeting friends and parishioners, announcing the raffles, prizes and who had won at horseshoe tossing. Children were busy licking sticky fingers and playing tag with each other. They were ducking in, around and under adults, showing that turn of pace and fleetness of foot that only an eleven-year-old could generate, never breathless, constantly moving.

Danny was watching all of this, a wry smile on his face, puzzlement in his brain. How could ordinary people live like this? He wasn't sneering, but he just knew that such a lifestyle would probably lead him to guzzling down a whole bottle of bourbon in one go and then send him lurching in search of the shotgun to suck down next.

He wandered amongst the stalls, wondering why he had actually turned up. Did he like Father Simeon that much? Well… yes. Did he respect him that much? It would seem so. Danny had turned up for his friend, the priest. No two ways about it. But how on earth could Sim think that such an event had anything of value for Danny? That was a mystery yet to reveal itself, if it could at all.

The stall in front of him was festooned with homemade comedy hats. The kind that could make you look like a dog with floppy ears, and a nose piece to complete the transformation. Or you might gain an instant set of dreadlocks, or stag's antlers, glistening with tinsel that was bound to be a hit come Christmas time.

Two women had stopped, trying on matching tam o'shanters that provided them both with shocks of instant ginger hair. They were both leaning into one another, taking a selfie. Danny was struck, not for the first time, that he didn't understand the twenty-first century compulsion to take pictures of yourself at every turn. Had we become so self-obsessed that every time a person so much as took their dog for a walk, they felt an irresistible desire to record the moment for posterity? As he thought this, one of the women turned towards him, taking the hat off as she laughed.

It took Danny a second to recognise Amparo Sosa, especially as her hair was off-kilter and not pulled back in a regulation bun. Plus, she was dressed in civvies, with no sign of her Monroe County uniform.

"Hello, Danny… what are you doing here?"

"Eh…"

"*Lo siento*… that sounded rude… I just didn't expect to see you at an event like…" She trailed off.

Danny laughed. For some reason, he liked to see her disarmed as she dug a bigger hole for herself. "Nice social skills there, Deputy. Are you always this charming? Like a little ray of sleet?"

"Sleet? What is… is this another British thing?"

He laughed again. There was endless fun to be had here, but he was interrupted by the second woman clearing her throat.

"Oh, sorry again… This is my friend, Cheryl Costanza. We came to support the charity, her grandmother suffered from Alzheimer's."

"A pleasure to meet you…?"

"Danny Franklin. I seem to be Amparo's pet Brit. She keeps me around so that I can teach her how to speak English properly. Sorry to hear about your grandma."

"Thank you, and with that accent, I might ask for an English lesson myself, Mr Franklin."

Amparo turned, looking incredulous at how forward her friend had just been.

"I only deal in one pupil at a time, Ms Costanza. Languages can be tricky, you need that one-on-one touch."

"Ignore my so-called *amiga*. She is a little eager to make new friends…" This earned Amparo a playful punch from her friend.

"Have you tried on any hats, Danny? I could see you in one of these doggy ones."

"I'm not sure it's my kind of thing, Deputy."

"Don't be boring, *hombre*."

Before he could stop her, Amparo was plucking one of the hats from the display, reaching to place it over his head. Danny was feeling uncomfortable, but when her friend raised the camera phone, he objected. Danny never wanted to be caught on film, digital, mobile or any other kind.

In scrambling to avoid the hat and turn away from the camera, he ended up pinning Amparo's arms to her sides. It was an awkward embrace lasting just a beat too long before both broke apart.

"Jeez, that was almost a touching moment, you guys. Amparo hasn't had so much male attention in a long while." Cheryl was laughing.

Danny was irritated. He couldn't be sure he'd avoided the camera's stare.

"Here, try a different one, Danny. How about a knitted Marlins hat? You like baseball?"

Cheryl threw the beanie at him, but he didn't catch it. The word baseball triggered his memory. His night with Harkness. A flash of blood arcing up a wall. A hot feeling of his own hair singeing at the side of his head, so real he reached up to touch where the scab was still healing under his hairline. His face turned a little ashen, and suddenly, all the self-loathing shame that he had been able to distance himself from came rushing to the front of his mind.

In a heartbeat, he went from irritated to feeling sick. It was disgust at how he had revelled in the mayhem, how he had enjoyed the strain on his muscles as he cracked the bat across another person's knees.

And Amparo saw it. He knew she did. The distress his memories were causing. Right there, etched across his face.

"Hey, Cheryl… go get us a couple of beers."

"What? *Hermana*…? What'd I do?"

Amparo flicked her head impatiently, Costanza taking the hint and walking off in search of the beer concession.

"You okay, Danny? You look a touch pale… you feeling *chuke*?"

Danny was breathing deeply, eyes clamped shut, trying to stop his mind from racing, to keep a panic attack at bay. And then, he felt a touch on his face, gentle, calming. He opened his eyes. Amparo was standing before him, looking up, a concerned expression on her face. She took him by the hand and led him to a nearby bench, sitting him down.

"Hey, *muchacho*, relax, okay. Take a deep breath. You want some *agua*?"

Danny cleared his throat. He was beginning to feel embarrassed, which he took as a good sign, his panic starting to fade. "No, no, I'll be all right. I've just had… a touch of a cold, or something…"

"Are you sure? Because to me that looked like someone just walked straight over your grave. You went kinda white, which is saying something for a *gringo*."

Danny looked up at her and started to softly laugh. "Thank you for your concern, and your gentle touch. That was…"

Danny stopped himself. *What the fuck am I doing? With everything going on right now, I can't be flirting with a woman… let alone a sheriff's deputy. Madness…*

An awkward silence followed until Danny found it possible to stand up. "I ought to find Father Simeon. I was supposed to help him cook ribs…"

"*Sí, sí*… I think he's the one with the microphone." She nodded over Danny's shoulder, as he turned to see his friend in full MC swing. "I'm off today and tomorrow. If you want to talk about whatever made you look like a ghost, you could take me for a drink, later?"

It caught him off guard. He turned back, not quite sure what to say. "I… I um..."

"Oh, excuse me… now I'm the one being forward, it's *simpatico*, maybe some other…"

"No. No, I'd like that. A drink, yes. How about Schooner's Wharf? In Key West?"

"On Williams Street?"

"Yeah, they have music and stuff… it's fun."

"Okay… eight pm?"

"That would be nice…"

Nice? Jesus, Danny thought, *you know how to charm a lady.*

"Great. See you later, Danny."

Amparo walked off to find her friend, leaving Danny to feel equal parts excitement and trepidation at what he had just done. He wanted to have that drink with her, but equally, he knew it was nothing but trouble.

"I thought you were gonna help me cook up some damn tasty ribs…"

Simeon cut through Danny's thoughts. He had a huge grin on his face, cigar ash cascading from a massive stogie jammed in his teeth, leaving little grey tracks on his black shirt and white priest's collar.

"How could I miss that? Let's go, big man."

"You all right, Brother D? You look a little… I dunno… preoccupied?" Simeon turned his head to watch Amparo catch up with her friend, turning back to Danny. He had an arch to his eyebrow.

"Aren't you supposed to be a man of God?"

"Hell, yeah, and one who has taken a vow of chastity with it, too. But, sometimes, I can feel a little envy. I mean, God made us in his image, didn't he? Even the weaker parts…"

"You're the second person to tell me that recently."

"Really? You been having philosophical conversations behind my back? I'm hurt, Brother D!"

Simeon's deep, throaty laugh warmed Danny over, leaving him feeling a bit more like himself.

"Come on. I'll help you cook and eat those ribs."

The next few hours were spent over a hot barbecue, alternately basting and turning pork rib over the coals, laughing, chatting and enjoying a Dr Pepper with his friend, the priest. The laughter was long and genuine. The families were nice, and the food was tasty. Eventually, Danny had to admit he was having a good time. As the light turned in the sky above them, the crowds ebbed away, and Danny found himself at a picnic table. Father Simeon was nursing a beer while he finished his plate of sauce-laden ribs.

"Okay, I give in. Why did you invite me here, Sim?" Danny licked a bit of sauce off his top lip.

"Brother D, you think you have this religion thing all tied up. You think it's all about oppression and rules. Brainwashing, making people behave through fear…"

"Something like that, yeah."

"And I promised you a look into a different version to that. Every single person turned up here today to do a little bit of good. We need a lot of money to fund a day care centre for those in need. Yes, they had fun. Yes, they got great ribs, a little dance, played some games, but they also put their hands in their pockets, and they gave money. Money that the St Thomas More boys will use to build that new centre to help families who are living with the challenge of Alzheimer's. That might just seem like charity to you, but if people didn't have the nudge from their church or priest, they might not make that little bit of effort. They might not look to do a little iddy bit of good in this world."

As Simeon finished, a young woman accompanied by a much older woman approached them.

"We came to say goodbye, Simeon."

"Martha, Martha, thank you. Thank you for coming and thank you for bringing this lovely creature here with you."

The lady was really old, Danny thought. He looked at her trying to place an age for her, settling on late eighties, at the very least.

Simeon took her hand. "Did y'all have a beautiful day?'

"I certainly did, suh. I certainly did. You know, I once had a son, young man, looked just like you. He's not a good man like you are. No, suh, he's in the wind, never payin' no mind to his Momma... Can you believe it? In this day and age? No respec'. I get no respec'."

"Oh, now, ma'am. I'm sure he's out there somewhere, right now, thinkin' on what he done, probably making his way back home to say sorry to you."

"My ass. Excuse my tongue, Preacher, but he's a sorry, no good wastrel... I ever see him again, I'll give him a piece of my mind instead o' a piece o' pie."

Simeon gathered her into a bear hug, his huge frame threatening to swallow up the little woman. "Never mind, never mind. The lord loves you just as much, anyway, even if you are angry at your son. You go have a good night's rest now... go on..."

Martha also said her goodbyes, taking the old lady off towards a people carrier.

Simeon sat back down, taking a long pull from his beer as he did so. Danny took a moment before he said what was on his mind.

"I get where you are coming from, Sim, I do. But what puzzles me is the blind faith. The blind acceptance religious people have about their world and their God. I mean, if God loves us so much and is so benevolent, why do we even need a centre for Alzheimer's? Why do we have any disease at all? If he created all of us, why bother with the stuff that causes us so much pain?"

"It is supposed to be a planet of free will, Danny. We don't just get to live it up all the time. We are sentient, conscious beings… we have to make our own choices. God shows us what's possible when we make the right ones. Helping all those families cope with the loss of a loved one who still happens to be living and breathing right in front of them, that's gotta be one of our better endeavours… and if we do it because our church encouraged us to… that's religion at work, right there, my man. I know I appreciate it."

"You would, you're a priest. It gives you a little feedback from the congregation, right? See them turn up here. Bet you never hear anything back from God when you're praying…"

"Brother D, that's where you're wrong. These people showing up is God answering my prayers. And you know how I know that fo' sure? Because that little lady cussing out her wastrel son… That's my momma, and I'm the supposed wastrel she thinks she never sees. She don' know if it's Tuesday or Tishomingo. And I sure as hell need help dealing with the heartbreak of that every single day."

It was all Danny could do to drop his eyes to the ground, regretting every word he had said to someone who was the closest thing he'd had to an actual friend for a very long time.

20

❖ Simple Truths ❖

"They're going to rob you."

Ines Zedillo was looking incredulous, despite being a vision in white linen. The apple martini was paused halfway between the table and her lips.

Harkness enjoyed the moment. He liked that he'd managed to cut through her studied 'sangfroid' with his little revelation. They were sitting at a corner table at Azul, one of Miami's top restaurants, where you needed a bit of pull to snag a table, and even more to get a quiet one.

He deliberately took a sip of his own drink, an Old Fashioned, milking the pause in the conversation for full dramatic effect.

"Stop fucking with me, Harkness. What do you mean, 'rob me'?"

"What do you think it means? They are going to steal your money at that big holy Joe bollocks they are holding next month, the one where they launder a shit load of cash for you. They are going to blag it and try and put the blame on someone else... the Dominicans, the Mafia, whoever the fuck you Mexicans hate most this week."

"That would be the president..."

"He's not worth your energy. But there it is. That is what they are going to try and do."

"How do they even think they could get away with it? *Muy loco... Madre di Dios.*"

"Because June Cardell has asked me to sort it. And I know someone good enough to help me do it."

And there it was, the delicious hook in Harkness's tale for Señora Zedillo. He knew that by being honest with her, she would listen to him for real.

"There is a lot of face to be lost here, Ines. People would think you'd misplaced your balls if this were to happen. But, as I told you the last time I saw you, I can help."

Zedillo set her glass on the table with meticulous care. She smoothed down her skirt and then turned slowly to look Harkness full in the face. "And why on earth should I trust you, Harkness? *Porque*? Eh?"

"Because I think we could both benefit. I can help them pull off the robbery and then return the money to you. We make a deal. You tell your 'Barrio' buddies that they managed to make off with more than they actually did while you and I walk into the sunset a little happier and richer. That's why…"

She snorted, derision obvious in her tone and her face. "You are a more foolish *cabrón* than I gave you credit for. *Chingate, amigo*. Stealing from my own bosses? It would be easier to get away with killing that *pendejo* Trump than to steal from *mi familia*…"

"Except are they *familia*, sweetheart? They act like they are because they climbed out of the same shithole, but you had the brains and knew how to put their money in a nice orderly pile for them up here in Miami. How long, though? How long before one of your bosses has a son or a daughter who covets the old *Yanqui* lifestyle? Wants to walk down South Beach, stay in fancy suites at The Delano, and eat dinner in places like this? How old are you, Ines? Fifty-five? Your clock is ticking. Don't tell me you haven't got a little stash growing somewhere in the background. A little early-retirement fund. I can top it off nicely for you, you can hand the reins over to some younger, meaner Culiacán dog…"

Ines dabbed at her lips delicately with her napkin, gently folding it, placing it to the side of her martini glass. She reached for her handbag. Keeping her hands under the tables, she pulled a Smith and Wesson 686 revolver from it and sat forward to push the muzzle of the gun into Harkness's crotch.

"*Oye, pendejo*. You never, and I mean *nunca*, ask a lady her age. And never forget who you are dealing with here. I was once a Culiacán dog. That blood runs in my veins and means more to me that any *loco* plan some fool like you might bring me. As for money, yes, I am planning for my future, and yes, I might just take advantage of this situation. But never forget, you are dealing with Ines Zedillo. You will be my little British Bulldog. Set it up, keep me informed, and if you so much as yank on the leash I'm putting on you, I will skin you alive before I kill you."

"Last night. Florida City. Counting house. You lost some money, a few barrio boys who will only be able to drink soup through a straw for the next few months. Sound familiar? I bet it does, sweetheart. That's how deep I am into your little organisation up here in Florida. You didn't even see me coming."

Harkness calmly drained his glass before standing up, leaving her gun pointing at his chair and a look of surprise across her face.

"I want forty percent of the take. You get the rest, however much you declare to your bosses is up to you. For that, I'll deliver the Cardells and my thief into the bargain. You can skin them alive and post them back to Mexico, for all I care… and next time you pull a gun on me, be prepared to use it, Ines."

Harkness could feel her eyes on him as he walked away, pretty sure that she was already planning ways to kill him along with the Jesus freaks.

There was much to think on in the coming days.

Danny was careful to arrive early at Schooners Wharf in Old Key West, not wanting Amparo waiting in the bar on her own. The place was as crowded as it usually was, tourists and locals all enjoying the great atmosphere, with music being played by a chain-smoking man playing an acoustic guitar on the little makeshift stage, a huge and very old Labrador sitting patiently at his feet. The only time the dog moved was when it had to avoid the ash dropping off his master's cigarette. It didn't surprise Danny at all to hear the guy had a growl of speaking voice, a bit like a bike chain being dropped onto a metal bin lid.

Danny was feeling nervous. He was contradicting every single rule he had previously held about his personal life. He had always avoided distractions of the relationship kind. He barely committed to furniture, let alone a girlfriend. And yet, here he was, waiting on a girl. A girl who was a policewoman, to boot! Was he so tired of his chosen path? Was this an early onset mid-life crisis? No. It wasn't as clichéd as that. He just felt it. He felt he deserved a touch of affection in his life. He wanted to indulge himself. To feel. As to why that was the case? He didn't have an answer to that yet.

When she did arrive, suitably ten minutes late, Danny spotted her instantly. She dodged customers in the entrance way, looking around, trying to spot him in the bar area that was partly open to fresh evening air. He caught her eye, and, smiling, she made her way to where he stood at the end of the bar.

"*Hola*, Danny… how ya doin'?"

She shuffled onto the barstool he had pulled out for her. He wasn't sure whether to chastely kiss her on the cheek or shake her hand. He felt like an awkward teenager, something he'd never really been. He opted for the kiss, and she responded except they both misjudged, and it almost ended up being a kiss on the lips as they got their cheek directions confused. They stopped and looked at each other, laughing.

"Sorry, Amparo, let's try that again, shall we?" Danny lent in, clearly telegraphing the direction of his face this time, being rewarded with the touch of her skin on his face and the sweet, musky smell of her perfume. "What can I get you to drink? I've got one of these awful, fizzy beers you Americans seem to like."

"Don't diss the king of beers, they're delicious!"

"You're kidding, right?"

"*Claro*. I'll have a margarita, please, Janey knows how I like mine…"

The bartender winked at her, and Danny couldn't help but smile. He may have suggested the venue, but it was now clear he was on her turf.

When her drink came, it was in a plastic cup placed inside another plastic cup with a Schooners Wharf beer mat jammed in between. Danny was puzzled, and it showed.

"The beer mat? It means I'm a local."

"Oh, okay… and I'm not." Danny gestured to his single plastic cup.

"No, you're not. You get the '*touron*' prices!" She giggled, taking a sip of her margarita through a straw.

"Now it's your turn to translate. '*Touron*'?"

"Sí… '*touron*', half tourist, half moron, usually how they show up round here." She laughed again.

Danny thought how much he liked the sound. "Okay, I get it… We call them grockles in England. They aren't much liked. Their money is always welcome, though."

"True, true…"

"Speaking of truth, why did you ask me out for a drink, Amparo?"

"Can't a *chica* ask a nice boy out for a little fun?"

"I suppose…"

"Listen, I always liked the bad boys, the ones who are a little *mysterioso*. And you intrigue me… it must be the cop in me…"

"Is this some kind of alternative interrogation technique?'

"No… no, I just like conundrums."

"You like being a cop?"

"*Si… me gusto*. It's the best job in the world when it goes right and you're making a difference."

"Is that important to you? Making a difference?"

"Definitely. When I was young, my *hermano*, my brother, he got involved with the wrong people. He ended up in a gang, selling a little marijuana, boosting the odd car… relatively small-time shit. Except it wasn't small enough… He was shot, lost an eye. It was a drive-by, gang feud over some stupid stuff, a girl or money or something. From that day on, I wanted to try and stop the small stuff before it became the big stuff. Before someone got hurt."

Danny signalled the bartender. He had decided to dump the terrible beer, switching to a Blanton's on ice. He took a sip, savouring the smoky aroma on his tongue.

"And what about you, Danny? How come you wanted to be a fisherman? You like tuna?"

"Ha! I just wanted a quieter life."

"You need money to drop out these days… you must have been a lucky man in the past. Or is that part of your mystery?"

"What can I tell you? I'm an international bank robber living off the proceeds of just one big job."

Amparo laughed, and Danny sipped his drink to disguise his own amusement at how he'd just told her the truth. He could see that she hadn't taken him seriously.

The evening wore on. The two of them chatted, easy with each other's company, crossing from subject to subject, everything from why Americans didn't understand kettles to why the British drank warm beer. Danny was enjoying the warmth of her presence. Only now and again did he catch a flash of his own discomfort, a tinge of worry that he was getting to know this woman, a police woman no less, at a time when he was about to embark on a dangerous new phase in his life. A phase that would almost certainly lead to him either being dead or, at the very least, running the hell out of town.

And that was when he realised it. He was getting to know her. He was flirting, because deep down, he knew it might be his last chance at experiencing something other people were able to take for granted. That was why he was feeling close to Father Simeon. That was why he was feeling lonely. His life choices were putting him on a path to this point. A point where his options were going to grind to a halt. Soon, he would either have to kill or be killed. And for a time, even if it was going to be a short one, he wanted to feel friendship. Companionship. Maybe even a little love.

"Danny? *Que pasa*? Where you gone?"

He had been busted, staring off into middle distance, coming to terms with why he was even here. "Sorry, Amparo, I was just off with Alice for a second there."

"Who's Alice? Should I be jealous already?"

"Ha-ha... no, I mean off in wonderland... like Alice."

"Oh, *amigo*... if I am boring you..."

"No... no, really... I was actually wondering about something really important."

"*Digame*... tell me..."

"I was wondering, as you're a local, if I walk you home, would you let me kiss you goodnight?"

Amparo reached for her drink, tossing it back in one sizeable swig and, without speaking, started to pick up her little purse, standing up off her stool. "*Hombre... vamos*. Let's get walking..."

And they both laughed. Danny felt like the luckiest boy in class who had just been allowed to hold hands with the pretty girl.

21

❖ Daydream Believer ❖

Danny was daydreaming. He was thinking about kissing Deputy Sheriff Amparo Sosa. He caught himself thinking about the night before. How she had felt in his arms. Her perfume. The sheen of her hair. The fact that he had turned into some kind of infatuated puppy from a 1950s pop song.

He liked the fact that she had not invited him in for the proverbial "coffee". He had been left with an inane grin on his face as she closed the door on him, and he'd stood there for a full minute and a half before walking away. Here he was, replaying the scenario in his head and enjoying every second.

A revelry that was instantly spoiled when the woman sitting next to him grabbed his hand and forced him to stand up, along with the rest of the congregation. The church was massive, with an altar to match, decked out in obvious plastic plants and a deep-pile scarlet-red carpet. To one side, a band had launched into a version of *Are You Washed in the Blood,* except their version was a quasi-heavy metal one, complete with screaming guitars and a drummer who thought he was in AC/DC. Jolted back into the here and now, Danny thought, not for the first time that morning, that this was the very definition of mass hysteria.

As he watched the musicians, Danny moved his mouth in a fake low-level sing-along. The lady next to him was belting out the words.

"*Are your garments spotless? Are they white as snow? Are you washed in the blood of the lamb?*"

Bloodstains are hard to remove, love. I know better than most, thought Danny as the woman tugged his hand about in the air in time with the racket the band was making. It puzzled Danny.

How could you put all those hours of learning and practise into playing electric guitar only to then use it playing "Christian Rock"? *If it were me, I'd be on the road, banging for Britain in every town we visited.*

Sitting towards the back of the altar, June Cardell was looking every inch the dutiful preacher's wife. Dressed in a cornflower-blue twinset, she wore a pearl necklace to complete the look. Danny nearly burst into laughter at the next line of the hymn: "*When the Bridegroom cometh, will your robes be white?*" He reckoned June hadn't worn that kind of white for at least twenty years.

When Danny had climbed into the blacked-out Escalade that had arrived at his home earlier that morning, he truly had no idea what he was letting himself in for. The service had been going on for over an hour and a half. On... and on... interminable. Danny didn't know how much more he could take. So far he'd seen a little white-haired lady tell the gathered faithful that "Global warming isn't the work of human hands. It's God telling us to mend our ways." This had been followed by a tall man in cowboy hat and boots. He was introduced as a 'modern day Hank Williams with a bible in one hand and guitar in the other.' He had sung three songs about the evils of alcohol, at one stage proclaiming whiskey to be the "Devil's buttermilk". All he managed to do was make Danny crave a Blanton's on ice.

Finally, Vincent Cardell entered. He took centre stage. The room had fallen eerily silent, an expectant hush signalled that he was the main act here today. *Except*, Danny mused, *for the majority here, this is no act. This is a way of life.* These people literally believed every single phrase, word, doctrine and epithet that had been cast from the altar. The notion terrified him.

Cardell had been like a whirlwind. Starting at the pulpit, he strode about the raised dais. His message became ever more strident. He preached about the purity of the Bible, how many had tried, but not succeeded, to taint the Christian legacy. He condemned Catholics, politicians and scientists. Even Darwin got a pasting. All for the sake of Cardell's version of religion. His was, to Danny's mind, a vengeful, capricious and bigoted version of the "All-powerful.' Cardell spoke of reckonings, of cleansing fires, floods and pestilence. At one point, he argued that only Americans would survive the apocalypse. Only they would see the true face of God. And when Danny thought Vincent might be on the brink of some kind of seizure, so intense was his tirade, he suddenly stood still. The silence in the church became claustrophobic. Cardell slowly and deliberately surveyed the whole room, taking in the two thousand or so people; he looked around as most hung on his every word.

His final volley was then delivered in whispered tones. "Know this, my fellow believers. His judgement upon us will be swift and relentless. We have built a world that worships false gods. We have been complicit in allowing these ungodly weeds to proliferate in the Garden of Eden. But His word still rings true. Romans, chapter one, verse eighteen. '*For the wrath of God is revealed from heaven against all ungodliness and unrighteousness of men who suppress the truth in unrighteousness.*' Are you suppressing? Are you living His truth? It's time we abandoned false idols. It's time we returned our America to good old Christian values. It's time we tell our leaders to lead so we can follow them back to the path of righteousness. When you leave here today, it is your calling to tell your politicians that is what you want. It is what we all here want. Because it's not me simply spouting from a pulpit. No. It. Is. God's. Will."

Cardell paused, letting his message settle on the congregation. "We do not want to anger him. We do not want to invoke God's wrath. We want to execute His will and see the glory of His second coming. We can return our nation to God's favour. God bless each and every one of you… and God Bless our America."

The congregation had been silent until this point. They were rapt at Cardell's fervour. As soon as he stopped, the crowd went ballistic. The last time Danny had heard a noise like it had been at a world title boxing match, the challenger severely cutting the incumbent champion's eye, with bloodlust fuelling the wave of noisy euphoria that followed.

A few more acolytes had taken to the pulpit, but none had held the sway Cardell had. Danny's thoughts had wandered off to Amparo, and now, he hummed along to a heavy metal hymn he neither knew nor cared for. As the song neared its frenetic, guitar solo-ed climax, a tall man in a suit appeared next to Danny. He bent to half-shout, half-whisper into Danny's ear.

"Come with me now, Mr Franklin."

At first, Danny hesitated, not recognising the name, but quickly remembered that he went by Franklin these days. It may have been a year-and-a-half since he'd left London, but he still had moments where his cover name sounded unfamiliar.

They picked their way through the rows of congregants, Danny struck at how they looked cut from the same cloth. The men were wearing a kind of uniform – chinos, white starchy shirts and old-fashioned ties. The women were in long skirts and blouses that buttoned right to the neck, despite the humidity inside the huge Floridian church. They looked like an army.

The tall man led the way to a door at the right-hand side of the altar whilst the host preacher wrapped up the day's worshipping, trotting out earnest "thank-you"s to his guest speakers. Once through the door, a maze of beige-coloured corridors, multiple doors on either side met them, until they came to what looked like a fire exit. The tall man pushed through it, and a stretch limousine was on the other side, engine running, a chauffeur stationed at the open rear door.

"Get in."

Danny was about to smart-mouth the tall man, but then thought better of it when he heard June Cardell's voice call him from inside the huge vehicle. "Come on in, Danny. The air-con is struggling."

He ducked into the car. His eyes adjusted from the sunny glare to muted tones of the interior. The door closed behind him. June was sitting at the far end of the limo. She patted the seat alongside her. "Sit here. That way, when he arrives, you will be able to see us both."

"I feel like a pet dog."

"Behave, and I might give you a treat later." June winked. "Now remember, my husband is a little… intense. And he will be terse with you. He always feels exhausted after delivering a sermon."

"I can imagine… the weight of all that bullshit."

"There's no need to take that tone, Danny. What I'm offering you is a fabulous opportunity. Play nicely."

"What you're offering and what your husband is offering are two different things."

"Remember what I told you, Danny." June cocked her index finger and thumb like a gun, pulling the imaginary trigger.

Danny ignored her. "Why can't I mention Harkness?"

"When you plan to dupe someone, do you normally furnish them with the plan and a list of names of those involved?"

"I'm still not fully on board with your little game here, June. Just remember that. You might think you hold all the aces, but I'm not even playing just yet."

"Would it help if I told you a number?"

Danny shot her a look. He had been considering for some time that there must be a significant amount of cash at stake. Why else would Harkness be sniffing around? Why else would a woman like June embark on such a risky venture? Danny looked at her, being careful not to remain poker-faced.

"Try me."

"Around eighteen million dollars. The mission only rakes in about half that… but then… we launder."

Nine million dollars laundered in a little over seventy-two hours. That's time and efficiency in motion right there, he thought. *Who knew a little Gospel could take you so far?*

"That's a lot of money that Jesus is missing out on."

"And you could have your share… if you behave."

"You mean, if I misbehave, June. Misbehave on your behalf…"

"I'll make it worth your while… in all sorts of ways."

Danny was about to answer when he heard the chauffeur grip the handle of the car door.

Vincent Cardell climbed in. Despite his energetic performance, when Cardell sat down opposite Danny he looked remarkably calm and fresh.

"It's Mr Franklin, isn't it?" Cardell then looked down at his right hand. He inspected his fingernails, which, to Danny's mind, looked long for a man. He then slowly offered it to Danny.

Danny shook it, unsurprised by the wan, limp handshake that he received. "You don't like to touch strangers, do you?" Danny tightened his grip a little towards the end of the shake in order to see the preacher's discomfort flicker up a notch. "I'd like to say it's a pleasure, Mr Cardell. But compulsory invites are not ones I usually relish or comply with."

"Really? Why are you here, then?"

"Let's just say that June can be a persuasive person."

Cardell glanced at his wife. There was no obvious expression on his face, but Danny knew something had passed between them.

"My wife seems to think you are the answer to our prayers. Is she right?"

"Depends on what you are praying for. I can show you a fabulous day's fishing."

"Danny..." June tutted at him.

"Have you ever killed a man, Mr Franklin?"

The question took Danny by surprise, and before he could answer, Cardell continued.

"I think it might be the closest feeling of being a God that man can ever experience. The thing is, if you do kill, you had better make sure that it is in God's name. Otherwise, he might have a problem with you. Everything we do should be in God's name. Let's cut to the chase, Mr Franklin, shall we? You are a thief. We want something... appropriated. You will be handsomely compensated, should you decide to help us."

Danny took a second to answer, still feeling nonplussed by Cardell's words. "If I don't choose to help you, Mr Cardell, that would make me, somewhat, a loose end. I'm sure you don't risk leaving many of those lying around."

June interjected. "In the past, we may have trusted in a few individuals too easily and too quickly. This has caused us to accelerate our game plan. But we think you are a more professional risk."

Danny was getting a clearer picture now. They had to make their play as they had sprung a leak somewhere. The cartel they were stealing from was on to them. High stakes. Danny's stomach did a little flip.

"You do leave loose ends lying around, then. Why should I help?" Danny enjoyed pretending he knew less than he did.

"And why shouldn't you help us, Mr Franklin? Do you believe in Jesus? Did you gain any insights from this morning?"

Danny sighed. He felt like he had been explaining his relationship to God a lot lately. "Here's the deal. I won't talk to you about your God, and you don't need to ask me about my feelings on the subject. You wouldn't ask a car mechanic if he believed in UFOs now, would you?"

"The question still stands. This will be a relationship that, whilst professional, will require a large degree of trust, Mr Franklin. If we cannot gauge the mettle of your character, how can we be expected to place our faith in you?"

June's eyes went wide. Danny could see that she had assumed this might be a little more straightforward.

"Do you like the cinema, Mr Cardell?"

Vincent and June both looked puzzled.

"There's a great film called *Angel Heart*. In it, Mickey Rourke plays a private detective who takes on a missing persons case for Robert De Niro. De Niro's character is called Louis Cypher. Ring any bells?"

Vincent opened his mouth to reply, but Danny didn't let him.

"In one scene, he meets with Mickey. De Niro's peeling, in a very deliberate manner, a boiled egg. Once peeled, he sprinkles the egg with some salt and says, 'You know, some religions think that the egg is a symbol for the soul. Did you know that?' And then, he takes a huge bite out of it, pure malevolence in his eyes."

"This is all very well—"

Danny cut him off again. "As far as I'm concerned, you, and all your kind, are exactly like that. You're all actors pretending to understand religion, God and souls. You are showmen, no better than actors playing a role. If God turned up here, right now, you'd just about shit your pants. Never ask me again about God, faith, religion or eternal damnation. As for being trusted? If I decide to collaborate with you, I will bear more risk than you ever will. I will have way more skin in the game. That should be your guarantee. Not whether I fall to my knees, join hands and sing alleluia."

Silence descended on the interior of the car, tension sitting in the air. It was June who finally broke it.

"Whether you believe in God, fate or the collective consciousness, I know that you find yourself in front of people at certain times in your life, and their presence is no accident. You are that type of person, Danny. And we are the same for you. This is an opportunity for us all to benefit. You have a sterling reputation for this kind of work. My husband does not trust easily. He relies on meditation, prayer and divine guidance. But on this occasion, I'm going to ask him to trust me. Rely on me. I will vouch for you, Danny. And Vincent, if that's not good enough for you, I don't know why we're married."

The irony was supreme. Danny almost guffawed at what she had just said, but he recognised the play to be the right one. And Vincent didn't disappoint.

"Very well. At least I have had the chance to look you in the eye, Mr Franklin. If June speaks for you, so be it. But remember one thing. I may be a man of God, but I am not to be underestimated. I have a greater plan… Nothing will stop me from achieving it."

Danny wondered if that warning was as much for June as it was for him. "Okay, Mr Cardell. Tell me. What is it you want me to steal?"

22

❖ How'ya? ❖

The weather played ball. It was tricky enough piloting a boat in the dark of the night without having to contend with a swell or high winds. Danny thanked his lucky stars that the elements had decided to have a quiet night.

He'd reached the agreed co-ordinates with plenty of time to spare, and was now enjoying the bump of a gentle swell, having weighed anchor. He blew on the tea that he had poured for himself from a small flask. It wasn't exactly cold out here on the Gulf of Mexico, but it was chilly enough to find comfort in the brew. And anyway, old habits die hard. He had always enjoyed the ritual of tea at certain times. It was why he liked smoking the odd cigar. The need to light it properly, turning the stogie in the match flame and timing your puff so that you gave it enough oxygen to light but not so much that you inhaled. He learned never to tap the ash end of a cigar into an ashtray, instead he left it to fall off as it burned naturally. Convention considered it vulgar to flick cigar ash.

The same with tea. He relished using loose leaf, pre-warming the pot and giving it time to infuse. Decanting it into the flask was not part of the normal process, but now, he was completing his own little tea ceremony, blowing on the brew, making sure that when he added a dash of milk he achieved the colour of the drink exactly the way he liked it. This wasn't easy in the gloom of his boat at night, especially as he was moored in the middle of nowhere with all his lights extinguished so as to avoid attracting any unwanted attention.

As he drank his tea, Danny reflected that he considered pulling a job to be a ritual, too. It followed a pattern. The search for an opportunity. The planning, scouting the location, making meticulous notes, both mental and physical ones, being careful never to store them any place they might get found, no laptops, tablets or mobile phones for him… way too easy to trace and give you away. Following the planning with days of observation. Watching the patterns around a job. If there were security personnel, what was their routine? Their foibles? How often did the older guard need to pee? How distracted was a younger guard by their mobile phone or reception computer? Were there members of the public around and, if so, at what time of day? All of this type of information helped Danny to plan a job in his mind like a ritual. To build a picture so complete that he could readily begin to predict scenarios and how they might play out once his plans intervened. He could spot the patterns of human behaviour and predict changes and reactions in them with almost eerie accuracy. It was what made him an excellent thief. And he enjoyed the ritual of it all. Just like making tea or enjoying a fine Cuban Robusto.

And the most satisfying thing about these rituals? When they came together to form a plan that would go off without a hitch. That night was no different. When he had contacted his lawyer to set the wheels in motion, he had hoped that the help he was asking for would turn out to be available. Danny had been amazed at how quickly it had all come together. The last bit of that cry for help would be completed out here on the Gulf.

After an hour of waiting, Danny saw a single, solitary light in the distance. He was calm, but expectant, as he watched it grow a little larger, finally switching on his own single spot when he judged the time was right. In an almost old-fashioned gesture, he blinked his spot not once but three times. The oncoming light did the same.

Soon, a small fishing craft havered into view. A short man, dressed as though he were on board an ice-breaker instead of a boat on the Gulf of Mexico, stood at the prow. This made Danny chuckle as it reminded him of Leonardo DiCaprio and Kate Winslet in *Titanic*. He was even wearing a bobble hat and gloves.

The fishing boat pulled alongside. Danny used a boathook to steady the connection while the other pilot tied the two vessels together. Danny handed him an envelope that contained a sizeable wedge of cash. It was only then that the pilot stood aside to allow the heavily swaddled man to step awkwardly from the fishing boat onto Danny's craft.

"Fuck me. Is that you?"

"Hmmph, fecking hmmph," came the muffled reply.

"You know we're on the Gulf of Mexico, right? Not the Arctic Circle. No Northern Lights round here, mate." Danny was laughing.

The short man unwound the scarf that was wrapped high around his face and neck, slowly but surely revealing a truly electric shock of ginger beard. Danny was laughing, thinking it was the bushiest face fuzz he had ever laid eyes on.

"Jaysus… it's not fecking natural… if we were meant to be out here over deep water, God would have given us fecking flippers. I was fecking freezin'. I felt like your man… Col Abram?"

Danny was howling. "What, you mean the eighties pop star who sang 'Trapped'?"

"What the feckin' Jaysus are you bletherin' about? No, no, no, the boy who hunted the big fuckin' whale."

Tears were pouring down Danny's face. "You mean Captain Ahab? *Moby Dick*?'

"I don't care what size his dick was… I don't like it… boats… floating… I've no webbed feet, ya know…"

"Ciaran, it's a delight to have you back in my life…" He wrapped the Irishman in a bear hug. The pair of them thumped each other's backs, genuine affection was obvious in their reunion.

"How'ya, Danny… is it yourself?"

"It is, Ciaran, I'm chuffed to bits that you decided to come. Welcome to Florida."

"Ah now. Stop it. Don't be getting ahead of yourself. I only came because I want to go to Disney World. I've always wanted to meet thon' yoke Mickey."

And they laughed heartily.

Danny wasn't joking when he had said he was chuffed at Ciaran's presence. They had a bond that had been strong for years, and the events surrounding the robbery and mayhem in London had only served to cement and deepen it for both men. Danny couldn't think of a better right-hand man than Ciaran. And with his help, Danny could start to feel more optimistic about his chances of solving his Harkness problem and surviving to tell the tale. If Ciaran was still willing to be involved once Danny had laid it out for him.

It had been a bit of a long shot contacting Ciaran. After London, all Danny knew was that he had returned to the west of Ireland to keep his head low and enjoy the spoils of the robbery. He only had Ciaran's mother's address as a point of contact. He'd instructed his lawyer to FedEx a note to her from Danny himself and to include a plane ticket from Ireland to the Dominican Republic and, from there, a boat, to make the relatively short hop north to the Florida Keys. All the note had said was:

Ciaran,

Paradise has been lost. Unwanted company. Need your help. Use the ticket. You'll be met and transported the rest of the way. May the road rise to meet you…

Danny.

The last line had been their agreed code. If they wanted to contact each other, they had to include the line from the ancient Irish blessing. That way, they would know the message was genuine. And even with such scant context, Ciaran had still come. The old double act was back together.

"Now, so, who has found ye, Danny? Someone I could guess?"

"Have a go…"

"Yer man, Harkness… he'll be like a dog with a bone… can't be botherin' to let go."

"Correct. Took him eighteen months, mind you."

"I'm sure some of those were spent at her Majesty's pleasure."

"It seems the connections from his murky past managed to shrink that time to an almost insignificant period."

"How'd ya think he found ya?"

"There can only have been one way. He followed the loot. I was having Barry Blount send the money in drips for about six months."

"Wha? Yer man, the reality TV boy... he's dead."

Danny looked at his friend, a grim expression on his face. Had his actions added to an already long death toll surrounding the London job?

"Before she commissioned the robbery, Dexy had asked me to do a little number on Blount for a separate client of hers. I had him scared shitless. When I revisited him after we pulled Dexy's job, I knew he would do anything I asked of him."

"He died a few months back. All over the papers. They said it was an accidental drug overdose."

But Danny knew better. Barry must have given up the address that he'd been sending the money to, a rented post box here in the Keys. From there, it wouldn't have been that hard for Harkness to find his way to Danny's door.

"Right, so, when are we going to kill him? I'll enjoy doing that fecker. Especially after the way he played our boy Enda and his explosives."

"Harkness may have manipulated him, but Enda still planted them, despite us asking him only to throw London into chaos, not blow it to bits."

"Aye, right enough, but Harkness knew the buttons to push. He knew that Enda was still mad Irish Republican. 'A nation once again' and all dat. Feckin' nuts about it, he was. But, sure, he got his comeuppance. I saw to that."

They had both realised that Enda had to be disposed of in London. The amount of death and destruction he caused would have made him Britain's "most wanted". He had to be dealt with to protect the others. Danny had been willing to do it, but Ciaran felt it was his job, especially as he'd brought him into the robbery in the first place.

"So, if Harkness has found ye, why are you still walking round, breathin' like?"

"Oh, he doesn't want to kill me... yet. He's wants me to pull a job."

'Ah, Jaysus, Danny... you must be fuckin' kidding me."

"I know... crazy, right? But he didn't reveal his presence until after the people with the gig had contacted me."

"But ye knew it was him, still?"

"Let's say, he left a trail of breadcrumbs, and I followed them."

"Wha's the job?"

"Okay, stick with me on this. We're going to rob a church."

Ciaran's eyes widened. "I know we're going to burn in hell, Danny, but wha'? You tryin' to make feckin' doubly sure?"

Danny laughed gently. "The church is a bit of a big deal. The married couple who run it are evangelical celebrities. Every year, they hold this big mission in Miami. Thousands, and I mean thousands, show up and pray with them, get healed, whatever the fuck they do at these things, and..."

"They make donations... cash donations. The oul plate going round."

"Yes, as old-fashioned as that sounds, that is exactly what they do. In their world, they call it tithing. You don't buy tickets to these events, but you are expected to pay tribute once you've felt God's holy light rustling around inside your wallet."

In the distance, the lights of Key West twinkled gently on the horizon. They would soon be making land.

"And we're going to steal from them? I don't know, Danny... I still like the odd priest... My ma would kill me just for having this talk!"

"No, they want us to rob them."

"Jaysus, the night and day! What now? They're in on it?"

"Yes... kind of... It's complicated."

"I only arrived a half hour ago and my head's already thumping."

"The money they make at these services is mostly cash. One of the couple, Vincent Cardell is his name, harbours political ambitions to go with his religious fervour. In order to realise those, he needs a shitload of money. So, he has a bright idea. He decides that he can help a Mexican drug cartel launder their dirty money by swelling his donation coffers with it. They load their cash in, the Cardells process it through their charitable foundations and, slowly but surely, through bogus initiatives, the money is cleaned up and trickled back to the cartel."

"The sweet Lord Jaysus moves in mysterious ways here in Florida..."

"That's not the whole story."

"There's more? Holy bejeesus."

"In his wisdom, Vincent has been skimming off the top from the cartel money."

"When's the next flight to Ireland?"

"Oh, I'm still not done. Vincent's wife, June Cardell, who happens to be English, suspects that the cartel suspects... and she wants me to rob the money and give it all to her, not to her husband. She was the one who knew Harkness, and he pointed her in my direction. Oh, and I've banged her too..."

Incredulity was painted all over Ciaran's face.

"Jaysus Christ on a bicycle! If I'd known church was as good as that these days, I would still be goin'. You're some boy, Danny Felix. And you, like a madman, are going to play ball with dis lot?"

"I have no choice. Harkness fingered me for the job. They revealed their hand to me. I'm a loose end now. If I passed, they'd have to deal with me, and Harkness would try too. But being involved gives me a shot at Harkness. It's like you said. He'll be like a dog with a bone until he kills me. It is hunt or be hunted now, plus, and I hate to admit this, but I've been feeling a little bored. I'm missing the kick."

Ciaran nodded, as if Danny's logic made sense to him.

"Now that you know all the complexities, do you still want to get that next plane back to Ireland?"

"No. Ye've promised I could meet Mickey Mouse. I'll wait and do that. If ye need my help with your other crazy shit in the meantime, I suppose I'll muck in."

He grinned, his smile penetrating the thick ginger beard he had grown since Danny had last seen him. In that moment, Danny knew they were definitely back in business.

"Ye know me, Danny. I'd probably follow ye to the ends of the earth and beyond. You'll do for me. Oh, but one other ting?"

"Name it, Ciaran."

"At some stage, can I get a ride, too? It's been a while… The west of Ireland is no place for loose women…"

And they both laughed. Danny pointed his little boat north towards home.

23

❖ Wicked Web ❖

"You want to kill him, don't you?"

"You know the old joke about the pig that saves the farmer and his family from a fire? When asked why the pig has only three legs, the farmer replies, 'A pig that useful… you only eat him a bit at a time.' Danny has his uses, but when I'm done with him, I will be done."

June sat up in the huge bed, reaching for the champagne bottle on the bedside table. She topped up her glass, then did the same for Harkness. The suite at the W Hotel in Miami Beach afforded spectacular views of the Atlantic Ocean. The long beach stretched off into the distance, sun reflecting off the water. It was a perfect day.

Harkness watched. He was enjoying the view of June, rather than the one on the other side of the huge picture windows.

"That has always irritated me. You know the way in the movies, after a sex scene, the actors hold the bedclothes to themselves like their lives depended upon it."

June clinked her glass to his. "Ludicrous, isn't it? They have just fucked, after all. I'm glad you like the view, James."

He leaned forward and kissed her, a long, deep kiss. She was enjoying herself. She suspected Harkness was, too.

"He knows you want to kill him. That is hardly the best way to motivate our 'Danny boy' to do his best work."

"Maybe, maybe not. He wants to return the favour. That's how I sold the job to him. I told him he might get a swing of the bat at me."

"And what if I decide to kill you both? We are talking an awful lot of money, after all. I might decide I don't feel like sharing." She said it playfully, a twinkle in her eye.

"That will be a second and third murder for you, my dear. Have you got the stomach for all that blood?"

"Second and third?"

"You are going to kill your husband, aren't you? You want to..."

"Does that shock you?"

"This is me you're talking to, darling. If I perceive something or someone to be an obstacle...' He made a slicing motion with his hand across his own throat.

"I did love him. In many ways, I still do. But I have learnt my lessons the hard way. You can only depend on yourself. What he has done with the cartel and their money started out smart, but then became stupid very quickly. I can't have that level of irrational behaviour in my life. I'm not willing to leave my fate in the hands of a man who would be so arrogant. Jesus may be our guide, but I'm beginning to think that Vincent sees himself as invincible because of it."

"And you think robbing them is a better way to proceed? A lesser risk."

June swung her legs out of the bed. Walking naked to the windows, she took in the sun worshippers and the surfers, who looked like they were making the most of the beautiful day. "The damage is done. I'm sure Ines Zedillo knows that Vincent has been skimming. In the chaos of a robbery, I'm confident that I can make my exit stage left. It will be Vincent she wants, anyway. Not me. I've never been the fox in the henhouse."

Harkness joined her at the window, standing behind her. "As long as that exit doesn't preclude me, sweetheart. I'm not putting this together to see you fuck off over the horizon with the dosh, leaving me to face the Mexicans all on my lonesome. Threatening to kill me and take the cash doesn't motivate me that much."

He leant his weight against her, pushing her, naked, against the glass. June caught her breath at the sudden cool sensation, then realised that he was pinning her there. She couldn't move away easily, even if she wanted to. She slid her hand up to shoulder height on the glass, trying to push back against him, but he just crushed her harder against the window.

Harkness whispered into her ear. "Don't become an obstacle, June. Don't ever play silly games with me, or make me second guess your moves."

He kicked her legs wider apart, taking a handful of her hair to hold her in place, bending his knees, then pushing himself up and against her sex. She struggled, but Harkness just tightened his grip, forcing himself into her.

"You're playing with big boys now, June. I can make you and your Pharisee husband bend to my will. I have reach, June. I am everywhere… I can snuff you out like blowing out a match. Do you understand?"

Her breathing was coming in halting sobs, struggling to stop him from raping her. Trying to force her limbs to act, fight back, but he felt like a wall of stone against her.

"Tell me you understand, June. Let me hear you say it."

"You're hurting me. You're—"

"Oh, I know I am, love. I'm showing you what happens when you try and weave a wicked web that is meant to trap me as well as the others. Now say it, June. Say you understand…"

He shifted his weight, making her face press harder against the glass, making it rub the window with every thrust he made. At some point, she stopped struggling, realising it was pointless, but also finding a deep resolve inside of her, a single thought that she knew she would never let go of: *I will cut off your balls and then kill you, James Harkness. I swear it.*

June Cardell was the first to leave the hotel, waiting for a few minutes while the valet brought her car to the front door. Danny noticed she looked uncomfortable. Delicate in her movements, she was constantly adjusting her sunglasses, dabbing at her eyes with a tissue. There was a scarf up round her shoulders and head, despite the fine temperature of the day. Danny had not been surprised at her arrival, having earlier followed Harkness to the same spot.

Danny had found Harkness easily enough. Amongst a few other contacts, Danny had put a call in to the mechanics who serviced his boat, asking if anyone had heard of a new British face had been seen around the Keys. His mechanic friends had said no but to check back with them in twenty-four hours. When he did, they had some information for him. A big, ugly looking Brit had rented a houseboat they regularly serviced. They even gave Danny the mooring address. He wanted to follow Harkness, to try and get a clearer picture of what he was up to. He had found the houseboat easily and was delighted when, at around ten the following morning, Harkness had emerged and used a little motorised skiff to come ashore. He then climbed into the black Ford Mustang he and Danny had used the night of the baseball bat fight, and Danny simply followed. He recalled how, back in London, Harkness had been slack about checking he was not being tailed. It seemed the madman had not learned the error of his ways.

It was another forty-five minutes before Harkness exited the W Hotel. It took Danny unawares, as he hadn't seen the black Mustang being brought to the door for Harkness. From his spot in a public car park right across the street, Danny only caught a glimpse of his target when he came out under the canopy of the hotel and strode purposefully across the road. He was going somewhere on foot.

Follow the money, Danny thought, recalling the line from *Magnum Force*, Clint Eastwood excelling in the role of the uber-violent, huge gun-toting cop. Waiting a few minutes, Danny slid out of his converted jeep, only stopping to pick up a rucksack off the passenger seat. He crossed to the other side of the road to follow Harkness at a distance. Because he was so big, and ugly, the task of keeping Harkness in view was an easy one.

They were only walking for about ten minutes when they came to a crossroads. Harkness was delayed by the pedestrian light with two runners and an elderly lady with a tiny dog on a leash. Opposite the high hedges, the front entrance to the Delano Hotel beckoned. Danny hung back, standing diagonally opposite his target. When the cars were finally held back by the lights, Harkness crossed and headed straight into the luxury hotel. Danny darted through traffic to the hotel's side of the street, not quick enough to see Harkness, but Danny was fairly certain his prey had gone inside.

He glanced at his watch. It was almost three in the afternoon. He was convinced that Harkness was meeting someone. The question was, who? He could stick around and watch, but there was no obvious place to sit down and wait it out. He had another idea. Opening his rucksack, he fished out a large SLR type camera and swung the bag back over his shoulder. He then reached into his trouser pocket and pulled out a one-hundred-dollar bill. He made his way over to the bellhops who were congregating at the right side of the door.

As he approached, Danny folded the bill, making sure the one hundred was face-up when he slipped it between his index and middle finger. One of the bellhops spotted him and broke away from the group.

"May I help you, sir?"

Danny smiled. Trying his best to look affable, he cleared his throat and spoke in his broadest cockney accent. "All right, mate. Listen, I'm 'ere trying to get a few shots, famous faces, that kind of thing. Any one interesting inside today?" As he said it, Danny raised the money under the young man's nose.

"We don't really encourage—"

Danny cut him off. "Come on, mate. I know how this works…"

"If you did, asshole, you wouldn't be handing me a hundred in full view of the security cameras…" The bellhop was pissed off.

"Take it easy, guvnor. Just trying to get a jump on the game 'ere."

"Meet me round the side in fifteen. I'm on a break then... and bring the hundred with you."

Danny pocketed the money and turned away. He was kicking himself. The bellhop was right, he'd charged in like a teenage boy on a first date. He made his way down the side of the hotel to kill time walking on the beach.

Danny was suspicious. Harkness didn't make mistakes, but his arrogance did provide him with a few blind spots. And Danny had been thinking this through as though he were Harkness himself. He'd skated from London, managed to track Danny down, somehow avoided immigration and entered the United States. Either at the same time or by pure fluke, June Cardell had then reached out to him. A job. One that had multiple layers of treachery involved. It served up a chance to make some money, take a run at Danny and have some twisted fun along the way.

But what would Harkness do next? Danny thought he knew. He suspected Harkness wouldn't be playing fair. He would be trying to work angles. And one of the angles he loved the most was to play from the top and bottom of the deck simultaneously.

Beautiful people jogged past him. A few rollerbladers glided by, with older couples strolling their little dogs on leads. All of them enjoying the intense blue of the sky and the gentle sea breeze that was tempering the afternoon sun. In such a pretty place, no one would suspect that he was standing amongst them having ugly thoughts.

When the time was close, Danny headed back towards the hotel. He spotted the young bagman at the side of the building, lighting a cigarette, his tie removed for the ten minutes or so that he was off duty.

"All right, mate?"

The bellhop studied Danny for a second, a look of barely concealed disdain on his face. "You were pretty clumsy back there, man. I get caught talking to a pap and taking a tip, my ass is canned right there and then."

"I know, I know. I only arrived here a few weeks ago, still trying to get the hang of how this all works..."

The bellhop shook his head and then put out his hand. Danny raised the hundred-dollar bill into the space between them, but as the kid went to take it, Danny withdrew his hand a little.

"Ha... you're not that green, are you?"

Danny laughed. "Information first, then if it's worth the tip..."

"Okay. The hotel is fully booked, today and through the weekend. P. Diddy, or whatever he calls himself these days, is here. Penthouse. He's due to go to some Versace benefit tonight at eight. I know because we have to cordon off the right-hand side door for him and leave space for his limos."

Danny nodded, pretending to be excited by the name.

"Then, in the private dining room tonight, Dr Steve Simon is hosting a little event."

"Why do I care about him?"

"You're fucking kidding me, right?"

Danny shrugged, trying to look eager.

"He's Miami's primo plastic surgeon. He's had his hands all over the most expensive tits, asses and jawlines on the East Coast. As a result, when he throws a party there is always a gaggle of porn stars, Playboy models and pop stars in attendance. His guest-list is kept secret, but it always delivers. That's a nine pm start."

This was all so-far-so-what to Danny. No names that could possibly interest Harkness or him.

"What about now?"

"What about now?" the bellhop repeated.

"Is there anyone of real note in the hotel right this second?"

"I told you... P. Diddy..."

"Yeah, but anyone else? Any Miami royalty? Socialites, that kind of thing?"

"Not that I know of. The other penthouse has the property developer lady in."

"Who is she?"

"She's Latino… Mexican, I think. Her name is something like Centeno… or something like that. She builds high end hotels and condos."

"Mexican. Is she legit?"

"Legit? In this town, there's no such thing as legit. You're either big money or Johnny No-Stars. But with her, now you mention it, there are a few whispers."

Danny's interest was piqued. He was joining dots in his own head before the bellhop completed the picture for him.

"Some say she's a front. Her investment capital comes from the black market. More specifically, the Mexican black market… But I didn't tell you that. Those are serious dudes. I wouldn't mess with them if I were you. Stick to porn stars and rappers… you feel me?"

Danny went to hand the kid the one hundred dollars, but again stopped short. "Her name? What's her name?"

The bellboy groaned, searching his brain for a second. "It's… I think it's Zedillo. Yeah, that's it. Zedillo. I remember now, I signed for a FedEx for her room yesterday morning."

He got his cash, Danny clapping him on the shoulder after handing it to him. "Thanks, mate… what days do you work?"

"Depends, I'm in college… so I work round my classes…"

"Okay, I'll keep an eye out for you. You're a good man."

"Yeah, whatever… just a little less obvious next time."

Danny walked away, returning the camera to his rucksack. His head was spinning. Harkness was playing all the angles. He had to be. Why else would he have left one hotel and June Cardell only to head straight to meet one of Miami's rich elite? It was too likely to be a coincidence. At least he had a name. Danny could now do a little more due diligence while he tried to figure out exactly what Harkness was up to.

As soon as Harkness entered the cavernous suite, something didn't feel right. Nothing obvious, but he couldn't quite put his finger on it. One of the bodyguards led him into the lounge area. Ines Zedillo sat on one sofa, gesturing for him to sit down opposite her on the other.

"*Buenos Dias*, Señor Harkness. Please, take a seat."

As he did so, he noticed the iPad on the seat next to her, lying screen down. As soon as his ass hit the chair, the bodyguard locked his arm around Harkness's neck, the feel of cold steel at his skin. He didn't need to see it to recognise the feel of a knife pressing against his carotid artery. He immediately regulated his breathing, relaxed into the hold and waited for Ines to speak. If there was going to be a time to fight back, this was not it.

"*Ahora*, Harkness. Part of today's meeting is to show you how we do things. I want you to fully understand how we like to work. *Trabaja, trabaja… siempre trabaja.*"

She picked up the iPad, typing in a password of sorts, her manicured nails clicking against the screen as she dabbed at it.

"You know how *los niños* have 'show and tell' in school? *Hoy*, we shall have our own little show and tell. I want to share with you some pictures of people who tried to dictate to us, to tell us how our business should be conducted."

She flipped the iPad round to face Harkness and show him the file she had opened. The screen was filled with a picture of a man who had been hung upside down. He was naked, his body covered in cuts, some small, some long, deep incisions. The blood had flowed and gathered from them, turning the entire corpse into a dripping scarlet mess. But the most startling detail was that whoever this man had once been, his head was now staring up at his own decapitated torso, eyes open but lifeless.

"And *otra vez*." Ines swiped at the picture to show the next.

It took Harkness a moment to realise it was a corpse dumped on a street. Another dead man, this one had something stuffed in his partially open mouth.

"You want to taste your own severed cock in your mouth, Harkness?"

She swiped again and again, a total of twelve images all showing corpses that demonstrated long periods of pain before they finally breathed their last.

"I think you now understand, no? We take business very seriously, and any deviation from our agenda only leads to unfortunate ends. It is also worth knowing that all of the individuals in these pictures also lost close family members. We are nothing, if not thorough."

Ines nodded, and the bodyguard released Harkness from the grip, making sure to just nick his skin with the knife as he did so. Harkness didn't even flinch. Calmly, he fished inside his jacket pocket and produced a handkerchief. He held it against the spot of blood from the cut the knife had left behind.

"All very theatrical, Ines. What? Did you watch *Scarface* over the weekend or something?"

Zedillo just stared back, not showing any reaction to his patronising line. "Harkness, I am going to indulge you. I will allow you to help clear up our little challenge. But you will do so on our terms. They will rob the money from the Christian mission in Miami, yes?"

"Yes."

"We will allow the robbery to happen. But I will want to know every detail of the plan well in advance. Then, when the meeting is held to distribute the stolen money, we will be your surprise guests. I will allow you to leave, with your percentage, when we know that the Cardells and your master thief are both in our hands."

The bodyguard returned, dropping a mobile phone in his lap.

"What's this? I don't use…"

Ines cut him off. "It is a burner phone, from Mexico, hard to trace. You are to use it to update me. All such calls must last less than three minutes and should be made from different, sterile locations. Like the mall or the beach, never the same place twice. I want daily updates, even if there is nothing to tell. You still call. And finally, you will text message me, using the WhatsApp on that phone at the beginning and end of every day, your location and agenda for that day."

"Now, listen…"

Ines waved him off before he could get started. "*Pendejo*, I have been *claro*, no? I expect to hear the plan for the robbery soon."

Harkness was silent. He was trying to judge what was leverage he might bring to this meeting that had run away from him like no other he had ever had.

"The plan is still… evolving."

"I know, señor. I know. Which is why I called you here today. To set you on the correct path and to leave you in no doubt as to who is running this particular show. And, by the way, we will follow you from time to time. I am so slow to trust, señor. Please, forgive me."

Ines stood and dismissed Harkness with a desultory wave of her hand. The bodyguard once again appeared at his side to escort him out. Harkness took the hint.

As they arrived at the door of the suite, Harkness stepped to one side and brought his elbow sharply up in the air, expecting to feel the contact of bone on bone. But nothing. His arm simply flailed through the air, as Harkness turned to see that the big guard had anticipated his move. Harkness was then on the point of the knife again. The guard smiling from behind it.

"I have had a few coffees this morning, cabrón. I was awake to your thought before you even had it. Now leave, before I slit your worthless throat."

All the way down in the lift, Harkness could barely contain his sense of anger mixed with embarrassment.

Vincent was in his office when his security manager knocked softly on the outer door. "Come in, Greg."

"Good afternoon, sir. I have the updates you requested."

"Thank you, Greg. But before that, I want you to arrange something for me."

Cardell held his hand up, reaching behind his desk to switch on a radio, making sure to turn the volume up loud. Norby looked a little confused until his boss pointed to a sheet of paper on his desk. He lifted the sheet to read the note that had been handwritten on it.

Norby, I want you to organise for that friend of ours that we met after church on Sunday to be shown around the Miami Urban Conference Centre after hours. Preferably this week, but as soon as is humanly possible. This is to be done with a high level of discretion, please.

Vincent gestured for him to hand it back. He instantly passed it through a shredder.

Vincent leaned closer to Norby so that he could be heard over the radio but didn't have to shout. "Do you understand who I mean?"

Norby nodded.

"You know where to find him?"

Another nod.

"Good. Now, update me on June?"

"We now have a fix on her new cell phone, sir. She has spent part of today at the W Hotel."

"Who with?"

Norby spread his hands in a gesture which indicated he had no idea.

"I think it's time we started to stick to June a little more closely, don't you, Norby?"

The security manager nodded his agreement again.

"See to it. In the meantime, I will pray on it. We are living in interesting times. Stay focused please. We have our Lord's important work to do."

Once alone again in the office, Cardell switched off the radio and sat heavily into his chair. His mood had suddenly darkened. His resolve tightened in his gut, turning into something much harsher. He picked up a framed photo of him and his wife on their wedding day. In the picture, she was smiling, her happiness somehow making him feel even more angry. In that moment, he wanted to hurt her. Hurt her very badly.

Nothing... and, by God's will, I mean nothing, will stand in my way. Don't doubt me, June.

24

❖ The Happiest Place on Earth ❖

Danny's tea was tasting particularly good when he heard the crunch of car tyres on his drive.

An early morning visitor was the last thing he wanted as he stood on his deck watching the sun slowly climb into the morning sky, but it sounded like he had no choice in the matter.

However, when he made his way round to the front side of the house, he was pleasantly surprised to see the green and white sheriff's cruiser parked on his drive. Amparo climbed out of it, raising her hand to him as she did so.

Danny smiled. *If there's trouble brewing, a copper rarely gives you a little wave.*

"Good morning, Deputy. Isn't this a pleasant surprise?"

"*Buenos Dias...* I'm just ending my shift. Got any coffee on the go?"

"I'm sure I could arrange something."

It was then that Amparo noticed the Harley Davidson Electra Glide parked just in front of the carport. Danny saw the question form on her face before she spoke it aloud.

"I have a good friend staying."

He could see disappointment replace the puzzlement in her expression, and his stomach did a flip at the sight of it. Had she turned up hoping for a little more than coffee?

"I see. Maybe I should not disturb you? I can come see you another time."

"Come on up. My friend, he's not one for alarm clocks."

She stepped up on to the decking, and Danny bent to kiss her hello. He aimed for the cheek but was thrilled when she angled her head and kissed him on the lips. It turned into a long kiss.

Setting his mug of tea on the rail of the porch, he reached his arms around her, pulling her close, enjoying the smell of her. They stayed that way for a few minutes. Kissing, like teenagers. It wasn't until Danny's arm brushed against the automatic pistol strapped to her waist that he thought how stupid he was.

Gently, he stepped back from her, a huge smile on her face as he did so.

"Have I earned my coffee, *muchacho*?"

"Oh, I think so. Come on round."

They walked around the outside of the decking that surrounded the little clapboard house, finally coming to where the kitchen door opened onto the view which stretched out over trees and into the Gulf.

Danny flicked his kettle back on to boil, reaching for a cafetière.

"*Hombre*! I get the French press? I must be special."

"I like to treat local law enforcement every now and then. You know, to keep in their good books."

"How many of my colleagues drop by for coffee?"

"It's a regular java stop round here, madam."

They laughed at his joke as the smell of coffee grounds filled the little kitchen.

"So, *Ingles,* I thought I would stop by and ask you for another date. Seems to me I'm doing all the work, but if a girl don't ask, she don't get."

"Is that what we're doing? Dating?"

"Better that than being investigated, eh, *amigo*?"

"Except if I'm being investigated, you might have to frisk me. See? Every cloud… silver lining."

"I am investigating. You'd be helping me with my enquiries… and my next one is 'how good a dancer are you?'"

Danny held his hands up in mock submission. "Me and dancing never quite got along. My sister used to call me 'knock kneed'."

"Knock what?"

"Kneed. When I dance, I look like someone gave a flamingo a triple bourbon on ice."

"You just need a good teacher. I could be your *profesora*."

Danny stopped what he was doing and looked at her. He was enjoying himself, relishing the flirtation, pleased she had dropped by, but at the same time, he could feel his heart sinking. A tinge of sadness started to grow in his chest. None of this could be his. He neither deserved it nor could sustain it. *I need to stop this. Stop it now.* And yet, he couldn't, didn't want to, even with all the risk it entailed. He felt torn.

"I'm, eh, I'm not sure I'm quite up to dancing lessons, just yet."

She instantly looked crestfallen, as if he had just told her to piss off. Awkwardly, he handed her a mug of coffee. The silence was brittle between them.

"Okay… I just thought… I mean…"

"Look, Amparo, you have to excuse me. I'm not really any good at this kind of thing. Not only am I knock kneed but when it comes to… what I mean is, I'm a bit of a useless wanker around women. I never know what to say or…"

"Or do? Did we not just kiss? That felt like you knew what to do… *Oye, amigo*!"

She smiled, and he returned it, feeling the pleasant buzz of affection, followed instantly by a mixture of doubt and sadness. Danny went to speak again when she stood up. She stepped close to him and put her index finger on his lips.

"Señor, you have the right to remain silent. Anything you say can and will be used against you in a court of law. You have the right to an attorney. If you cannot afford an attorney, one will be provided for you. Do you understand that you are going to go dancing with me?"

Danny shook his head, starting to laugh.

"Don't make me cuff you, *hombre*."

"Now, girl. Can ye tell me, are you arrestin' this eejit, or are ye playin' some kind of weird, dressy-up sex game?"

Ciaran stood in the doorway to the kitchen, wearing nothing but a pair of boxer shorts and more ginger hair than both Danny or Amparo had even seen in their lives.

"Cos, if it's the latter, I've got at least five outstanding warrants and a price on me head…"

Ciaran winked at them both and made off towards the bathroom, leaving Danny gobsmacked and Amparo blushing like a schoolgirl.

They dissolved into fits of laughter that soon went into another deep kiss.

"Are ye feckin' mad? A copper? Talk about poacher and gamekeeper… Ye live long enough, ye feckin' see everything."

Once Amparo had left, Ciaran had emerged from the bathroom and left Danny in no doubt as to what he thought of his friend's flirtation.

"I know, I know, I'm a twat. But it just kind of… happened."

"When I was young, that was the kind of thing ye said to your ma right after ye'd showed her the pregnancy test."

"Ciaran! I'm not sixteen."

"Exactly! Have you lost all sense of who ye are? Who we are? Do you remember? Stand and deliver… Yer money or yer life?"

"I'll deal with it."

"Deal wi' it? Danny, it is a she, and she's a feckin' sheriff's deputy. No wonder ye asked me to come. Yer feckin' losing it."

"I'm not. Trust me. I know it's wrong, but I will deal with it. We both know, whatever way this job plays out, I have to up sticks and get the fuck out of here. So, in a way, there is nothing to deal with. I'll be in the wind in a matter of weeks."

"If ye don't end up with your trousers round yer ankles. Mind ye, I tink she'd quite like that."

"It changes nothing. We have a job to do, and it will soon be time to do it. I think I now have a fix on what Harkness is up to. I'm going to see a friend today, one who will be able to confirm what I suspect."

Ciaran looked at him. "Another 'friend'. What kind is this one? A CIA agent?"

"Actually, this one's a stripper."

"Have ye' turned into some kind of sex maniac? If this were home, I'd be getting the priest out to ye!"

Danny couldn't help but laugh. "No, I haven't, and you wouldn't believe me even if I told you."

"Told me wha'?"

"The stripper… she's in her seventies."

Ciaran looked aghast. "Aw, sweet Jaysus. Let me smell your breath. Have you been at the poitín? It's still only eight in the morning."

"I'm serious. She's a bit of an institution."

"So's Pamela Anderson, but she's not still droppin' her drawers for a livin'."

"Speaking of drawers." Danny stood up and crossed to dresser in the corner of the small kitchen. He opened the top drawer and took out an envelope. He handed it to Ciaran.

"Wha's this?'

"A little folding for you."

Ciaran looked inside; there was a thick sheaf of hundred-dollar bills.

"Now, I suggest you climb on that motorbike you hired for yourself and take a couple of days to drive north. Go and see Mickey Mouse. If you don't do it now, you might not get the chance."

"There's a shitload o' cash here, Danny. I don't need this much."

"You've obviously never been to a theme park. It takes a lot of dosh to buy a ticket into, what is it Disney call it? Oh yeah, 'the happiest place on earth'."

"And the happiest place after earth, at least that's what them yokes we're going to rob seem to think, anyway."

Ciaran had Danny laughing again.

"I will finish up the research here. Be back by the weekend, we'll need to start putting our plans into action by then."

"I promise to be back on time, as long as ye promise ye won't go on a date with a federal prosecutor… grand?"

"I've got my eye on a cute district attorney. Does that count?"

Ciaran made a playful swipe at Danny's head.

❖

June Cardell was in tears. Just moments before, she had felt raging anger. It had been this way since she had left the W Hotel a couple of days earlier. She felt like a latter-day King Lear, railing against the storm, tortured by her own choices, tormented by her own frailties. She was enraged by the man – men – who had seen fit to use her, to play with her like a dog does a toy. To violate her at their will.

She wanted to claw Harkness's face off with her bare hands. She wanted to plunge a knife over and over into her drug-dealing ex's chest, the man who had set her on this life of relentless opportunism. She imagined slitting Vincent Cardell's throat from ear-to-ear for giving her a glimpse of love and affection, only for him to turn out like the others – volatile, unreliable, self-obsessed. And just as quickly as the boiling fury would rise in her veins, she would then be dashed into despair, a feeling of powerlessness and self-loathing, diving deep into the notion that she was to blame. She had brought most of this to her own door.

She had to do something. If she didn't, this maelstrom would devour her. Everything she had endured, every play in her game, every desperate choice she had made would be for nothing. If she lay down under this blanket of shame and excoriating ire, then they would have won. She would have proven their point for them. She would be consigned to being labelled a weak, emotional, unstable bitch of a woman. Men could play power games, be described as 'ruthless' when they took what they wanted, be feted for their 'fearlessness' as visionaries when they defied convention or played hard and fast with the rules. But when women did it, they were 'psycho-bitches', they were 'fishwives' and 'witches'.

It was in the midst of her darkest hour when a moment of pure clarity came to her. A flash of inspiration. Wiping tears from her eyes, she dug her nails into her own hands, feeling them bite into her flesh, watching her knuckles turn white, her palms flush deep red. She'd see their revulsion and scorn and raise it by some measure. She'd show them just how powerful a woman could be. All at once, she intuitively knew how to deflect this clusterfuck right back into their faces. June Cardell was now mad. But more importantly, she was going to get even.

When Danny walked into Woody's Strip joint, his eyes took a few seconds to adjust to the dark. The sunny, spring afternoon outside might as well have been on a different planet. Inside, it was permanent midnight, coloured neon and thumping music robbing the customers of any sense of time or place.

It may have only been four o'clock, but there was a smattering of customers already chugging down beers, taking advantage of happy hour. Not that they looked very happy to Danny.

He took a seat at the bar, and without even having to ask, Sal the bartender set a shot of Blanton's Bourbon in front of him, ice on the side in a separate glass. The Red Hot Chilli Peppers were blasting out *Californication* while a mousy blonde threw herself into the dance with an energy that belied her surroundings. Danny was already jiggling his knee, hoping that it wouldn't be long before he could leave the stench of beer mixed with coconut body butter behind.

His wish was soon granted. Slow Tina emerged from behind a beaded curtain, like a latter-day silent movie star. She was slow and elegant with an air of haughtiness, despite the fact that she was dressed in nothing more than a translucent chiffon kaftan over leopard print lingerie. She spotted Danny and picked her way through the bar towards him as he caught Sal's eye, making sure Tina's drink was on order.

It arrived just a moment before she did. Danny winced at the electric orange concoction in the glass.

"Why, if it ain't my liddle English gennelman caller. I do declare, you look finer every time ah see you." Tina proffered a wrinkled hand, and Danny obliged, gallantly kissing it like a knight from an old-fashioned film.

"Tina, it is always a pleasure, never a chore."

"Are you here to indulge in your love of the terpsichorean arts or solely to flutter those long, dark eyelashes at me, Danny?"

"I'm here to bathe in your presence, Tina."

As he said it, he palmed a hundred-dollar bill into her hand. She smiled demurely and slipped into a tiny handbag. It was done with such efficiency, no one would have ever noticed it.

"I was wondering, Tina. Have you ever heard of a lady called Zedillo?"

Tina never usually did anything particularly fast, but the name caused her to swivel her head and look at him. "Now, Mr Danny, please don't tell me you are playing games with either me or her? She is not a lady to be trifled with."

"I thought she was a property developer."

"And Kim Kardashian calls herself a star, but we both know trash when we see it, don't we, honey chile?"

Danny chuckled in reply, even though he didn't know who Kim Kardashian was. "She's not doing business with me directly, Tina, but with an associate of mine."

"I did not think you were a white powder boy, Danny. I might be getting a liddle disappointed in you. People like you and I should stick to the glamorous vices: alcohol and filthy, decadent lovemaking."

"Don't worry, lovely Tina. I'm not into anything chemical full stop. I'm more of an accountancy type. I help people who have too much money."

"Ah, that's much more derring-do... a Raffles type. I enjoy separating men from their hard-earned cash too. My money maker's been shakin' much longer than yours though, my darling."

"It's still a sight to behold, Tina. For clarity, then, Ms Zedillo is not a bona-fide developer of condos and hotels?"

"Oh no, my dear, but she is. She builds the most luxurious dwellings and hostelries. But her – how shall I phrase it? – seed capital is much more prosaic. You can clean a lot of messy money up in construction, sweet pea. Ms Zedillo is rumoured to be very efficient in such dealings."

So, Harkness was playing both ends of the deal. Treachery. It ran in his veins. It also upped the ante beyond belief. Bad enough that Danny was about to swipe drug cartel cash. But even worse, they probably knew he was coming. This was going to have to be an incredibly precise job. Danny's thoughts were interrupted by the music changing. Some awful dance track clanged in his ears.

"I'm going to change the subject a little, if you don't mind, Ms Tina. At the risk of sounding crude, when did you last have some real fun?"

"Why, I'm shocked you'd ask a lady with such an artistic bent a question so earthy."

"I don't mean... sins of the flesh type fun. I mean a little excitement, the flush of a little risk?"

"Sweet pea, my face may be angelic, and my body a little less holy, but trust me. My mind is always primed for a calculated risk. How can I help? Will it be excitement of the financially rewarding kind?"

"It certainly will, Ms Tina. And I may need the help of some of your more artistic friends too. Boys and girls."

"I can supply a whole troop of creatives, all bursting with artistic ambition and questionable morals."

"That is good to hear, my dear lady. I'm still figuring out the details, but I will be in touch soon."

Danny downed the bourbon, the caramel heat of it giving him a slight glow on the way. Tina reached out and put a hand on his.

"No time for a liddle bump and grind before you go? My dying swan is a joy to behold."

"Ms Tina, the pleasure would be all mine and, of course, a privilege. But business calls..." He stood and kissed her cheek, Tina resting her hand there after he had stepped away.

"All work and no play makes Jack terribly dull. I do declare. What does a southern belle have to do round here to nab a seat on a young knave's lap?"

"Next time. I promise."

"I'm not after a promise, sweet pea. Just your filthy cash."

Danny had no answer to that. He felt exactly the same way about life himself.

25

❖ Bless Me, Father... ❖

"Y'all sent a friend to Disney World? Yo sho he's still yo friend?"

Father Simeon laughed at his own joke around the edges of the huge cigar he was smoking as he sat in the fighting chair at the back of Danny's boat.

"I didn't send him, Sim, he wanted to go of his own accord. He said he'd always wanted to meet Mickey."

"Dude, too many kids. I do a christening? The baby cries, I order a cab, take my ass outta there."

It was Danny's turn to laugh. Simeon shifted his position and checked the two fishing rods he had on the go. Nothing.

"We've had all the luck of the Chicago Black Sox today. I'm startin' to think yo is some kind of jinx. I might have to re-think this arrangement!"

Danny looked at his friend and saw an opportunity to start a chat he didn't really want to have. "Funny you should say that…"

Simeon's head whipped round, a look of concern on his face. "What chu sayin'?"

"My circumstances may be about to change. And it's outside of my control."

"Yo never struck me as a brother with outside controllin' influences…"

"Everybody's got a boss, Simeon… even you."

"Alleluia to that, brother! But mine is little less controlling and little bit more encouragin'. Ya feel me?"

"I do… but I'm serious. I think today may be our last opportunity to fish. I'm going to have to move away."

Simeon looked at him, an expression of extreme puzzlement on his face. He repositioned the cigar between his teeth without taking his hands off the rods. "Y'all in trouble."

It was a statement, not a question.

"No, no, nothing like that."

"Brother D, I ain't no fool. I have always seen a shadow over yo. I may be a priest but I ain't no jackass. Talk to me, dude."

"I'm not sure I'm comfortable with where this is going, Sim."

"Yo' sayin' yo' don't trust me…"

"Simeon… don't do this."

The big priest took a moment, looking out to sea before he spoke. "Repeat after me."

"What? Simeon!"

"Repeat, dammit! Bless me, Father…"

"I'm not…"

Simeon stood up, pulling himself up to his full height so that both of them were almost eye-to-eye. Danny could tell he was deadly serious. "RE-PEAT! Bless me, Father…"

Danny sighed. "Bless me, Father…"

"For I have sinned."

"For I have sinned."

"My last confession was… make something up, Danny…"

"My last confession was in 1999."

"Good enough… now go ahead. Whatever you tell me now is bound by my holy vows. Tell me Danny, what the fuck is goin' on?"

"It's… complicated.'

"Life is complicated, Brother. I can't help yo' if I don't know what to help wit'…"

Danny felt sick. Worse. He felt trapped. Not by Simeon, not because he was out on the boat in the middle of nowhere. He felt trapped by himself. By his own actions, his own choices that had led him to that moment. The reality of it crashed into him. He felt a flutter in his chest. The horizon tilted in front of his eyes, he felt his heartbeat rocket and his breathing became instantly laboured. It was another attack.

His lungs went tight, as if someone was winding piano wire around his torso. Then, as always, the sounds began. He could hear the screams. The booms of explosives, the cries of people begging to be helped. He didn't realise it but he had sunk to his knees. The big priest scrambled to try and help him before he collapsed fully, at risk of cracking his head on the side of the gunwales. Try as he might, his eyes could not focus. Everything was a blur as he gasped and gasped, fighting to get air into his lungs. He was only able to suck in what felt like a tiny sob's worth with each heave of his chest.

"Brother! Brother Danny! Look at me, look at me."

Simeon looked wildly around him, searching for anything he might use to shock Danny out of whatever funk he was in. He spotted the open drinks cooler just a few feet away. Stretching past Danny, he dragged it towards them. Once in reach, he grabbed Danny's arms and plunged them both into the icy water, bottles of beer and Dr Pepper spilling out the side.

It did the trick. Danny's eyes pulled instantly into focus, and he took a deep, rasping breath. It sounded like a cartoon character preparing to blow up a comedy balloon.

And then, the tears came. Big fat ones dripped down his face, as his body seemed to fold in on itself. He wept, his sobs sounding heartfelt and intense. Simeon sat heavily on the deck next to him, folded his huge arms around him and held him tight for what felt like an eternity.

They sat like that for a half an hour. Some of the time, they were in silence. Some of the time Simeon gently prayed, his words barely audible, a mixture of the Hail Mary and the refrain "Jesus was lost, Jesus was found."

When he could finally move, Danny shuffled to rest his back against the side of the boat.

"They're… they're panic attacks. I've been having them off and on for quite a while now."

"What dark shit yo' got in yo' life, Danny? You might as well tell me, now, cos I sure as hell know it's bad."

"I'm a thief."

It was a revelatory moment for him. It was the first time he had ever heard his own voice speak his truth. It also felt like a huge chain had been lifted from his shoulders.

"Because of me, an evil man was able to cause the deaths of a lot of people in London almost two years ago. And now, when I have one of my… episodes… all I can see and hear are their voices, their pain. I didn't mean for them to suffer. But I have no doubt, I more than did my bit."

Father Simeon looked astonished. Danny didn't blame him.

When he eventually spoke, it was Danny's turn to be astonished.

"God forgives you, Brother. He forgives you. He knows that you got entangled. But he also knows it was never your intent to end those souls' lives."

"I was carrying out a robbery. A big one. I got away with it, but the price… fuck me, it was a high price. There's no god I know would forgive a man for that. I can't begin to forgive myself."

The tears continued, as the full force of his remorse, shame and anger came out in him. It was as if the bottle he had tried to contain them all in had just been shattered into a thousand pieces simply by acknowledging the truth out loud.

"What I'm gonna say to you next won't make no sense right now. But I tell you, Danny, I swear to you on my momma's life it's true, and it will mean everything to you when you've had time to think on it." Simeon took Danny's face in his hands. When Danny tried, gently to resist, Simeon slapped him. Not a full-blooded face-slap, but enough to focus both their minds.

"No man, and I mean no muthafucka, is defined by a single act or a single day in their life. Things happen to a person, and things happen because of us. Because of the things we think and feel, say or do. Some of those things are moments of weakness. Others are instances of great heroism and generosity. But as iddy biddy moments, they mean nothing. They do not define us. Not in God's eyes. He doesn't pick holes in a life because we fucked up now and again. He sees us as a totality. He sees us for who we really are. In our hearts. You might have done bad things, Danny. But it ain't ever too late to stand up and say you're sorry and start again. Make a change. Re-direct your life. Y'all have a good heart, Brother Danny. God sees it. I seen it. You just need to remember it too… and then try to keep it pure.'

Danny was stunned. He sat there, looking at his friend, believing he had just heard the most generous thing anybody had ever said. Not just to or about him. But about everybody. It was then that he realised that Simeon truly believed in his version of God, and it had made him a better person. They sat in silence for another while, both watching as the twilight gathered in the sky above their heads. Simeon spoke first.

"Have you been discovered, Brother D? Have the po-leece found you?"

"No, Simeon. It's worse than that. The evil man I mentioned?"

Simeon nodded, a look of dread gathering on his face.

"He's found me, Sim. He has. And now, I'm going to have act. I have no choice. It's him, or it's me. And I can't let him take any more lives along the way."

"You could always go to the po-leece. You could make it their bidness… not just yours."

"I did that last time, back in London. But this man's reach is broad and far. He didn't spend very long in their custody. And now, he's back, and I know that it's down to me."

Simeon looked at him long and hard until he sighed. "In that case, all I can do is pray for yo', Brother D. I'll pray for yo' and pray to keep the rest of us outta yo' way."

By the time he had piloted the boat home and shared a sombre goodbye with Father Simeon, Danny was exhausted. He didn't even stop to offload spent supplies and used equipment from the day's fishing. He simply trudged from his little dock, onto the decking and straight into his house.

Once through the door, he shed his clothes, kicking off shoes, dropping his trousers, flicking off his underpants and pulling the T-shirt over his head, discarding it in the doorway to his bedroom. He looked down at his feet and immediately conceded defeat by collapsing face down onto his bed. He was asleep in seconds.

But it wasn't to be a peaceful rest. His dreams were a kaleidoscope of explosions, death screams and mayhem. The violent images bombarded his subconscious, becoming ever more frantic, their intensity ratcheting up like the heat of a house fire. Soon, they seemed ready to consume him, until he awoke with a start. His bedclothes were sodden, the reek of his own sweat bitter in his nostrils. Usually when he dreamed, be it pleasant or, as was more common these days, nightmarish, he could never quite remember the last image that had assailed him.

But this was different. The last image his limbic brain had conjured up was a vivid one. It had been an image of Harkness's face coated with sweat, close up, spittle flecking his lips, his eyes wild and rheumy. And as the image widened, like a shot from a film, it revealed a pair of white-knuckled hands clamped around Harkness's neck. And they were tightening even further.

Danny knew.

He knew they were his own hands.

He knew that his primal self was telling him what must be done. This time, he had to show no mercy. This time, he had to kill Harkness.

26

❖ Details, Details, Details ❖

Ciaran looked an absolute sight. He had returned from Orlando with every piece of Disney-branded clothing the mouse machine had ever cared to dream up.

A baseball cap that gave the wearer the long ears and teeth of Goofy sat atop Ciaran's mass of wiry red hair. A T-shirt that had Mickey's front on the front and his backside on the back was next. On his bottom half, he had a pair of horrendous plaid shorts with Mickey silhouettes secreted in the pattern. And to complete the look, the coup de grace: a pair of Crocs on his feet that were festooned with whistling Mickeys. Danny laughed so much that tears had appeared in his eyes.

"Ye can feck aff, ye feckin' fecker. These are an absolute revelation. Have you ever worn a pair? They call 'em Crocs. It's like walking on feckin' air."

"You look like you were caught in a Disney shop during a fucking hurricane, Ciaran. Did you try everything on in the dark?"

"It's your fault. Ye gave me too much money. I tink ye've lost yer inner child. Where's your sense of innocent wonder? Have ye forgotten the pure joy of childish fun?"

"I'm not sure I ever had an inner child, but I know I'm not colour blind. You'll have to change before we go out later."

"Yer taking me out? Ye have to ask nicely, I'm no hooer."

Danny was reminded why he liked Ciaran.

"Don't get excited. It's not that kind of night out. We're going on a recce. We're off to see where this church mission meeting is happening."

"See! No sense of fun… Yer all about the business, so ye are."

"At the minute, yes. I have another delicate matter to discuss with you, not just your ridiculous clothes."

Ciaran levelled a look at him that told Danny he was in no mood to be trifled with. Danny thought his friend was genuinely offended. "It's like the boy, Yeats said. 'Tread softly because you tread on my dreams'."

"It's the beard."

Ciaran's hand shot to his chin in a defensive move. 'What's wrong wit' me chin?"

"I'd like to see it. Your hair is bad enough but that beard makes you stand out like Samuel L. Jackson at a KKK rally."

"Ye want me to dye it? I'm not sure strawberry blond takes the old dye wild easy."

Danny creased up, laughing hard. "I don't want you to dye it. I want you to shave it!"

"I'm wounded. This is my pride and joy… It's taken me ages to perfect my look."

"That's no look, mate. It's not so much a fashion statement as a question mark."

"Ye can go an' fuck yerself."

"I'm serious. If we're going to pull a robbery, you don't need that beard acting like a big 'look at me' arrow on the way through."

"I'll wear a scarf.'

"Jesus! You're in Florida. I've seen you sweat just flicking on a light switch."

"I'm not shaving… I don't care who the feck ye are…"

Ciaran flounced out of the room, leaving Danny to his tears of laughter and a hope that when he saw him next, his friend wouldn't look like a walking advert for the Mouse House.

It was just gone midnight when the black Lincoln MKX crept down his drive. Danny was on the deck waiting. As far as he could see, there was only the driver inside. But Danny had asked Ciaran to stay out of sight until he knew who he was dealing with.

The car swept right up to the foot of the steps and Danny could see, sitting behind the wheel, the tall grey-haired man who had led him behind the altar when Danny had first met Vincent Cardell. He appeared to be alone. Danny descended the steps, cautiously. Knowing now that Harkness was playing all the angles, he was taking no chances.

The passenger window of the SUV glided down. "Get in." The driver leant over.

Danny turned to look back at the house and whistled. Ciaran stepped out of the shadows and lightly jogged over to join him.

"Who's that?"

Danny looked at the driver.

"He's with me. No him? No me…"

The grey-haired man grunted and hit a button on the dash that unlocked the doors. As he and Ciaran climbed into the car, Danny couldn't help but feel they had both just crossed some kind of Rubicon.

The grey-haired man told Danny he was Cardell's head of security, but he wasn't so forthcoming with a name. Danny was fine with that. If he really needed to know he could find out through Harkness or June.

"I've had to pull some strings to get us this after-hours access, so we play it cool once we arrive."

"The amount of money the Cardells are paying that convention centre, you should be able to get in any time you like, day or night."

"And we do, but I don't think you guys would want to be seen by too many night staff on the way round."

Danny just nodded. He knew the man was talking sense.

Ciaran hadn't shaved, but he had changed out of his Disney attire. *Small victories,* Danny had thought. The journey to Miami was made in relative silence. Ciaran took the opportunity to snooze, whilst Danny watched out of the window, marvelling at the flow of traffic even at this late hour, pondering what everyone was doing.

After ninety minutes, their destination came into sight.

Even in the dark of night, the Miami Urban Convention Centre was impressive. Lit up like an architect's Christmas tree, the complex looked like a twenty-first century cathedral. Glass and white painted steel girders shot into the air, meeting at impossible angles at dizzying heights. Visible as it was from the interstate, Danny was looking for exits. He was pleased that it was so close to easy-access infrastructure. When the time came for them to get the hell out of there, the proximity of the freeway was going to be nothing but a blessing.

The bulk of the centre itself was a simple rectangle shape. Being crowned by not one but two huge glass and steel spires, it meant the eye was drawn upwards when looking at it, therefore concealing the brutal efficiency of the huge box of the building underneath.

Danny was assimilating information about the outside of the centre as fast as he saw it. His mind flicked through various options open to them for access and egress. He subconsciously timed the drive from the Interstate to the boundary of the complex. He noted where the stoplights were, the road layout and the positioning of the concrete bollards that heralded the realities of living in an age of suicide bombers and lone wolf terrorists who might drive vehicles into crowds at speed.

Running around the outside of the arena was a four-lane ring road dissected by pedestrian crossing points and ramps that led to underground parking garages. This was another feature Danny liked. If a job went south, complicated parking structures were always a good spot to do two things: he could firstly evade capture on foot using the parked cars to mask his progress, and second, steal a car when it was time to complete a swift exit stage left.

What he didn't like was the dividing meridian between the lanes of the ring road which had been planted with mature palm trees at intervals of about fifteen feet. Punctuating them were huge spotlights mounted at the halfway point between each tree. If a high-speed getaway did become necessary, crossing lanes to reach the nearest exit against traffic flow was going to prove tricky.

An automatic traffic light halted their progress near the main front entrance to the centre, and Danny felt a nudge at his elbow. Ciaran was pointing to the eaves of the building where the steel joist met the glass canopy over the doors. Every ten feet or so, small security cameras hung in pairs, angling away from each other to guarantee that no inch of pathway around the structure was not covered.

"Feck me," was all the Irishman could say, a gentle awe in his voice.

"Can you make a complete circuit of the outside, please?"

"I think it's an interrupted route. At the back of the building, there are security gates. Authorised vehicles only. Do you want to go inside straight away?"

"Okay, take us as far round as you can. And, yes, let's go in. I'm going to be back here in daylight anyway."

Their grey-haired driver had been right. Three quarters of the way around they were met with security gates which were manned by several men in beige uniforms.

"Are they packing?" Ciaran couldn't quite make out until one of the guards approached their vehicle.

"Fuck." Danny was disappointed. They were packing, not just pistols on their hips, but he could also see pepper spray canisters hooked into the guards' belts too. That upped the ante for them right off the bat. He had to consider being armed. He had been hoping to avoid that, with his keen aversion to collateral victims.

"Good evening, Mr Norby. Little late for you this evening?"

Danny almost laughed out loud. The guard had just given the grey-haired man's name away, despite his careful efforts to not reveal it.

'Yes, sir. We've had a few audio-visual questions come up last minute. These engineers here will hopefully have a solution for us."

"Are their names on the manifold?" The guard looked like every other retired cop Danny had ever seen. The guard started pointing his torch directly in his face, blinding him temporarily.

"Like I said, this is all a bit last minute, but these boys should be on your list. We phoned 'em in earlier."

"Excuse me while I check. Who'm I looking for?"

"Mr Luke and Mr Matthews."

Danny tutted under his breath. *Shit, even our aliases are biblical references. These guys aren't even subtle.*

Once they were allowed in, Norby parked them up in a spot next to a huge articulated trailer that had been backed up against the loading dock delivering Coca Cola. Before they exited the car, Danny and Ciaran put on baseball caps, pulling the brows low over their eyes. No sense in making TV stars of themselves from the get-go.

Standing by the car, Danny couldn't resist a little mischief. "Nice to meet you, Mr Norby."

"Go fuck yourself, you Brit piece of shit. You need to know I don't like this idea… any of it. I think Cardell is nuts for trusting you. Just so we're clear…"

Danny was about to answer when Ciaran stepped between them.

"Now listen to me, big man. How ye answer my next question will determine whether you get to eat normally ever again or be fed through a wee tube down yer throat. Are you going to be a problem? Have we already got a rat in the pantry?"

Norby was immediately flustered. Ciaran may have only come up to his shoulder, but Norby wisely didn't push his luck with the Irishman.

"My loyalty lies with Mr and Mrs Cardell. That's all you need to know."

Danny touched Ciaran on the shoulder, the gesture calling on his friend to stand down. "Let's go inside, gentlemen. We need to get on with it."

It took them an hour to walk around the inside of the structure, Danny and Ciaran making mental notes all the way. They tried to memorise where fire exits were placed. They counted out the steps from the centre of the cavernous room to the nearest doorways, and toilets. Inside the gents, they noted the lack of windows or direct access to the exterior of the building, which Danny didn't like.

After about twenty minutes of quiet measuring, Danny suddenly had a thought. "Hold on. Will this entire space be used?"

"We will have over fifteen thousand pilgrims per night, so yes. And they will be seated."

Ciaran swore under his breath. Once they had established the rough pattern of the seating rows, they did their walking measurements again. A couple of times, Danny could hear his accomplice mumbling under his breath.

A few minutes later, when they were some feet away from Norby, Ciaran spoke outright what he'd been grizzling to himself about. "I don't like it, Danny. It's like a big, feckin' coffin to me. All these cameras, all these people, all the bollix of the trees and the spotlights outside. And have ye had a chance to look up?"

Danny nodded, taking the opportunity to glance up above their heads for probably the twentieth time in the last hour. Whilst the ceiling was high above them, the overhead lighting gantries which hung from it were clearly visible and festooned in not just lights, but more security cameras, too.

"Ciaran, what have I told you before?"

"Get a feckin' shave."

Danny grinned as he replied. "No. We turn disadvantages into advantages."

"I can't see how a bollock load of cameras can ever be an advantage."

"We'll find one. I promise."

Next, Danny asked Norby to show him where and how exactly the stage would be laid out, again walking the perimeter of its boundaries. He and Ciaran then tried to judge where it sat in relation to everything: exits, toilets, and then the most important one.

"How do you go from the main altar area here out into backstage?"

"I'm not exactly sure where the access points on the dais will be."

"There's going to be a band, right?"

Norby nodded. "On the left-hand side of the dais from where the main pulpit will be."

Danny walked over towards that end of the huge room, trying to predict which of the doors at that end would lead to backstage.

"I'm going to need a full stage plan, Norby. On paper… I don't do emails or mobile phones."

"I'll see if Mr Cardell is happy for you to have access to it."

"Ye'll just feckin' deliver."

Danny cut across his friend before he could warm to his theme. "Is there going to be a sound and light desk?"

"Again, I'm not sure…"

"Do ye know feckin' anyting?"

"Leave it, Ciaran. We'll need to know that, too. We need everything you can give us in advance. How many security personnel on the floor? How many personal security for the Cardells on or around the stage? Every detail. If we are to pull this off… the devil is in the details."

"I'll see what we can do."

They continued on with the tour of the facility, taking in the backstage area, which included various rooms that could be used as dressing rooms, meeting spaces, storage areas. They even looked through the locked glass doors of a canteen area.

As they walked away, Danny's stomach growled. He couldn't remember when he'd last eaten. This was a sure sign that he was in flow, preparing for a big job. It wasn't a discipline matter. He was simply so occupied, he forgot to eat. In each new area they visited, Norby used a credit card-sized piece of white plastic to open locked doors. Danny made a mental note. They would need some of those.

Danny realised, as they worked their way back towards the car, that Norby had been methodical with his tour. He had taken them to the furthest point for their transport and slowly worked them back towards it, without leaving an area unseen. It made Danny think. *Norby, you're either ex Old Bill or you were a tea leaf, just like me.*

Danny could sense they were close to finishing. They were by a block building that was only about sixty yards from the loading dock. Three floors high, with its own front door and set slightly aside from the main structure, Danny guessed these were the administration offices.

Norby confirmed it. "This is where the convention centre runs its business. Do you need to see inside? I'm not sure I can get access."

"It's absolutely where we need to go."

Norby arched a quizzical eyebrow in response.

"To quote Tom Cruise, Norby, 'Show me the money'. You've pointed out everything except where they are going to store, keep and count the donations. Logic dictates it will be in these offices… probably in a basement that is accessible by a tunnel from the convention building. Not holding out on us, are you now?"

Norby looked deflated. Danny could only guess that he had been hoping the two thieves were amateurish and would not have spotted the most important detail. He really didn't want the job to go ahead.

"Open the feckin' door, or I'll open it wit' yer head."

Danny's instincts were proven correct. Norby showed them through a maze of corridors that led to a door at the foot of a stairwell. But there was a problem.

"My passkey does not open this one. It has a punch key system." Norby pointed to a numbered keypad to the right-hand side of the doorframe.

"What's behind the door? The counting room?"

"Yes, and it has another door on the other side of it that leads to the tunnel that you anticipated. It links to the conference hall.

The money is brought through there in carts and deposited through a timed slot in the wall, straight into the count room. Once we are done totalling it, an armoured transport arrives at the end of the day to take it away to the bank."

"How is that done? The money will weigh a lot."

"They have a freight elevator that rises up to ground level behind this building."

"Makes sense," Danny mused. "It keeps the money van away from the main conference building. Do they have their own exit out onto the freeway?"

"Yes and no. They have one that takes them away from the conference centre ring road, but it doesn't lead straight to the freeway. They still have a half-mile of public road to navigate. But at least it's quicker."

Ciaran and Danny looked at each other. Was that short stretch of road the ideal place to put the hit in?

They spent a few more minutes measuring distances and trying as best they could to count the number of security cameras. After about ten minutes, they exited the office block and made their way back to the loading dock where their car was waiting.

As they reached it, Danny nudged Ciaran. "Count the security cameras here, too, mate. I want to look at something."

Norby waited as Ciaran walked around the loading dock. Danny climbed up onto the dock, using the cab of a forklift truck to boost himself up. He then paced out the dock, measuring the distance roughly in his head.

Ciaran joined him. "Not as many cameras here. Mostly covering the dock doors, so they can see if someone sneaks in during a load."

"What do you think of it all now, Ciaran?"

"I feel a bit better. I think I can see where we might get busy…"

"Oh, I do too. For the first time, tonight. In fact, for the first time in a long time."

Ciaran turned to Danny, puzzlement written on his face.

"I was never quite sure if I wanted to pull this job. But after tonight, I do. I know exactly how we do this… I just need a few more details."

"That's feckin' nice for ye… When the time's right, I trust ye'll share wit' the group?"

"When the time is right, Ciaran, I will. But I know one thing for sure."

"Wha'?"

"You will definitely have to shave off that fucking mess of a beard…"

"Ah, ye fecker…."

27

❖ Of Mice and Men ❖

"I hear you brought a little helper with you the other night."

With a burnt orange sunset flaming in the sky above them, Danny, Harkness and June Cardell sat in the Lorelei Cabana bar at a table that was slightly removed from the crowd enjoying their rum cocktails and the gentle live music. Right on the sea front, the outdoor bar was popular, always busy, and a good place to meet that would not attract second glances.

Danny ignored Harkness's statement, not seeing Ciaran's presence was any of his business. "There are a lot of gaps. Your husband's head of security, Mr Norby? He thinks our criminal enterprise is a load of bollocks."

"He's Vincent's plaything, not mine. I engaged you, not my husband."

June had an unusual steel in her voice that evening. She seemed preoccupied. Danny didn't like it. He wondered if she had been spooked. Had her husband discovered her real intentions? Had he challenged her? Had Harkness changed his deal with her? Danny didn't know, but whatever it was had her pulled tight like piano wire in a hitman's grip.

Harkness sat forward, a slight grimace on his face. "Is he going to be a problem? Do we have a trust issue here?"

Danny stopped before answering. Depending on the answer he gave he might set Harkness off on one of his lone wolf missions. "Unnecessary roughness" they called it in American football. Danny didn't need that on his conscience.

"No, he's playing ball, for now. If that changes, I can control him."

"You thought you could control your friend Enda, Big Man Boom in London… remember?"

Danny ignored the insult and turned his attention back to June. "Do you want to know what I'm thinking?"

"Every detail you have."

"I'll give you the important parts. If you want to know the whole plan we could be here 'til midnight."

"He's like this… won't share… 'does not play well with others'. Do you, Danny boy?"

"If you speak across me once more, I will plant my fist into the middle of your face, Harkness."

June sighed. "Once you arseholes have finished measuring each other's dicks, can we please get on?" She took a gulp from her martini like a man lost in a desert. It was her second. Danny's curiosity flicked up another notch. She was stressed.

"They move the money from the conference hall to a counting office via a tunnel. The counting office is protected by a keypad system, unlike the rest of the setup which is all keycard. I'm presuming the door code is on a need-to-know basis. That's a problem, but one we can cope with. Once the dosh is counted they send an armoured van to pick it up. I think it's a Loomis they use. The counting office is in the main admin building, and it has a separate exit out onto the public roads. Makes sense, as it allows money, supplies, deliveries, all that shit to leave without having to battle the ordinary traffic. Once out, it has about a half-mile stretch of private road before re-joining regular traffic and onto the freeway. As soon as it's on that last stretch, we will hit it and liberate the cash."

"Liberate… I like it. Aren't armoured vans too difficult to get in and out of nowadays? Airlock systems, fingerprint and iris recognition?" Danny and Harkness turned to June as if she had just spoken for the first time. Her knowledge surprised them. She bridled at the looks on their faces.

"Oh, for fuck's sake. I'm a woman, not a fucking Neanderthal. We do know things these days, you know. How do you crack it?"

Danny was embarrassed that he had shown his surprise. He looked away as he answered her question. "We have our ways.

We create a situation where the guard and the driver have to make a choice… Open the doors or suffer."

"How? Explosives? Accelerant?"

"It all depends. First, we will block its way with larger vehicles, usually HGVs of some kind, front and back. If it's an older van, we'll ram it with a heavy vehicle, or we flip it over using a digger or such like. This would allow us to access the bottom of the van to gas them out, or to burn a hole in the escape hatch. The Loomis vans have them in their roofs. Once we know what type of van services this route, we'll have the plan complete."

All the way through this, Harkness was nodding agreement. Danny wanted to be clear with both of them.

"Don't they have trackers? Silent alarms inside them? You'll be very tight for time."

Harkness answered. "I think you'll find Danny has done this before."

"Time is of the essence, June. But as Harkness is inferring… we are pros. But now I have a question for you. When and how do you take delivery of the extra cash? The drug money?"

"It comes in overnight before the last day. They usually deliver it hidden amongst bible leaflets. They surround the bags of cash with boxes of printed flyers. We only allow our team to unload them. The drug money then joins the rest in the counting room, sent in dribs and drabs by our people, to make it look just like more donations. We wouldn't want convention centre staff to become suspicious."

"Which of your team members oversee the count?"

"That would be Greg Norby, our head of security."

Danny shot a look at Harkness. "So, we have no choice but to leave him in place, whether we trust him or not."

June answered with a sigh. "If he's a problem, say the word. Vincent and I can handle him."

"We aren't there… yet. Leave him in place, please, June. Anything that deviates from normal procedure might cause members of the public to become suspicious. We don't need any extra eyes on us."

"That just leaves the most important part of the plan, Danny boy. When and where do we do the handover?"

Danny reached out and picked up his glass of Blanton's bourbon. The smoky amber liquid seemed to complement the sunset that had reached its most flamboyant point in the sky. He sipped the drink, sweet charcoal fire on his lips and tongue. "That all depends."

"Danny, don't fuck around. On what?" June stared intensely at him as she said it.

"On the amount of heat we generate."

"If you do it right and get away, the police will take at least twelve to eighteen hours to catch a lead on you. I know how you work, Felix. You don't fuck around, and you don't hang around."

"And how do you know you can trust me this time, Harkness? Remember the little welcoming committee I had set up for you in London?"

June's expression became wide eyed. "What in Jesus fucking Christ's name is that supposed to mean? Harkness, you told me he was solid."

"Lower your voice, woman. I've told you, you're playing with men now, not boys…" Harkness's tone made June recoil. It was slight, but Danny clocked it. He thought he knew why June was skittish. Something had happened between Harkness and June. Something she may have started, but Harkness had most likely finished. It can't have been pleasant. Had she underestimated Harkness? Had she tried to play him and ended up burnt?

"Danny and I got off on the wrong foot in London. Bad blood. We have… clearer lines of communication now. Wouldn't you agree, Mr Felix?"

Danny stayed quiet, taking another sip of his drink.

"When I said heat, I wasn't referring to the police. I am much more concerned about our Mexican friends."

"All the more reason to do the divvy-up as soon as possible. Then, fuck off out of it, lickety split."

Danny was intent on talking to June. "You do realise you are at risk, don't you? We will have to tell your husband one thing when we meet to apportion the money and then do something entirely different and quickly. At that point, he will come after you. Us. He may even rat you out to the Mexicans. Then, we'd have the cops, the drug dealers and your husband to contend with. But my guess is, he'll want to draw a bead on you first."

"If he has the chance to. Don't worry about my husband. I will deal with him."

The way she said it, Danny knew she was focused and serious. It was not a matter for discussion. Is that what had made her edgy? Had she and Harkness come up with a plan to kill Vincent Cardell at their earliest convenience? Did that plan extend to killing him too?

"I will let you know about the divvy-up in due course, but only once you've given me the answer to all of the questions on this list." Danny stood up, finished his drink in a single swallow and looked down at the two of them.

"I'll need the answers the next time we meet. See you both in a week. And let me be clear. I don't want to see either of you, individually or as a pair, until then. This time, next week, at Wahoo's Bar and Grill. Arrive separately."

June stared dumbly at the handwritten list of questions Danny had handed to her. Harkness tried to stand up, but Danny put a strong hand on his shoulder, pushing him back into his chair.

"No, you don't, matey boy. This is my job now."

Danny left them to it. One was looking frustrated, the other seething. *He won't be able to just fucking leave it, will he.*

He was expecting the tap on the shoulder as he crossed over to the car park opposite the bar. As soon as he turned, Harkness was full into his face.

"What the fuck are you playing at, sunshine? Your job? I fucking brought you this. I let you live when I could have snuck into that shitty little house of yours and gutted you like a pig."

"But you didn't, did you? Just like I didn't back in London. Now, you're stuck with me. You want this money. I can tell. You may have been able to get the hell out of London and come looking for me, but I'm guessing it cost you a bit more than you anticipated. You need cash. I'm the way you're going to get it. So, back off, Harkness. Or else I'll take my chance and walk away."

"You think you'll get your chance, don't you, Danny boy? You think you'll have an opportunity to take me off the board."

"Harkness, make no mistake. Whilst my days of killing are done, I kept one last slot open… especially for you."

Danny cocked the pistol that he'd been holding just below Harkness's side from the moment he had turned around to face him. The noise raised a flicker in Harkness's eyes. He'd missed it.

Harkness laughed, just as Danny remembered. That deep, throaty bellow was accompanied by the slow clapping of his hands. "Bravo, Danny. Bravo. Bring it on, my son. You just try and bring it on…"

Danny had seen and heard enough. He walked off.

But he didn't put the gun away until he was back inside his jeep.

Amparo was looking lovely. She was wearing a long, white linen skirt paired with a cropped purple linen top, sleeveless. Her hair was down, a freesia just above her ear. Danny was a little speechless as he kissed her on the cheek.

"Ay, *hombre*… what was that?"

She grabbed the front of his polo shirt and pulled him into a longer, proper kiss. As always, he was thrilled by the smell of her perfume, the softness of her skin against his face. When they parted, Danny was beaming.

"Where we eating?"

"We're going to Sarabeth's, *mi amigo*. The best seafood in Key West… and their beet soup is delicious."

"Great, I'm starving. I haven't eaten anything for a few days."

"Really? How come? You need to look after yourself, *hombre*."

"Sometimes, I just forget."

"At least I know you're not a '*touron*' for sure now. They do nothing but eat."

She'd been right. The beet soup was amazing, as was the shrimp. The conversation flowed, Danny finding himself being charmed at every turn. It caused him at one point to think of how Ciaran would admonish him, how "no feckin' good" could come of this. But he didn't care about what was right or wrong. In this moment, he was content to just hang, convince himself he was normal, even if it was for just a few hours.

Danny asked for the bill, their server having to make sure he meant the cheque. Amparo laughed.

When it came, Danny paid in cash. He noticed Amparo's face change, just for a second.

"What? What's wrong with cash?"

"Let me see your wallet."

Danny hesitated. Wrong move.

"*Hombre*! Let me see it."

"I… I don't have a wallet."

"Bullshit."

"Frisk me, if you want to. I don't own a wallet."

"What about credit cards? Your ATM card? Driver's licence."

"My licence is in the car."

"And the others?"

Danny could see more awkward questions. "What? You think I'm secretly married or something? Carrying a picture of another girl around?"

"Danny… I already know where you live. There's no girl in that little house. It doesn't have a female touch to it."

He thought he'd diverted her attention, but it was only for a moment.

"The only guys I know that pay for everything in cash are drug dealers, *muchacho*."

"See! There's that cop instinct again. Always ready to think the worst. If I were a dealer, I'd have mobile phones coming out my ears."

"*Sí, sí… pero* it must be something else. It doesn't stack up… You don't stack up."

And then, she said it. The words Danny didn't want to hear.

"Why did you lie to me about the truck? The one I came looking for after the fight in the Tom Thumb?"

He'd been right. She had clocked the GM truck key on his fob that day at the coffee shop.

"You were in that store that night, weren't you?"

Danny took a moment to look at her. He was at a crossroads. It had happened in a heartbeat. He had a choice now. Lie to her and then walk away. Tell her the truth and watch her walk away. The little bit of romance he'd been enjoying was about to flutter from him like the answer to a vital question that was on the tip of your tongue but never quite spoken aloud.

"Yes, it was me. I was the one who stopped the robbery. I was the one told the kid behind the jump to wipe the security video, forget the cops and most importantly, forget me."

She met his gaze, her expression not changing from one of intense scrutiny. She was looking for a tell, a moment when he deviated from the truth with something on his face that would indicate it to her. He decided to plough on. He might as well; he thought all was lost anyway.

"I have been honest with you. When you asked me what I did, I told you the truth. I told you. I'm an international thief. I'm on the run, hiding. Hiding here in the Florida Keys."

Amparo blew out her cheeks, a sadness in her eyes. It was at least a minute before she spoke. "We have a saying down here. Florida Keys… It's a sunny place…"

He completed it for her, "…for shady people. I've heard another that goes 'We're here because we're not all here.'" Danny tapped the side of his head as he said it.

She allowed herself a rueful smile.

"Would it make any difference if I told you I'm a changed man? If I trotted out all the clichés, despite the fact that, in this case, they are true?"

"Leopards… spots… *hombre*. You might think you're a changed man, but…"

"Didn't your brother want to change? After he'd been shot? Didn't he see the world he was living in for what it truly was?"

"He did, but he's not still living off the proceeds of crime. Are you?"

"What's that phrase they used to use about gay people in the American military? Oh, yeah, 'don't ask, don't tell'…"

"That's not an answer that makes me real comfortable, *muchacho*."

"What do you want me to say, Amparo? Your cop instinct led you to me. Then, your female intuition led you further. You found me attractive. I find you attractive. We took it somewhere. Yet, I think you always knew. You told me yourself, you like a bad boy. I'm not the worst; I'm trying to get better. But I'm not a saint."

Danny did not want a scene. He didn't want his last memory of Amparo to be some kind of semi-row. He certainly didn't want that to be her last experience of him. But what could he do? How could he reclaim a bit of that evening?

But then, Danny had an idea. He returned to his regular source of inspiration. "Have you ever seen a movie called *Out of Sight*?"

He could see the question was a bit of a curve ball, but he nodded at her to answer, despite her puzzled expression. "Called what?"

"*Out of Sight*. Stars George Clooney and Jennifer Lopez. Great director…Steven Soderbergh."

"*Hombre*? What has this got to do with–"

"Everything! He's a thief, she's a cop… They have a thing… chemistry. They kind of find a way through…all the…tricky stuff."

"You're trying to square off your context with a movie? Ay… *que pasa*…eh?"

"I know it sounds crazy…but I'm serious. Make me one small promise. Before you consign me to the bin… sorry, the trashcan… watch the film and have one more drink with me."

She looked astounded. But he pressed on.

"What harm can it do?"

"Only my job…"

"You knew I was some kind of bad boy… You were here anyway. Watch the film. Please."

He saw the first chinks in her armoured attitude. He reached across the table and gently took her hand. She looked him in the eye, her expression softening further.

"I guess it can't hurt… *Muy loco… muy, muy loco.*"

Danny felt it was a victory, a small one, but a victory no less. He wasn't ready to lose this little slice of normality just yet.

Danny walked her home. It wasn't the same, but still, he walked her home. There was no hand holding, but she did link his arm which he took as a good omen. The evening air was refreshingly cool. Each time the breeze blew, he was able to enjoy little bursts of the smell of her perfume. At this point, he was enjoying all he could.

In the hallway of her duplex, she stepped back from him and looked up into his eyes. "What's the movie called, again?"

"*Out of Sight*. It has the sexiest seduction scene I have ever watched."

"Don't get ahead of yourself, *chico*."

"I wasn't… I didn't…"

"*Alto*! I'm teasing. I'll watch your stupid movie. Then, if I change my mind, I'll leave you a note in your mailbox. Now, I know why you have no phone."

"I never liked them anyway. By the way, before I go can I just…" He leant in towards her, looking like he was about to kiss her, but he actually plucked a newspaper from one of the pigeonholes. It was a freebie, full of nothing but supermarket coupons and local advertising.

"I thought you were going to kiss me."

"I thought that might earn me a slap…or worse."

"It would have…"

"I just need the paper. I think I may have stepped in something unpleasant…"

"Oh…*bueno*. So, this is goodnight…"

"It is. Despite everything, I had a lovely time, Amparo. I hope I have a shot at another one."

"*Quién sabes*? Who knows…"

She stood on tiptoe and kissed his cheek and held the door for him to go.

"Goodnight, Amparo… but I'm not saying goodbye. Not yet."

He turned and left. As he did so, he rolled the newspaper into a tight cylinder in his hand.

Danny crossed the road away from her apartment complex and took an immediate right turn. This took him down a road that ran along the back of two rows of similar duplexes. It was darker and each side was lined with parked cars and rubbish bins. About fifty yards in, Danny ducked behind a parked car, making sure his feet on the ground were hidden by the wheels.

About thirty seconds later, a second person came down the same alleyway. As he drew level with the car, Danny leapt.

Using one end of the newspaper, he popped the guy just below his Adam's apple. He went down on his knees, his hands immediately around his own throat, gasping for air. Danny then used the paper again, this time mashing the end of it onto the bridge of the guy's nose. There was enough paper wound tightly to break bone. Now, the man at his feet had two problems, and both were fucking up his airways. To finish him off, Danny brought the end of the newspaper roll right down onto the crown of the guy's head. Danny had no doubt his target would be seeing stars.

He leant down and grabbed him by the collar. He wanted to grab him by the hair, drag him all over the alley, but the guy was shaven-headed. On his neck, Danny could see a gang tattoo. He wasn't sure of its meaning, but he knew a gang tattoo drawn in prison ink when he saw one.

"Why were you following me? Eh? *Que pasa, hombre*?"

Danny played out a hunch. Through garbled gasps for air the man spat out a string of Spanish swearing. The last one being *cabrón*. Even Danny knew what it meant. And being proved right made him feel sick.

"*Chingate*, you wanker. Don't come near me… or her, again." Danny didn't want to kill the guy, but he knew he had to send a message. He stood over the gasping man and brought his foot square down onto his ankle. With force.

The crack sounded like a whip. The man's scream split the air, pure agony.

Danny exited the alley the way he went in, but this time at double speed. They had sent an amateur to follow a pro. They had been arrogant. He was a Mexican, no doubt. And now, Danny had a big problem. He'd been followed. Followed with Amparo. He hadn't clocked the tail until a hundred yards from her front door. At least he had acted after leaving her. But still. They had followed him to her door.

They would spot a weakness in him as surely as he would an opponent's. They would spot Amparo as his.

Fucking hell! What the fucking hell have I done? But he knew. He was well aware of the answer to his own question. He had put Amparo at risk.

28

❖ The Third Law ❖

"I look ridiculous."

"I tell ye, Danny, ye never looked finer."

"And why do we have to be the 1960s TV *Batman and Robin*. Couldn't we have been more up to date."

"Listen, ye spoilt pig. Get real. It's comic-con. All the local fancy dress stores were bunged. We were lucky to get anything. We might've had to go naked and claim we were wearing the emperor's new clothes."

"Small mercies…"

"Feck off… ye can speak for yerself… nuttin' small in my case."

They were driving north to the convention centre. There was a geekfest happening. Miami's version of comic-con where cosplayers turn up in their thousands to buy superhero toys, meet Z-list science fiction stars and try their best to outdo each other on the dressing up front. More importantly, for Danny and Ciaran, it gave them another chance to roam around the inside of the centre. Danny was squeezed into the Adam West-era, Lycra monstrosity, whilst Ciaran was rocking the Robin outfit complete with little cape and huge ginger beard. Danny had still not won that particular contest.

It was an entirely different experience walking around the convention floor whilst it was bustling.

"Have ye noticed how many security guards they have in here? These feckers aren't taking any chances. And they're all packing, too."

Danny had noticed. Was this a regular amount, or was this just for an expo that had so many members of the public present?

Would a Christian function be quite so heavily patrolled? "Do you think Vincent Cardell's will be this heavy-handed?"

"Hard to say these days, mucker. I never know if this is to keep order inside, or keep disorder out? The IRA played a bit fairer. At least back in our day, we left a warning. Most of the time, anyway. When we didn't, some fecker had cocked up."

"I suppose. Now, a load of Christians all gathered in one place is a huge target."

About to respond, Ciaran was tapped on the shoulder by a very convincing Wonder Woman.

"Hey, Robin, would you be a cutie and take our picture, please?"

Given his height and the Wonder Woman's build and stature, Ciaran was momentarily lost for words.

Danny, laughing, had to poke him in the shoulder to break the spell. "Hey, Boy Blunder… take the picture…"

"Oh aye…"

It was only then that Ciaran spotted Wonder Woman's friend. A tall, willowy Poison Ivy wearing less than her friend. He whipped his head back round to Danny for an instant. "This may be the greatest job recce we've ever done, Danny. I love my job."

As Ciaran set about taking the super women's picture, Danny was approached by a young man dressed in a red and white uniform. The brow of his ill-fitting baseball cap was covered with a Coca-Cola sign. It reminded Danny of the huge trailer they had parked beside when they had first recced the centre the other night.

"Hey, Batman, want a soda? You can have a regular for two bucks or a souvenir cup for five."

Danny took him in, amazed by the kid's get-up. "They make you walk around like this all day?"

"Yeah, I only go back for refills, and I get a break once every three hours. My back is killing me. You know how it is; you gotta do what you gotta do. But I did get to meet George Takei earlier, so that's cool."

Danny gently spun the kid around. On his back, he was carrying what looked like the pack that Neil Armstrong wore walking on the moon, tubes coming out the top and over each shoulder.

"It's kinda cool, though. The left side of the pack has the gas and the other side has the soda. I'm diet, my buddy over there is full fat."

'I'll take a regular, please." Danny wasn't thirsty, but he wanted to see it in action.

The kid pulled a regular cup from a tube hanging off his belt and, using one of the tubes, he filled it. Then, from a pocket in his trouser leg, he retrieved a straw and a lid. Danny assembled it and took a sip.

"It's cold! How much Coke do you think you sell a day, kid?"

"Who knows, mister? This thing holds ten litres, and I refill about twenty times a day. And that's just me. You do the math."

Danny handed him a five-dollar bill and told him to keep the change.

"Holy tips, Batman! Have a great comic-con. Is your buddy okay over there?"

Danny turned to see Ciaran in the middle of a gaggle of super women. Wonder Woman and Poison Ivy had now been joined by a Storm, a Supergirl, a She-Hulk and, finally, a Batgirl. They were all giggling as Storm tried a group selfie.

"Ladies, ladies, I've never felt so much girl power in all me life, I tell ye that for nuttin'."

"Hey, Superjerk, we've got make a move."

Poison Ivy was the first to respond. "Aww, don't take away our Robin. He's so cute. That accent is divine. I wanna make him itch."

"D'you hear, Batman? She'll even help me scratch it!" They all dissolved into ribald laughter.

"Ladies, put him down. He's only little. I'm saving you from yourselves…"

More laughter as Ciaran detached himself from the group, an exaggerated look of chagrin on his face. "We'll save the world together another time. Who knew Batman was such a ball-breaker?"

As they climbed back into Danny's jeep to drive home to the Keys, he asked Ciaran a question that had the ginger Robin confused. "How much Coca-Cola can a place like this sell at an average event?"

"What's that got to do wit' the price of bacon? Is that one of those details you were on about t'other day?"

"Maybe I'm just curious."

"I was curious about Poison Ivy, but you didn't help me out wit' that one."

Danny smiled. "Who'd want to kiss a beard like that?"

"And I thought Batman was supposed to be Robin's friend."

June walked into Vincent's office and sensed his foul mood instantly. "You wanted to see me?"

Vincent looked up at her, peering over a pair of very old-fashioned, half-moon spectacles. She hated them on him. They made him look old and, to her mind, creepy. Mind you, who was she kidding? She knew there were many things about her husband that were creepy. He gestured to an envelope on the desk in front of him.

"Here. That's for your…" he paused looking for the right word, "acquaintance. It's a list of the answers to the questions he passed to you. You can thank Norby for collating it."

'Thank you. I'll see he gets them."

"I'm sure you will."

June noticed the sarcastic tone in the reply. "What's that supposed to mean?"

"As if I need to answer that. Is he any good?"

June went to reach for the envelope intending to then turn and leave but then thought better of it. "Do you really want me to answer that question? Do you want to know?"

She came around the desk, perching her backside on it, making her husband sit back a little.

'He's very good, Vincent. He's strong. He's muscular and fit. He has big, rough hands that felt harsh on my skin. I felt them, especially when he pulled my panties aside so he could bury his head between my thighs."

"Now listen here…"

"No, Vincent. No. You listen. You listen as I tell you all about how I unbuckled his belt, practically ripped his button flies open. My eyes almost popped out of my head. He was so big… and ready. And I was too. I couldn't sit on him quick enough. And he fucked me. Long and hard. Like a porn star. He made me beg for more, and then, he gave it to me. And I begged again and again. He made me see stars. It was so satisfying, Vincent. So delicious to be with a man who didn't need some handcuffs and a shit load of pain to get it up…"

Vincent stood and raised his arm in the air. But June surprised him. As he drew his arm back, she punched him square in the solar plexus, putting all of her body weight into, enjoying the solid contact she had made. There was a look of absolute shock that turned to pain on Vincent's face.

He flopped back into his chair, gasping for air. June stood over him, hands opening and closing at her sides, waiting, daring him to try and stand up. She knew he was probably becoming aroused, but she wanted to hurt him, needed to make him feel real pain.

"You… you will never raise your hand to me again. If you do, at a time in the future, it may be one week or a month or two months, when you're asleep, I will cut you. I will cut you badly, and you will bleed. You holier than thou son of a motherfucking bitch."

She grabbed his hair and bent down. Speaking directly into his ear, her spittle flecked the side of his head. "I'm busy putting your fuckwit mistakes right. If that means I have to do a little fucking to achieve it, then that is my choice. Besides, how else does a woman get an orgasm around here?" As she said it, she grabbed his cock and balls, not surprised to find him erect. She gave them both a vicious twist.

June stepped back from him, took a moment to fix her hair and picked up the envelope off the desk. But before she could turn away, Vincent found his voice, despite his pain.

"I saved you. I picked you up from out of the gutter and gave you a life. I gave you Jesus. I gave you redemption. If you are going to double-cross me, or stand in the way of my plans, my plans that are built on God's will, then make no mistake. I will have you killed. And it will not go easily for you."

June tutted. "Really, Vincent. Do you think God wanted you to piss off an entire Mexican drug cartel? And by the way, when he made me come, I screamed for Jesus like I was at one of our missions."

And then, she walked out.

After stopping for a takeaway at Jersey Boardwalk Pizza on the way home, Danny and Ciaran were sitting on the porch with cold beers in the hands and full bellies under their respective fancy dress costumes, content to sit in silence, listening to the breeze create music in the trees around the house.

Ciaran finally broke the sound of the night air. "I can hear yer brain whirring away from over here… All that planning… scheming."

"You like me better when I'm thorough. I still have a few loose ends to tie up. Plus, I'm trying to weigh up a calculated risk."

"Our whole feckin' lives are about calculated risks, for Jaysus' sake."

"This one is more a calculated play more than a direct risk…"

Ciaran sat forward, interested. But the sound of a car coming down the drive interrupted them.

It was June Cardell's car. Danny stood to meet it, the headlights cutting across him as he descended the steps. It was only then that he remembered he was still dressed as Batman minus the cowl.

When June stepped out of her car, she was already laughing. 'I didn't think I would even smile today, Danny, but you have changed all that. Looking handsome. I thought you were a criminal, not a crime fighter."

"Believe it or not, this was all in the line of duty."

"Oh, come now, Danny. Are you sure? Mind you, I wouldn't have put you down as someone who likes to dress up."

"What are you doing here? I thought I told you, no contact."

"I don't have a bat signal... so I couldn't summon you." She held the envelope from Vincent's office out in front of her.

"And that is?"

"The answers to your list of questions."

Danny took it from her. He opened it to find a typed list. "This was done on a computer."

"And?"

"Jesus, June. Think. It may have been saved on the computer. That then becomes evidence. Malice aforethought."

"Norby created it. He was the one got you your answers."

"Then, you have to get him to delete it, and I have to treat the answers with some suspicion. He's not on our side."

"As I told you, he's Vincent's man. He's loyal to Vincent, and believe me, Vincent wants this robbery to happen."

"Were you careful? On the way here?"

"What do you mean?"

"Were you followed?"

"Who might be following me, Danny?"

"Look, June, from here on in, assume everyone is an enemy agent. Okay? You're playing—"

"With the big boys, now, huh? Is that what you're about to tell me? Because I've heard that one already this week. Again, you are underestimating me because I'm a woman. Grow up, Danny. This is the twenty-first century."

"No, I was about to say 'playing with fire' if you aren't assessing everything and everybody as a potential risk. You are in a high stakes process, June. Every step from here has risk attached."

"I'm more than ready and able for this, Danny. Don't doubt my capabilities nor my resolve."

"What happened?"

"When?"

"Your demeanour. It's changed. You are less seductive 'femme fatale', and now, you're more 'business-like bitch'. What spooked you? What changed your play? Is it because I'm all the way in now? Or did something else happen?"

"I'm approaching this with a clear head, Danny. Isn't that what you have just demanded from me?"

"No, June. I can feel it. Something or someone has clipped your wings. I think it has something to do with Harkness."

And there it was, even in the light of her car headlights, he spotted it. A momentary flicker in her eyes. The rest of her face was taut and composed. But her eyes had given her away.

"I'm tired of you boys and your macho bullshit. You have your list of answers. I will see you next week with Harkness as arranged. You boys can go back to playing dressy-up now. Goodnight, Danny."

Harkness had done something to her. Something that had scared her. And worse too. He'd made her angry. And on this job of conundrums, that made June an unwelcome variable. Danny watched her drive away, his thoughts clouded by all the possible consequences. Sometimes, Danny hated Isaac Newton and his damned law.

29

❖ I Will Follow ❖

It had been four days since Danny had taken delivery of the list from June Cardell, and once he and Ciaran had pored over the answers, they went to work.

Ciaran had spent most of his time shadowing the routine of one of the names on that list: Marvin J. Quantick III. Marvin was in his fifties, balding but trying desperately to cover it with a comb over that bordered on the comical. He was married but had no children. In other words, an average Joe.

Ciaran had been tracking him from very early morning until very late at night. The aim was to gather as many details as possible about Marvin's everyday schedule as he could. Then, they might be able to find his weakness and, therefore, have the leverage they needed to persuade him to help out with the upcoming job.

The man was a walking cliché. He lived in a modest suburban home on a typical Floridian street. He drove a Volkswagen Jetta. His wife even saw him off to work at the door every morning, handing him a packed lunch and blowing him a kiss.

Ciaran would then follow him on his Harley Davidson, taking exactly the same route every day, being caught in the same traffic snarls and stop lights. It was the kind of existence that would have driven the Irishman to a mental breakdown. Each to his own, he supposed.

Once Marvin was safely ensconced at his place of work, Ciaran would then track back to Marvin's home and watch the wife's routine for a while. On the first day, she went to the gym, driving there in her Chevy Spark. The first time Ciaran had seen her pull the car out of the garage, he had felt nauseous. The car was not only small and ugly, but it was lime green. To him, this was an offence to the entire American motor industry. After the gym, the wife met friends for coffee.

Just before lunchtime, Ciaran would then ride back over to Marvin's work, checking that his Jetta was still parked in the employee car parking lot. Then, using a pair of binoculars, he would locate him, sitting at his office desk, busting open the lunch bag his wife had given him. Ciaran was not surprised to see that Marvin chewed his food with his mouth open, like some kind of caveman. It made Ciaran retch involuntarily to watch, but, ever the pro, he kept the binoculars locked on his target, deeply unpleasant though it was.

The afternoon went pretty much the same. Marvin sat at his desk, working on his computer, making calls, talking to the odd colleague who came and perched on his desk. Now and again, Marvin would get up and leave Ciaran's line of sight. He presumed these occasions were trips to the gents, the longer ones perhaps a meeting or an office gossip.

At the end of the office day, Marvin would climb back into his Jetta and drive home. The traffic snarls and stop lights obstructed just as they had in the morning. Once home, his wife would be waiting, and they stayed in.

Day two had been identical. On day three, Ciaran was settling himself into the bushes of the park that faced Marvin's little home and began to think that he might die from boredom. The morning went off exactly as the other two had. Marvin went to work. His wife went to the gym and then Starbucks. That day, there was a deviation. And what a deviation it was, too.

As he rode his motorbike back to Marvin's office, Ciaran was surprised to see Marvin's Jetta pulling out of the employees' lot. He thanked his lucky stars and wheeled the big bike around to follow his target.

The journey wasn't a long one. The Volkswagen ended up in a small residential community about three miles from Miami Beach. Careful not to be too close, Ciaran left enough space between himself and the car, so that when he was parked up and climbing out of it, Ciaran rode past.

He stopped in the mouth of the next street, turning his head in time to see Marvin ring the doorbell of a house. The front door opened, but Ciaran couldn't see by whom, the occupant staying behind the door, shielded from the street.

Ciaran spent the next fifteen minutes riding around, trying to find a vantage point from which he could watch the house. He cursed the fact that he had chosen to follow on a bike. You could slump down and watch from a parked car. You couldn't do that on the back of a Harley. Then, he had a moment of inspiration. He rode to the nearest strip mall, which was only a half mile away, and parked up the bike. He then jogged back to the street. The car was still there. Opposite, there was another house. It had a big Chevy Suburban parked there on the drive. Ciaran had to take a risk, but it might be worth it. At least this was a bit of excitement, given the tedium of the last two days.

Once settled under the big car, Ciaran began to do what he did best. Sweat. The heat of the day swirled around him, reflecting off the brick-paved drive he lay on and bouncing back down on him from the underside of the car. He was wearing his Mickey shorts and a T-shirt. He could feel moisture gathering around his head and slowly making its way down his face, ending in a drip from the end of his bush-like beard. *Come on, ye fecker… Don't keep me under here long…*

Marvin did keep him waiting, at least another forty minutes. But when he finally emerged, Ciaran was ready. He snapped the binoculars straight to his eyes when the door opened. And what he caught a glimpse of made his heart soar.

Ye dirty wee fecker, Marvin, thought Ciaran.

In these same three days, Danny had been doing a similar job. But he had bigger prey to track. Ines Zedillo. He'd made his way to the Delano Hotel on the first day, again using his paparazzi persona. He once again found the young bellboy who had helped him out before.

He established that Ines was not in residence, but she was due back the next day. Danny took the rest of that day to drive all the routes around the Miami Urban Convention Centre, familiarising himself with all the alternate 'ins and outs.' Where did the major roads lead to from the complex? Where did they intersect with other major routes to take you away to the north and south of the Florida peninsula? He drove them all. Spending nearly an entire day behind the wheel, he drove home to receive an update of tedium from Ciaran and fell asleep on the deck of his house, a half-drunk Blanton's in his hand.

Day two was better. Ines Zedillo arrived at the Delano at exactly the time the bellboy had said she would. Three black Mercedes SUVs heralded her arrival, the hotel staff fluttering around her and her team, showing the right amount of deference to a lady who really did have clout in this town.

Once inside, Danny caught his bellboy's eye, nodding towards the street that ran down the side of the hotel. The bellboy responded by flashing five fingers at him, once, twice and a third time. He would be on a break in fifteen minutes. That worked for Danny just fine.

"She's here for two nights. That's how long she normally stays. Tomorrow night is a bit different, though. You'll have plenty of use for your camera."

Danny handed the bellboy a fifty-dollar note. "Oh, really? How come? An event?"

"Yep. Big charity fundraiser. Ms Zedillo is hosting. The great and the good of Miami Beach are gathering. There's a dinner, an auction, Mariah Carey singing – the whole nine yards."

"Celebrities?" Danny was trying to still sound like an actual pap.

"Oh sure. Nicki Minaj, Ryan Seacrest is in town for it, Will Smith… It's a big deal. It is for Ms Zedillo. She's got a stylist coming tomorrow afternoon with a bunch of dresses for her to choose from. She's gotta look a million dollars. I'm on duty tomorrow, so I know. I've been told to bring up the dresses."

"Who's the stylist? If I can get a shot of the dresses, I might get a fashion scoop. I could sell it to *Miami Online*."

"I dunno. But I do know they are due to arrive at two-thirty."

"Can you get me next to them, the dresses?"

"I'm not sure, man…"

The flash of a one-hundred-dollar bill seemed to clear the bellboy's mind.

"Be here tomorrow at two. And bring a couple more of these." The bellboy waved the money at Danny.

"For sure." Danny would be back the next day. He couldn't believe his luck.

The next day, Ciaran waited under the Chevy Suburban. What he had seen when Marvin had emerged from the house the previous day made him think that he might have a shot at entering it sooner rather than later. His hunch paid off. He glanced at his watch. It said two twenty-five. A car pulled up, a red corvette, all shiny and sleek. It parked where Marvin had. Ciaran scrambled out from his hiding place.

A middle-aged, balding man climbed out of the sports car. He was old enough to make Ciaran think mid-life crisis.

As the man beetled his way to the door of the house, Ciaran half jogged until he was right behind him. Staying light on the balls of his feet to avoid detection, the Irishman made his move as they reached the door to the house. Ciaran stuck the muzzle of a gun into the base of the guy's spine.

"What the fu—"

"Now, you listen to me, loverboy. Yer gonna ring the doorbell, and as soon as herself in there opens the door, yer gonna get the fuck away from here as quick as ye can. Geddit?"

Ciaran dug the gun into the man's back to emphasise his point.

"I…I geddit… Don't hurt me man… I'll do it…"

Ciaran pushed him to the door. Crouching down behind him, he kept the gun firmly at his spine.

He rang the doorbell, and after a second, the door opened, the person shielded by it. Ciaran pulled the man to one side and quickly stepped through, his gun raised at ninety degrees from his chest.

The woman behind the door let out a scream. Ciaran convinced her to be quiet by bringing the gun closer to her face. He put his fist against the inside of the door and punched it closed.

The woman was in her forties, a brassy-looking bottled blonde. She was dressed in a matching black bra, suspenders and stockings, her high heels shiny as fresh liquorice.

'I don't have any money. Mister, I swear it, please don't hurt me."

"Calm down, woman. I'm not here to hurt ye. I just want a little info and maybe some help. Yer mistake was to give me a flash of stockinged leg when ye let the last punter out."

She was starting to calm down a little. Her look of abject terror was abating slightly.

Ciaran gestured with the gun towards the inside of the house, and she took the hint, leading him into a lounge that was lit almost entirely by candles. Seductive music was playing. Ciaran thought he recognised it, but he couldn't quite remember the singer's name.

In the middle of the room was a massage table covered in towels, a hole in one end for a person's face to recline into.

"I… I only do massage… Nothing else."

"Dressed like dat, love? Who ye kidding…"

"I do happy endings… Let them touch me a little but nothing else!"

"Put yer dressing gown on, love. I'm not here for any of dat."

The blonde did as she was told while Ciaran went and turned off the music.

"I want to be fair to ye… How much would that man at the door have given ye?"

Now she was really puzzled. 'I don't… I…"

"How much business have I just cost ye?"

"Oh… erm… two hundred bucks."

Ciaran pulled a wedge of cash out of his back pocket and peeled off four fifty-dollar notes. He handed them to her. "Now, I'll give you another five hunnerd if ye tell me all about one of yer customers… His name's Marvin."

The blonde woman's eyes went wide, and she started to talk as quickly as she could.

At roughly the same time, Danny was in the loading bay at the back of the Delano hotel. He had arrived as instructed and his favourite bellboy had shown him in through a staff entrance.

The plan was this. The bellboy was to help unload the dresses. They came on large castered dress rails that were draped in heavy canvas covers from top to bottom. They would be put into a service elevator and brought up to the penthouse, where the stylist would let Ines Zedillo try them on. Adjustments, if needed, would be done there and then by the stylist.

The bellboy had told Danny he would have about a minute alone with each rolling rail while he went to fetch the next one. He would distract the stylist on Danny's behalf, allowing him to take some pictures.

At least that's what the bellboy thought the plan was. But as soon as he went to retrieve the third rail, Danny wheeled the first two into the service elevator himself. He then ducked under the canvas of the first rail, balancing himself on the bar that ran along the bottom while holding onto the top bar for stability. He was soon squeezed into place amongst the couture dresses.

When the bellboy came through with the final rail, he seemed surprised not to see Danny. He didn't have time to wonder what had gone on, because the stylist came directly behind him, shooing him along to push the last trunk into the elevator.

As the doors on the lift closed, the bellboy must have assumed that Danny had taken as many pictures as he'd wanted and left.

Danny had to tense his core muscles all the way up in the lift to be careful not to slip off his precarious hiding place. He heard the lift doors open and the stylist greeting someone on the other side.

"May I have some help rolling these in, please?"

"Yes, ma'am."

The voice was deep. Danny assumed a bodyguard was about to help. There was a grunt as the guard was taken a little by surprise at the weight of the first rail.

As soon as the rail was left in place, Danny slowly lowered himself out from under the canvas. He was in the bedroom of the Delano suite. His luck was holding… He was alone. There was a closet on one side of the bedroom. He climbed into it as quickly as he could. He left the closet door open a crack so he could watch what was happening.

Once the rails were all in place, the stylist went about peeling off the canvas covers. The dresses were all bagged in heavy plastic, zipped bags. She proceeded to open each one, turning the dress outwards on their hangers. Each rail had five dresses, fifteen to choose from in all.

When Ines Zedillo came into the room, Danny held his breath. He was going to have to pick his moment carefully. He was struck by how elegant she was, how she carried herself, poker-straight posture, head held high. Her manicured nails blazed red, her long legs lean and tanned.

Ines and the stylist spent the next forty minutes debating the gowns. She dismissed five straight away. Colours or details not appealing to her. She then tried three on. Each time she disrobed, Danny looked at his feet. He was uncomfortable at the voyeuristic nature of what he was doing, but he knew needs must.

The final dress Ines put on was a shimmering, emerald green one. Off the shoulder on one side, fitted to the waist with a lavish skirt which splayed out to form a long train at the back. Danny had to admit it was stunning, and she only made it better.

Ines agreed, as did the stylist. They discussed possible tweaks and shoes to match. They had their winner. Ines asked the stylist for some shoes from the Gucci store.

"Have them sent over. They know my size. I have an account."

"I'll go phone them now, Señora Zedillo."

The stylist left the room, and Danny saw his chance. He produced an ugly-looking Sig Sauer pistol from the waistband of his jeans and stepped out into the room, careful to do so before Ines could start to undress.

"Good afternoon, Señora Zedillo."

She gave a startled gasp and was about to shout when Danny waved the gun at her, placing a finger over his own mouth.

"Shhhh. I'm not here to hurt you. I just want to talk."

She considered him for a second, then her face flushed with anger. "I know who you are. You are the thief."

"I am. And I'm not surprised that you know who I am. You were having me followed. Until I broke your man's leg. Then, I decided to become a little more vigilant."

"Are you surprised that I wanted to keep tabs on you? I have an investment, no?"

"An investment in me is one thing. Poking around in my private life is another."

"Ahhhh. The woman. You are worried that we saw you with a woman."

Danny held his breath. He wondered if that was all they knew about Amparo. Ines answered that for him with her next breath.

"A little cavalier, consorting with a policewoman, Danny. I have to say I was surprised."

Danny's heart sank. "There is no need to involve her. She knows nothing."

"And I'm to believe that? I'm to take the word of a thief? *Muy loco...*"

"We are not enemies, señora. I just want to establish some ground rules. Boundaries."

"No enemies? Yet here you are in my hotel bedroom pointing a gun at me."

"This is about respect. I have things I wish to keep separate from our arrangements. You have a need for those arrangements to go off as planned... without hiccups. By showing you I could get in here at will, that is just my way of illustrating my level of expertise and... commitment."

"Are you threatening me, señor?"

"No. Rather I'm showing you what I'm capable of."

Danny then played out a hunch. He lowered the gun, replacing it in the back of his jeans.

"Tell me, señor. Tell me about the robbery. You will hit the armoured cash van, I believe."

"Yes...that's the plan. Harkness shared that with you, then?"

"*Sí, sí.* What do you make of our Señor Harkness?"

Danny thought before he answered. He decided honesty was the only way to proceed. "I want to kill him. He wants to do the same to me."

"Ah... *bueno.* Is he a threat to the success of your plan?"

"Not the robbery itself. But after... perhaps."

"Shall I have him killed?"

"To be honest, I think that is probably best left to me. I have some thoughts on the matter."

Ines laughed at his choice of words. "So, what do you want from me *ahora*, señor? You have *cojones* for getting in here like this."

"Stay away from the lady cop. Stay out of my life, and I will deliver the money and the Cardells to you."

"Your *amigo*, Harkness, has already promised that to me..."

"And do you believe him? Do you believe he will deliver?"

"He smiles like an alligator. He also wants a cut of the *moneda.*"

Danny looked at her with a steady gaze. "I have enough money. No cut for me."

Ines raised an eyebrow at him.

"I will walk out of this suite now, untouched. Leave my life and my friends untouched. Let me do my work and deliver the money and the Cardells to you. And then…"

"Then, señor?"

"I kill Harkness, and I disappear."

She took a moment. He knew she was making a choice. He hoped it would be the right one. She crossed to the bedside table and wrote a number down on a piece of paper.

"When your plans are set, call this number and tell the man who answers every detail. Do not disappoint me. *Comprende*? *Ahora*, I will walk you out myself, Señor…?"

"Felix. Danny Felix."

"I will escort you to the door of the suite myself, Señor Felix. But the next time we see each other, you had better be delivering all those promises you just made."

"*Muchas gracias*, Señora Zedillo."

Ines pointed towards the door, and Danny's heart rate began to return to somewhere near normal.

Danny was already on the porch in his favourite chair, savouring his Blanton's, when Ciaran's bike came roaring down his drive. The Irishman took little time to join his friend, pouring himself a shot from the bottle that sat on a little table next to Danny.

"Mission fecking accomplished."

"Really? What did Marvin have to offer us today, then?"

"You'll never guess. He goes for a wank at lunchtime every Wednesday and Friday. A woman called Anastasia. She dresses all sexy like, swears she doesn't do anything but the oul' five finger knuckle shuffle."

"Ah… and the wife is none the wiser, I presume."

"Not even a hint of it. He tells Anastasia his wife doesn't understand. He's been going to see Anastasia for about two years. Buys her flowers now and again. Tries to push his luck."

"Do I want to know how you gathered all this intel?"

"No one was hurt in the making of this scenario. Promise, scout's honour, on my sainted white-haired mother's life."

"So, all we have to do now is front poor old Marvin?"

"And I know exactly where and when. It'll be grand. With what he does for a living and with what I know about his lunch breaks, he'll help us pull this job, no bother."

"I hope you're right, Captain Gingerbeard."

They clinked glasses. Danny finished his in one gulp.

"How'd ye get on yerself, like?"

"Oh… about as well as you. I think."

"Really? Share wit' the group?"

"I met Ines Zedillo today. The boss of the cartel we're about to rip off."

Ciaran almost dropped his glass. His mouth hung open, his eyes wide and panicky. "Ye did wha'?" He involuntarily crossed himself.

"Some Catholic you are. You just blessed yourself with the wrong hand."

"I'm holding me drink! Anyway, feck dat. Why'd ye go and see her?"

"Harkness. He's playing all the angles. So, I thought we'd better, too. She knew all about the armoured van… the back road. He's been sharing everything."

"Aw, Holy Mother of God. These things are hard enough to pull off."

"Oh, there's no need to worry. I have most of it worked out. I just need one more player to help us. Just one more."

"Who's dat, then?"

"I better tell you the plan first, hadn't I? At least then, you'll know why I need them."

"Aye, right enough."

"Have you ever wondered how to pull off a robbery where there isn't a robbery?"

"Ye've gone a bit mental on me there."

"Let me explain…"

And Danny did. He laid the whole job out as he saw it in his mind. Everything from start to finish, even down to how he thought all the parties would react.

And when he was done, Ciaran poured them both another shot.

"Jaysus, if I didn't know you were a feckin' Englishman, I'd swear you were a cute enough hoo'er to be Irish. God bless you, Danny Felix. Let's get into trouble together…"

And for the second time that night, they chinked glasses.

30

❖ Finishing Touches ❖

Woody's strip joint was a little sad even at the best of times. When all the neon was switched on and the music was pumping, it had a robust dinginess about it. But during daylight hours, when the house lights were on, and the doors were open to let some fresh air in, it seemed more down at heel.

That day it was more than fit for purpose. Danny was in front of possibly the strangest crew he had ever put together. Slow Tina had helped to gather this rag-tag band, so he shouldn't have been too surprised at the variety of the bunch. Still, he hadn't worked with a six-foot transvestite, a huge black guy who was as camp as Christmas and another eight peroxide blonde women of varying sizes all at once before.

Rounding out the contingent were Ciaran, Slow Tina and the guy who played the music and fixed the lighting for this august establishment. His name was Rusty.

Danny had just laid out most, not quite all, of the plan to them. He'd walked each of them through their piece of the operation, using floor plans of the convention centre, images courtesy of Google Earth all printed off at the local library in Islamorada.

Ciaran also went through the route that the armoured cash van would take. He had spent three days identifying and then tracking the right van, following it from base to pick up, to drop off, to base. The drivers, to his mind, had been lazy. They hadn't bothered to vary their approaches, not even once, especially as their route took them past 'The Salty Donut' shop in Wynwood.

"Jaysus, but they love their donuts, these boys..."

As usual, questions had been asked, answers given. Scenarios were discussed and debated. By the end of the two-hour session, everyone agreed that they were about to take on a great adventure.

Danny praised them all for their willingness and enthusiasm, while assuring them that they were all at the low-risk end. The high-risk portion was preserved for Ciaran and himself.

"Thank you, ladies and gentlemen, truly thank you. Two last things. We have just four days to go until the 'Holy Joes' start their gig at the convention centre and a further two days until we spring into action. In the interim, please, keep your heads down and your noses clean. I don't want to be losing a team member this late in the day. And finally, here's the uniform we are all going to wear."

Ciaran started to move amongst them, handing out T-shirts, baseball caps and sunglasses.

The huge black guy held his T-shirt up, reading aloud: "I♥JESUS. Who y'all kidding? I never did like a man with a beard."

Ciaran instinctively stroked his own ginger fuzz at that point.

The baseball caps all had a diamante cross on the brow and "Jesus is my homeboy" embroidered over the airgap at the back.

"We must keep the caps and the sunglasses on at all times, even you guys who are performing on the big night. There are too many security cameras in this place, so we need to hide in numbers. The hats and glasses will do that for us, since most of the cameras are in the ceiling void. There can be no customisation of the hats and T-shirts, and no way out of wearing them." Danny had on his most serious face.

"And last, but not least, here is a little pre-game 'thank you'. You will get more of the same after the job, I promise." Ciaran was distributing again. This time, it was envelopes containing ten thousand dollars for each of the assembled team members.

"If anybody has any last-minute doubts or concerns between now and the day, Tina will be glad to help, and she knows how to get a hold of me. That's it, everyone. Stay safe. See you at the convention centre."

The little group gathered their things, and Danny went over to talk to Slow Tina. "Tina, I can't thank you enough. You've been great."

"Honey chile, with this, you've already started to thank me handsomely." She waved the envelope at him as though it were a fan. "And besides, I haven't had this much excitement since one of my gentlemen callers introduced me to one of those rampant rabbit contraptions. My, that was an afternoon of entertainment."

Danny couldn't help but laugh. "I am sure it was, Tina. And you're happy with your part of the plan? Not worried about putting your little dog, Morty, at risk?"

"That liddle, damned dog has more grit and determination than any so-called shining knight I ever met, sweetie. We'll get your job done, no doubt. By the way, that other individual you wanted to meet? He should be here any time now. I explained to him you needed his assistance for which he would be well remunerated. He's a salty old fool, but I know a greedy boy when I see one. He'll be here. Now please, excuse me. I have to run. My chiropodist and I have a hot date. I flash him a liddle ankle, and he assesses my bunions. Don't grow old, dear. It really is a bore."

And with that, the oldest stripper in Florida, possibly America, was out the door.

Rusty the DJ came over, a CD in his hand. "I can convert this to an MP3 file. It will make my job a lot easier on the night."

"Thanks, Rusty. Just as long as you're clear about when and how."

"Clear as day, mister, clear as day. I must say, I am a little curious. How did you manage to get a hold of the preacher's own running order for the night? That's smooth work, right there."

"Rusty, let's just say the Lord moves in mysterious ways."

"He surely does. God bless us all. And thank you for this envelope. My wife has been dropping hints about a vacation to Cabo for months. You have just made that possible. Every time she treats me nice down there? I'll be thinking of you, mister."

Danny didn't know if that was the type of tribute he wanted, but he said thanks, all the same.

Once everyone had gone, Rusty locked the building and left Ciaran and Danny in the parking lot.

"Do ye think they'll be okay?'

"I think so, Ciaran. Tina is a woman of many talents who has lived many lives. Despite her artistic endeavours, I suspect this might not be her first 'job'."

"D'ye know, I thought that too."

"And all we have left to do is meet the last piece of our puzzle."

"And then, I can look after Marvin, the dirty wee fecker."

Before Danny could respond, a huge lorry pulled into the parking lot, festooned in lights and pulling along behind it a trailer that was painted red and white, the Coca-Cola logo bright and shining in the sunlight.

"And here he is. Give me that last envelope, Ciaran, and let's see if our truck driver friend here will help us."

31

❖ Life Changer ❖

When Marvin J. Quantick III left his home to go to work that day, little did he know that his life was about to be fucked with.

The radio was playing *Manic Monday*. The DJ was trying to be ironic, blinding the working-Joe to the misery of another mundane week with the inanely chirpy song. Marvin drummed his fingers along to the tune, remembering how hot Susanna Hoffs had been when she recorded the song with The Bangles.

Who could blame Prince for gifting her the song? I mean she was… damn hot. His next thought was also a damn, as the stoplight he was hoping to pass through on the first go changed and blocked his progress. It was the same every morning, but, somehow, Marvin had forgotten. He happened to look down, noticing a stain on his plaid patterned tie, one he had never spotted before. He silently mouthed the word "fuck", licked his finger and started to rub at it in vain. That was when he heard it. TAP. Something metallic on his car window.

Marvin looked up, expecting to see some street seller trying to offer him oranges or flowers or to wipe his windshield. At first, his brain couldn't quite compute what he was looking at, but once it did, Marvin felt his guts turn to liquid and a sweat break out on his brow. It was a gun. A big one. TAP. The holder gestured with it, signalling they wanted the window opened.

Marvin knew he was fucked. There was another car in front of him, at the lights, with many more behind. The man with the gun sat astride a huge Harley Davidson, blocking that route out, more traffic on his inside.

TAP TAP TAP.

This time, the motorbike guy cocked the gun. With trembling fingers, Marvin lowered the window. Just a crack, not all the way. As if that made a blind bit of difference.

The motorbike man leant over. Marvin could see for the first time he had a bandana across his nose and mouth, mirrored aviator shades and a cropped crash helmet, the type that looked like the one the Germans used to wear in World War Two.

"Pull the fuck over at the next junction, or I'll ride up and blow yer brains out. Nod if you understand."

Marvin was now in the full-on shakes. In a daze, he slowly nodded. The light changed, the cars began to move forward. He looked ahead, trying to see if there was a way he might drive off, evade this madman. Had he cut the biker up? Had he almost wiped him out with his Jetta, to make him angry enough to draw a gun and threaten him?

But Marvin knew. Between the weight of the traffic and speed and agility of the bike, he knew that if he tried to make a break for it, the Harley would catch him, and things would go south from there.

So, he did as he was told. Switching to the inside lane, the bike matching his move, he stayed alongside.

The next turning was the entrance to an abandoned gas station. The motorbiker moved slightly ahead and used his front wheel to guide Marvin into it. As he pulled in, Marvin's heart was hammering in his chest. He felt his guts churning, his mind raced. What the fuck had he done? What was going on?

As he pulled to a stop, he contemplated abandoning the car, to fling the door open and run like hell. But as soon as the thought occurred to him, his brain shut it down, a self-loathing, small voice laughing in his own ear. *You? Run? Give me a fucking break*.

And then, it was too late. *TAP TAP TAP.* The motorbiker was at the passenger door of the Volkswagen, demanding to be let in.

"Listen… Mister… I… if… I cut you up, or crowded you on the road, I… I didn't intend…"

"Open the fuckin' door."

The gun looked awfully big and black to Marvin. He'd never owned one. He'd never even shot one. Lots of his friends did. They said it was for personal safety. He now regretted he hadn't taken up their invitations to learn how to handle one.

Noticing the furious shake in his hand, he reached out and pressed a button, the doors clicking open.

The motorbiker sat next to him. Marvin couldn't take his eyes off the gun. It was laid there, in the biker's lap. The guy wasn't even breathing heavy. He was cool, calm. Not angry. What was this about?

"Hello, Marvin. How are ye today?"

"What…? I…I don't understand."

"Look, ye can calm down. If this little chat goes as it should do, I'll have no need to use this on ye. We clear, Marvin?"

Marvin, petrified though he was, managed a nod in agreement. "How… how do you know my name?"

"Ach, Jaysus, Marvin. It's not just your name I know. I know you have a wife… I know she drives a green piece of shite car. I know where ye work. I know ye have a wee packed lunch every day at yer desk… see? I know lots about ye. Yer wife goes to the gym a lot, doesn't she?"

Marvin stammered. "What's this got to… g... g... g... got to do with her? You leave her alone!"

"Now don't be getting all 'ants in yer pants', Marv. I know ye love yer wife. She keeps herself trim for ye. Works hard at it, she does. And ye probably worship the ground she walks on. But sometimes… sometimes, a wee wife just isn't enough, now is it?"

"What are you talking about…? I don't…"

And then, Marvin stopped cold. A thought had just crashed to the front of his consciousness. His mouth went dry. He tried to swallow, but it created an involuntary croaking noise instead.

The biker opened a pocket in his cargo shorts and brought out what looked like a photo, but Marvin couldn't be sure, as it was face down. But Marvin knew in his heart of hearts it was a photo. He knew before the biker turned it over that it was a photo of him.

"Sometimes, ye just need a wee bit of fun on the side, don't ye? Like this, maybe."

The biker brought the picture up in front of Marvin's face. He was staring at himself. Buck naked. Face down on a massage table.

"That… that could be… anyone…"

"Ach, now. That's not what Anastasia says. She says yer a regular. She says ye bring her little gifts, try to touch her up, now and again. Mind, who could blame ye."

Marvin's heart sank even further. The biker had another photo, this one of Anastasia kissing him goodbye at the front door, wearing nothing but a smile and probably some of that perfume he bought her. Now that he thought of it, he'd wondered that day about how brazen she had been at the door. She'd normally hidden behind it. She usually didn't even give him a kiss.

"But, Marvin. This need not be anything more than a bump in the road for ye. As I said at the start of this chat, we can both be calm here."

"How… how…"

"How did I stumble across all this info and lovely pictures?"

"No… I fuck… I fucking know how."

Marvin spat the words out through gritted teeth. He felt like a fool. He'd blurred the lines between emotional connection and someone he paid to jerk him off twice a week. What a cliché.

"Then what? If not that, Marvin?"

"How… much? How much do you want?"

"Oh. No, Marvin. You misunderstand me. I just need a few wee favours. Nothing much. And, if you do as I ask, then all this… unpleasantness can be forgotten. Mind you, by the look of those tatas," the biker waved the photo at him, "I'm not so sure it was all unpleasant for ye, eh? But if ye don't do what I ask, I think ye might have some explaining to do to that wife of yours. Oh, and if you try and go to the police? I'll just hunt ye down and kill ye. Clear?"

"What do you want?" Marvin mumbled, resignation descending upon him.

"Ah, sure yer a grand lad. Now. It's about where ye work…"

The end of the afternoon had been marked by dark clouds gathering over Danny's house. He could feel the atmosphere change in the air, as he rhythmically punched out sequences on the bag in his carport.

He hadn't been in Florida all that long, but he still recognised the tell-tale signs of an oncoming storm. A long shower followed by a brief update from Ciaran when he arrived back from Miami Beach rounded out his day. Danny took to his favourite seat on the porch and said goodbye to his friend as he descended the steps of the house.

"I'm only nipping down to Woody's… Ye know… bit more research, like."

"Really? Nothing to do with that bottle blonde who was fluttering her false eyelashes at you during the meeting the other day?"

Ciaran looked bashful for a moment, then pulled himself upright. "A man has needs! Yer all right, ye've had a bit of tomfoolery lately. I'm still waiting."

Danny reached into the pocket of his shorts, pulling out the keys to his jeep. "Here, take this. It's going to storm. And you might need a roof over your head as you drive to her place."

Danny tossed him the key ring and Ciaran caught it one-handed. "Yer a good man, Danny Felix. I don't care what everyone else says…"

Once the taillights of the jeep had faded off into the night, Danny poured himself a large Blanton's and sat back, beginning to think through every aspect of the job for the umpteenth time. Soon, he could hear the first ticks of fat raindrops on the roof, a thunder rumble not too far off in the distance. The night sky pulsed every so often, electricity trying to find its way from the clouds to earth. Danny stopped thinking just for a moment, sat back and enjoyed God's light show. The thunder crept closer, growing in volume. Which meant he didn't hear the car creeping up his drive. A small Subaru. At that moment, the heavens chose to open. One thing Danny had learned was that when it rained in Florida, it really rained. Great sheets of water tumbling out of the sky, filling the senses, clearing the atmosphere.

The Subaru stopped just shy of the steps, and Danny's heart leapt as he saw it and recognised who was behind the wheel. He went down the steps and met Amparo as she stepped out of the small car.

"Hello, you. I didn't think I'd see you again. Let's get undercover."

But as he reached for her, she stopped him, grabbing his arm and holding it tight.

She pulled him directly in front of her, both of them getting drenched in the storm.

Amparo stood on her tiptoes and had to half shout to be heard over the clatter of the rain. "I watched your film. *Out of Sight*? You were right, it's great. And yes… it is a very sexy scene. J-Lo and Clooney make it really hot."

"I'm glad you liked it… Why don't we…"

"*Cállate, hombre*. I'm not finished. What I wanted to say was, I loved the movie, but it's just a movie. I'm a cop. You're playing fast and loose with the rules. When I joined the sheriff's, I made a promise. A promise that I would never get caught up in the kind of shit that *mi hermano* did. So, I can't be some kind of movie romance for you. Some kind of fairy tale ending."

"Amparo… I…"

"Shhhh. But what I can do, is this. I can find out. I can find out, just for one night, what I might be missing."

"Amparo, let's talk about this."

"Talk? *Madre de Dios*! Danny, let me be *claro*, okay? This isn't for you. This is for me. This is so I don't spend months, maybe years, wondering 'what if?'. Now, take me inside and rip these wet clothes off me."

She was right. They were both soaked. Danny's T-shirt was plastered against his chest and stomach, rain dripping off the end of his nose. He could make out the colour of her bra through her blouse, her skirt clinging to her legs, her long hair thickening with rain as she pushed it back off her face.

She looked down and grabbed his hand. She led him into the house, the two of them leaving wet footprints all the way to the side of the bed. She pulled his T-shirt up over his head, and he bent down to kiss her, enjoying the contrast of the warmth of her lips and the cold of the rainwater running down his face. She kicked off her shoes, quickly unzipping her skirt at the side and let it drop to the floor. Danny peeled off his shorts, surprising her with the fact that he wore no underwear.

And then, she stopped him, holding his face tight in both her hands. "Danny, this is a one-shot deal. I'm not kidding. We can't be. There is no us. But there is an us right now. Let's make the most of it."

And she jumped up, knowing he would catch her as she wrapped her legs around his waist, pulling his head into a kiss that was deep and passionate. And as she tightened her thighs around him, she was in the perfect position to kick the bedroom door closed just before they both collapsed onto the bed.

In the morning, the world felt very bright and new. The storm had swept away the humidity of the day before and left the full force of spring in the air. Danny had woken alone in his bed, but the smell of coffee and the clink of cups told him he hadn't been abandoned just yet. He rolled out of bed, stood up and walked out into his kitchen, a smile on his face followed by a stretch and a yawn, expecting to see Amparo.

"Jaysus… would ye put that away? Ye'll have somebody's eye out with it. Coffee will be brewed in two shakes…"

Danny turned away from Ciaran, going back into his bedroom. Nothing. There was no note. No forgotten piece of clothing.

No earring left behind by mistake on the bedside table. And then, Danny felt it. Felt his heart sink and world become that little bit more closed.

Amparo had meant what she said. Every word. And his loneliness settled on him with hateful familiarity. He'd wanted something more. He'd fooled himself into fantasising that something more was possible. But at that moment, that morning he felt hollow and angry. Angry at himself, because he realised it was his own fleeting optimism that had led him to this point. These emotions.

A connection. Affection… even love. They weren't supposed to be available to a man who had made the kind of choices he had. He couldn't even have a relationship with God. Danny was thousands of miles away from home. He was embroiled in dark plans, some of them his, some of others' making. And he had nowhere else to go. Nowhere to be. No one waiting on him to say a kind word or graze a kiss on their lips.

He sat heavily on the edge of his bed, the tangle of the sheets taunting him. Brief memories of passion, of wanting, and of being wanted.

Danny ran his hands over his face, pushing his fingers into his eyes, and sighed loudly.

A song drifted into his head, appearing from the deepest reaches of his brain.

"A taste of honey's worse than none at all… ooo little girl in that case I don't want no part. I do believe that would only break my heart…"

Honey? Danny thought. *I never knew it could taste so bitter.*

32

❖ For the Love of God ❖

The first two days of the mission had been frosty as far as June and Vincent Cardell were concerned.

In front of their assembled pilgrims, they were all warmth and togetherness. They preached side-by-side, they sang hymns, they prayed. To the outside world, they were the perfect evangelical couple, loving God and each other.

In private, there was a foul atmosphere between them. Uncomfortable silences, glares, and when they did speak, it was to deliver some malicious swipe. Not directed at each other but definitely about each other. It was poisonous.

But on the Saturday night, in front of the gathered faithful, Vincent surprised her. In a section of the proceedings that was supposed to focus on the sin of envy, the preacher asked the congregation to indulge him for a moment.

On the big screen behind him a huge image of him and June on their wedding day came into view. Vincent walked over to June who was standing on the altar and took her by the hand and led her to the centre.

"Pilgrims, in the good book, in Proverbs, the Lord says this, chapter twelve, verse four. '*An excellent wife is the crown of her husband.*' Can you imagine the day, the day when I first laid eyes on my June? How my heart leapt that the grace of God had brought me into the presence of this angel. She keeps a beautiful home for us. She keeps me on an even keel when the storm of modern life attempts to blow us off course. Pilgrims, she reminds me, every single day, that God's love finds its way into our lives via many routes, but none are more purely felt that the love of a wife for her husband."

The crowd was clapping, applauding the words of love from a man of God for his life partner. They felt reaffirmed, reassured. Couples in the audience turned to one another, hugging, some kissing, saying they loved each other and praise be to God for it.

"And as I don't often get the chance to give thanks to both our Lord and my beloved June, I wanted to take this chance, in front of all of you, to bear witness to her incredible dedication to me and the word of God."

Vincent took both her hands in his, turning so that they were staring into each other's eyes. He produced from his inside pocket a little box. "June, this is my way of thanking you. Thank you for being my wife. Thank you for journeying with me. Thank you for your devotion to me and to my vocation as God's instrument on earth. And thank you for being involved in every, and I mean absolutely every, adventure in my life." As he said it, June saw a cold glint in his eyes.

He handed her the box. She opened it, the crowd now on their feet, clapping, whooping like they were at a rodeo. Inside, it was a simply designed, gold cross on a gold chain. It was weighty, so she knew it was not cheap. Turning to look at the congregation, she held up the cross, knowing that one of the many cameras on the altar would capture the moment, transmitting it onto the screen behind them. The noise from the crowd went up another notch.

June turned back to Vincent. He put his arms around her and pulled her into a tight embrace. With his face on the side of her face away from the applauding pilgrims, he whispered to her, careful not to let his microphone pick out his words.

"And, June, darling, the other half of that proverb quote goes like this. '*but she who brings shame is like rottenness in his bones.*'The cross… it symbolises what I will do to you if you bring me shame… I will crucify you. Tomorrow is a big day. Our day. I hope you have not done anything to disappoint me."

And he then kissed her, the throng whistling and cheering as he did it.

It was all June could do to stop herself from retching into his mouth right there and then.

Danny wasn't at all surprised when Harkness showed up. He knew that the control freak could never have resisted a final visit. To reinforce that he was in charge of the overall situation.

"All right, my son? Are you ready to weave your dark magic in Miami tomorrow?"

He took the steps up onto Danny's porch two at a time. Despite his tall, athletic frame, he was remarkably quick and light on his feet. His damaged eye seemed to shine brightly white in the gathering twilight. He held his hands wide in front of him, grinning.

Danny stayed in his seat, a cup of tea in his hand. "Why are you here, Harkness? What part of 'stay the fuck away' do you not understand?"

'Oh, now, now, Danny. You know me. I like to remind colleagues of what's at stake, and who is pulling the strings on a job."

"And are you? Do you really believe that?"

"I have told you before. Why have a dog and bark yourself? I like it when you do my barking for me, Danny. You're so very good at it."

"You think you have all the angles covered, Harkness. Yet, your arrogance and supreme self-belief are your biggest weaknesses."

Harkness was about to reply when he suddenly felt cold, hard metal being pressed into the base of his skull. The unmistakeable sound of a pistol being cocked loudly followed it. Ciaran had managed to sneak up the steps behind the big man. Danny was amazed, as it took stealth to mount the creaky, wooden steps.

"See? Not all your angles are covered, Harkness. Now, answer me this. Why should I stop my Irish friend here from pulling that trigger?"

"You'll never get away with their money, if you take me out of the equation, sunshine."

"Do I really need their money? Do I really want it?"

"Oh, feck this shite, Danny. Just let me kill this cunt, and we can all get on wit' our lives."

Danny could see light dancing in Ciaran's eyes. Realising that his bloodlust was up, Danny saw that he wanted to pull that trigger more than anything else in the world.

But Harkness still had one last trick up his sleeve. He raised his right arm slowly in the air. "If I may be so bold… take a butcher's at this, Danny boy." He had a mobile phone in his hand. His thumb moved over a sensor, unlocking the device. He then slowly reached out and handed the phone to Danny, Ciaran being careful to maintain the pressure of the gun on the back of his head as he did so.

Danny knew what he was about to see before he even looked at the screen. It was photo of Deputy Sheriff Amparo Sosa. He felt sick.

"You see Danny, Ines and I talked about your little girlfriend the other day, and even though you thought you'd cut a deal with her… let's just say we think you do your best work when you have something at stake in this game of ours. Good luck tomorrow, Danny. And now, would you mind asking this pigfuck Irishman to take his gun and shove it up his arse."

Ciaran hesitated. He didn't know what Danny had seen on the screen, but he knew it could not be good. Before he reluctantly lowered the gun, he leant in and whispered harshly in Harkness's ear.

"Listen here. '*Go mbrise an diabhal do chnámha.*' Do you what that means in Pig Irish, ye cunt? It means 'may the devil crush yer bones.' I'm gonna see to it, at some point, that he gets the feckin' chance."

As he descended the steps away, Harkness shouted over his shoulder, "Say your prayers and get some sleep, boys. The love of God is going to bring us all a lot of money tomorrow. Make sure you enjoy yourselves."

And then, he sang in that clear, luscious voice that he had exhibited the night he and Danny had gone to work with those baseball bats. "*Amazing Grace… How sweet the sound… That saved a wretch like me….*"

33

❖ Driving Ms Tina ❖

The 1975 Pontiac Grande Ville was, by modern standards, more of a cruise liner than an average car. It was huge. It was light blue, and Tina had been driving it since day one, a present to her from one of her gentleman callers.

It was funny, when she thought about it. She had never been in love, but plenty of men had proclaimed the undying type for her and lavished her with gifts. But, if she was honest, she held more affection for this car than any of the men who had attempted to woo her. The only problem was, that as she grew older, with the car not having assisted steering, it was much more difficult for her to manage.

Still, she loved climbing into it. She adored the feel of the big leather bench seat. She liked to run her hand over the heavily creased and dimpled leather where it folded every time she slid in to drive it. How many times had she lain down on that seat, entertaining some young beau for the price of good meal and a ticket to the drive-in? How many times had she driven it away from a secret assignation at some motel just off the freeway? How many times had she taken it to the beach, parked up and listened to the sound of the waves as she smoked a long menthol cigarette, feeling like a French film star in some impenetrable arthouse flick that was full of long looks, tense silences and frantic outburst of angry passion?

Yes, Tina loved her Pontiac. Many of the stories of her life were ingrained in its upholstery and so many of her miles travelled had passed under its wheels. But today? Today, it would be the end of their beautiful love affair. Because today, she was going to wilfully do something to write off the car. She needed a new one. Her days of battling with the heavy steering were numbered. And living in Florida it might be nice to have some air-conditioning. And writing off the car would mean she could afford whatever damn car she liked.

Success would be all in the timing. So, she was concentrating on the road in front of her. Making sure not to miss the other vehicle she was waiting on. Morty wasn't helping, though. The Chihuahua was safe inside her handbag, but as all he could see was the traffic passing by, he couldn't help voicing his disdain for all humans with the exception of his mistress. He barked and barked, causing Tina to admonish him on at least three occasions.

"I do declare, Morty, if I didn't love you, I'd have just about wrung your neck by lunchtime today."

Morty whimpered, showing her that he knew he was making mischief.

The traffic seemed to be whizzing by faster than usual as she sat parked illegally on the corner of a street that intersected the main road that led from to the highway. From there, it was only another five miles or so to the Miami Urban Convention Centre. But she didn't want to go there today. Or let another, specific, vehicle arrive there, either.

Tina could see for at least three blocks and watched all the cars, buses, trucks and motorbikes, waiting for her target to come into view.

She was dressed in her best old lady outfit. Not that she liked wearing it very often, but Danny had been very specific in his instructions. She usually reserved it for winter and funerals, the latter were becoming uncomfortably more frequent in her life. So, here she was, in an A-line skirt and a blouse with a horrid floral print pattern, high-collared and long-sleeved. The overall image was bumbling old woman. It would help with the chaos and the aftermath of what Danny was asking her to do.

She had also decided to bring Morty along because his barking and frantic reactions would only serve to deepen the confusion once she had carried out Danny's instructions. She knew she could keep him safe in her handbag, so that was no problem. She glanced at her watch. It was almost just after five in the afternoon, her target would be there sometime between then and twenty minutes past.

Tina had been thinking it all through for days. She knew she had to ensure that the collision was big enough to halt her target. They'd offered her a hire car for the mission, but she'd refused. She knew that her beloved Pontiac had become too much for her. What finer way than to go out with a bang? And be helping desperate men achieve desperate measures? The derring-do of it appealed to her.

And then, she spotted it. Coming over the brow of the hill, three blocks away. They were in the outer lane, so she would have to time her pull out carefully. Morty started to bark again. She hushed him to no avail. She started the ignition, listening to the enjoyably throaty rumble, a noise she would miss. Her target was closer... two blocks now, the traffic slower, busier, helping her and hindering her all at once. She flicked on her indicator, edging the car towards the junction.

And then, a piece of good fortune. A taxi cab decided to switch lanes, going from the inside one nearest to her and out into the middle. She eased the Pontiac into the traffic. She locked her eyes onto the rear-view mirror, tracking her target and holding her breath as it pulled nearer to her. She indicated again, pulling into the same lane as her target, putting it directly behind her. Morty's barks reached a new pitch. She glanced ahead, spotting the stoplight, exactly where Danny had told her it would be. Now, this was where her timing had to be immaculate. She could see it was red. She slowed a little, the target gaining on her. She counted to ten, then sped up, her prey speeding up with her. They both anticipated that they would make it through the light, it would change to green just before they reached it.

Tina reached across and grabbed her handbag, Morty settling deeper into it at her as she did, an extra bark to show his curiosity. And then, Tina bit down on the gum shield that Danny had given her.

The stoplight turned green in front of her. The target vehicle immediately behind her sped up a touch more. As she reached the junction, Tina slammed her brakes on for all she was worth. The big boat of a car left rubber on the road, as it squealed to a heavy stop. Anticipation caused her to tense her shoulders as the armoured cash-collection vehicle behind her did what physics demanded. The collision pushed the Pontiac into the middle of the junction. A Toyota Corolla that had the misfortune to be behind the armoured van smashed into it, pushing it and Tina's car even further forward. Morty howled at the noise and ferocious jolt. Tina immediately spat the gumshield out into a handkerchief and slipped it into the glovebox. When a witness from one of the cars alongside hers came and tapped on her window, asking her if she was all right, she nodded slowly. She put tears in her eyes as she did so, reaching into her handbag and retrieving an unhurt Morty and clutching him to her chest. She looked the epitome of a crazy old lady driver.

That van would not be picking up any cash from the Miami Convention Centre that evening… and Tina felt very proud of herself, if a little sore. She'd perfected her best crusty old woman act for that moment, knowing she would have to lay it on thick when the cops arrived.

The last thing she did was to click on the small walkie-talkie Danny had given her. She was to press a button on it and say one word three times. Then, later that day, drop it into a trashcan somewhere far from where she lived. She did as she was told, saying loud and proud, "Crash, crash, crash," as she thought of the money and a long slow slip of her favourite electric blue cocktail.

Danny was in the gent's toilet at the Convention Centre when he heard the walkie-talkie in his hand crackle into life.

"Crash, crash, crash." *Game on*, he thought as he flushed the little radio down the toilet.

As he exited, he pulled the brim of his baseball cap down a little lower, making sure his sunglasses were still firmly in place. Walking fast, he scanned the congregation until he saw the face he was looking for. It was also wearing a baseball cap with a cross on, sunglasses and a white 'I ♥♥JESUS' T-shirt.

Danny nodded. The other man nodded back. It was about to kick off.

34

❖ Organised Chaos ❖

Returning to his seat in the congregation, Danny nudged Ciaran, who turned to look at him through identical sunglasses. "I can't believe you did it."

"Wha'?"

"Shaved off the beard. I'm not sure what was brighter, your mad ginger hair or your whiter than white chin… Jesus."

"Feck off! I'm strawberry blonde."

"Oh, and by the way. It's about to become interesting in here. Hold on to your hat."

"Have I ever told ye? Yer great craic to work wit'. I insist on only working jobs with ye from now on."

"Don't go soft on me, Irish. I'm going to need the tough version of you in the next forty-five minutes." Danny winked at his friend, feeling ready, confident.

Which was just as well.

Rusty the DJ adjusted his baseball cap and made his way along his row. Danny had given him the nod, so it was his turn to start the fun. His stomach was full of butterflies, but he had to admit he was looking forward to messing with this event. "*Fucking self-righteous, pain in the ass Christians.*" Ever since his mother had forced him to church as a child, he had detested the idea of religion. To him, it felt like a set of rules that spoilt your fun. Not today. Today, he was going to start the fun… big time.

He made his way towards the very middle of the big room, aiming for where the sound and light booth sat. On the altar, Vincent and June Cardell were talking with a guest preacher, swapping theories about how the bible was the only book a home needed. The timing was perfect. Rusty knew that whilst they were preaching, it would be easier to distract the technician. If the band had been playing… a whole different matter.

He reached the barrier that separated the sound and light booth out from the congregation, circling around it until he found the gap that allowed the tech guys to come and go. Rusty mounted the single step into the booth, the techie standing with his back to him. Rusty cleared his throat loudly.

"Hey, buddy… buddy…"

The tech turned.

Rusty smiled. "Do you believe in Jesus, like the rest of this crowd?"

"Praise be, I do, pilgrim, but you need to sit down."

"Pray with me… just for a second, friend."

Rusty knelt down on one knee, his head bowed. The tech hesitated, glanced at the altar and figured they weren't about to burst into song any moment. He then made the mistake of taking to a knee alongside Rusty.

The Vipertek VTS-989 is a particularly nasty but effective little bit of kit. It's a handheld stun gun that can produce a ferocious burst of electricity with just a flick of the switch and a pull on the trigger. Its manufacturers claim it can deliver up to fifty-three million volts. It also has a flashlight and is rechargeable. Rusty liked it. He liked the fact that it fitted into his jeans pocket, and he really liked it when he touched it to the tech guy's midriff and worked the trigger.

As the sound tech, without any sense of irony, cried out for Jesus Christ and collapsed unconscious in a heap on the floor of the booth, Rusty went to work. He found a laptop beside a stack of sound equipment, scanned it for an input USB, which he found within seconds. He quickly jammed in a little blue pen slot, waiting for what seemed like an eternity for it to then open a window on the computer screen. The tech guy was mumbling at his feet, starting to come round.

The laptop screen showed a window. The pen drive had loaded. Rusty scanned the myriad faders on the sound desk in front of him. Each are connected to a different sound source. If you wanted the source to become louder, you pushed the fader away from you. Quieter? Pull it towards you. Helpfully, and Rusty had been banking on this, most sound technicians label their different faders with a chinagraph pencil. This meant that if a microphone malfunctioned or a musical instrument started to feedback, it would be easy to isolate the problem and turn it off. Rusty scanned the rows of faders until he found the one marked laptop. He pushed it all the way to ten, then turned back to the computer. Using the touch pad on there, he double clicked an icon on his pen drive window. A music MP3 file appeared. He right clicked that and selected the word 'play'. His work was almost done.

He turned and gave the tech guy another jolt from the Vipertek. This one was received with a moan and another collapse. Rusty reckoned the dude was good and out cold for at least three to four minutes. More than enough time. Especially when he heard the scream. It wasn't from anybody in the congregation. It was from the music that he had started playing.

A scream followed by a thumping bass drum line. Anyone who loved their music and loved it raunchy could recognise Prince's hymn to hot, sweaty sex. *Gett Off* boomed out across all the speakers and over the heads of the devout Christians in the conference hall.

Rusty ran his finger over the chinagraph writing across the entire top row of faders, making it difficult to remember which one pertained to the laptop and then did what Danny had told him. *"Get the fuck out of there."*

Danny and the dancers from Woody's had chosen the track mainly for two reasons. Firstly, the scream at the start was such an unmistakeable and clear sound, it would act perfectly as a cue for action. Secondly, they found the thought of such a sexually charged song was simply too deliciously funny to ignore.

As soon as the scream sounded and the drum kicked in, the dancers leapt from their seats in the main congregation and sprinted towards the altar. The sudden change of the audio pace in the room caught the security guards by surprise. Puzzlement was their initial reaction; not really knowing why the hell the funky tune had drowned out a discussion of how Darwin's "Origin of The Species" was purely a work of evil. By the time they suspected something was up, they were too late to stop what happened next.

The huge black gay guy, the tall transvestite and the eight blondes had all stormed onto the altar. They were, of course, all wearing the baseball caps, sunglasses and hats that Danny had given them. What they were wearing underneath all that and their jeans was another matter entirely.

To the incessant beat of the Prince song, they shed their clothes, save the glasses and hats. The group were a blur of stockings, suspenders, peephole bras and nipple pasties.

Vincent, June and the guest preacher could do nothing but stare in disbelief at first – the bacchanalian scene unfolding in front of them was too surreal to compute.

At first, the security guards tried to physically remove them, but the tall cross-dresser and his imposing black friend simply batted the guards away. They continued to shed clothes, until it was obvious the transvestite was a pre-op and his mate fulfilled every stereotype about the African American male you had ever heard.

The girls were doing their bit, too. Three of them were writhing in a steamy clinch while two more were trying to seduce the guards who were unsure as to how best tackle women wearing flimsy lingerie and wicked smiles.

The congregation were in uproar. Some women were covering their husband's eyes, others wondered if you really could have twenty-two positions in a one-night stand, like the song said. Some of the younger men in the building were tutting furiously whilst not being able to drag their eyes away from the debauched tableau in front of them.

The sound tech was struggling to stand up in the booth. He knew something weird was going on, and at the back of his addled brain somewhere, he vaguely knew that he needed to stand up and put something right. But at the moment, for the life of him, he couldn't grasp what.

Security also knew they were collectively missing some important point as they grappled with how best to stop the happy band of strippers on the altar, until someone yelled into their radios, "The preachers! Protect the preachers!"

Four security personnel stopped tussling with the scantily clad stage invaders and made a bee-line for Vincent, June and their guest, bundling them away from the dancers who were now gathered in a circle, can-canning their way through what was left of the track, all G-strings, bouncing boobs and balls gyrating in time to the music.

And whilst this was going on, no one noticed. Not a single human being spotted the two men wearing baseball caps and sunglasses, one of them carrying a small backpack, making their way to the side of the hall to a door that was marked "*Staff Only*".

"This is where we make our leap of faith." Danny nervously reached into his pocket and brought out a small plastic card which he held against a larger square of plastic on the frame of the door. For a second, nothing. Ciaran was holding his breath. Danny could hear his heartbeat. It was suddenly loud and fast in his own ears. And just as Prince was declaring that "*Tonight, you're a star… and I'm the big dipper,*" they both heard a click, and Danny put his weight against the door. It opened and through they went.

"Jaysus. We're in this far…"

Back on the altar, the guards had managed to corral the dancers, slowly pushing them to one side, while the preachers had been safely shepherded to another door that led to the backstage area. They had made it to "safety".

❖

Just before the chaos had erupted out in the auditorium, Greg Norby was in his seat in the security hub of the Convention Centre. Banks of TV screens displayed every possible angle of the property, and when he saw three black Escalades arrive at a personnel entrance at the rear of the arena, he was instantly on guard.

"I'll be back in a minute, keep your focus on the auditorium."

'Yes, sir."

He grabbed a portable walkie-talkie from a charging bank by the door and made his way to the personnel door that led into the building. *Was this it? Was this the start of the robbery he knew his boss wanted and had allowed to be planned?* He had a bad feeling. It was the stupidest plan he had ever heard. He had tried to urge Vincent to cut some sort of a deal with Ines Zedillo. With people like her, there was always a price. Equally, there was always a deal to be done. But Vincent was too focussed. Too single-minded to be deflected from his political ambitions and his hunger for power.

Norby hurried through the maze of service corridors as quickly as he could, expecting to encounter the thieves. But it wasn't until he was nearly at the door he'd seen the group enter through on camera that he came face to face with them. But it wasn't who he was expecting. Where was the tall, good-looking Brit? No sign of the crazy little Irishman. Instead he was standing in front of six Latino men and a tall, shaven-headed man who was busying himself spray-painting over the lens of a security camera. When he turned, Greg noticed two things. First the man was holding a white security key card, one which had given them access to the building. And second, the tall man had a mangled eye, it looked like ruined boiled egg in its socket.

"Who the hell are you?"

"We, my dear friend, are here to see your bosses. And you are their security manager, are you not?"

"Not another Brit..."

"Yes, another fucking Brit. But this one is grateful. You've saved me the job of hunting for you."

Norby's face went white with terror as he saw the man with the horrible eye produce a pistol with a very long silencer on the end of it. He heard the slap of it being fired just milliseconds before feeling the round hit him square in the chest. Norby fell to his knees, his hands reaching towards his heart, not able to catch a breath.

Harkness bent down over the stricken man. "I heard you didn't like any of our plans. I heard you told Vincent we were trouble. Matey boy, at least you now know how right you were."

And then, he shot him twice in the head, the corridor filling with the smell of cordite and burning flesh.

"Right, let's get on, chaps. We've business to conduct."

As they were eventually hurried through the door to the backstage area, Vincent was having trouble concealing his excitement. He had realised almost immediately that the madness erupting on his altar had to be connected to the robbery. June's Englishman had evidently embarked on his plan. But Vincent's excitement was to be short-lived.

Having made their way to safety, they were immediately confronted with a group of seven armed men. The security guards who had helped them off the altar didn't know quite what to do next, one of them reaching for his radio, on the verge of asking the control room what next.

But one of the seven armed men stepped forward. "It's okay, gentlemen, we are part of Mr and Mrs Cardell's elite security team. We can take them from here. If you could escort the other preacher to his dressing room until we get a security all clear."

Vincent was about to protest, but June spoke across him. "What are you doing here, Harkness? Why are you even here?"

"Oh, June. You had to speak out of turn."

Harkness calmly raised his silenced gun and shot first the guest preacher and two of the security guards without a moment's hesitation. The other armed men finished the job, their silenced guns filling the air with oily smoke as they did so.

Vincent instantly went into panic. He couldn't believe that he'd just witnessed the death of a fellow preacher and four guards. His eyes were wide. Was this part of the robbery plan? He'd never envisaged the killing of a fellow preacher. He thought it would have been much cleaner. And how did his wife know this man with the putrid looking eye? He glanced down at the corpses, the blood leaking from them causing him to involuntarily lick his lips.

June spoke again. "What the fuck are you doing, Harkness? For Christ's sake..."

"Is it for Christ's sake, June? I thought this was all about dirty money, sweetheart. Let's get going. Ms Zedillo is expecting you both..."

And those were the words that made Vincent's guts twist and his heart skip at least ten beats.

35

❖ The Good Lord Provides ❖

Danny and Ciaran found themselves in front of the first keypad door. It would give them access to the money tunnel. From there, it was a straight shot to the administration offices and the counting room in the basement.

It was another hold-your-breath moment. Had they been given the right codes? Had they been sold down the river? Had the discovery of Marvin Quantick III's dalliance with Anastasia the masseuse been a defining moment? Because it was Marvin who was the security co-ordinator for the Miami Urban Convention Centre. He had given them the keycards and the passcode for the doors. It was Marvin who had parted with the information in return for silence about his louche lunchtimes.

Ciaran reached out to the keypad. Carefully, he punched in the numbers. Zero. Seven. Seven. Nine. Nine. A little light on the front of the pad had been solid red until the last nine was pressed. It flashed red twice then turned green. The door clicked. It was open.

"Jaysus, Marvin… yer some boy…"

Danny put his hand out to stop Ciaran. "Hold on a second. If we go in there now, there's no way out. We could be sealed in. They could lock us in place. The door closes, the code at the other end is changed and at this end, too. We could be trapped. Marvin might just have us."

Ciaran's expression clouded. "Ah, feck, Danny. Why'd ye have to say that out loud? He was shite scared when I braced him. I had him convinced. If he fucked wit' us, his wife… ye know…" Ciaran ran a finger across his throat.

"Yes, but he's had time. What if he was wracked by guilt? Came clean to his missus? He could have spilled to his bosses. They are the only link in the chain we've not covered. He doesn't work for the Cardells, nor the Mexicans." Danny was appalled. He'd let a ball drop. He'd failed to spot a weak link in the process. Never mind the fact that everyone was expecting a different plan. He'd broken one of his own rules. Cover every single fucking angle.

The two friends stared at each other for a second longer. It was Ciaran who broke the silence.

"I'd just as well be hung for sheep as a lamb. We've come this far together. This is what we do. We take risks. Aye, we minimise them, but let's be feckin' real here. We love takin' dem… don't we?"

"Tell me again why I chose to work with a crazy Irishman? Let's go."

They pushed through the door. Before they let it close, Ciaran reached into his backpack. He pulled out a Smith and Wesson Sigma 40V. Danny was impressed. He'd not seen the gun before. It had a composite frame topped by a stainless-steel slide. The gun looked hardcore. Ciaran steadied the door with his foot.

"Get back a wee second, Danny."

Raising the gun in one hand and shielding his face with his arm, Ciaran fired. The explosion was ear-splitting, especially when combined with the bullet mashing into the lock mechanism on the door.

"They can fecking try and lock us in now."

"And they know we're coming."

"Sure, feck it. We were gonna show up anyway."

They sprinted to the other end of the tunnel, knowing the gunshot meant they needed to get the hell on with it. Marvin had been scared. The same code that had opened the other end of the tunnel worked at this end, too.

Ciaran had his gun out. Danny was carrying another Vipertek stun gun, like the one Rusty had used earlier. It took Danny's eyes a few seconds to adjust, such was the brilliance of the white neon strip lighting overhead.

Ciaran's radical door policy had been a blessing and curse. The staff who had been working in the counting room had all backed away to the far end, away from the door. Danny quickly took stock, counting six people in there, two women and four men. The curse came in the shape of one of the men pointing a gun straight at them.

"Now, hold on a second..." Danny had his hands up and out in front of him.

"No, you hold on, mister. I know how to use this... I'm not going to let you terrorise any of my colleagues and sure as hell ain't going to let you leave this room with so much as a single dollar."

Danny would have preferred the element of surprise, but that was long gone. "The only way anyone will get hurt here is if you keep pointing that thing. Please... and I'm asking nicely, put the gun on the floor."

One of the women whimpered. They had all gathered behind one desk in the far corner of the room. Between them and Ciaran and Danny was an array of desks, each with a counting machine on. In the very centre of the room was a pallet upon which sat a huge bale of counted money. Lots of it. And then, in the other far corner, was the door to the goods lift, a hydraulic trolley for shifting the money pallet right next to it.

"I always knew a day like this would come. We've always had a lot of cash come through here. It was only a matter of time. I'm ready... I tell you, I've always been ready to handle people like you."

The man with the gun was yammering. Danny knew it was nerves. He was trying to "talk the talk" whilst not being sure that he could "walk the walk". Ciaran made to move forward, but Danny held up his hand. He had this.

"Are you? Are you really ready?"

"Clarence... don't be stupid... It's only money... Let them have it... We can all walk away." Ciaran glanced towards the new, clearer voice of reason, recognising it instantly. Marvin was in the room, too.

"Clarence... have you seen the *Dirty Harry* movies?"

"What? What the hell does that have to do with anything. Don't take another step, mister, I'm serious, I'll blow you away."

"Oh, come on, Clarence... Answer my question. Dirty Harry? Clint? That big old handgun? Blowing people away for fun?"

Danny was slowly edging closer.

"You're...you're crazy, mister..."

"Am I? You think? Maybe I have to be to be a thief, Clarence. But maybe you're the crazy one. Pulling a gun, a big one, mind, on a desperate man. A man willing to commit crime, and you point a gun at him. You think you're *Dirty Harry*, Clarence? You think you're some kind of vigilante?"

Clarence's shake was becoming more pronounced, the gun quivering in mid-air. It looked like an older model gun, so it was probably heavy. And Danny estimated that it would feel like a hundred tons to Clarence. Two of the women were now openly weeping. Clarence was blinking, not at a normal rate, but like a man in a sandstorm with no sunglasses on.

Danny decided to finish it. "You ready for the blood, Clarence? For the ear-splitting bang, the buck of the recoil on that big old gun of yours? The smell of burnt flesh? Are you? Are you like *Dirty Harry*, Clarence? You feeling lucky?"

"Shut the hell up... just shut up... I will pull this trigger..."

Danny was close enough to see the sweat rolling down Clarence's forehead and into his eyes. He was close enough to reach out and touch him. But Danny wanted to be sure. He didn't want any doubt, no chance that Clarence might fire off a panicked round, maybe hit one of his own colleagues. "Because if you are feeling lucky, Clarence... you'd be wrong. There isn't a gun in the world will fire, if you haven't taken the safety off."

Clarence's face fell, his hand shook, he didn't know what to do. Was he being bluffed?

He flicked his head down, couldn't resist the urge to check, he could do it in a nanosecond. But it was all that Danny needed. The Vipertek was out and delivering a crackling hot shot of electricity to Clarence's wrist before he even got the pistol turned all the way around.

He screamed, the gun dropping. The women screamed, too, and one of the men called out, "Sweet Jesus."

Danny scooped the gun off the floor. Damn, it was heavy. "Okay, you people, no more fucking around wasting my time. Who's in charge?"

Marvin stepped forward. Ciaran didn't say a word. He didn't want Marvin to connect his voice to the little meet they had had days earlier. No point giving cops any extra information if it ever came to it.

"How much is in the room? Counted?"

"Err… Megan, where'd we get to?"

Megan was in a weeping mess on the office floor.

"Megan! How much?"

"I… I… can't be sure now… I…"

Danny crossed to where Megan sat, her face running with a mixture of sweat and make-up. He bent over her and clapped his hands close enough for her to react like she had been slapped. "Megan! You know. Answer your boss."

"We… we got to seventeen… seventeen million and change."

Danny was happy enough with that. He nodded at Ciaran. "Okay, here is what is going to happen, people. My friend here is going to gaffer tape your hands and feet together as well as your mouths. As long as no one resists, no one will be hurt. We got that?"

"Tell… tell that to Clarence." One of the men was beginning to feel angry. Danny couldn't have that.

He walked over to where the angry man was trying to care for Clarence, who looked like he was just coming to from his Vipertek experience.

"Hey, mate? Remember this?" Danny thumbed the trigger on the Vipertek. The resulting crackle was loud and menacing in the room. "Keep your shit together, and I'll do the same, okay?"

Mr Angry was suddenly a bit quieter.

It took them a full five minutes to get everyone, except Marvin, bound. He was to be last. Danny told Ciaran to get the hydraulic trolley while he had a chat with Marvin.

"Okay, boss man, what's your name?"

Marvin started to answer. "But you know…"

Danny touched Marvin's wrist discreetly, giving Marvin the smallest of shakes of the head. Danny couldn't believe it. *For fuck's sake, Marv… don't implicate yourself in front of your esteemed colleagues.*

"Marv… Marvin."

"Okay, Marvin. Is there a code for the goods lift over there?"

He nodded.

"Is it the same as the ones we deciphered to get in here?"

"No."

Fuck. Danny's mind was racing again. It had been another loose end. Why did they not know there was another code to be used? Plus, going up in the lift could be another potential trap point, especially if he and Ciaran went up together with the money. Danny was getting angry with himself, but right now, that was pointless. Once again, it was just as well that he'd not shared all of the true plan with anyone except Ciaran.

"Are we in for any nasty surprises when we go up there, Marvin?" As he whispered the question, Danny gripped Marvin's wrist and squeezed. Marvin looked dumbly down at his own arm, the pressure from Danny's grip communicating its own message: *be honest or else.*

"No. No… there isn't. Four, zero, one, two, nine."

"Wise move, boss man."

Danny taped him up, hands feet and mouth. And just before he left him, he whispered something in his ear.

Ciaran had pushed the hydraulic trolley into the slats at the bottom of the pallet and was jacking the handle back and forth, slowly raising it off the floor and allowing the wheels on the prongs to take the weight and do their work.

Danny went over and found the keypad on the goods lift. He punched in the code and heard the motor start to wind the lift compartment down to the basement. It felt like it was taking an age.

They were about to embark on possibly the trickiest part of the job. When they emerged from the lift, what would they find? Would the dancers have caused the conference centre to empty? Would the entire place be festooned with police? Or would there be enough time to execute the final part of the plan? His reverie was interrupted by the huge door sliding open in front of them.

Together, they pushed the trolley into the lift, the metal wheels clanging loudly on the steel floor.

Danny turned back to look at the room, the staff huddled together, Clarence in particular looking pathetic and lost.

"You did the right thing, people. Sorry to have made this a horrible day for you. But, sometimes, you just have to roll with the punches."

Ciaran hit the ground level button and the door slid shut. The lift started its slow ascent.

Danny looked down at the money on the pallet. There was an awful lot there. He whistled softly. "Fuck me, Ciaran. There's a lot of dosh to be made in Jesus's name."

"Aye, right enough… the good Lord provides… or rather a load of people who need a wee bit o' Jesus something to make them believe their lives have a feckin' point to dem."

"Fuck me, I'm in a lift with an Irish Leonard Cohen."

"Gobshite! By the way, what did ye whisper to oul' Marvin?"

"I asked him if Anastasia's happy ending technique was worth it."

And they laughed, as much from nerves as from Danny's question.

36

❖ Sleight of Hand ❖

When the lift doors opened, the first thing they could hear was the sound of evacuation announcements inside the convention centre. The voice was calm but firm, stating that due to technical difficulties beyond the organisers control, today's event was ending early. That was a good start for Danny and Ciaran.

The lift emerged at the rear of the administration building right by a side road that was intended to allow cash vans to arrive and leave with ease. Due to its function, it was covered by four cameras. But Ciaran had an answer for that.

Before stepping out of the lift, he fumbled once more in his bag and produced a very old-fashioned solution. It was a catapult. He stretched the elastic on it once to check it was all intact and then fitted a small yet heavy rubber ball into the sling. Next, he pulled his hat firmly down over his forehead and adjusted his sunglasses. Danny noted the sweat ring that had developed around his friend's baseball cap. It was a sign that not only was it a muggy day, but he was feeling the stress. Outwardly calm, but still sweating his bollocks off.

Ciaran and Danny had both memorised where the cameras were. Dropping to one knee and bracing his shoulder against the doorframe of the lift, Ciaran took a deep breath. Then, he ducked out and aimed around the corner. With quick, controlled movements, his first shot took the first camera lens out cleanly, a whoosh and a crash announcing his success. He repeated the process twice more, three cameras down in a matter of thirty seconds. Fitting ball number four into the sling, he could feel the perspiration stinging his eyes.

"Holy bejesus. This is fecking hot work."

He took another deep breath, trying to regulate his heartbeat, and steadied his hands.

The fourth shot was the most difficult. It was the furthest camera, so his margin of error was next to nothing. Ciaran crossed to the other corner of the lift door and knelt. He slotted a ball into the sling and after a brief pause darted out. He didn't fire. His balance wasn't right.

Danny looked at his watch. Time was against them. It had taken longer to exit the counting room. Thanks to Clarence and his fucking gun, they really needed to get a move on. The police were bound to show up sooner or later.

Ciaran ducked out once more and let loose. There was no satisfying 'crash, tinkle, tinkle.' "Feck! Ye fecking fecker…"

"Calm, big man… Breathe… This is vital. We can't let them follow the money. You can do this."

Ciaran fitted another ball in his sling shot and rolled his shoulders, trying to relax them. "Holy Mary, Mother of God… gi' us a hand here…"

He ducked out, taking a beat longer than before and then let loose. The crack and crash the ball caused was one of the finest sounds Ciaran had ever heard.

He stood, a beaming smile on his face. "See? The power of prayer, Danny… the power of prayer."

Danny only snorted in reply and started to pull on the hydraulic trolley that they had been using to jam the lift doors open. There was still more trickiness to come.

They needed to haul the money over the loading dock where they first parked when they arrived for their recce weeks earlier. Again, they wanted to keep what happened to the money a mystery. There were more cameras over there for Ciaran to deal with. They should be easier because they weren't as high or far away as these ones, but there was a bigger risk. Witnesses. This was the one point where they might encounter security staff, members of the public and, most problematically of all, police. Danny realised that Ciaran wasn't the only one feeling the tension now. His own forehead itched where the hat band stretched across it, the hair at the back of his neck damp and sticky.

Once around the corner of the administration building, it was a straight line across a two-lane road over to the loading dock that had a space in front of it allowing large vehicles to turn. Ciaran peeked around the corner and saw no one between him and the dock.

"It's clear, wait here. I'll do the fecking cameras."

Ciaran sprinted across the road and the open space. The small backpack jiggling across his shoulders as he did so. It was only halfway across when he remembered the pistol was in there, and he couldn't recall whether he'd left the safety on or off.

"Be fecking embarrassing if I shot meself on a job," Ciaran muttered to no one in particular as he fished around in the bag until he had hold of five more rubber balls. It was a surprise to him when he had found them in the toy shop just a few days earlier. He wanted something heavy duty to fire at the cameras, and he recalled superballs from his childhood. He hadn't wanted to use metal because of the noise they might make in his bag, plus the weight. He never believed he would find the small rubber balls from his youth. But lo and behold, they still made them. And they were still small, light, hard as hell and bounced like crazy. Perfect for disabling the cameras.

Using the huge Coca-Cola trailer for cover, he dropped again to one knee and made short work of the three cameras that covered the loading dock. He then turned his attention to the forklift truck parked next to the big trailer. If there was one thing he was good at, it was hotwiring. The diesel exhaust of the forklift was soon puffing out foul smoke under his touch. Ciaran then turned it in a tight, quick circle and took it across the loading space, over the road, and met Danny at the side of the admin building.

"Good man, you were quick. Anyone?"

"Nah, not so far. Pull that trolley out from under the pallet. Let's crack on."

Danny did as he was told, and then stood back as Ciaran carefully slotted the prongs of the forklift under the pallet of money.

"All aboard the Skylark!"

Danny jumped on. As they trundled across the road towards the dock, they both heard them. Sirens. Police sirens.

"Fuck...we knew they'd come. We just have to double time it from here."

"What's it dem rappers say? '*Fuck Da Police*'? I'm right wit' dem."

They had arrived at the ingenious part of Danny's plan. The Coca-Cola trailer. The soft drinks were delivered in two forms. Firstly, as canisters of syrup that when mixed with carbonated water became Coca-Cola. Secondly, a smaller consignment of small vats that were used to refill the sellers who literally carried the drink around their back during events, like the kid Danny had tipped so heavily.

When they had done the recce, Danny had wondered why the trailer had been left on site. He had taken a second to look inside it that evening and spotted that the trailer was full of canisters and small vats. It had been an easy matter to get Slow Tina to introduce them to the guy who delivered coke to Woody's. When he had turned up in his truck after they had finished the team briefing, what he had told Danny was music to his ears.

Because the events at the convention centre were not constant, but fitful, the soft drinks would be delivered in a trailer which was left there to cover a period of a busy week. During that time, the centre would unload what they needed from the trailer each day, loading the empties back onto the same trailer. The manufacturers would then simply take the trailer away when the busy period was finished or supplies ran out, whichever occurred first. And that was where Danny's cogs had started to turn. A robbery where there isn't a robbery.

The trailer was a tautliner, meaning it was not hard-sided. It was covered in the kind of plastic/canvas that made the vehicle lighter and therefore more fuel efficient. The taut cover was secured at the bottom by a series of retaining straps, through which was laced a long cable that was then attached to a lock. But, as Danny already knew from the recce, they left the straps unlocked for speed and ease of access when loading and unloading the containers.

He started loosening straps as quickly as he could. He listened all the while to try and gauge how close the sirens were, and if, indeed, they were getting closer. Who was he trying to fool? They could only be headed to one place… here. Ciaran joined him, both of them working frantically, whilst also constantly scanning their surroundings to see if there were witnesses.

So far, so good. They had unclasped enough of the plastic curtain on the trailer to make a big enough access point. Danny then climbed inside and moved the canisters and small vats around. Once a space had been cleared, Danny ducked his head out of the trailer.

"Load it up…"

Ciaran lifted the pallet, the money heavy and enticing. He had to be careful. Such a load could throw out the balance of the forklift. If it were to topple, they would be in huge trouble. For the umpteenth time that day, seconds passing seemed like hours. The slow, monotonous rise of the pallet appeared to be glacial in its pace. Danny's foot was tapping uncontrollably, his T-shirt now drenched, sweat stains causing it to become moulded to his torso.

Finally, the pallet was at the right height. Carefully, Ciaran edged the forklift forward, while Danny waved him in. He then dropped it gently onto the floor of the trailer. All he had to do now was reverse out. But the angle wasn't quite right and, as Ciaran pulled back, the pallet shifted, too.

"Hold it, mate!!"

Ciaran applied the brakes.

"Left hand down, Irish, then come forward a smidge."

"What the feck is a smidge?" He shifted forward a little.

"Now right hand down, all the way. Then back."

Ciaran did, and this time the prongs of the forklift were clear.

But it was a delay too far.

They both heard it at the same time. A car. A cop car.

The cop driving pulsed his siren to let them know he was there. Danny emerged from the back of the trailer. Ciaran stayed put. He hoped the lifting mechanism of the forklift was at the correct angle and obscuring the money from the policeman's line of sight.

The cop spoke to them through his car loud hailer system. "Gentlemen, let me see your hands please."

They both complied, slowly.

"Okay, now are you loading or unloading?"

Danny affected his best American accent. "Loading empty canisters, officer, lotta people drank a lotta soda tonight."

"Did you guys see anything strange back here, tonight? See any unusual activity?"

"No, sir. We've been loading for at least thirty minutes." Danny had no idea how long it usually took to load empty Coke containers, but he was trying to cover them off from their timeline. You never knew if someone in security had seen something they didn't like from a camera they had missed.

"It got pretty wild inside, guys… women and men shedding their clothes. We think some kind of protest."

Danny responded with a shrug.

"Okay, thanks anyway. If you see anyone suspicious, call it in, boys."

And the car pulled slowly away. Ciaran took a very large breath and when Danny looked round, he realised that his friend's hand had already been resting on the butt of the Sigma pistol.

"Close one. Let's get finished."

Danny jumped back up into the trailer while Ciaran returned the forklift to its parking position. He was careful to repair the wires he had earlier pulled so he could start the engine.

In the trailer, Danny covered the money pallet with the empty canisters and vats. He pushed the full ones, of which there weren't many, to the back of the trailer. Once he was satisfied, he then set about re-securing the curtain siding of the tautliner, making it as smooth as possible.

When the job was done, Danny looked at his watch. From the moment the Prince song had started up, the job had taken a touch under forty-five minutes.

"We've been lucky, Irish. There were gaps here."

"Isn't it done? Give over, there's always them tings, whatycallem? Intangibles..."

"You know me, I don't like intangibles... Let's get out of here."

But as they turned to go...their cop friend was back. But this time at speed.

Again, from the loud hailer. "Gentlemen. Stop! I need you to put your hands above your heads and turn around. Once you've done that, kneel."

Danny responded. "What seems to be the problem, officer?"

"Just do as I ask. We are getting reports of a violent crime. Now on your knees, guys."

They were both puzzled. Had the counting room staff been discovered already?

A taser shock wouldn't be enough to provoke this level of reaction from a cop, surely?

"We better do it. As he gets close, I can taser him, I think," Danny whispered.

Ciaran shook his head ever so slightly. "No, mate. He's seen us. He knows we were at the trailer."

"No, Ciaran..."

"Danny, my soul's black already..."

"Ciaran..."

But he had to shut up then, because the cop was creeping towards them, his gun drawn and pointed, a flashlight along with it.

"Okay, gentlemen. Just stay still and let me come round in front of you. Easy does it."

"What's going on, officer?" They could hear more sirens now. Danny's instinct kicked in. He knew something big had happened.

Something other than what he and his friend had been engaged in. And he knew. It could only be one thing.

Harkness.

The cop's radio chirped on his belt. "Ambulance en route. Multiple casualties."

He was in front of the two of them now.

"Okay, you on my left. I want you to slowly reach down and throw that bag to my feet. Slowly, mind."

Ciaran started to bend. Danny could feel his heart beginning to race. His breath was laboured. *Not now… for fuck's sake not now…* But he knew. He knew it didn't matter how hard he wished it. He could feel the panic coming. He could feel the stress rising in his own chest. He heard it in his ears, and his arms, tucked on top of his head, started to shake. And then the tears. And suddenly he was gasping. Gasping for air… trying gulp in lungfuls of it, but nothing would come.

The cop looked confused then suddenly became alarmed. "Sir? Sir? Are you all right, sir? Please, can you stay still?"

"He has panic attacks, officer."

"What?"

"Panic attacks. Severe anxiety attacks. They stop him breathing."

The cop was both confused by Ciaran's accent and by what was happening to Danny.

"If you would let me, officer. I have his inhaler. In me bag."

"What? Oh, inhaler?"

"Sir, he'll choke, if I don't…"

"Okay, toss the bag to me. I'll get the inhaler."

Ciaran did as he was told, gripping just inside the bag. He had to get this right. There would be only one chance. He tossed the bag, but as he did so, he held onto the Sigma. The cop missed it, he was focusing on the trajectory of the bag itself. He registered the gun too late.

'Jaysus, I'm awful sorry." And Ciaran meant it, as he shot the cop square between the eyes.

❖

First, he bundled the cop's body into the back of his cruiser. Then, he went back to Danny. He was sitting in the middle of the road, staring dumbly into space, drying the tears that were streaked down his face.

"C'mon, Danny. We have to get out of here. We're not taking the bikes, we'll use the cop car. C'mon, up."

Slowly, Danny stood. They had a change of clothing and two bicycles stashed nearby. They had reasoned that the convention centre would be evacuated, and they intended to calmly cycle away amongst the fading crowds, trying their best to look like disappointed attendees.

But that was all shot to fuck now. The cop car was the right call. It would transport them far enough away at pace. Reach their actual vehicles, the jeep and the Harley, where they originally were going to cycle to and then split up. They could rendezvous much later on.

As they drove away, Ciaran was fiddling, trying to identify the switch that would activate the siren should they need to really move at speed.

Danny was inconsolable. "I fucked up, Ciaran. I fucked right up."

"Ye could never have anticipated that cop coming by and then coming back. We thought we'd dealt wit' him."

"No, no, no, no. It was Harkness. Harkness has done something. I gave him too much leash. We should have killed him the other night. He's done something that brought more cops than was needed."

"Like I said… it's on me. My soul's black as tar anyway."

"No, Ciaran. It's on him. This time. This time… he dies."

Danny wiped the snot away from the end of his nose. He tried to clear his vision and started to think. He started to plan how he could execute what he should have done all those months earlier in London.

37

❖ Judgement Day ❖

Ciaran couldn't believe the United States. You could buy almost everything across the counter. For a start, the Viperteks. They had a kick like a mule and could put a target down for at least ten minutes. Amazing. And what had they cost? Under thirty dollars. Seriously?

And when it came to discussing plans, it had come as no surprise to the Irishman that when he asked for a night-scope and a sniper's rifle, Danny had just shrugged and said okay. They'd then driven to a gun store, Danny had flashed a fake ID, and twenty minutes later – most of which Ciaran had spent like a kid in a sweetshop, having trouble making up his mind – they left with a Barrett M82 that could do amazing things from up to two thousand yards away. For a rifle that had been first manufactured in the 1980s, Ciaran was impressed.

Lying here on the roof of an abandoned house in the Florida Keys, waiting for the players to show up, he had to admit he was feeling a little nostalgic. He had trained with the IRA's top sniper, a woman who turned the borderlands of Crossmaglen into her very own hunting ground. She was a legend amongst the paramilitaries on all sides, able to hit a target from a mile away without so much as missing a heartbeat.

He'd spent a week with her, both of them freezing their backsides off, picking off rabbits from thousands of yards away for sport. Only once was he given the opportunity to spot on a live target. Ciaran had been her watchman that day, keeping an eye on the target's surroundings whilst she concentrated on assassinating a prison officer who had been known to sexually abuse those under his watch. The hit had been commissioned by both the IRA and the Loyalist UVF, such was the hatred for the man in her crosshairs. She had gladly done the job, and Ciaran had happily assisted. The pause between the report of her shot and the man's head exploding was a testament to the distance and her skill. As soon as Ciaran had confirmed the kill to her, she popped some chewing gum in her mouth and told him she had to rush home. "The wee'ans will be wanting their tea."

And that evening? Ciaran knew he would have the same cold expertise. To his mind, with the exception of Danny, any of the people he swept his sights over that night were worth a bullet. All he needed was a calm evening, a little luck and a direct line of sight. He could show them God's retribution, teach them the meaning of biblical justice.

Lying on a rooftop in Florida was a lot warmer than a barn in County Tyrone. He bent his head, fitting his eye to the scope, slowly sweeping the area where they were due to meet. Some were expecting to divide up money. They were in for a shock.

He steadied the crosshairs on the back of the head of one of the bodyguards who had been there for at least fifteen minutes. He was sure they worked for the Mexican lady. Drug dealers. For feck's sake. They had nothing but machismo to them. No training, no discipline. There were four of them and each of them had smoked at least two cigarettes since arriving, swaggering about the place with their TEC-9 machine pistols. They might as well have hung a sign over the heads saying, "*Shoot here!*"

He expected there to be at least another two when the Mexican lady showed up, but once he started shooting, he expected chaos to give him a helping hand. He had enough height to see over most things, and if the worst came to the worst he had distance, time and patience on his side. Danny knew the play; they had worked it out together. Between the two of them, they would rain down holy judgement as sure as the big man with the white beard would on the last day.

The only tricky one would be Harkness. Ciaran knew what he was about. Feckin' bastard. But then, Danny wanted that pleasure.

And who was Ciaran to deny him it? At the very least, he made for excellent backup should his friend run into trouble with the hateful ex-copper.

He continued to observe the scene through his scope, sweeping back and forth, left to right, watching to see what other vehicles arrived. He didn't have to wait long. A big black car, an Escalade, bounced slowly across the waste ground they'd chosen for the rendezvous. The patch of land had been purchased by a developer who had been planning a luxury hotel until his wife caught him in bed with the office help… two of them. The divorce was still not through, but it was clear to all parties that the man wouldn't be spending investment cash on a luxury anything any time soon. The house he was lying on was part of the purchase and due to be demolished to make way for a spa. It was set off to one side from where the main hotel would be.

Harkness emerged from the driver's side, another bodyguard from the passenger seat. He opened the rear doors, and out came June Cardell and her 'holy Joe' husband. With each new face in his scope, Ciaran made a soft bang noise with his mouth.

"Welcome to the feckin' party, ye eejits." But then, "Uh oh, now who's dis?"

The guard had brought a third person out of the Escalade, but this one came from the boot of the car and was slung over his shoulder. The person was smaller, and they had a black bag over their head, hands secured behind their back somehow, feet bound together, too. Ciaran zeroed in. It was a woman.

"Aw feck… That'll be your copper, Danny."

At that, another vehicle arrived, this time it was a Mercedes SUV.

"Now here comes La Mexicana… nice car, love."

He swept the scope over Ines Zedillo's face. "Bang…" There was also another bodyguard with her. He passed her a huge handbag once she was out of the car.

And then, last, but by no means least, he spotted Danny. He was on foot, a gun in his right hand, walking into the meet like the sheriff from *High Noon*. Gary Cooper walking to meet his fate. Ciaran watched him through the scope, marvelling at how calm he looked, especially given his new habit of breaking down in tears at exactly the wrong moment.

Ciaran counted up in his head. Four bodyguards over there, one with Harkness, another with the lady, the two Cardells, and Harkness. Nine targets, plus Danny and his lady cop. Everyone had showed up. He glanced to his left. Three speed-loading magazines with ten bullets in each sat on the roof next to him. More than enough.

"Okay, boys and girls, ladies and gentlemen… I do believe it is fecking showtime…"

They were all gathered in a circle, the space illuminated by the headlights of the various parked cars. Danny was trying to regulate his breathing, especially after seeing Amparo. He knew it was her, despite the black bag over her head. She needed him to be buddha level calm and he intended to oblige.

"Where's your little ginger leprechaun, Danny boy?"

Harkness… as always, the first to speak, enjoying his own fucking voice, Danny thought.

"He's in the wind. He's got his cut, he knows when it's time to piss off out of it. What did you do, Harkness? Why did the cops come screaming in to the convention centre so quickly?"

"My orders were to secure Vincent and June. Ms Zedillo asked me nicely. Sadly, some security dicks and a preacher got in the way." He made a gun with thumb and forefinger, pulled the imaginary trigger a few times.

Ines spoke up next. "Enough! I'm impressed, Señor Felix. You managed to blindside us all. No hit on the armoured van. You took the harder route, no? Inside the centre itself. *Muy dificil.* But where is my money?"

"We'll get to that in time."

Despite hearing and reacting to his voice, Amparo had said nothing so far. Danny realised her mouth was probably taped shut under the bag.

"No time like the present, Danny boy."

"What's going on here? What is all this about, what money?" Vincent was trying to act the innocent in front of Ines.

"Shut the fuck up, Cardell. Your race is run. Señora Zedillo, how many of these losers came to see you, to talk about this so-called robbery?"

She looked at Danny and shrugged. There was no need to play games anymore, they were all here now. "You did, Señor, as did Harkness…"

"In matters like these, a good copper's instinct tells you to manage upwards. I felt I had to cut you in, Ines. As I promised. You have the Cardells, you have my thief. If only he would tell us where the money is."

Before Danny could respond, Ines crossed the space between her and Harkness, with June and Vincent next to him. "Yes, you did promise me all of that, Harkness. So did Danny. But there was another who came to see me."

Before she said it, Danny did. "June. June came to see you, too, didn't she?"

"Clever. Your thief is a clever one, Harkness. And yes… June did come to see me. And yes… we struck a deal. Didn't we, June?"

Ines fished around inside her huge handbag and produced a large handgun from it. She handed it to June, who took it readily.

"Yes, Ines, we did make a deal." June checked the safety on the side of the pistol.

Danny, Harkness and even Ciaran, watching from afar, realised what was about to happen all at the same time.

June Cardell raised the gun and shot Vincent. Right in the crotch.

He screamed and crumpled to the ground. His hands tried to cover the gaping wound that she had just inflicted on him. June stood over him and very deliberately spat on him.

"How's that feel, Vincent? How's that pain? I thought you liked a bit of pain? Is this not turning you on? Can't you stop screaming, Vincent? Jesus didn't scream, did he? He didn't scream when they nailed him to his cross. Where's your Jesus now? Where is he, now?"

Harkness had backed away a little. Danny had spotted it. He thought he knew what might be coming next. Harkness was reaching under his jacket.

Danny chose to speak up. "June?"

She stopped haranguing her soon to be ex-husband and turned, first to look at Danny who nodded in Harkness's direction. She instantly understood.

Harkness had his gun only part way out of the holster he kept at the small of his back when June shot him. She was once again aiming for the crotch, only this time, she was a little high and the bullet took him right in the gut.

That'll still work, was all Danny could think.

Harkness went down, dropping his gun in the process, his face twisted in pain.

"And now. It's your turn, Harkness. You thought you could rape me? Thought I was a little woman, just playing at messing with the big boys? Isn't that what you said? The big boys? All you fuckers… you can all be cut down to size. And I just did it. And I'm not finished."

She walked back over to where Vincent was still curled up in agony.

"Vincent. Vincent… look at me." Her voice raised to a shout. "Look at me!"

He swivelled his head. His eyes were full of tears, cold sweat across his brow, his skin the colour of concrete as the blood flowed out of him.

"You always wanted to enter the Kingdom of Heaven. To meet your precious maker. Next time we see each other? It'll be in hell."

And June shot him again. This time in the head.

Ines walked over to her, placed a hand on her shoulder. "Señora, it is time to finish business."

"Harkness…"

"He is gut shot. He will die anyway. To business. The shots… they will have been heard."

Danny knew it was his turn. But the gun wasn't pointed at him. Instead, it was placed against the black bag over Amparo's head. She fell to her knees. June simply adjusted the angle of the gun.

"The money, Danny. The money. Where is it? Tell us and you live and she lives."

Ines joined in. "You are in no position to argue, Señor."

Danny looked at both of them and then calmly raised his hand into the air and made a thumbs-up gesture.

Ciaran acted on his cue.

The shot rang out and struck the ground at Ines's feet. Shock flashed across her face, and June took an involuntary step backwards. The bodyguards started to make a move, but Ines held her arm up.

"No, Ines, I still have skin in this game."

Danny's thumbs-up had been their agreed signal. It meant a shot across the bows, a warning shot. After that, the killing was to start on the second thumbs-up.

"My men will kill you, and her."

"But you won't know where the money is, and you'll all die in the trying. Believe me, if my friend had wanted to make his shot count, he would have."

June looked confused. "That's not how this ends, Danny. I didn't go through all of this for nothing."

"I'm not suggesting you did, June. But I have achieved what I wanted out of this, or, at least, you helped me do it." He gestured towards Harkness who was passed out on the ground next to them. "I'm a businessman. I am happy to make you a deal." Danny was looking at Ines now.

"Do you realise who you are crossing, Señor? We are a cartel for a reason."

"No, you crossed me. You all were happy to have me do the dirty work, but I know Harkness had sold my ass to you for afterwards. I know June here fucked my brains out and then expected me to roll over, do her bidding like a puppy. I wanted none of this."

Ines considered him for a second. "Terms?"

"There was seventeen million in the take. You can have half of it back."

Ines snorted at him.

"It's my only offer."

"We will kill you, and your friend."

"No. No, you won't, because this is business. I'm not the first person to try and rip you off, and I won't be the last. You will be busy with another Harkness or Danny Felix in six months' time. If your bosses don't kill you first. You could tell them that whilst you killed Harkness and Vincent, the money was never found. Your bosses will say you did the right thing. It is important to send a message that says don't fuck with us, even if the money disappeared. And then, you get to pocket the eight and a half million I'm offering you. It's the only deal on the table."

"And what about me, Ines? What about our deal?" June looked panicked.

"You were going to steal from me. I let you kill the men you wanted to kill. Be grateful you lived long enough to do it."

"You fucking bitch."

The bodyguards raised their guns in unison, all of them trained on June.

"Ah, ah… June, stop and be sensible for a moment." Danny pointed at her. She stopped.

"What if I take your deal, señor? My guards here, they will know the truth."

Danny knew she would say it. He had discussed the possibility of it with Ciaran.

He stuck a thumb in the air and then dropped to one knee. He shot the two immediately behind Ines with ruthless efficiency, a military-style double tap. Ciaran took out the one next to Amparo. The guard's head exploded like something from a horror film, and then, Ciaran popped another as he tried to dive behind one of the cars. The bullet caught him in between the shoulder blades and punched him into the dirt. The last guard came at them, raising his TEC-9, screaming in Spanish, when June stepped into the fray once more. She shot him twice in the chest, the impact dumping him onto the ground, his chin slumping onto his chest, leaving him to look like a sulky child in death.

The last guard, the one who had come with Ines, was thinking about starting in. Ines held her hand up.

"Solecito! No! You stay with me."

The guard, an obvious favourite of hers, did as he was told. Danny also raised his arm in the air.

"That makes this a much more even negotiation. It's almost like a proper business deal." Danny chuckled darkly.

"You are an impressive thief, Señor Felix."

"I try, señora. The casualties will make your story look plausible. And now, I will make a further compromise. Leave June with me."

June's eyes went wide. "What the fuck…"

"I will look after her from my take. She can walk away. She didn't start this. Vincent did. Me, my sniper friend, June and Amparo. We all walk."

"When will I get the money?"

"Three days. Hand delivered to your suite at the Delano."

"That's a long time, señor. A lot of trust."

"Would you trust me more if I told you I didn't steal it?"

"*Que*?"

"Never mind. You'll get your money. Trust me. I could have killed you, or at least had you killed, in the last five minutes. I may be a thief, but I'm not a preacher. You can take me at my word."

Ines stepped forward and shook his hand. "We have a deal, Señor Felix. Do not let me down."

"I won't, señora."

"Have you ever been to Mexico, señor?"

"No."

"Really? I could have sworn you were a Culiacán dog, just like me."

"English through and through, and I have no plans to visit your homeland…"

"*Nunca*! Never say never, Señor. Solecito, we will take Vincent and Harkness's bodies. *Vamos*."

"Come on, June. Help me."

Once he had removed the duct tape wrapped around Amparo's ankles and taken the black bag off her head, he could see that she had indeed been gagged, too. There was no gentle way to remove the tape over her mouth, he told her so and then yanked it off as quickly as he could. He then freed her arms, and instantly, she began to flail at him, punches, kicks, a stream of invective pouring from her in Spanish. He took every blow, every kick and every punch until she eventually dissolved into his arms, tears pouring from her.

Danny eventually walked her and June back towards a stolen Chevy Suburban. "June, do you have a cell phone?"

"Yes."

She handed it to him, and he handed it to Amparo.

"Here, can you remember your friend's number?"

"Cheryl? Yes…"

"Call her, get her to meet us on Collins Avenue, Miami Beach."

She made the call as he drove there. The nightlife was in full swing, the traffic slow. Forty-five minutes later, he could see Cheryl approaching.

He stopped the car and asked June to hold on a second.

He went around and opened the passenger door of the car, helping Amparo out.

"You were right. Amparo. I am too far gone to have any chance of anything normal in my life. I'm toxic. I put you at risk with a daydream of a relationship. You won't believe me, but for that, I will be eternally sorry."

She could only stare at him.

"Go back home, or go to a station house, raise the alarm, do whatever you think is best. But you won't catch me and you won't ever see or hear from me again. Cheryl will look after you for now."

"You… you. All those people. Shots… death…"

"You're probably in shock, Amparo. I'm sorry. I have to get back to my life now, whatever that is."

He kissed the top of her head and climbed back into the car as Cheryl rushed to grab her, both of them crying.

Danny drove away. It was the hardest thing he had done in his entire life.

As he drove, it was June's turn to rail at him.

"What the fuck's going on? You patronising wanker. I don't need your white fucking knight act. I had a deal with Zedillo."

"Shut the fuck up, June, and listen."

"Who do you think you are? I—"

"Shut up and listen. I just saved your life. Zedillo wanted heads. Yours would have been one of them. Mark my words, Vincent's head will be found on Miami Beach tomorrow morning. As will Harkness's. They will want to send a message. Don't fuck with the cartel."

"And what? You don't know what she and I had agreed. She let me kill the two of them. She would have stood over…"

"You were entertainment, June. To her, you were a woman scorned whose anger could do the dirty work for her. Listen, here is what's going to happen. I'm putting you on a boat—"

"A fucking boat?"

"Yes… a boat to the Dominican Republic. You need to stay fucking low for at least a year before you try coming back to the United States or anywhere else the cartel has reach. If you stay where I have arranged, then you will be sent money… at least a million."

"What? Why the fuck are you doing this? Why should I trust you?"

"Because, I owe you. Because you brought me the opportunity to put Harkness down. And even better than that, you then did it for me."

She fell silent for a minute, taking it all in, until another question formed in her eyes.

"Go on… ask. I can tell you want to know something."

"What did you mean, back there? About you didn't steal the money."

"We didn't."

"What? What does that even fucking mean?"

"The money. It's still there, at the convention centre. And it will be for at least another forty-eight hours until the police are finished trying to work out who killed those security guards and the preacher. Mind you, Harkness's head turning up will help. But the money? It's still on site… but no one realises it. Now, settle back. We have to meet Ciaran, and it's going to be a forty-minute drive to get there."

They travelled in silence, until just before they arrived at the rendezvous point. June turned to look at Danny. "You're right. If it had been me, I'd have killed me too. Ines would have had my head on a stick."

"No doubt."

"But, as it turns out, I was right all along."

Danny cocked an eyebrow at her. "You. You were a Godsend all along."

Epilogue

Forty-eight hours after the robbery, the police began to allow access to the convention centre again. This meant the resumption of business, including delivery of supplies. There was a show the following week, some YouTuber was holding an event. Mass crowds were expected, kids showing up to see another kid tell them stuff they already knew. And a lot of soda would be drunk.

The big rig that showed up with its tautliner trailer full of Coca-Cola was driven by a man who had been delivering such loads up and down the Florida Coast for many years. He had delivered to everywhere. Hotels, restaurants, the convention centre and even a place called Woody's down in the Keys.

With a minimum of fuss and a little paperwork, he drove away the old trailer filled mostly with empty soda canisters and small vats. Plus, just over seventeen million in dollars.

Nobody ever thought to take a look inside the trailer. Just as Danny had wagered.

"D'ye think she'll stay put?"

Ciaran and Danny were in a Denny's in Louisiana. The money had been delivered and divided out amongst the players. They'd then made their way north and west, seeing where the wind would blow them.

"Who?"

"June… the preacher woman…"

"Some vicar's wife!"

They both laughed.

"I dunno. My friends will tell me. If she does, we'll send her some money. When I say we, I mean I'll have my lawyer to do that."

"Feck me… trusting a lawyer. Ye can't even trust the preachers these days."

"And what about you, Ciaran? Isn't your mammy expecting you?"

"Ah, she's grand. I've sent her a few quid, she'll be all right. I have seven brothers and three sisters there to look after her."

"Okay. What do you think you'll do? You're a bit richer, now."

Ciaran put the last bite of syrupy waffle in his mouth and washed it down with a slug of coffee before he answered. "I'm going to stick wit' ye. Ye need looking after more than me Mammy. What with the broken heart and the shit fits and all dat you got going on." He punched his friend on the shoulder and winked.

Danny responded with a rueful smile but he kept his thoughts to himself. *Shit fits? Well, they've not surfaced for a week or so now. But the broken heart? That one will never mend.*

"Awww, feck."

"What?"

Ciaran handed Danny the newspaper he'd been reading over breakfast. He poked the page, pointing to an article on the bottom half of the front page.

It was a gruesome story. A head was found by a tourist on the shore in Miami Beach.

Danny read one line aloud. "The decapitated head is believed to belong to the preacher Vincent Cardell who, along with his wife, have been missing since their Miami mission was robbed last month."

Danny repeated his friend's earlier sentiment. "Aw, fuck."

There was only a mention of one head. Where was Harkness's?

Amparo spent days giving endless statements and pleading to be allowed on the taskforce investigating what the press had begun to call "The Bible Bandits". But her requests were refused amid rumblings of conflict of interest and questions as to why the perpetrators had chosen to kidnap her in the first place. She had been careful as to how she characterised her relationship with Danny. They had taken her word at face value, but she knew that their concerns remained.

She knew then and there that her career in Florida law enforcement was over, and she cursed all the times she had joked with her friend about the sexy Brit with his funny accent. He had taken her career at home away from her and, at some level, also broken her heart.

She was later accepted into a sheriff's office in Arizona, a position that was dedicated to relations with the tribespeople of a local reservation. It was honest work and interesting. Slowly, she began to rebuild her life.

June Cardell did stay put and received her money. But a million dollars was not enough to build the kind of life she wanted. She knew that. But what could she do? She bought some land and grew crops. Specifically, marijuana, using all the tricks she had learned from the ex-boyfriend that she had sold out back in London all those years earlier.

Within eighteen months, she had become a serious player on the Dominican drug scene. But her ambitions didn't stop there. It would take some courage and a leap of faith, but she knew it would be worth it. She wanted to build her operation. She wanted a joint venture, open some new markets, maybe even diversify. June contacted Ines Zedillo.

"Ines…let's make another deal."

Father Simeon would always be curious. About a number of things. Where had his fishing buddy gone? Had his criminal life caught up with him? Had he fled? Did he ever find peace of mind to stop the panic attacks that Simeon had witnessed? It was a mystery to him, but he prayed for his friend all the same.

But one day, the questions were answered… sort of. A parcel arrived at his church. It was wrapped in plain brown paper, sent through the regular mail. There was no return address on the outside. But when he opened it up, Simeon nearly fainted. It was money. Lots of money. And a handwritten note that read: *"I still don't believe in God, but I do know a good man when I meet one. Put this to good use. Use it to build your dementia centre."*

It wasn't signed, but he knew who had sent it, nonetheless. Father Simeon blessed himself and started to count. It took quite a while. There was half a million dollars in the parcel.

The police were never able to establish a direct link between what became known as 'The Stripper Protest' and the 'Bible Bandits,' so the participants got away with a slap on the wrist. Having already been given ten thousand dollars each for their trouble, they were all happy enough, but when envelopes arrived containing another twenty thousand each, Woody's was unexpectedly closed for a night, and a spontaneous staff party that would go down in legend kicked off.

A few weeks later, Slow Tina received a parcel containing one hundred thousand dollars. She went out and bought a new car. It wasn't small, but it did have power steering. She thought she looked great in a red Ford Mustang. Morty seemed to like riding in it, too.

Ines Zedillo was listening. The satellite phone was buzzing. She waited for it to be answered on a sun terrace at a Villa in Fayence, the South of France. Her boss, Alvaro Montoya, had sent a message. He wanted to talk.

"*Bonita, buenos dias.*"

"*Buenos dias, jefe.*"

"I will make this quick. The man. The one who helped himself to some of our candy. Candy we never found."

She tensed. Did her boss know about the deal she had made with Danny Felix?

"*Sí, señor?*"

"He was a clever man, no?"

"The candy. It is still missing… and so is he."

"Find him, *Bonita.*"

"Do we want to… express our disappointment to him? In the normal way?"

"No, no, señora. A man that talented can be useful. I have a job for him. And he owes us for the candy, no?"

"*Sí, jefe. Es verdad.*"

"*Bueno*. Find him, *Bonita*…"

And the connection went dead.

Danny Felix will return…

THE END

Acknowledgements

Clichés are clichés because they always have a seed of truth at their core, so it seems fair to me to trot out the age-old expression that goes "many hands make light work".

As with all creative endeavours, I could not have written Godsend without the help of a bunch of very special "hands".

Firstly, and as always to HJ. None of this happens without you…deep gratitude.

My thanks and joy go out to the Bloodhound Books team: Betsy, Fred, Alexina, and Sumaira, for making this book happen. It is simply great to collaborate with you guys.

My partner in crime, KT Forster, must always be acknowledged for her help, support, encouragement and creepy crime news stories…she keeps me on the straight and narrow…if that is ever possible.

Another whose wisdom and insight always makes a difference is Morgen Bailey, thanks for smoothing over my cracks.

I was also very blessed to get incredible assistance from the Monroe County Sheriff's Office in Islamorada, Florida. My time in the Keys was invaluable in the writing of this book, so my gratitude is deep and sincere. Thanks to Captain Corey Bryan and Lt. David Carey and their team for answering all my dumb questions, sharing their stories and making sure I didn't miss any of the local colour that helped bring this story to life. I hope I wasn't too much of a 'Touron' and that one day I may qualify as a 'Mangrove Monkey'.

Appreciation also goes out to Sophie Goodfellow and all the Book Bloggers and reviewers who have become so vital to the publishing world. Your dedication is inspiring.

And last but not least thanks to the readers…keep turning those pages and touching those Kindle screens.

I hope I have delivered a Danny Felix book that furthers his story, deepens his character and keeps everyone on the edge of their seats…until next time, thankyou.

J.A.Marley

February 2018.

Lightning Source UK Ltd.
Milton Keynes UK
UKHW03f0224100418
320753UK00001B/141/P

9 781912 604197